# TALES FROM THE ANDERWELT: THE SPARK OF REBELLION

SCOTT SWAINSTON

This is a work of fiction. Names, characters, places, and incidents either are the product of the author's imagination or are used fictitiously. Any resemblance to actual persons, living or dead, events, or locales is entirely coincidental.



First edition June 2022

ISBN 978-1-7396093-0-6

# 1

A cold night and a thick mist filled the forest where Kurt Bauer had made his home. A crudely constructed cabin standing amongst the stumps of the trees that had helped make it. The misshapen hovel with its overly large front door stood out awkwardly in the clearing where it dwelled but despite how the cabin looked, it was a sturdy home. A small pile of firewood stood underneath the only window on the place, the slightly cracked glass letting out a tiny creak with every passing breeze. Emanating from the window was a soft orange glow that pierced into the darkness surrounding the cabin.

Inside, firelight made shadows dance across the entire room. The cabin's interior was only a singular space with everything a person would need to live crammed inside. In one corner, several piles of folded clean clothes lay on the cold wooden floor, while some discarded used clothes were left nearby, based on their worn state it was almost impossible to tell which was which. On the opposite side lay a dishevelled kitchen, a generous word for what was essentially a wooden cabinet, two cooking pots and a few jars of odd-smelling herbs. The whole place was covered with moving lights and shadows because of the dingy fireplace built into the wall. Several flames in the blackened hearth struggled to keep burning as they consumed the last hunks of wood. The lights danced over the young man laying in the bed that took up an entire side wall of the cabin. Even with the fire warming the place, the man and bed were covered in several brown fur blankets, so worn down with use that you could barely tell they had come from a deer. The young man in the bed was Kurt, tossing about restlessly in his sleep, the distress from a bad dream echoing throughout his rough-hewn home.

Meanwhile, just outside the cabin the various creatures of the night went about their normal instinctual routines; a family of grey rats were scavenging for food, several owls flew overhead searching for stragglers amongst the rodents, there was even a deer at the treeline staring curiously at the glowing window, all of them completely unaware of the ethereal turmoil that was transpiring inside.

Within his mind, there was a stench of rot that had surrounded Kurt and as he looked down a cold grey hand grabbed his arm, sending a wave of ice shooting up his arm. Kurt sat bolt upright with a terrified yell, the sound echoing outside, scattering the nearby animals with almost half the terror that Kurt was still reeling from. As his senses started to return, Kurt looked down and wasn't surprised to find his hand gripping a knife. Letting out a relieved sigh, he pulled himself out of bed, allowing the chilly night air to wash over his naked body and fully wake him up. The dying fire did nothing to warm him as he walked over to the kitchen to place the knife atop his only plate. It wasn't a particularly dangerous weapon, almost blunt and barely a few inches long, but Kurt often found he didn't like to be without it when he was trying to sleep, not that it was much of a comfort in his dreams. Knowing that if he tried to return to bed, he'd likely just wake up in another cold sweat, Kurt sat down in front of the fire and tried to soak up the last warmth it could give before the flames disappeared completely. He looked to the window, hoping to see some hint of morning light but was soon disappointed as all he could see was his own reflection on the dark glass. It wasn't the most flattering thing to see first thing in the morning, pale, unshaven, short yet unkempt brown hair and clearly in need of a good meal.

As he was sitting in the cold, Kurt thought about throwing some more wood on the fire but when he looked over to the hearth he noticed that he'd used the last of it already. Not wanting to go outside, he decided to get up and start his day proper. His spine made several reluctant cracking noises as he stood up, which Kurt ignored while he grabbed his discarded clothes from the night before. After a brief sniff he was satisfied that they'd be fine for another day. Once he was dressed he looked around his kitchen for something to eat. It didn't long for him to find a hard chunk of something that could have been called bread at some point. As he gnawed away, doing his best to ignore the slightly bitter taste, the tiniest slivers of light began to appear at the window. The sunlight gradually started to push the shadows out of the cabin giving Kurt a clear look at the state of his home while he ate. The place wasn't in the best condition, small drafts came in from all over and Kurt had lost count of how much food he'd lost in the gaps between the floorboards but this was his cabin. He'd had help from some people from the nearby town to build it and while he didn't own many things to make the place feel much like a home, Kurt was still a little proud of what he'd built. Building the place from nothing reminded him of when he was child, going into similar forests to build forts. He was glad his skills had improved since then, as that young boy's first few attempts wouldn't have survived the first bout of rain this cabin had struggled with.

The last bite of the stale bread snapped Kurt's attention back to reality. Seeing no point in waiting around, he went to the side of his fireplace where a small bucket of cold water stood. After splashing a little on his face to clean himself, he threw the rest of the water onto the last smouldering embers. Satisfied that the place wouldn't burn down in his absence, Kurt walked over to the door. Standing there waiting for him was a pair of thick fur lined brown boots which were probably the most valuable thing in the entire cabin. Kurt always made sure he had good footwear, if there was one thing from his youth that he took to heart it was the value of good boots, especially as it was a long time before he owned a pair of his own. Hanging on a hook by the door was his jacket, a dark and ragged looking thing with a heavily worn-out fur lining but it was reliable at keeping him warm regardless of the weather.

Finally ready, Kurt opened the door to the outside. The cold morning air rushed into his skinny frame and washed away any remaining tiredness from his restless night. He took a long and deep breath before closing the door behind him, the metal clang of the latch echoing out over the clearing. He'd never bothered to put a decent lock on it as he never had visitors and the only other denizens of the forest that he'd ever seen were animals. Kurt then began his journey into town, walking down the path through the forest that only his feet had worn in over the year since he'd arrived.

After a few minutes the small clearing where Kurt had made his home had completely vanished from sight. As he strolled through forest breathing in the fresh morning air, he thought about the day ahead. He was already feeling tired from his restless night but that wasn't an uncommon feeling, as he rarely slept well but something about the cold air made each step he took feel sluggish and more difficult than normal.

Other than the occasional sound of a nocturnal creature scurrying back to their nest, the walk was peaceful. It wouldn't be more than a couple of months longer before all the green around him would fall away to a dead dry brown, so while Kurt walked down the path, he slowed down to take in more of the sights around him. After an hour of walking, Kurt emerged from the forest. Below him, his path led down a grass covered hill where he could see his destination, nestled in the centre of the valley was the mining town of Bismurr. Surrounding the town were green and yellow fields, where either food was grown or livestock would graze, the colours only breaking where a road of dirt and stone led to the mountain on the opposite side of the valley, the shadow of which would loom over everything come noon.

Even from where he stood Kurt could see figures moving around already, as some people started their work before the dawn. Soon enough he was marching his way between the wooden and stone buildings that made up the townsfolk's homes. As he passed by people coming and going Kurt did his best to keep out of their way, even after a year of living and working in Bismurr he was still a stranger to the town. As he got closer he could make out a few familiar faces, not that he knew many people by name. A dwarf gave him a slight nod as a greeting when he strolled by. When Kurt had first arrived in town, the sight of a dwarf was a shock but it quickly became clear that dwarves were the least strange part of this place.

As he reached the centre of town, most of the streets were now so busy with people beginning their morning work that Kurt had trouble reaching his destination, the town's bakery. A small wooden building with a wide brick chimney jutting out of its roof which was breathing out a steady thin stream of smoke. He opened the door and hastily stepped through. Once inside, the smell of baking bread instantly surrounded him, making his stomach growl in reply. Ignoring the noise, Kurt wiped his boots on the floor and walked past the stacked barrels that flanked the entrance and into the bakery proper. At the back of the room, a stout dwarven woman was working in front of the large oven that took up most of the wall. She was juggling a sack of flour with one hand while carrying a metal tray of freshly baked rolls in the other.

"Morning Cali." Kurt said loudly, as he took his jacket off to place on a hook sticking out of the wall alongside a small collection of somewhat dirty aprons. Cali looked up and gave a quick smile before putting the hot tray of rolls onto a cooling rack.

"Morning, take this flour would ya? Got some big orders to fill today!" She then tossed the sack with ease, the force of which caused Kurt to stumble back as it almost winded him.

Not one to waste time, he immediately went to a side table already coated with flour while Cali went to grab various other ingredients. Between the two of them the work was easy and as a few hours passed the pair chatted about nothing whilst making dozens of rolls, sweet cakes and even a few pies. Kurt wasn't much of a baker but thankfully his job was mostly keeping the place tidy while Cali worked. It was only once the cooling rack was full that the pair finally stopped for a break.

"Good work this morning Kurty." Cali said as she wiped the flour from her hands onto a small rag. "You fancy taking this out for delivery soon? Got more orders to fill here."

"Sure," Kurt replied, picking up the crate of rolls he'd help fill. "Where is it going?"

"Over to the mine." Cali paused for a moment and her tone shifted anxiously. "They've got an inspection today, so they'll want everyone working and not waiting around for food."

Kurt knew why there was a slight nervousness in her tone. He knew what an inspection meant, there would be an elf in town.

"I'll be quick, be back here before you know it," Kurt said, trying to put Cali at ease. She let out a small relieved sigh and stood up to begin baking once more. Still warm from the work, Kurt left his jacket in the bakery and began the short journey to the mine. As he walked past the townsfolk going about their own jobs, he thought about the times he'd seen the elves around Bismurr.

When he'd first arrived in town and was still learning about the world around him he quickly discovered that Bismurr was under the control of the elves. Kurt was familiar with what a military occupation looked like but what was strange about this place was that the force who controlled the town rarely made an appearance. It seemed like as long as the people understood their place and the mine kept up with its regular shipments then the populace would be left in peace. Things seemed pretty fair, at least until Kurt first saw how the elves treated the people of Bismurr.

It was just after Cali gave him a job at the bakery and he was still trying to learn the language of the land, an elf came to town. Like with most of their visits they had come to discuss something about the mine. This was the first time Kurt saw their leader, the elf was a slender fair-haired man, clad in pristine white clothes that, by design, stood out amongst the dirt, dust and stone near the town. The foreman of the mine apparently disagreed about something and the elf took exception to that, so in response he raised a hand and made a nearby pickaxe rise up and crash down through the dwarven man's foot. It was the first display of magic that Kurt had seen but certainly not the last. The dwarf was soon replaced by another more 'agreeable' foreman and the elf didn't reappear for another four months.

As Kurt began to leave the town area, still being careful to keep out of the way of the busy townsfolk, he thought about his second memory of the elves. This was the first time he had seen anything resembling an elven soldier. Once again the elf that had disagreed with the first foreman was in town, apparently planning an expansion of the mine into some recently discovered tunnels. Several of the older dwarven miners gathered to raise the concern as those tunnels might belong to an orc clan. The white-clad elf ignored their pleas and ordered them to get back to work, gesturing at two armoured individuals nearby. In contrast to their commander, these elves wore a black metal armour which was so form-fitting it looked almost chitinous and their faces were covered by dark blue silken scarfs. They raised their hands and marched forward, causing the dwarves to run into the mine terrified. Several of those dwarven men were found dead a few days later, and the mine expansion was halted. Apparently a few weeks later a contingent of elves went into the mine and returned with a dozen charred bodies, and the mine expansion was sealed off permanently.

Kurt could now see the entrance of the mine and the several wooden buildings nearby, workers busily moving large carts filled with metal ore. As he marched on, keeping out of the way of miners, Kurt thought about the third time he'd seen the elves in town. This wasn't long ago, Kurt had been around the town for about a year and was more familiar with how to live in Bismurr. His anonymity was important to him so when he saw the white-clad elf for the third time, he chose not to get involved with the scene before him. The white-clad elf was marching through town with some dwarves escorting him, discussing the state of mine and the future of the people on the whole. As they walked on a nearby man stumbled forward and a small amount of dirt landed on the boot of the elf. Barely a moment passed before the elf, in a rage, used his magic to fling the passer-by into a nearby wall. He then stormed off, and left the town immediately, leaving his escort to tend to the poor man. Apparently he was injured for weeks before he could return to work, yet the other people in town made sure his family didn't go hungry. Kurt hadn't seen a community come together like that since he was a small boy.

Once he had finally reached the largest building outside the mine, the canteen and bunk house, Kurt stopped dwelling on the past and drew his attention back to his task. He walked through the large doors into the canteen area. It was empty save for a human man mopping the stone floor, cleaning up the food debris from breakfast.

"Those the bread rolls? Take 'em out back, drop 'em anywhere," the man spoke with a monotone as though he had repeated himself a dozen times already.

"Sure thing." Kurt replied, doing his best to avoid the clean patches of floor as he made his way to the open kitchen in the back. He placed his delivery atop another pile of crates before he made his way back out of the canteen. He thanked the lone worker and walked back out into the morning sun. Before he could start heading back to the bakery however, a commotion was beginning at the large entrance to the mine. The familiar white-clad elf stood silent while a large elderly dwarf was berating a younger worker. The older of the two gestured towards Kurt's direction while yelling about an irresponsible and stupid idea. Kurt looked around and spotted a teenage looking boy shifting nervously next to the bunkhouse. He walked over to the boy giving him a slight wave and leant against the wall next to him.
"You alright?" Kurt asked.

"Y-yes, sorry, am I in the way?" The boy nervously replied, and started to move away before Kurt shook his head.

"You're fine, I don't work the mines." He nodded towards the argument. "That about you?"

The boy replied with a nod. "My father doesn't want me to work in the mines, but apparently they need more people down there."

"Tough job," Kurt replied sympathetically. "But a young lad like you? You'll be fine."

"Sure," said the boy as he shifted anxiously and looked down at his feet.

"Tell you what. Come by Cali's bakery later, I'll get some cakes or something for you." The boy's eyes widened excitedly upon hearing that. Kurt began to walk away, distancing himself as the arguing dwarves' attention began to land on him.

"Thank you!" the boy called out after him. Kurt didn't look back but waved a hand regardless.

"You're welcome," Kurt muttered mostly to himself as he started to head back towards the town. Seeing someone so young being made to work was a little too familiar but he pushed his thoughts aside. It wasn't his place to interfere.

The walk back to the bakery was uneventful. The rest of the day's work with Cali also seemed to fly by as Kurt grew somewhat contemplative. He'd been living in Bismurr for about a year now and while he found ways to keep busy, he still wasn't sure what he should do with himself. Despite being lost in thought he took the time to bake a few extra rolls and some sweet pastries, bag them up and leave them aside. Soon enough the work was over, and Kurt took the packed food and gave Cali a farewell pat on the shoulder before grabbing his jacket and walking to the front of the bakery. He wasn't waiting long before he saw a sheepish teenager shuffling along with his head down, trying to avoid everyone around him. The boy was now covered with dirt and the skin on hands looked a little raw, but otherwise seemed to be alright.

"Hey!" Kurt called out.

"Hello again," said the young man as he jogged over. Kurt swore he could hear a stomach gurgling, so with a smirk he handed over the pack of treats. Gratitude spread across the boy's face and Kurt started steering him away as some passers-by began to stare.

"Better get home quickly, otherwise you might have to share," he said, giving the boy a slight push to move him along. The young one obliged and began rushing down the street clutching the food tightly to his chest as he ran home.

Kurt waited and watched the young man until he disappeared around a corner. Satisfied with the day, Kurt began to make his own way home. He pulled his jacket closed and braced himself against the evening chill as the now-setting sun took away the warmth of the day. Just as he got past the outskirts of town he noticed several elves riding on horses nearby. Kurt knew a military patrol when he saw one. He stared as he walked, curious as he had never seen the elves performing a task so ordinary. They seemed to be taking note of the outskirts of the town itself, almost like they were sizing something up. Before he could speculate any further they rode out of sight leaving Kurt alone as he hurried towards the forest's edge, eager to get home before the night descended on him.

Once he arrived at his cabin Kurt grabbed an armful of wood chunks and went inside. He started up a fire, tossed his jacket and boots across the room and sat down to warm himself for a short while. As he stared into the flames, he thought about the day just gone and felt a sense of frustration growing in the back of his mind. Seeing the elves in town was something he'd gotten used to, but he'd never seen them push to recruit children into working the mine. This thought swirled around in his head as he grabbed a few scraps of dried meat from his kitchen. The taste was so bland that he couldn't identify what animal it had come from but Kurt didn't care, his mind was elsewhere. Without realising he found his eyes being drawn to a small chest he kept stashed under his bed.

Kurt shook his head, trying to shake the thoughts. It was fine, nothing to be worried about. Normally he'd be unsatisfied with such a meagre meal but as his thoughts kept going over the elves' presence in town, Kurt found himself too distracted to pay attention to his grumbling stomach. Sitting down in front of the fire, he took off his boots and closed his eyes as the heat from the flames drifted through him. Slowly his thoughts faded away and tiredness crept over him, taking him gently to sleep.

*An all-too familiar scene began to form around Kurt as he found himself standing in a field surrounded by fog. In the distance he could hear shouting and panicked voices. Without thinking Kurt found himself walking towards the noise but no matter how quickly he walked, the voices stayed distant. Then an orange glow began to fill the fog surrounding him and a smell of burning cascaded around him. He tried to cover his face but the stink of it seemed to push through his hand. The fog started to become smoke and fire, flooding the area as the flames stretched all around trying to reach towards him. Kurt crouched down and covered his head, like a child trying to hide from parents. The heat faded away but he kept still as he knew what was coming. He felt a cold hand touch the back of his neck and as he turned he caught a glimpse of an unrecognisable face covered in burns.*

# 2

Kurt jerked awake from the cold floor. The light from the embers in front of him, made something glint in his hand. He angrily tossed aside the knife he'd somehow grabbed in his sleep. Looking up at the window he could see the faintest trace of dawn starting to appear outside.

He started getting dressed, ignoring the cold sweat that tried to cling to his clothes. Kurt paused briefly as he put his boots on, wondering if the dream would ever stop coming. It didn't come every night but he felt like whenever he tried to rest, it was waiting for him. Between the dream and the elves in town, Kurt felt a knot growing in his gut. He tried to push it down as he walked outside to start another day in Bismurr, but the feeling kept its grip on him for the entire journey. Once again as he arrived at the outskirts he noticed the same elf patrol making their way around the town. They were talking quietly amongst themselves, but even from a distance Kurt could see them gesturing towards some of the buildings, like they were planning some changes.

Seeing the elves discussing their plans for Bismurr had always left a pestering thought in his mind. It was something that bothered him since hearing about the elf control over the region, how could so few control so many? Even with their 'magic' it seemed unlikely, but Kurt made sure to keep his curiosity to himself, as he didn't want to draw attention to himself. The town was uncharacteristically quiet as he walked to the bakery, but Kurt did notice a few people standing in the door frames of their homes, every person he passed seemed to be looking around, shrinking back somewhat when they caught a glimpse of the elf patrol nearby.

The town seemed to be on edge but he stopped thinking about it as he hurried inside the warm bakery. It was then immediately clear that Cali had been working for a while already, judging by the dozen or so trays of bread rolls standing nearby.

"Started early today Cali?" He asked curiously.

"Aye, got double orders of everything and I need you to get this out for delivery." She gestured towards two full crates filled with rolls and sweet treats. "The elf inspection went well, in a manner of speaking, so they practically doubled the workers for the mine."

"Yeah, that boy I had drop by yesterday was being drafted into work. I imagine there's a lot of other children being sent in if they're strong enough to work," Kurt replied, not trying to hide his disdain about it.

"I don't approve either, but when the elves are around you have to do as you're told and keep your head down," Cali sighed sadly. "It happens from time to time, but then things go back to normal. Small price to pay as far as I'm concerned."

"I guess so," Kurt replied as he picked up the crates.

"Now get going, They've got a shift that's gonna finish soon and they're bound to be hungry." She smiled a strained smile before turning away to continue working. Kurt wasn't eager to leave again so soon, but he did as he was told, hurrying out of the bakery with the two crates of food.

He made his way back to the mine, except with a hurried pace since he suspected the elves wouldn't care about a hungry workforce. While Kurt walked he once again noticed the people seemed to be keeping off the streets. He didn't see any sign of the elf patrol but based on how this day was going he expected to see them at the mine. Increased workers often led to unrest so a show of force could help people keep cool heads. Kurt had seen those tactics before and despite how uncomfortable they made him feel, he did his best to keep his mind focused on his own task. It wasn't his place to argue about it.

It didn't take long to reach the mine and as Kurt approached he saw a gathering of miners surrounding something. He soon heard a raised voice that was the source of the commotion. Doing his best to keep his head down, Kurt carefully made his way forward until he was at the back of the crowd. One of the older miners, a dwarf, had injured his hand and was talking with one of the elven soldiers.

"You mean to tell me you're incompetent as well as lazy?" the elf said with amusement in his tone.

"Sir, please, I just need a day to recover," the older dwarf replied through gritted teeth, cradling his hand that had turned a deep shade of purple.

"Now that just won't do. You people have constantly been slow to meet the deadlines we set for you." The elf patrol-man started to look around at the small crowd that had gathered. "In fact this could be a good lesson for all of you." The elf then turned and punched the old man in the gut, sending him to the ground struggling for breath. Kurt dropped his delivery and stepped forward.

"He's just an old man, leave him be," Kurt muttered to himself. The elf spun round to look at who spoke and the crowd backed away from both of them.

"What was that? I couldn't quite hear you," said the elf, stepping forward slowly but confidently.

Realising how many eyes were on him, Kurt lifted his head and did his best not to mumble. "You should leave him alone. I'm sure after a day of rest he'll be back to work soon enough."

The patrol-man stopped approaching and laughed. "A bold human and a stubborn dwarf, what a joy. You don't look like a miner, so just run along back to whatever hole you crawled out of and leave us to discuss the real work here."

Kurt looked around and saw that no one else was stepping forward, no one wanted to draw attention to themselves. He nodded slightly and turned away but as he was crouching down to pick up his delivery, the elf spoke once more.

"Now I hope all you filth will take the example of this human here and remember who runs Bismurr. Remember who controls your lives. Remember who is the superior race." His voice grew louder with each word, as though he was reinforcing his own beliefs as he spoke.

While the elf revelled in the crowd backing away out of fear he didn't notice that Kurt had stopped moving. *Superior race... why those words?* he thought to himself. A chill snaked its way down his spine, the same one that gripped Kurt in his dreams but something was different about it this time. Once the chill hit his stomach it disappeared, only to be quickly replaced with anger and fire. The heat spread throughout his body and he walked towards the elf, clenching his fists so tightly that he could feel his nails almost piercing the skin on his palms. The elf finally turned, still laughing to himself but before he could do anything else, Kurt exploded.

He threw a punch carrying his rage into the elf's face, instantly breaking his nose. The force of the blow flung the slender man to the ground but Kurt didn't stop, he leapt forward and landed atop his foe. He then slammed fist after fist into the elf's face as the words 'superior race' played in Kurt's head over and over again. Each blow landed with a wet crunch spreading blood over Kurt's hands. It wasn't until his chest grew painfully tight that Kurt finally stopped to take a breath. The air filled his lungs and rushed straight to his head. The fire he'd felt in his gut faded away, leaving Kurt feeling sick as he realised what he'd done. He looked down at the pummelled face before him and leapt back. The elf was lifeless and the crowd stood motionless, no one knew what they should do next.

Two of the miners eventually stepped forward and started to check the lifeless body in the dirt. A dwarf from the crowd stepped forward, approaching Kurt, he then nodded towards the bunkhouse and began steering Kurt away from the crowd. The next few hours were a blur; the dwarf cleaning and bandaging Kurt's hands, being taken back outside and walked to the outskirts of town and finally left alone to head home. Kurt stumbled slowly back through the woods in a daze until he arrived back at his clearing. It wasn't until he was standing outside his home that Kurt finally felt the weight of what he had done. He dropped to the floor and sat down with his back to the door. Kurt looked down at his hands, staring at the bloodstains on his bandages. He felt like he should scream or cry but instead he just found himself feeling adrift and numb. While staring at his hands, he didn't notice the elderly dwarf from before approaching until he stood right in front of Kurt. He felt too hollow to react to the dwarf looking at him, but after a while the silence seemed almost painful so he forced himself to meet the gaze of the stranger.

“What you did today, no one here has ever struck out against the elves.” The old man said, his tone was serious but had a hint of warmth.

“I didn't....I just...” Kurt stumbled through his words, knowing he couldn't say anything that could change what he did, he took a breath to steel himself. “How long before they come for me?”

“What?” the old man asked. Kurt looked up to see his confused face.

“After what I did? You told the others what happened, right?” Kurt asked, panicking. “You have to tell them what I did or they'll punish everyone if you...” The old man raised his hand and shook his head slightly to silence Kurt before he rambled further.

“We already hid the body in the mine.” The old man then crouched down and met Kurt's gaze. “You did something no one else felt able to do. I'm grateful, the others are grateful.” He patted Kurt on the shoulder before standing up. “Just come into town as normal tomorrow, draw away any suspicions.”

"I don't think that'll work. You have to tell the others. Please," Kurt pleaded.

"What's your name son?" the man asked, ignoring the begging of the younger man in front of him.

"Kurt," he replied, feeling defeated as his pleas went unheard.

"My name is Jacob. You did a good thing and while there may be consequences for all of us, we're all going to face what may come. Together. So rest up, come to town tomorrow and hopefully this'll be over soon enough." The old man smiled warmly as Kurt sat still, his mouth agape.

Kurt watched as the old man walked away and sat in the dirt until darkness surrounded him. When he felt the evening chill in the air, he entered his home and shut the door quickly. Exhaustion quickly flooded through his body and before Kurt could think any more on the day, he stumbled over to his bed and simply fell on to it. As he sank into the soft blankets and furs, his vision blurred as he slipped into a thankfully dreamless sleep.

# 3

Kurt awoke with dawn, feeling only a small hint of exhaustion from the previous day crawling throughout his body. He didn't bother changing his clothes as he set about readying himself for the day ahead. Kurt grabbed a small hunk of bread to eat even though he didn't feel particularly hungry. As he left his home and absent-mindedly chewed the food, his thoughts drifted onto the townsfolk and how they'd react to him.

Once Kurt reached the outskirts of the town, he saw one of the armoured elves standing in the middle of the street. The elf was watching people going about their daily duties, scrutinising each passer-by, searching for anyone looking out of place. Kurt kept his head down and tucked his bandaged hands in his pockets, hoping to look inconspicuous amongst the crowd. Mercifully, Kurt passed by the guard without even a second glance. Not wanting to take a chance, he kept his head down until he was safely out of the elf's eyeline. Despite Kurt's nervousness, everyone he walked passed was acting like this was just another ordinary day. After what felt like hours of trying to get there, Kurt finally arrived at the bakery. Once he stepped through the warm threshold, any delusions Kurt had about the entire town keeping up this ruse were immediately ended.
The moment Cali laid eyes on him, tears began streaming down her face. She rushed forward and with a little hop pulled Kurt down into a tight hug, easily dragging him down onto his knees.

"Oh Kurt, my poor boy," Cali muttered. Slowly she pulled away so she could look him in the eyes. "What are you going to do?"

Kurt pulled away and kept her at arm's length. He had hoped not to have this conversation.

"I need to answer for what I did," he said. Cali looked like she was about to rush forward again but with some difficulty, he kept her still. "The others at the mine, I think they want to hide what happened. Gratitude I guess, but it isn't right."

The dwarven woman held back her tears, knowing they weren't going to help. "Why do this? I don't think the others will even find anything. You could just be making yourself suffer needlessly."

"You and I both know they'll find out." Kurt then turned to leave, hoping to end this quickly. "And it wouldn't be needless. Someone should always make sure people like me get what we deserve."

Before Cali could stop him, Kurt walked back out into the daylight, letting the chill in the air sweep over him. While still within earshot he could hear sobbing from behind the door, Kurt wanted to go back and apologise, to share his gratitude for everything Cali had done for him for the past year, but he knew that was just going to delay the inevitable. Steeling himself, he pushed ahead and began his walk to the mines. Kurt noticed the few other townsfolk walking the streets were all walking in the same direction as him.

As he merged into the growing crowd heading toward the mine Kurt could hear a multitude of raised voices. Most of the people were arguing amongst themselves about being dragged away from their daily work while others were simply chatting amongst themselves like it was any other day. Kurt made his way through the crowd and found his way to the front of the gathering. His stomach dropped when he saw the well-dressed elf slowly pacing in front of his three compatriots and a couple of the miners. The elf was silent but looking at the people gathered before him with a piercing gaze, his eyes darting to the next face in the crowd when he came to a decision of some kind. Kurt stared and kept quiet, not wanting to exacerbate the situation for the people around him. After a few more moments of pacing the elf came to a stop and took a long breath.

"So. Just for my own clarity let us go over this one last time." His voice was frustrated but also eerily calm. "One of our number goes missing, you people know nothing about it and not one of you have found a single sign of him? Is that the entirety of the situation?"
One of the elves nodded and before anyone else could speak up the lead elf raised his voice to talk to the crowd.

"It would seem you filthy creatures have proven once again that you simply aren't worth the very air we allow you to breathe. Having been the Governor of this mud hole for far too many years, I realise I have been giving you far more freedom and peace than you clearly deserve."

Acting quickly, Kurt pushed forward through the crowd drawing the attention of everyone.

"Stop. It was me. I... I hurt your man." He looked around at the now silent people, thankful no one was stepping forward to contradict him. "I hid the body deeper in the mine." Kurt dropped to his knees and stared at the floor. "I acted alone. So you only need to punish one person here."

Everyone gathered grew still, holding their breath with nervous anticipation. The elf walked forward slowly, each step soft but firm as he approached Kurt. He stopped only a few steps away and made a small gesture with his hand. Kurt felt a strange push underneath his chin, forcing him to look up at the now smiling elf.

"No." The elf then made a gesture with his hand and Kurt felt himself being forced down, face-first onto the ground.

"Please. Just do what you want with me and let that be the end of this," Kurt said, his voice muffled by the dirt as he was held in place.

"You seem to misunderstand your place in all this, you pathetic little man, so let me explain." The elf flicked his wrist and Kurt was pulled up onto his knees. "I am Orlan Lysander. A name that holds some weight with my people. That is why I was given control of this mine and I have ruled over this hole of a town long enough to know that you disgusting creatures aren't capable of doing anything on your own." Orlan looked out to the crowd. "And since all of you feckless animals allowed this atrocity to occur, I think it only fair you all be punished accordingly."

While still using his power to hold Kurt down, Orlan used his free hand to gesture at the other three elves. A thin stream of black smoke started to stretch out from Orlan's fingertips and surround the soldiers. The three began to convulse and clutch at their chests while groaning in pain. Their limbs began to twitch and stretch, ripping through their clothes as they grew taller. Their legs started to bend backward and with a loud crack snapped, taking on a feline shape as the new bones began to form. The elven armour buckled under the stress as the transformation was taking hold and within a few moments the three elves had writhed their way free from the metal and leather that could no longer contain them. The elves' arms almost shifted into a longer shape with sharp claws replacing their fingers. Their skin also quickly darkened to a dark purple colour that looked like it could tear at any moment as it stretched painfully over enlarged muscles. Finally, with one last pained yelp, their faces morphed as fangs pushed out of their mouths at odd angles.

The crowd started to panic at the sight of the three monstrosities, everyone started to push each other as they did what they could to run away. A twisted smile spread across Orlan's face as he watched the chaos start to unfold.

"They killed one of us. Go and lay waste and don't spare anything." He then lowered his hand and the three creatures immediately began sprinting towards the town, their enhanced speed instantly apparent, violently throwing people aside as they moved. Orlan then turned his attention back to Kurt. "But what to do with the piece of filth who committed such a vile act?"

The elf slowly walked towards the helpless man, still maintaining his power to keep Kurt down. Orlan raised his free hand once more and with a weaving gesture formed a ball of flame out of the air itself. As he created his fiery weapon, Kurt could feel the strange grip on him weaken a little. His mind raced, trying to think of any way to get out of this situation so he can do something, anything to help the townsfolk. He lowered his hand just to his side where the elf couldn't see and scooped a handful of dirt, clenching it tightly in his fist.

Satisfied that the orb of fire was ready, Orlan slowly approached Kurt, coming to a halt only a few steps away. Using his power, the elf then raised Kurt's head so that their eyes met. A sadistic smile spread across Orlan's face as he raised his fiery orb above Kurt's head. Before the elf could move any further however, Kurt threw his fistful of dirt into his eyes. Blinded, Orlan stumbled back, his grip on Kurt releasing as the flaming orb disappeared. Jumping into action, Kurt lunged forward and shoved the elf with all his strength, sending Orlan sprawling backward onto the ground. Kurt seized the opportunity he'd made for himself and bolted towards the town, leaving the elf scrambling in the dirt.

With each step Kurt took the sounds of screaming and chaos grew louder, as the creatures had begun tearing their way through the town. As he ran, a chill started to creep its way up his spine when he started to see the carnage the three monsters had already caused. The few people who hadn't quite made it into the town were gathered around the first victims of the creatures. Some of the fallen were screaming in pain at the bloody wounds they'd received while others were completely still, terror now permanently attached to their lifeless faces.

Kurt slowed to a halt and took a moment to breathe and tried to focus his thoughts. Seeing how many people had been hurt already made one thing clear to him, he needed a weapon. Looking around his gaze soon fell onto a body nearby, a dwarven man laying on his back with his throat torn almost clean in half. The dead man was gripping a small pick, still covered in grey dust. Resting his hand on the dwarven man's shoulder, Kurt pushed his guilt aside and pulled the tool free. Makeshift weapon in hand Kurt got up and continued running after his quarry. He didn't have to run far before he encountered the first of the three monsters. Standing over a fresh victim with blood splattered all over its face, the large creature was ferociously ripping at the planks of a wall, trying to tear its way inside a building. Kurt could hear several people screaming from within but he ignored their cries as he charged forward. He leapt upwards and landed on the creature's back, plunging his weapon deep into its neck. As its dark blood started to gush out, the creature started swinging around violently, almost sending Kurt flying but he kept his grip and pulled back on the pick hard. More blood sprayed out of the wound and the creature's angry swipes started to slow. Despite its rapidly dwindling strength however, the creature still managed to reach back and grab Kurt's collar. Its grip tightened and the monster dragged Kurt off its back and slammed him into the wooden wall with enough force to splinter some of the weakened planks.

Even with the wind knocked out of him, Kurt didn't relent, he gripped his weapon tightly and pulled it with all his might. As the pick tore away a large chunk of meat from the creature's neck, its blood now pouring freely onto the ground, the grip on Kurt loosened enough for him to break free. The monster became still as it fell onto its knees, gargling as it struggled to take its final breaths. Kurt gritted his teeth and leapt forward, pushing the creature's large frame back as he embedded his weapon into the centre of its malformed face. He took the handle of the pick into both hands and with an enraged scream, Kurt ripped his arms upwards, tearing the monster's face in half.

Kurt finally gave himself permission to breathe normally and as he stepped away panting, he could hear more screams from further into town. He looked up and could see smoke starting to rise up in several different places, chaos was spreading quickly and he'd only taken down one of the monsters.

After one more deep breath Kurt took off running, his now-bloodied weapon gripped tightly in his fist. As he ran through the streets he saw more bodies, some people just injured but some far worse off. He ignored it all and kept moving, running towards the loudest sounds of violence echoing through the town. Kurt didn't have to move very far through the streets before he found himself facing down the second creature. This beast was holding a human arm above its head, letting blood pour down its throat.

Scattered around the monster were several dead bodies, all of them dismembered with their blood pooling together at the creature's feet. As Kurt looked on in horror at the gruesome sight the monster stopped feasting and its yellow eyes fell onto the small human. With a monstrous roar the creature rushed forward, using all four of its stretched limbs to pick up speed quickly. Kurt shook off his disgust at all the bodies around him and raised his weapon.

He waited until the creature was close before rolling to one side and whipping his hand out to slash at the creature's leg. Kurt managed to dodge away from the monster's swipe but his pick was instantly snatched from his grasp as it embedded itself into the muscular flesh of the monster. Having missed its prey and suddenly gaining a deep leg wound, the creature fell awkwardly and slid through the dirt until its large frame smashed into the side of a building, cracking and splintering the wood with a sickening crunch.

Furious at its failure, the creature roared as it got back onto its feet and once again charged forward. Kurt wasted no time and ran towards a narrow alley nearby, far too narrow for the creature to follow. As he was sprinting towards safety Kurt could hear heavy footfalls rapidly gaining on him but just the sounds came too close he dived forward, barely dodging a swipe from the monster. Kurt moved ahead, frantically looking for anything he could use as a weapon. The creature, raging at the entrance to the alley, was wildly slashing at the walls, ripping out large chunks of wood as it tried to squeeze its way closer. Panic rushed though Kurt when he discovered the only things in the alley were a pile of dirty sheets and an empty bucket. Before he could accept a bloody fate however, Kurt could hear shouting from the streets nearby. Distracted by the noise or eager for new prey, the monster stopped its assault on the walls and turned away from the alleyway.

Four people had rushed into the street, each of them brandishing knives while shouting at the monster to draw its attention away from Kurt. The creature rushed forward to attack the newcomers only to be met with wild slashes that left it screaming in frustration as it struggled to shield itself. As Kurt was awkwardly stepping over the pieces of wall on the ground a familiar face appeared at the entrance to the alley.

Jacob, now sporting several cuts on his arms and face, reached out and pulled Kurt out onto the street. Neither man said anything as together, they turned to face the monster. Despite being outnumbered, the creature had managed to pin a dwarf under its large foot while swinging wildly at the other attackers. Unable to reach anyone with its savage swipes, the monster roared with anger. Before the creature could turn its attention downward, Kurt dashed forward and tackled the creature. Together, they tumbled away from the trapped dwarf and skidded to halt nearby. Before Kurt could go back on the offensive, the creature slammed an elbow into his stomach. Struggling to take a breath after the blow, Kurt barely managed to get out of harm's way as the creature thrashed around in a fury.

When he looked up he saw Jacob and two of the other men had rushed forward, screaming as they slashed wildly at the monster. The creature's long arms quickly became a shredded mess of torn flesh as it struggled to block the attacks. Before the attackers could move closer, the creature let out an ear-piercing scream and lunged forward. Knocking aside two of the men with ease, the monster bit down into the shoulder of the dwarf it had pinned down moments ago. The creature then reared its head back, ripping out a chunk of meat from the dwarf. As the attack sent the man sprawling onto ground, screaming in agony, Jacob appeared behind the monster. Somehow he'd found Kurt's lost pick and with a hefty swing, plunged the weapon into the side of the monster's skull.

Keeping his grip tight, Jacob kicked the large lifeless monstrosity away, its body landing with a heavy wet thud into the blood caked dirt. The two other men began to help their wounded friend, one man tearing off parts of his clothes to wrap his wound. Kurt didn't stay to help, after seeing the damage two had caused in such a short time he could only imagine what chaos the third had caused. Despite wanting to rush away and find the last monster, Kurt was starting to feel exhausted. It'd been well over a year since he'd last exerted himself so much and his body was not happy about the sudden stress.

While he took a few moments to catch his breath, Jacob grabbed a hammer from the floor and handed it to Kurt before joining his injured men. Kurt watched as the small group left the street, carrying their injured to safety. It wasn't until he was left alone that Kurt finally felt like he could start moving again.

Struggling to run, Kurt hobbled onward, heading towards the towers of smoke emanating above buildings nearby. His footfalls had grown heavy but with each step he picked up his pace until he had broken out into a jog. As he moved through the town searching for the last creature, Kurt saw the damage he had caused. Homes had been ripped open, furniture and lit pieces of firewood now scattered all over the streets, while the bodies of the townsfolk now littered the streets. The chill in his spine and the guilt that had been tormenting him were now a distant fog to Kurt's mind. All he felt was a fire of rage pushing him forward.

Further away, he could see the silhouette of the large misshapen abomination feasting on a body of another victim, wet crunches and dripping viscera echoing eerily nearby. As Kurt kept to the shadows, trying to think of a plan to attack, he heard shuffling from a small side street nearby. Lit by the orange glow of the scattered fires was a family, mostly children, trying to hide from the monster ahead. Kurt met their terrified gaze and he knew it wouldn't be long before the creature would find them. After one last breath to steel himself, Kurt marched out into the street and once he was out of sight from the hidden family, he screamed at the top of his lungs.

The creature stopped and turned, growling slightly as it left its meal. Unlike the previous two creatures, this monster did not rush to attack its prey. It moved forward slowly and carefully, its long limbs spread wide to block most of the street as it crawled over the blood-soaked dirt. Kurt waited until the creature grew close before raising his weapon. The monster came to halt only a few steps away and started to regard the prey that was challenging it, tasting the air with its long tongue. While the pair stared each other down, Kurt noticed the creature was covered in scratches and wounds, maybe even enough to make it slower than him. The pair stopped moving and after a few pained breaths, Kurt lunged forward. He tried to bring his hammer down into the creature's skull but it was still fast enough to dodge the blow. With an enraged roar, the creature whipped its arms upward and sent Kurt flying. Despite the force of the strike, Kurt managed to roll backwards when he hit the ground, awkwardly returning to his feet. The monster rushed forward before Kurt's momentum ran out, causing the two to crash into a wooden wall. Now close, Kurt tightened his grip and started to swing wildly with the hammer. He managed to land several heavy strikes into the creature's head causing it to reel backwards with a pained yelp. Kurt didn't let up. Ignoring the pain in his back, he pounced onto the creature, landing blow after bloody blow. Kurt screamed with rage as he kept striking, each attack bringing the monster closer to the ground. His blows continued long after the monster grew still and lifeless, each hit spreading blood and bone further away. Kurt's savage attacks didn't end until his hammer snapped clean in half. His hands now covered in dark blood, Kurt stood up, breathing deep painful breaths as his lungs and chest struggled to choke down the cold air. Looking around, Kurt saw people had started to venture out from wherever they had been hiding. Some of the townsfolk started to do what they could to put out the fires. Others started to crowd round bodies, trying to find their loved ones amid the injured and dead. Even with the scattered fires surrounding him, Kurt felt cold as he began hearing anguished cries echoing out across the town.

Townsfolk started to emerge from the shadows trying to make sense of what had happened as they tended to the wounded. Kurt knew it wasn't time to rest however, not while there was one more monster still standing. He picked up a piece of wood and started making his way back toward the mine. As he walked, people began to gather and walk with him. Some with weapons, some tearful and angry, and some just afraid to be left behind. Kurt ignored them, he ignored everything except what was ahead. Despite the exhaustion and pain settling in, he still managed to walk ahead of the gathered crowd. Sooner than he would have liked, Kurt found himself approaching Orlan. The elf was slowly pacing back and forth, only looking up when he noticed the approaching crowd.

"I see you've all saved me the trouble of gathering you once more." He spoke with confidence, not surprised to see Kurt and the others gathered before him. "I presume the three transformed have expired by now? Such a waste, though I am a little surprised you managed to muster up the courage to fight them at all."

An older man stepped forward from the crowd. "Is this over now? Blood shed on both sides, will you please let the rest of us be?" The man's tone was almost begging. The elf turned his gaze upon the man and smiled, the same twisted smile Kurt had seen before.

Orlan raised a hand and a glowing orange sphere began to form, floating gently above his palm. The ball of fire took shape quickly and the elf reached back ready to throw his magical weapon. A lit torch, thrown from someone in the crowd, then smashed into Orlan's face, dissipating the magic orb and sent him reeling back grabbing at his face whilst roaring in agony. While some people started to step back in fear, Kurt dropped his makeshift weapon and sprinted forward. He tackled Orlan to the ground, straddling him with ease, and grabbed the torch from the floor.

"You could have punished just one deserving man. I want you to know that," Kurt spat as Orlan struggled to break free, still writhing in pain.

Struggling to keep hold of the writhing elf, Kurt tightened his grip and slammed the torch down. He used all the strength he could muster to hold the flames against Orlan's right hand. The elf screamed, with a pitch high enough to make some of the crowd almost wince in sympathy. He flailed and scratched at Kurt's arm with his free hand but couldn't find the strength to break free. It wasn't until the flesh on Orlan's palm was almost black that Kurt finally released him. The elf started to let out pained groans as he tried to awkwardly scramble away.

The crowd looked on silently, unsure of how to react to the pitiful sight of their former master. Kurt however, just felt more rage building. He didn't feel any sympathy for the injured elf. Kurt then stepped forward and with a hard swing, smashed the burned-out torch against Orlan's head. The elf was knocked unconscious this time, landing in a crumpled heap with half of his face now red raw. Kurt threw the torch away and grabbed the elf's leg. He started walking away from the mine and the town, dragging Orlan behind him, making no effort to protect the limp body from the rough road.

Kurt kept walking until the ground changed from rocks and dust to grass and trees. He continued for a short time, looking back now and again to make sure he wasn't being followed. Once Kurt was satisfied that he'd travelled far enough, he propped the unconscious Orlan against a tree. He then found a tree of his own to lean against and waited for the elf to regain consciousness. It wasn't long before Orlan roused frantically, wincing with pain as his senses returned. The elf quickly noticed him and spat onto the ground.

"Letting me live was a mistake you pathetic rat! I'll kill you, I'll kill every last one of you!" While his words were filled with venom, the elf struggled to stand and was in no shape to take action.

"No. You won't. You're going to go wherever it is that you call home and tend to your wounds." Kurt's reply was quick. He turned away and began the long walk back to his cabin. "I'm not stupid. You'll come back to assert your authority here, but if you try to hurt anyone but me, I won't drag you to safety again. I'll just kill you."

He didn't wait for Orlan's reply. While the elf muttered something under his breath, the tired and injured Kurt kept walking, letting the enraged elf's ramblings fade away into the forest. Finally, exhaustion caught up and hit Kurt hard; his arms felt heavy and numb, his chest stabbed with pain with every step, and his legs felt like they'd give in before he could get back to his cabin. Regardless of the state he was in, Kurt still opted to walk through the woods around the town so as to avoid facing the townsfolk, who no doubt wanted someone to blame for everything that had happened.

Night gradually settled in while Kurt spent a few hours hobbling home and when he finally arrived at his cabin, a stranger was waiting outside his front door. He didn't recognize the dwarven man but he wasn't surprised to see him, Kurt had been half-expecting someone to come find him at some point before the day was through. The visitor smiled meekly and slowly approached, causing Kurt to halt in his tracks.

"Evening," the dwarf greeted Kurt with a calm tone, catching him off guard. "Me and a few others wanted to talk to ya, we decided I should be the one to come here. Name's Melrose. You're Kurt right?"

"That's right," Kurt replied, nervously looking around the clearing.

"Mind if we talk inside? It's a tad cold out here." The dwarf's tone was still calm. Once he was satisfied that no one else was going to jump out and attack him, Kurt nodded and relaxed a little, he was too tired to argue and would rather be sat down if he was about to be berated.

The pair walked inside and the dwarf waited while Kurt got a small fire going. Once the room was warmed Kurt gestured for his guest to sit on one of his only two chairs. After gathering some strips of dried meat and two cups of water from his kitchen, Kurt joined the dwarf and handed him a share of food which he accepted politely.

"So lad, I think we'd better deal with this outright. Who exactly are you?" Before Kurt could even take a breath to reply the dwarf spoke up again. "And don't say you got lucky today. The moment that bastard turned on everyone, you kept your head and helped us all. I know you've been here for some time and clearly want to be left alone, but after today? I think you'd agree that you owe all of us an explanation."

Kurt sighed and took a sip of water. He looked over at the chest stashed under his bed and that familiar chill crept down his spine.

"Alright." Feeling either too tired from the day or emotionally drained from hiding this for so long but either way decided to share his story. "When I arrived here a year ago, I said I was from somewhere far to the west. That's not true. I actually have no idea where my home is, because I don't even know where here is. I have no idea how I got here, but a year ago I woke up in the woods near Bismurr, a stranger to this place, and I was barely able to comprehend the language, the people or the rules here."

Kurt took a moment to have a drink, Melrose remained silent, waiting for the story to continue. "Thankfully you all took me in and I was able to make a home for myself here. Gradually my past life began to seem like a memory, or maybe a dream? But today I was reminded of who and what I really am. Where I'm from I am a soldier, like the elves who served Orlan.....perhaps too much like them." Kurt paused for a moment to give the dwarf time to react, but the kind older man calmly waited for the story to continue. "The... things... I... that I ran from led me here. I saw how this place was being treated by the elves and I thought it wasn't my place to do anything. This town, it's so different from my home and I really thought things were better here. So I chose to do nothing and let life pass by. It seemed like I was given a chance to live peacefully." Tears started to form and fall as Kurt spoke. "But after today? More people have suffered because of me. People died because I got involved."

At this point Melrose raised his hand to stop Kurt from talking.

"What you did since you arrived here was what we have been doing for decades.

What you did today was something many of us have been hiding from doing for just as long. Whatever your past and your involvement here, what happened today has been a long time coming," Melrose sighed, a hint of disappointment in his voice. "All that being said, a few of us gathered and are starting to prepare the town for what is to come. And after what you did today? A few of us decided that you should join our first meeting. You're going to help us be ready for what will come our way."

"There's no other way forward but violence is there?" Kurt asked, drying his tears on his sleeve. The dwarf shook his head and took a moment before replying.

"We have time at least. That elf will have to head back to his allies before returning here. The council we've formed is going to meet first thing tomorrow, you're expected to join us." Melrose stood up and began walking to the door. "Whatever decision we make for the town tomorrow, I truly believe you did the right thing Kurt. I'll return tomorrow to take you to the others, so rest up."

The dwarf smiled weakly as he left and Kurt responded with a simple wave. Alone once more, Kurt's exhaustion barely left him the strength to get into bed. As his head hit the pillow, Kurt briefly thought about getting undressed but found his body had finally given up on following his orders. Within a few seconds he was snoring soundly, drifting deep into a dreamless slumber.

* * *

The next morning, dawn's light trickled in through the window and gently roused Kurt. For a few moments he lay still, warm and comfortable, but when he did try to sit up, pain seemed to wash over every inch of him. Groaning like a man twice his age as he got up, Kurt set about making himself presentable. As he moved around the cabin, his aches started to recede, giving him the reprieve he needed to feed and wash himself.

A short while later, with a full belly and clean clothes, his aches and pains fading to the back of his mind, Kurt finally had time to think. While he thought about the past couple of days, a strange feeling began to circulate in his mind. He felt a drive building, a drive to be a part of something. Despite everything that had happened, Kurt found himself feeling energised for the day to come. Knowing that he'd be leaving soon, he eagerly pulled his boots on and sat down to wait. Within a few minutes a tentative knock echoed through his home. Kurt didn't delay, opening the door hastily to reveal a tired Melrose.

"Morning," the dwarf greeted him with a slight smile. "Hope you're ready, we have a lot to get done today"

"Hello," Kurt replied, as he stepped into the morning sun. "I'm ready. Are you sure people want me involved? I expect most of the townsfolk won't be happy to see me."

"There's some tension of course, but it's just uncertainty about what to do. If anyone holds blame for you, they're keeping it to themselves. Now let's get going, the others want to get started as soon as possible." Melrose then started walking away, headed towards Bismurr. Kurt closed the door to his home and followed quickly. The pair walked in silence as they approached the town, both their thoughts racing about the day ahead and the plans that needed to be made.

# 4

As the pair walked into town, Kurt noticed that the streets of Bismurr were oddly quiet. Since work had stopped at the mine, the few people they did pass in the streets weren't following the routines Kurt had grown so accustomed to over the past year.

The people they did pass by stared at the pair, whispering amongst themselves once they were out of earshot. Kurt couldn't make out what they were saying, but judging by the glares they weren't discussing anything good. Thankfully no one seemed to want to do anything but talk, at least for the time being.

"I need to make one stop before we start," Kurt said, stopping Melrose in his tracks.

"I'll wait here, but be quick please." The dwarf then gestured in the direction of Cali's bakery, clearly knowing where Kurt planned to go. He gave his companion a quick nod before heading off. He broke into a jog and within a few moments he was stood at her front door.

The fighting from the day before hadn't come close to her home and business so he felt assured she would have been safe. He went through the door without knocking as he had done so many times before. Sitting on a small stool holding a steaming mug was a very tired Cali. She jumped as Kurt stepped inside and let out a small gasp before rushing across the room, tackling him into a hug.

"You're a silly boy, you know that?" said Cali, her voice muffled as she spoke into his shirt.

"I know." Kurt paused for a moment before breaking away from her. "I'm sorry. I never meant for any of this to happen."

Cali looked him in the eye with a stern look. "Listen here. You don't have to be sorry for anything. You took responsibility, you did what you could and you saved people's lives. I'm proud to know you."

Kurt smiled weakly before replying. "They're having a gathering today. I've been invited to be a part of deciding where the town goes from here."

"That's happening this morning? You'd best not be here then." She started to walk Kurt out of the bakery. "Pop back here when you're done."

With a final small hug, Cali let Kurt go. Moments later he was back outside walking back to where Melrose was waiting for him. The dwarf was looking down, deep in thought, until he saw the younger man approaching.

"Ready?" Melrose asked.

"As much as I can be," replied Kurt.

They didn't walk for much longer before they came to the largest building in the town of Bismurr, The Jumping Canary, the only tavern in Bismurr. Normally it was one of the few places people could find a reprieve from either farming or mining but today it had been cleared out and made into a make-shift town hall. Kurt and Melrose walked through the large entrance, passing by a few townsfolk that were waiting outside. Once inside, Kurt could hardly recognize the establishment he'd frequented a few times during his year in town. Almost all the furniture had been pushed to the sides, save for ten chairs laid out in a circle in the centre of the main room. While the circle was kept clear, the rest of the tavern was packed with people, most of them filling the balcony overhead. A lot of the people were talking amongst themselves whilst keeping an eye on the scene below, everyone seemed eager for the meeting to start.

Of the ten chairs laid out, only three were occupied. Two elderly human men and one dwarven woman were sitting near each other and muttering amongst themselves. One of the men gave the new arrivals a brief wave and gestured at two empty chairs. Once the pair were situated, Melrose leaned over to speak to Kurt.

"The lady there is Mary Clavis, she and her family tend most of the crops outside of town. The two gentlemen are Rick and Cole Berne, brothers, they deal with the construction work in and around town. Usually just people expanding their own homes but occasionally new buildings. They're the ones who got the supplies for your little cabin." As Melrose finished talking, a thought occurred to Kurt.

"Most work in town seems family run. What is it you do? Must be important if you get to be on this council?" He paused for a moment as a further realisation dawned on him. "Was it you who wanted me on this council?"

"It was my idea but no one disagreed with me. Regardless of how you value yourself, you're the best trained individual in town. That's a perspective I have no doubt will be useful to hear from during this discussion." Melrose paused for a moment to give Kurt a chance to respond, but after a few seconds of silence he continued. "As for my place on the Council? I come from the Higgs family – tailors. Nothing special, but almost all the clothes in town are made by me and my kin." Melrose chuckled. "Surprising how much respect you get when you literally helped clothe a person's entire family."

As they finished talking, Mary, who had finished her own conversation with the brothers, walked over to Kurt. While he was seated they were equal heights. She had a kind smile on her face and unlike some of the faces staring down at him from the balcony, seemed pleased with his presence.

"Before we begin today, I wanted to thank you. One of my nephews was almost attacked by one of those creatures last night but thanks to you he managed to stay hidden and safe." Kurt had no time to reply before she returned to her seat.

As Kurt watched her sit down, he caught the eye of one of the brothers, Cole, who gave him a slight nod. Kurt responded in kind before he started looking around the room. Most of the people were still murmuring amongst themselves, making sure to keep their voices low so they wouldn't miss anything when the meeting started. The hushed conversations stopped momentarily when another figure entered the tavern. An elderly dwarf hobbled his way across the room and after a quick look around, wandered over to sit as far from anyone else as possible. Kurt recognised him as one of the miners but had never heard his name. Once the old dwarf had settled into his chair the voices started murmuring once more.

"That's Oligard Braks, most of us call him Ollie, he's one of the oldest people in town. Used to work the mines, now he just oversees everyone else down there," whispered Melrose, patting Kurt's shoulder as he spoke. Knowing that he had something of a guide to help him gave Kurt a slight sense of comfort.

Only a few moments passed before more council members came in, once again sending a wave of quiet throughout the room. This time it was two human women, both were much younger than the other council members, probably only a few years older than Kurt himself. They sat either side of Ollie and immediately started a hushed conversation with the elderly dwarf.

"That's Jessie Canan and her cousin, Tessa Stone." Melrose whispered. "They're the town healers. Quite the experts in plants, far better than I've seen in some time. Since they took charge a while back, we haven't had a sickness grind this town to a halt like it used to."

While Melrose was talking, two men entered the room. One was a young muscular dwarf and the other was a human with a few streaks of grey hair. The older of the two scanned the room, seemingly judging everyone sat in the circle. His gaze lingered on Kurt for a moment longer than the others, but he moved on quickly enough.

"Ah, the town hunters. We've probably about a dozen hunters in all but those two are something quite special. The human one is Keiran Stone, pretty sure he's related to Tessa, I think maybe her uncle? The young dwarf is Pete Bowen, probably the best hunter and tracker in town. Between the two of them, they probably bring in almost half the meat we eat." The new arrivals took the final two seats opposite Kurt and Melrose. This time the silence that fell over the room lingered, as people waited for the council to begin talking. After a few moments of silence, Rick stood up and made sure all eyes were on him before he began to speak.

"Now that we're all here, let us begin." He paused to make sure all attention was on him. "I think for clarity we should get the obvious out of the way. Oligard, if you would?" Rick then sat down and gestured for the elderly dwarf to speak. Oligard stepped off his chair and took a deep breath that seemed to weigh his old body down.

"We have been under the thrall of a greater power for almost my entire life. While there are many days where we live peacefully and seemingly free, there was never a day where our lives weren't spent in servitude." While he spoke, he became more animated as his own frustration seemed to bubble over into his words. "For so many years, we have been visited by Orlan. The blood he spilt over the years has left us impotent, enraged and yearning for some kind of justice. Yet we did nothing. We let generations of our families toil and suffer because we believed that was our only option." His gaze then fell onto Kurt. "Then this man did what any of us could have done, but through fear we didn't. So I think I speak for all of us when I say that whatever the consequence, we will not go back to the way things were."

The emotional outburst seemed to tire him as the elderly dwarf slumped back onto his chair and waved a hand for someone else to speak. Keiran then stood up and walked to the middle of the circle.

"Well said, Ollie. Now for the harder to hear part. It'll probably take a few months for Orlan to get back to his people and then another few to get back here, and you can be sure he will return." Keiran took a moment to let everyone take that in. "This town isn't that important to the elves but they'll definitely want to silence any hint of resistance, so when Orlan does come back, he'll come back in force. While we hunters can track and fire a bow, we're not equipped or trained to fight whatever is coming down on us, for that we turn to you, Kurt. You kept a cool head, dealt with those creatures and even bested Orlan. What do you think we should do to prepare?"

Kurt took a nervous breath as all eyes turned to him. Before making a move Melrose caught his eye and gave him an encouraging nod. He then stood up and took a few steps forward to stand with Keiran.

"If everyone is set on fighting through this then I have some ideas. First, those who can't or don't want to fight need to be ready to leave town and hide, they'll need to practise so they can do it quickly when danger comes. Second, we need to train up as many able bodies to fight as we can, and arm them with whatever weapons we have. Finally, we need some way to have a warning before Orlan returns so we have time to put everything into action. If we get some of that ready, we can see what our situation is in a month and make further plans from there." As he finished talking, Keiran gave him a thankful pat on the shoulder and Kurt returned to his chair.

"Alright then. We'll make arrangements for some of that later. Even if we prepare well, people are bound to get hurt. Jessie, Tessa – do you think you'll be able to handle dealing with the injured?" Keiran asked.

The cousins had a quick whispered discussion before Tessa stood up.

"We'll need volunteers but we can definitely be ready. Just give us a week to gather supplies," she said, sitting down again to continue whispering with Jessie.

"There is something I want to ask," said a voice from across the circle. Everyone turned to Mary who was now standing, turning a slight shade of pink at the sudden attention. "I think it'd be foolish not to consider other options. Now we know that talking through the situation isn't really an option, but do we have to fight? What about simply leaving?" A brief silence fell over the room until Ollie coughed loudly, drawing attention to himself.

"Where would we go? The elves did everything in their power to make sure any settlements that weren't their own were separated and isolated. The closest place is the east, though that's where the elvish outpost sits, where our enemy has travelled. Or maybe you'd rather try over the mine and the mountains towards some northern village? It'd take at least three months to make that journey assuming most of us could survive it. The western wilds could be an option, except they are untamed. There are more than wolves and birds that prowl there, we would most certainly not make the journey to the ocean. As for the south, no one has heard from anyone there since before the elves arrived so there is no telling what would await us. It'd probably be pointless to travel anyway as we'd most likely be ambushed while we journey as Orlan would easily be able to track such a large group fleeing him."

"Thank you Ollie," replied Mary, a little dejected. "It'll be important that we keep farming what we can in the time we have. Winter will be here in the coming months and assuming we manage to defend ourselves from what's to come, we'll need to keep our food stores as stocked as possible."

"I think that's enough for now." Cole said, standing up to address everyone. "We'll meet again in a few days, but I think for now we have enough to get started with."

With that, the crowd burst into conversation with some trying to grab the attention of council members while others just began talking amongst themselves. Melrose patted Kurt's shoulder and gestured towards the door, quickly leaving before anyone could approach them. Once they were walking down the sunlit streets and getting further from the tavern, Kurt felt relieved. He'd thought that he would have had nothing to contribute and would have been left alone to be quietly judged by the townsfolk. Melrose on the other hand seemed to look more concerned than he had been before the meeting. The two of them walked in silence for a time before the older man spoke up.

"Things are going to become hard for us all in the coming weeks." He seemed to grow visibly older as they walked. He barely knew the man, but Kurt was getting the sense that Melrose was simply kind, no logic or reason for it, just trying to do his best for the people around him.

"There's no doubt there. But at least we're getting prepared, I think we might just see ourselves through to the other side of this." Kurt truly believed that. Something in his gut felt right for the first time in over a year.

"I suppose you're right," Melrose replied, smiling a little. "I think we're done for the day, go do as you please. I'll fetch you tomorrow"

"Thank you Melrose." Kurt paused for a moment. "Truly, thank you for everything today."

The old dwarf smiled a big toothy grin and walked away, leaving Kurt alone in the middle of the street. Not wanting to linger, Kurt took a deep breath and started making his way back to Cali's bakery. He took his time while he walked, processing everything that had happened. Compared to his feelings merely a day ago, he actually felt hopeful, though there was still a cold feeling creeping inside his gut. Kurt passed a few townsfolk as he walked and despite giving them space he still overheard them muttering about him. As he drew closer the strong smell of freshly-baked bread filled his nostrils. Cali had been baking up a storm, probably out of nerves. Kurt walked in through the front and saw dozens of rolls, pastries and small cakes lining every shelf on the cooling rack. Cali was nowhere to be seen, but he could hear clattering from the back as she was still hard at work.

"Cali!" Kurt called out, putting on a happy tone.

"Ooh, just a moment dear. Let me take this last batch out!" she called out from the back.

Kurt leant against the wall. The wooden boards felt warm and soft as he drifted back into thought while he waited. Within a few minutes Cali appeared from the back brandishing two mugs of tea, leaving a dusty trail of flour in her wake. While the town had been making plans, Cali had been busy filling as many orders as possible. Lots of townsfolk seemed to want to stock up on as much food as they could. Whether they were celebrating their freedom or preparing for the worst, Kurt couldn't say. In either case it left Cali working the hardest she had in months. When she was finished sharing her day, Cali refilled their drinks while Kurt told her everything that was discussed at the meeting.

"I really think you have to see this through to the end," Cali said as she sat back down. "You may not have wanted to change things around here. But this is where you are now."

"You're right," Kurt conceded, knowing better than to argue with her. "I just never thought that something from my past would be useful to anyone."

"That's life for you," Cali smiled as though an old memory had replayed in her mind. "Everything you go through just makes up who you are. What you do with all of it is up to you."

"Some lofty thoughts for a baker," Kurt joked as he drank the last of his tea. Cali punched him on the arm as she walked toward the back room.

"You'd best be off and get whatever you need ready for tomorrow," she shouted from out of sight.

"Don't want help around here?" Kurt asked. All he heard in reply was a huge laugh. "Alright, alright. I'll see you later."

He put his mug on a nearby shelf and left the bakery. Stepping out into the chill air he became aware of how late it had gotten. Not quite night, but evening was definitely creeping its way across the valley. The streets were almost empty and lights could be seen from windows as people were starting to light their candles and fires. Tucking his hands into his pockets to keep warm, he marched off home. Kurt didn't encounter anyone else as he left town, which he was grateful for after a tiring day.

It wasn't until he was far from the warmth and light of the town that Kurt realised what he had built here. He looked back at all the houses and even the mine in the distance. This place had been a home to him for over a year now and as he looked on, he started to feel more resolute in what he needed to do. The place had to not only survive, but be victorious over what was to come. His thoughts drifted back to before his time in Bismurr and the familiar chill crept up his spine. Kurt took one last glance at the town before shivering his way into the woods, trying in vain to keep warm.

Once he got inside his small abode, Kurt wasted no time and got a fire started. For a time he just stared at the flames, his mind hazily shifting between thoughts as tiredness gradually took hold. Kurt looked to his bed but before he could move toward it, his gaze fell onto the chest tucked underneath. A cold gripped him as he stared at the chest, forcing him to huddle closer to the fire. The warmth from the flames did their job, giving Kurt just enough comfort as his vision began to blur into darkness, sleep finally claiming him.

*Kurt once again found himself standing in the dream that had been tormenting him for so long but something was different. He felt strangely aware of everything and this lucidity felt wrong. Looking around, all he could see was a thick fog obscuring almost everything from view. With one exception, a figure nearby looking around as though lost. Kurt ducked down and cautiously approached. As he drew closer, Kurt instantly recognised the figure that came into view and the sight sent a wave of cold throughout his body.*

*"You know, I really wasn't expecting your mind to be quite as interesting as all this," Orlan Lysander said, turning to face Kurt.*

*The elf seemed completely unharmed, once again wearing clean white clothes that seemed to almost glow in the fog making him look almost ethereal. Something was off about Orlan, he seemed too perfectly presented as though he was a living painting wrapped over his own body.*

*"You can't be here. This isn't real." Kurt spoke the words trying to convince himself, but this was the first time he had dreamt of something different in over a year and it felt so invasive, so wrong.*

*"Your little human mind will never grasp everything my kind is capable of so don't even try." Orlan smirked as he turned back to the fog. "I truly believed you were just some pathetic creature who didn't know his place. But after looking at all this?" He gestured towards the fog as though he was seeing a grand landscape. "You've given me such a gift."*

*"What are you talking about?" Kurt asked, the chill in his spine shifting painfully,*

*like it was trying to swallow him into the ground beneath his feet.*

*"Oh don't be so foolish. This perfect world you and your original kin were building. Of course you had a few details wrong but I have to say, and I don't use this word lightly, it is beautiful." Orlan's eyes seemed to glaze over and that smirk changed into something sickening.*

*Kurt felt raw, exposed and something in his gut screamed that this intrusion had to end. The familiar chill he felt was changing once again. The rage he had before was nothing compared to what was building now. He lunged forward almost frothing at the mouth and tackled Orlan to the ground. Kurt screamed in anger as he raised a fist and punched down, but he simply hit the air as Orlan was now standing behind him.*

*"This is a dream you dolt. You can no more hurt me here then I you. I am surprised to see you act this way though. Your memories hold such amazing things and you seem to hate them? Maybe you are as pathetic as I first thought. More unique of course, but still pathetic." The elf then started to look around once more, seemingly losing all interest in the despairing human on the ground at his feet.*

*Kurt's mind raced, he was trapped in this nightmare and he couldn't think of a way out. As he began to think of ideas he noticed the fog around him began to swirl and move as though trying to form shapes. He stretched out a hand and focused on a singular idea, weapon, and in response the fog shifted and moved into the shape of a dagger in his hand. It gained weight and mass the longer he thought upon it. He looked up to see Orlan still staring into the distance, completely disinterested in what Kurt was doing. The young man then took the dagger and kept low as he tried to rush the elf once more. This time there was no contact at all, he just passed right through Orlan like he was made of the fog itself.*

*"You really cannot grasp the concept of what a dream is can you?" The elf asked, not even trying to mask his condescending tone. One other idea jumped into Kurt's*

*mind. He took the dagger and spun it round to face himself. Orlan's eyes widened and before he could take a step forward, Kurt plunged the dagger into his own chest.*

# 5

Kurt bolted up from the floor in front of his fire in his home, still cold from what had happened. He struggled to catch his breath for a moment and clutched his chest. As he looked at the where the wound would have been the memories of what had seen became very hazy despite a dull ache remaining in his chest. Kurt tried to spend the rest of the night awake, but as he was staring into the fire watching it dwindle to embers, sleep found him once more.

Despite his rest being peaceful, it was still short-lived as he was roused by the cries of nearby birds waking with the dawn. Kurt felt he had to be active and get moving so he didn't risk drifting off again, so he stoked the fire and put a pot of water above it to boil for tea. Soon enough he was sat with a slightly too hot mug and some stale bread he wanted to get rid of. Neither were pleasant but they did the job of fully waking Kurt.

Feeling a need to get moving, he went outside and walked around to the back of his cabin. Attached to the back of the house was a small shed. Kurt opened the hatch and checked the contents, a large axe with a pile of uncut logs. He dragged out the largest of them and set about chopping the wood into smaller chunks. Each swing of the axe helped Kurt clear his head and push away the memories from the night before. He lost track of time as he chopped his way through a few logs, only stopping when he heard knocking coming from the front of the cabin. Kurt stashed the firewood and axe back in their place and made his way around the house to see Melrose waiting for him.

"Good morning," Kurt called from the side, wiping his hands clean on his trousers. He buttoned his shirt, hesitating when he reached the dull ache on his chest. Kurt ignored the pain and straightened his clothes. He wasn't completely sure why his usual dream had been interrupted but he felt like sharing the experience was a bad idea.

"Up already? That's good. Ready to go?" Melrose was quick with his greeting.

"Ready as I can be," Kurt replied, jogging over to Melrose's side as he spoke. "You're in a hurry today."

"Oh just a little. I've been given some designs for some more practical attire for a few people. Should be a little protective too." As he spoke he looked Kurt up and down, sizing him up in his head. "Also something you should know: Pete and a few others have headed south to see if they can find someone or something to help us. They'll probably return in a few days, Pete's always been one for travelling quickly when he's on his hunts so he won't waste time."

"What do you think they'll find?" Kurt asked. He had never been too interested in travelling since he had arrived here, but now he was just as curious as the other townsfolk.

"Honestly? Nothing, I suspect everyone who had been around there either fled or were killed. No one here even knows the name of any village that might have been there. All we do know is that when the elves came to the region they dealt with whoever was there very harshly." Melrose took a breath and shook his head, as though shaking away whatever dark thought he was having. "But that's for them to worry about. You've got something else to be getting on with today. A whole group of people volunteered for whatever training you're going to give."

"Really? I would have thought numbers would be quite small, especially so soon after what happened," Kurt replied.

"The people of Bismurr aren't foolish, they know that if they want to survive they need to be ready. You left quite the impression during that attack, and we all remember that you spoke well at the meeting. People are taking notice." Melrose gave him an encouraging nudge in the side.

Kurt almost wanted to talk about his dream from last night, but as he thought about it his chest started to ache again, so he kept silent as the pair walked through the forest. Keeping that nightmare to himself for now felt like the right choice. Melrose trusted him, a feeling that Kurt found oddly comforting. The pair didn't speak as they walked the rest of the way, keeping the pace quite brisk. Soon finding themselves back at the outskirts of town. A gathering had formed on the grassy field just before the first few buildings. Several dozen people were all waiting, while a few were pacing back and forth impatiently, most were sitting down looking like they were about to fall asleep. Once a few of them saw Kurt and Melrose arriving, some started muttering and nudging one another to pay attention.

"Well here they are," Melrose said, slowing to a halt so his voice wouldn't be heard by the crowd. "Whatever training you had in mind, it's time to begin. Make sure you sound confident. Stick around town when you're done, I've got a few things I want to talk about."

The dwarf then walked ahead into the town, waving at the crowd as he went. Left alone with the eager group, Kurt took a deep breath and walked up to the crowd, sizing up a few people as he passed. They mostly looked to be in good shape, most of them had been hard workers for most of their lives. As Kurt was staring, people started mumbling among themselves again, unsure of what was going to happen next.

"Hello everyone," Kurt said loudly, making sure everyone could hear him clearly. "I'm not sure exactly what I can teach you, but I'm going to do my best to do right by all of you and I hope we make it through what's to come." The crowd murmured some more and from what Kurt could make out, it sounded like people were agreeing with him. "First thing we're going to do is split into groups so we can manage our numbers a bit easier. So gather into even numbers as best you can and pick a leader. When you've done that, all the leaders come and see me."

The crowd fell into a small amount of disarray as friends started grabbing one another and people started arguing about who should be in charge. Kurt was happy to watch the chaos while they sorted themselves. Recalling what he felt were decades old memories, not being able to choose who to follow had weighed on him through the years, offering them a choice made sense. After a few minutes the crowd had formed into seven groups and their elected leaders had gathered in front of him.

"The rest of you, go for a run around the town. Once you've done that you can go eat, if anyone doesn't make it the whole way, you don't get your lunch." The crowd briefly seemed dumbfounded until one person at the back started running and soon was joined by others until one by one the entire group had taken off. Kurt then looked over the seven leaders. Six of them were dwarfs, four women, two men and the last was a human man.

"I guess we should introduce ourselves?" said one of the dwarves as Kurt's gaze lingered on him.

"Yes you're right. Well, as you all know by now, I'm Kurt Bauer." He then gestured at the one who spoke up first.

"Name's Soren Heathfel," replied the dwarf. He seemed slightly shorter than the others but his black bushy hair and beard seemed to give him a much bigger presence. Soren's clothes hung a little loose as though they had seen a lot of use. His hands and forearms were covered in little scratches and scars from a lifetime of work. Soren also had a pleasant demeanour as he patted the human next to him on the back to get him to start talking.

"My name is Peyton Rinnenon." The tall human shifted uncomfortably as he spoke. He didn't seem much older than Kurt but he did have several grey streaks in his combed brown hair. Clean shaven and somewhat stiff, he had the bearing of an academic. His clothes were tailored well but not suited to a day of physical activity, yet he still seemed to have an imposing presence about him. Peyton then gestured at the next down the line to introduce themselves. One of the female dwarves spoke up.

"I'm Yvette Rossum. Probably the best shot with a bow against this lot," she laughed. The female dwarf had been smiling throughout this entire encounter, which Kurt approved of - keeping spirits up was going to be important during the next few months. Her dark brown hair hung messily down to her shoulders, like it was trying to connect with the small amount of scruffy chin hair she was sporting. Her clothes looked like they were going to fall apart but she had sewn brightly coloured patches over the various holes and tears to keep them usable.

"Lief Turner," said the next person in line. The voice came from a very strong looking young dwarf. Her red hair was tied in a ponytail that hung down her back. She was wearing a vest despite the morning chill and gave no signs she wasn't feeling comfortable. She was also sporting a jagged cut across one arm; a scratch from one of the creatures that had attacked the town. Lief looked along to the dwarf standing next to her.

"My turn? I'm Garet Colier." This male dwarf was much younger than the others around him, but he held himself with the same confidence. His dark brown hair and beard were both cut short. His clothes were the same garb that many of the hunters wore whenever they left the village. Garet also seemed more energetic than the others, constantly looking back and forth among the seven and Kurt. He eventually stopped looking around and stared at one of the remaining women.

"That just leaves me and my sister. I'm Meredith Sotum." The dwarf had long blonde hair that covered half her face. She was the skinniest among the group but looked just as strong as the others. Unlike the others more practical garb, she was wearing a bright red dress that looked brand new.

"I'm Sig Sotum." The last of the group was quieter than the rest and looked a little uncomfortable as she raised her voice. She had blonde hair like her sister but hers had been tied into a neat bun atop her head. While the two sisters looked similar, Sig was clearly the younger of the two. She was also wearing brand new clothes, but had opted for dark brown overalls that made her look a little bigger than her sister.

Once introductions were done, Kurt committed each name to memory as best he could, even going so far as to repeat them once more under his breath as he looked at each person in turn.

"So, each of you are now squad leaders. This means whatever I say and teach, you pass onto your squad however you choose." The group all nodded in agreement and kept quiet as Kurt spoke. "Once we know what each group's strengths and weaknesses are, we'll give each squad specific jobs, but for now you'll just be squad one through seven." He gestured across the group as he spoke so they would know their numbers. "To be ready in the time we have, we need to establish the trust between all of you. That means I'm not going to speak to the squads much, just you seven. Hopefully that'll keep things nice and clear."

"Seems about right. We do that whenever we go out hunting with someone new," Yvette said, and the others muttered in agreement.

"I think we should give you a title of some kind," said Peyton, causing a few murmurs of agreement. "I've heard the elves throw a few words around in the past. I think Commander seems the most appropriate."

"Agreed," a few replied at the same time.

"Commander it is then. I think the first thing we should work on is just getting everyone to follow orders and work as teams. Any ideas?" Kurt asked. He looked around the group, but wasn't waiting long as Lief soon spoke up.

"A small fighting ring. Everyone takes part, first person thrown out of the ring loses. Squads pick their fighter each time." Lief met Kurt's gaze as she spoke and didn't break it when she finished speaking, waiting for an answer.

"That's a good idea, and it's a good start for everything else we need to cover," Kurt replied, giving Lief a supportive nod.

"We'll need to be careful. We might learn a lot but we can't risk anyone getting injured," said Sig, causing more murmurs of agreement.

"That sounds like a good place to start. Can I leave all of you to organise that? I'm going to see what kind of weapons we're going to arm ourselves with," said Kurt. The squad leaders then turned away and started to discuss where to start their fighting ring.

Kurt smiled as he left them to their planning. He was feeling very pleased with himself, seeing a larger crowd of volunteers than he expected was nice to see and then getting somewhat organised was heartening. The talk of training and weapons was familiar to Kurt, giving him a sense of confidence about the whole endeavour of preparing the town.

As he walked through the town on his way to the blacksmith, he overheard a few people talking about the large crowd running around town. By most accounts it seemed like they were struggling but trying as best they could. He smiled as he heard about their progress and it kept him in pleasant spirits all the way to the smithy. It was an open building with several different people working around the forge, some stoking the flames, others measuring and drawing designs onto large sheets of paper. Kurt's gaze fell on a familiar man hammering away on a bright red spike. It was Cole Berne, wearing some heavy protective leathers and looking filthy with soot and sweat from his work.

"Morning," Kurt called out, standing a short and safe distance away from the red-hot metals. Cole looked up from his work and turned to shove the spike into a barrel of oil. He didn't leave it sizzling there for long and swiftly moved it to stand to cool. Once it was secure in a vice he stepped away from his work table and threw his heavy gloves down on a blackened table.

"Kurt," said Cole, acknowledging the younger man. "How goes the start of training?"

"It's started off well, hopefully it'll stay that way. I was just coming to see what kind of weapons we're going to expect? Knowing what we're working with will shape our plans," Kurt explained. "I wasn't expecting you to be here though, I thought you dealt with construction?"

"Hah, normally I do but now we need all skilled hands working hard, and for ten years I tended this forge so I'm something of an expert." Cole smiled, mostly to himself, thinking of old memories. "As for weapons, the only things we have moulds for are axes and arrowheads so we're making as many of them as we can. If anyone has any specific orders in mind we could try to make them. We're also working on some small metal plates to sew into clothes, see if we can make some better protection for your recruits, but we've no experience in that so we're not sure how they'll turn out."

"Good to hear. Axes and archery, I think we can work with that," said Kurt, already starting to think of ideas of how to train people with those weapons in mind. "Where are you getting all the metals for this? I can't imagine the elves left enough around to let you build many weapons."

"Thankfully we're set there, Orlan was about to take an ore shipment away during his visit, so we have plenty to work with for now," Cole replied. "We've definitely got enough iron to create the weapons and few other things but if anyone asks for more beyond that? We might need to mine some more, and people aren't exactly eager to do that."

"Understandable. What about maintaining the weapons? Have you got people on that?" Kurt was curious as there didn't seem to be anyone else around the forge.

"Maintain?" Cole then laughed and pointed to the barrel of oil. "You see that stuff? Those elves made sure we kept a huge supply of it. They call it Valentail oil. We don't know much about it or where it's from, but it makes the metals it's treated with stronger. Practically unbreakable, doesn't rust and if it's something like an axe it stays sharp much longer than normal. We've got dozens of barrels of it stored up at the mine."

"That sounds a bit miraculous," Kurt replied. "I'll leave you to it for now, though I'll probably be back at some point with some special orders. That Valentail oil is giving me a few ideas."

"Right you are," the older man replied. "You've really taken to this. You seem like something of a natural."

Kurt simply smiled and walked away. Though the smile dropped once he wasn't facing Cole. *A natural?* he thought. He felt a pang of guilt and did his best to shrug off the feeling as he walked through the streets, making his way to the mine. His thoughts focused on the Valentail oil. Various ideas for using it began to swirl in his head but he wanted to see what other supplies the town had access to before he made a decision about what to make.

When he arrived at the mine it was eerily desolate, having been bustling with work only days ago. Kurt approached one of the supply buildings that he suspected contained the barrels. Once inside he noticed a couple of wooden barrels in the corner. He opened the top of one and while he didn't find the oil he was searching for, he did discover a large quantity of black powder. A powder he recognised. Kurt very carefully replaced the lid and walked back out. Once outside he spotted an elderly dwarf marching up towards the mine.

"Excuse me!" Kurt called out. The old dwarf looked confused, but adopted a friendly demeanour once he saw Kurt.

"Hello. You're that Kurt boy aren't you?" The dwarf asked as Kurt approached.

"I am, yes. I was just looking around for that Valentail oil but I just found some black powder, what is it?" Kurt asked eagerly.

"The sparking powder? Just something we use in the mine. Gotta be careful with that stuff, you could bring half a mountain on your head if you put it in the wrong place," laughed the old dwarf.

"Are those two barrels all we have?" Kurt asked.

"At the moment. You find it in the mine, usually in chunks tucked between the iron ore and the rocks around it. We usually grind it up and keep it for later. Don't think we'll get much more any time soon though what with no one wanting to tend the mine," he replied.

"Would you mind if I took some?" Kurt responded, curious about what he could make from it.

"Of course! Whatever you need. I'll grab some of that oil for you too," said the dwarf as he walked toward another small building. "I'm Grezie by the way."

"Thank you!" Kurt called out as the dwarf disappeared inside. Grezie soon reappeared with two flasks in hand with one already sealed.

"There ya go. Hope you find out what you need to." Grezie smiled as he handed over the two flasks. "I'd best get back to it, gotta move all the food outta here and back into town."

Kurt smiled to himself while walking away and began his return journey to town. He pocketed the flask of oil as he walked but kept the sparking powder in his hands - if it was as potent as he thought it might be, being careful with it was his top priority. While he walked he heard a large crowd approaching from the outskirts of town and he could see his recruits finishing their lap of the town. Some looked drenched with sweat and red in the face while others looked like this was just a normal day. Kurt gave them a small wave that he hoped was encouraging before resuming his walk.

After a wrong turn and a small amount of backtracking he finally found the entrance to the small building tucked away between two large houses. Kurt walked inside, jingling a set of wooden chimes above his head as he closed the door behind him. The place was littered with bits of fabric and leather, several piles of neatly folded fabrics were spread across several tables and there were thick leather strips ready to attach to clothes nearby. The room had a slight musty smell that felt familiar to Kurt, but he couldn't quite remember a specific memory. As he made his way further inside, Melrose came into view, tucked behind a particularly large stack of fabric cuttings, sat by a window and sewing a leather strip to a jacket.

"Wasn't expecting you until much later," Melrose said, not looking up from his work but his tone was warm and welcoming as it always was.

"I actually wanted to make a specific request if that would be alright?" Kurt asked. Melrose set aside the fabric and moved over to a central table. He pulled out a drawer that Kurt hadn't noticed and grabbed a large sheet of paper. He continued to look around before sighing to himself.

"Dear!" he called out. "Where did I put my design things? Pen, ink and all that?"

"You put that pile of leather on top of it. I said that you'd need it later but you were so very sure I was wrong. I'll never understand why you don't just listen–" The voice of the young sounding woman trailing off as she walked away. With an exasperated sigh, Melrose then shifted a pile of leather sheets to reveal a measuring tape, a pair of scissors, a pot of black ink and a carved wooden pen.

"What were you thinking of?" Melrose asked, giving Kurt his full attention.

"I've got an idea for a weapon I might have built. Nothing particularly different, I just need the right arm reinforced with as much leather as possible with room to sew in some metal plates." As Kurt spoke, Melrose was drawing up a design. His pen seemed to dance across the paper and Kurt could see how experienced the old man was at his craft.

"Easy to do. Nothing else?" Melrose asked as he scribbled some unrecognisable letters next to his first draft.

"I'll need some new clothes, something a bit more protective than what I have. Make sure you get all the recruits ready first though." Kurt thought for a moment. "I think that's all for now, but I'm sure I'll be back here again pretty soon."

"Hold up now. Let me grab your measurements." Melrose said as he pulled out the measuring tape and started dragging it along parts of Kurt's body mumbling numbers to himself as he checked everything he needed. "And that's that. Don't need to see you later but come around if you want to talk."

"I'll keep that in mind." Kurt then turned to leave but did look back briefly to see the old man hop back to his previous work. "Thanks again Melrose."

Once he was back outside, Kurt thought for a moment about where to go next. He quickly decided that checking on the recruits should be his next stop and made his way back to where he left his squad leaders. By the time he found himself back where his day started there were dozens of people waiting for him. Most of them were either lying down or sat on the floor struggling to catch their breath. Kurt walked through the crowd to reach the squad leaders, giving a few encouraging nods as he moved past them all.

"Welcome back, Commander," said Soren. "We've told our recruits about the plans for the evening. Everyone seems keen."

"Good to hear. I've got some things I need to do but I wanted to check on you all first." Kurt looked out over the recruits to see many eyes on him. "Listen up. You're going to spend the afternoon with your squad leaders, they'll get you all ready for the tournament this evening. Everyone who loses has to go running around the town again first thing tomorrow morning. Whichever squad wins, you get to relax."

There was suddenly some hushed and excited whispers, which Kurt found heartening. He looked over to each of the squad leaders and gestured for them to follow him as he walked back into town. The seven gathered and the group was soon huddled together at the side of the main road into town.

"I've been assessing what our equipment is going to be. Looks to be mostly axes, bows and whatever custom orders you all want," Kurt informed them all.

"I was thinking about that," Yvette spoke up. "I reckon my squad will focus on our archery. We've got a few good shots among us, and myself of course. Would that be alright?"

"I think that would be just fine," Kurt replied. "Just don't neglect to practise for some up close fighting as well. We need to be as prepared as possible."

"With that being said, I've had an idea." Lief was the one to speak up this time, looking at everyone around her in turn to make sure they were paying attention. "I think we seven should train with our squads everyday. Some sort of basic fitness first to keep everyone strong. Then fighting and weapons training. Finally, squad training, to make sure we all work well together."

"That's very much like what I was going to suggest," Kurt replied. He was a little surprised at how quickly the squad leaders had taken initiative, Lief especially seemed to be the most natural at this among the group. "If you're all agreed, you should start that first thing tomorrow. I'll check in often and between all of us, we'll make ourselves into a strong force to protect the town."

The group all murmured their agreement. Kurt gave the group a nod and turned away to walk back into town. He heard the seven march back to their recruits and start sharing the future plans. Kurt couldn't help but feel a warm sense of pride building, somehow everything and everyone seemed to be coming together well. While he walked he looked at the flask of sparking powder in his hand. Several ideas that were floating through his mind had started to take form. Lost in his thoughts, Kurt wandered aimlessly for a time before deciding to head to Cole's smithy once more. As he approached he could hear the loud metal clanging of the smith's hammer. Once the forge came into view he saw Cole and two other humans he didn't recognize. The younger man and woman were hammering several metal plates into shape to form pieces of armour. Cole himself was working at a grinding wheel, sharpening an axe head into shape. He stopped his work once he spotted Kurt, doing his best not to interrupt the other workers as he walked across the workshop.

"Hello again," Cole said. "You look excited about something."

"I am," Kurt replied. "I've got a weapon design for you. It's a little complicated but I think you should be able to make it with no problems."

He then went to a table that had paper and some charcoal. Kurt drew up his design as best he could along with a rough sketch of the design Melrose was making. Cole looked over the designs whilst Kurt was drawing them and stared at the paper for a while after they were finished, his brow furrowed in confusion as he tried to make sense of it.

"What exactly am I building here?" Cole asked, turning to meet Kurt's gaze. "I don't understand what it's supposed to do."

"Well this is just an experiment," Kurt replied. "If it works the way I hope, it should give us something the elves have no defence against."

"That's all I need to hear," Cole said with a smile. "Still, this might take a few days. I've never built anything exactly like this but I'm curious how this'll turn out, so I'll make it a priority."

"Thank you. I appreciate that," Kurt replied. "I think that's everything for now. I'll be around town with the recruits when you need to find me."

Kurt left, leaving Cole to look over the weapon designs. Once he had walked back through town, Kurt began to hear the sound of cheering. As he rounded a corner he was greeted with a much larger crowd than he'd left behind at the outskirts of town. Kurt made his way past the crowd and did his best to not draw attention as he made his way back home.

He looked back when he reached the tree line and though the sun was still a few hours away from setting, the blue sky had already shifted to a soft shade of yellow that seemed to make the entire valley glow with warmth. Kurt continued his journey home and though he felt satisfied with the day, there was still a persistent chill creeping through his gut. He did his best to ignore it as he entered his cabin, settling down to a warm meal of mushroom soup and the last of his stale bread. The rest of the evening he spent tidying his small home until night crawled over the forest. Tiredness gripped him in tandem with the night's arrival and after warming himself by the fire he finally got into bed. Kurt spent a long while staring at his ceiling, unwilling to drift to sleep after the previous night, but a dreamless sleep gradually managed to take hold and force him to rest.

# 6

The next few days were a blur for Kurt. In between training and building wooden defences around the town, everyone was kept busy. The people of Bismurr had spread the workload across anyone able. Even Cali, who didn't like many people in her kitchen, had gathered a few people to help her at the bakery. Kurt himself had managed to have dreamless and restful nights thanks to how exhausted each day was leaving him.

On one particular day, as Kurt made his way into town, he looked over the various new structures that were coming up around the town. The whole place looked so different from what he had grown used to during his time in Bismurr. He wasn't happy to see such a peaceful place change itself to be ready for a battle. The whole situation was bringing back memories Kurt would rather keep buried. He shook away the thoughts and kept walking into town, passing by his recruits and other townsfolk hammering at some skeletal wooden walls under construction. The squad leaders had also become so organised that he knew whatever task they were busy with, it was all helping to get their squads into fighting shape. Kurt wasn't stopping to talk with anyone however, as he'd received word that his new weapon had been finished. He eagerly made his way straight to the smithy, ignoring any stares from people as he passed by. The mood around him had shifted over the past few days, but he still seemed to draw a lot of scrutiny when he wasn't helping the recruits train. He arrived at the smithy to see Cole waiting for him, a large wooden box resting at the older man's feet.

“Good morning,” Kurt called out.

“Good morning to you,” Cole replied. He walked over to Kurt and handed him the heavy box. "Should be perfect, I did make a few alterations just to make everything fit, but it's still your design."

"Thank you." Kurt shifted the box to under one arm to shake Cole's hand. "I'll let you know how it works out. You might end up making a few more."

"About that," Cole lowered his voice and looked around to make sure no one was listening in. "While I was looking over the designs, I think I understand how that thing works. I'm putting aside some time and resources to build some.." Cole paused as he seemed to be working something out in his head. "...let's say larger versions."

"Well don't start on that until I've made sure this works." Despite his warning, Kurt couldn't help but smile. "Still, this will give us something of an advantage over whatever Orlan might throw at the town."

"Indeed. Now, you should get out of here. I've got a lot to be getting on with today." He didn't even wait for the younger man's reply, leaving Kurt standing outside while he returned to his work.

Kurt didn't mind, he hurried back through town and thankfully wasn't stopped by anyone as he made his way to his cabin. Once Kurt returned to his clearing he strolled around the back of the cabin and onto a small training area he'd spent the past few days building. He looked over the large pile of straw he had gathered and shaped like a large man, giving it a thump to make sure it was still sturdy. Kurt then laid down the box and carefully opened the lid.

Inside was a large metallic gauntlet with several straps on its base. The top of the weapon was made up of two cylinders bolted in place and at the back of each of them was a small hatch. Just on its side was a small switch which - if it worked - should act as a trigger to create a small spark inside. Laying in front of the weapon were a dozen metal spikes, each one just shorter than the cylinders themselves. Kurt quickly ran inside and grabbed a bottle of the sparking powder. He'd been testing the powder for a few days at this point and was feeling confident about how much he would need to use. Kurt then picked up the gauntlet and started attaching it to his arm, the straps pinching his skin a little as they were tightened. The whole thing covered most of his forearm, but wasn't as heavy as he thought it was going to be. Lifting and moving his arm was a little more difficult, but as he moved around he got used to the extra weight. Eager to try it out, he picked up two of the spikes and loaded them into the cylinders. Kurt lowered his arm and shook it. Once he was satisfied that the projectiles were staying in place, he opened the back hatch to the cylinders and poured a small portion of the dark powder inside, locking it in when the gauntlet was full. He raised his arm at his makeshift target and took a deep breath. Kurt braced himself and flicked the trigger with his thumb.

There was a loud explosive bang that echoed across the forest, scattering dozens of birds nearby. The straw target was almost disintegrated under the force of the two spikes blasting through it. Even a thick tree nearby wasn't left unscathed - splintered wood had spread all over the ground and a gaping maw had been left in the trunk. The two spikes were embedded in the centre of the hole, completely intact.

Kurt was astonished, not just with the state of the pile of hay and the tree but with the fact he'd hardly felt the gauntlet fire. He had hoped to test it a few more times, but since his test target had been completely destroyed he decided to put the weapon aside for now. He retrieved the two spikes, cleaned the dirt and black powder coating them before putting everything back into the box. Kurt then stashed the box in his cabin, far away from his barrel of sparking powder.

On his way back into town, Kurt was surprised to see a few people at the edge of the forest near town but it looked like they were starting to construct a hidden watchtower amongst the trees. Passing by with a wave he continued on his way. By the time he reached the outskirts of Bismurr he noticed people were starting to gather at the south side of town. Curious, Kurt joined the forming crowds. The people parted as they noticed him trying to walk through, letting Kurt to the front of the crowd. Once he had moved past the last of the townsfolk he finally came face to face with what the people had gathered for.

Pete Bowen and his scouting party had returned. All of them had been injured but the worst of them was Pete himself; his clothes were shredded and he was now sporting a large bloody bandage across the right side of his face. Two of the hunters were dragging a very large cloth sack that was so heavy it was leaving a trail in the dirt that stretched back south until it disappeared from sight. Keiran Stone appeared from the crowd and marched toward Pete. The two had a brief exchange before turning to the crowd.

"Everyone please listen," Keiran spoke loudly. "Please return to your regular duties for now, let these people rest up before you all talk their ears off."

Some of the crowd started to disperse while the scouting party moved forward to greet their friends and family. Pete stayed behind, his strength wavering as he took a seat on the ground.

"Glad you're here. Saves us time." Keiran greeted upon spotting Kurt in the dwindling crowd. "Pete, tell him what you found."

"Hello again," Pete said, his voice hoarse as he struggled to speak. "You probably know already that we headed south to see what we could find."

"Yes, I'd heard," said Kurt, looking past Pete at the large sack, which looked damp with dark blood. "I'm guessing you found something?"

"You've got that right." Pete managed a half smile, wincing as he did so. He then pulled the sack open and dropped the fabric to the ground to reveal the carcass. It looked like the same warped monsters that Kurt helped to dispatch before, but almost twice the size. Everything about it looked more evolved: longer fangs, larger claws, stronger muscles and, despite its wounds, a thicker hide.

"And it took all of you to bring it down?" Keiran asked.

"That's right," Pete replied. "We'd just reached what looked like the remains of a village when this thing and two smaller ones ambushed us. We barely managed to bring them all down with this one leading the charge. I wanted to rest up and press on, but we spotted at least another five moving around the settlement. My men said we should grab this one, get out of there."

"Five more? And you managed to go unnoticed making your way back?" Keiran asked.

"They didn't spot us," Pete replied, his voice unshaken and certain. "Based on where the ambush happened, we don't think they stray far from the village."

"Kurt, what are your thoughts?" Keiran asked, turning to the younger man.

"I think..." Kurt paused for a moment but then an idea dawned on him. "I think this is a perfect opportunity to put our new recruits to the test."

"Good. I was thinking the same thing," Keiran replied. "Take whoever you need. If there is anything in that settlement worth taking, we need it. I trust you have this all in hand?"

"We do," Kurt replied. "I'll get some people together and leave today."

Keiran and Pete then turned to join the last of the hunters who were beginning to drag the body away. Taking a moment to collect his thoughts, Kurt watched them all leave. With one deep breath he turned toward the town and marched to where his squad leaders would usually gather. They had built a small open hut where they conducted their meetings. In the centre of the hut was a table with a map of the town, covered in markings showing the defences and ideas for how to repel attackers. The seven were already gathered as though waiting for Kurt.

"We heard about Pete and the others. What's happening, Commander?" Garet asked. The others all looked to Kurt, waiting for orders.

"We're going to finish what Pete and his people started," Kurt replied. "I'm taking two squads with me, two and four. The rest of you will stay here, keep training and getting the town ready."

"Only two?" Soren asked, a look of confusion on his face. "Surely we should all go and just get everything dealt with quickly?"

"No. If things go wrong, we need to make sure the town is still prepared," Kurt said. He then looked at each of the seven in turn before continuing. "We're moving out as soon as possible. So talk to your squads and get what you need for the journey. I'll see you at the south side of town in a few hours."

Kurt didn't wait for a response and left the hut to head home. As he walked through the forest, the chill still lingered in his spine. He did his best to ignore it and rushed back to his cabin to collect everything he might need. Kurt nearly tore his front door off its hinges as he ran inside. Grabbing a bag he packed some food and a change of clothes. Kurt then took his weapon, ammunition, and a flask of sparking powder and stashed everything into his bag.

Within a few minutes he was out of his home and heading back to Bismurr. Once he broke through the treeline he saw a large crowd of people had gathered at the edge of town. As Kurt approached he saw Cole and Melrose talking with the dozen squad members who were going to travel with him. Cole was handing out bows, quivers of arrows and knives to one squad, leaving the other to pick up axes from a box at his side. Melrose meanwhile, was standing next to a large pile of newly tailored clothes, handing each person several pieces of leather armour as they picked up their new attire. Kurt drew closer and spotted Peyton and Lief, both of whom had already received their equipment and were checking through the packs, making sure everything was ready for the journey ahead.

"Kurt my boy! I have some armour for you here," Melrose called out. Kurt walked up to the old dwarf and took the clothes he was holding out. It was a mix of tough leather, fabric and what felt like some hard metal plates sewn inside. It was also light, which Kurt was grateful for as he tucked it into his bag.

"Thank you. You managed to make enough for all of us already?" Kurt asked, surprised.

"Well, this is just about all we have so far, but we have a few people working at all hours now, so we'll have everyone else suited up soon enough," Melrose replied.

"I have an axe here for you as well," Cole piped up, holding out the large weapon which Kurt accepted with his free hand. The wooden handle was rough to hold and the axe head already had a few chips on the blade but the weapon felt sturdy enough for a fight.

"I'm guessing you and yours have been working through the night too?" Kurt asked, bracing the axe against his shoulder.

"Oh indeed. We're not stopping until we have enough weapons for everyone in this town," Cole replied with a smirk. "Do you think all of you are ready for this?"

"We'll find out," Kurt replied. He looked out at the men and women checking on their new armour and weapons, a small smile forming as he did so. "But I think we'll do just fine."

"Good to hear it," said Melrose. "Come now Cole. Let's leave them to it"

Cole picked up the empty boxes and followed Melrose back into town, disappearing around a corner. Kurt turned to the gathered squads and noticed a few eyes on him, waiting for instruction.

"Everyone check your packs, make sure we have enough food and water for the journey. We move out when you all say you're ready," Kurt said.

A few of the squad members confidently stood still but a few started checking their bags. One by one people started to call out and within a few minutes both squads were ready.

"Alright everyone. Let's move out," Kurt called out. As a testament to their recent training, the recruits immediately fell into lines as they began marching out. There were even a few cheers from behind them as some of the townsfolk had gathered to give goodbyes to their friends and family. As they crossed a grass-covered field and moved further from the town, the cheers grew quieter and quieter, eventually falling silent as the group marched into the trees.

They made good progress for the first few hours, the two squads kept themselves in high spirits whilst chatting amongst themselves. Kurt kept to the back and did his best to make a plan for when they arrived at the settlement. He became lost in his thoughts and only realised the group had stopped when he almost walked right in the back of Lief.

"We're near a river. Probably best to stop for a while," she said. "If we pick this up after some rest and travel through the night, we might be able to get close enough to scout the place before dark tomorrow."

"Sounds like a good plan," Kurt replied, ever-impressed at how quickly his squad leaders had picked up some initiative. "Get everyone settled in and make sure everyone has changed into their new armour before we move out later."

"Righto Commander," Lief replied before marching off to spread Kurt's instructions.

A short while later the two squads were gathered around a small fire, some napping, others talking amongst themselves and a few seeing to a small pot of stew for everyone. Once Kurt had received his own dinner, he sat down alongside Peyton and Lief, ready to discuss their plan.

"I spoke to a few of Pete's people about what they saw," said Peyton. "They managed to bring down that larger one and didn't see any others like it. The rest though? They didn't seem to stray far from the buildings, like they were guarding the area."

"If that's true, then squad four can spread out with our bows to provide a little arrow rain," Lief said with a menacing chuckle. "Course that means your lot will need to move in to drive 'em out."

"Not a problem," replied Peyton. "Me and mine will take down what we can and get the rest out into the open."

"Make sure not to risk yourselves, so stay within squad four's sight lines," Kurt said. "I'll stick with squad two and we'll make sure to call out each one we take down, then hopefully they'll be dealt with quickly. Once the five that Pete mentioned are dealt with, we'll all move in together to see what we can find."

"Well that all sounds fine," Lief said. "Now if you boys don't mind, I'm gonna get some sleep."

She then marched off to lay down near the edge of the camp. Peyton finished his bowl of food before getting up to join his own squad. Now alone, Kurt moved to the side of the camp and sat down to lean against a tree. While he didn't intend on falling asleep, he still found himself drifting into a short nap. He awoke later and judging by the orange light touching the leafy canopy above him, the evening had settled in. Looking around, Kurt noticed most of the recruits had donned their new armour. Some were still stretching and moving around, trying to make the stiff leather more comfortable.

Kurt changed into his own armour and soon noticed that his was designed differently to the others. His forearms had straps attached to tighten the leather, which seemed like it would make attaching his spike-launching gauntlet quick and easy. He also took note that his belt had slots for his spike ammunition and a large hoop was sewn to the top of the trousers to help stow his axe. As Kurt stood up, he found everything to be very comfortable, even with the stiff leather joints and metal plates sewn into the fabric. Melrose had outdone himself. After stashing his discarded clothes into his pack, Kurt went over to grab some of the food that his recruits had left out for anyone to take. It was somewhat bland but it did the job of filling up his stomach. Looking around, Kurt realised only a few recruits were still asleep, everyone else was packed and waiting to move out.

"The light won't be with us for much longer," said Peyton, somehow managing to sneak up next to Kurt, making him jump a little. "Think we should head out soon?"

"Yes we should. Get everyone ready, we've got a lot of ground to cover," Kurt replied. Peyton walked away and started getting everyone ready.

Walking to the edge of their camp, Kurt looked out at the sparse trees that surrounded them. The orange glow of the evening sun was dancing across the leaves above them, giving an odd sense of warmth to the cold air of the evening. It was a strange feeling, travelling away from Bismurr. Kurt hadn't considered doing it before today, and yet he found himself growing more curious about the world around them. While he was staring at this calming view, his thoughts scattered miles away, the recruits started moving out past him with Lief leading the way. Peyton gave Kurt a pat on the shoulder as he passed by, snapping the young man back to reality. After one last look around him, Kurt moved on as well, jogging to catch up with the back line of recruits.

The journey through the night was quiet but tense. A few recruits got startled at a few nocturnal birds fluttering in nearby trees, but overall the group moved unhindered until dawn started to break. They made a brief stop for some food and rest, but were back to travelling within an hour. The following day was tiring as they moved through the untamed forest and grasslands but the amount of ground the group covered was more than worth it. After cresting one final grass covered hill the group's destination finally came into view.

Keeping themselves in cover by the trees, the group looked down into a small valley to see around a dozen dishevelled stone structures. Rubble from the buildings was scattered all over, some pieces small while others were larger than people. As he scoured the site, Kurt couldn't see any sign of movement which was a concern. He gestured to Lief to come over to him.

"We need to rest up before we get down there. Can squad four spread out and stand watch while the rest of us get prepared? We'll switch places in an hour or so," Kurt asked.

"Can do. Thinking of clearing out in the dark?" Lief replied.

"I don't know. I at least want to confirm where our five targets are before we move in," Kurt said. "Whatever we decide, stay hidden and alert for now,"

Lief nodded and started whispering to each person in her squad to move into place. Soon enough they were all climbing up various nearby trees and making sure their bows were at the ready. Meanwhile Kurt and squad two moved further back into the trees and took some time to rest. No one wanted to relax too much, but they did manage to sit for a time and gather themselves for a tough fight ahead. By the time the group felt rested enough to move out, the light had faded and had begun to give way to night. Kurt noticed that a lot of the people around him were starting to look anxious, not helped by the fact that no one from Lief's squad had spotted any movement, putting everyone further on edge.

"I've been having a look around our camp and I can't find any tracks nearby," Peyton said in a hushed whisper. "If those creatures are around here they're certainly not coming out any time soon."

"I'm not eager to send anyone down there before we find those things, but hopefully the dark will put them at a disadvantage," Kurt looked out over the moonlit settlement and tried to think about the best course of action. "Do we have anything we can use to light some torches?"

"We have some of our campfire materials, along with the wood around here we could probably make as many as you need," Peyton replied. "It would give us away immediately though."

"True. I'm thinking we each take one and spread out," Kurt replied. "If squad two stays near the light and lures the creatures there, squad four can pick them off easily without being spotted."

"That could work," Peyton said. "I think we should double up and spread some torches on the ground as well. Get as much light down there as we can. We'll need to be quick but it'll give Lief's squad the best chance of hitting those things."

"Alright, let her know the plan and get those torches lit," Kurt ordered, trying to keep his voice sounding confident, despite his own nerves.

Peyton dashed around the squad whispering to everyone in turn and the recruits started to ready two torches each. Before lighting his own torches Kurt took the time to attach and load his wrist weapon. One recruit lit a small fire just out of sight and everyone from squad two gathered around the flames, ready to enact the plan. With one final glance at everyone, Kurt nodded. Everyone lit their torches in unison and started to scatter. Peyton, Kurt and squad two formed a long line as they rushed down toward the ruined settlement. Once they were halfway down the hill everyone slammed a torch in the ground in unison and continued running forward. Then after the planting of the second torch the forward line all drew their axes and readied themselves, while in the trees behind bows were drawn and arrows notched ready to be loosed.

Then there was silence, the stillness of night only broken by the soft crackling of the torches. As each moment passed the group grew more tense. A nervous chill started to run down Kurt's spine, but he pushed it out as he stepped forward toward the edge of the light. He could barely make out the ruins ahead of him, and the quiet stillness was threatening to swallow him.

Then Kurt screamed. Just a noise at first, but it quickly turned into a battle cry, a challenge against whatever was waiting in the shadows. The deafening quiet fell once more but only for a moment. From ahead of them, hidden by the stone structures, several piercing animalistic roars broke through the darkness. Kurt backed up into the light as the beat of footfalls started to echo around in the darkness ahead of him. Then the creatures came into view, each one rushing forward into the light, eager to attack the prey that had appeared so suddenly.

These creatures were more ragged and scarred than the ones Kurt had fought before, like they'd been beaten and starved for weeks on end. One charging toward Peyton was even missing a clawed hand, though using the stub at the end of its arm to move didn't seem to slow it by much. Within seconds of the monsters entering the circles of light, the sound of arrows raining down filled the air. The creature in front of Kurt took a hit to the shoulder causing it to scream in pain and stop in its tracks. Kurt didn't waste his chance, he jumped forward and swung his axe downward with all the force he could muster. The blow struck true as the blade smashed into the skull of the creature, embedding with enough force to slam its body into the dirt below, killing it instantly. Kurt looked up and realised each member of squad two had also dispatched their foes with help from the arrows still being fired from the darkness. Peyton was struggling to avoid swipes from the monster in front of him but the repeated arrows from the darkness swiftly brought it down. Seven monstrous corpses were soon littered on the ground - two more than they thought, but everyone was still standing. Kurt took a moment to let out a sigh of relief. He turned back towards the ruins and after a minute or so of silence, was satisfied that they were safe for the moment.

"I think we're clear for now," Kurt said. Almost in reply he heard Lief's squad in the trees start scuttling down from their perches while the squad on the ground took a few moments to catch their breath.

"Everyone grab a torch," said Peyton, still breathing heavily. "Once we're sure the ruins are clear we're going to make camp, but everyone keep alert until then."

"You lot do the same," piped up Lief to her own squad as they all jogged down the hill to join the others.

Reunited, the now larger group started to cautiously explore the stone structures, while two figures remained behind with torches to set about burning the corpses of the monsters. Judging by the silence that had fallen once again, it became clear that they were very much alone. Tensions eased as they started to explore the ruins. The structures were far older than any of them could guess and despite how dilapidated they had become, some still had clear markings on what would have been their entrances - though no one seemed to know what they could possibly mean. Every building was also covered in claw marks, some old and weathered while some were much more new.

"Those things must have been here for years," he said aloud.

"Indeed," replied Peyton. "Yet we never saw a hint of them until we explored here. I wonder what kept them here? Maybe they just stay dormant if they don't have orders? Whatever the reason, we know less about those monsters than we thought."

"Well they're dead now at least," Kurt said, trying to put his own mind at ease. He then raised his voice so everyone could hear him. "Time to make camp, we'll explore this place thoroughly at first light."

There were several cheers from a few recruits which echoed out into the night. Everyone was in high spirits as they set up a small camp against the wall of one of the larger structures. The two of Lief's squad who were disposing of the bodies returned, silhouetted by the bonfire they'd left on the nearby hill. The pair were greeted with more cheers as they joined their friends. Someone had even smuggled a small cask of ale to share around, spreading the merriment much quicker as the group settled in for the night.

Kurt smiled to himself while making himself comfortable at the edge of the camp. The cold stone wall at his back was a familiar sensation and memories started to swirl around his head. The cool night air was gentle and the sounds of celebration nearby was putting Kurt into a warm mood. Without realising, he slowly started to drift into sleep.

An all too familiar chill crept up his gut and clawed at his throat.

*When he snapped his eyes open he was once more standing in a dense fog.*

*"Hello again," said a voice from behind him. "You left so abruptly when you were last here, so maybe we should try things differently this time."*

*Kurt turned and saw Orlan standing before him, dressed once again in white clothes, with an ethereal quality to him.*

*"Haunting my dreams again?" Kurt asked, trying to keep his temper down. "I thought you were supposed to be smarter than this?"*

*"Sarcasm? Charming," Orlan laughed in response. "I commend your effort from before, even some of my own kind struggle to learn how to escape when their dreams are being viewed."*

*"Like this?" Kurt said as he tried to dream up a weapon to his hand. When he looked down however, he found his hand defiantly empty.*

*"As I said, we're going to try things differently this time," said the elf. "I'm not going to dive into your memories this time. You and I are just going to have a talk."*

*"And if I refuse?" Kurt asked.*

*"Then we can go around and around achieving nothing," Orlan replied. "But I'm willing to stoop down and talk to you on your level."*

*"How very kind of you," Kurt spat. "Let's get this dream over with then. What do*

*you want?"*

*"Straight to the point then. What I want is to scour your mind until I find any useful information," said the elf. "Then when I'm done, and the time comes, I'll grant you a quick and painless death."*

*"Generous," Kurt said as he stepped forward. "I think my answer is still going to be no."*

*"Well you can certainly try to refuse but I'll get what I want soon enough," Orlan then turned to face the fog. "I presume you already tried to discuss my presence here with someone? Did you find yourself unwilling? Did the words just simply not form? Think on that. I'll be seeing you."*

*A realisation dawned on Kurt but before he could say anything further he was ripped out of the fog.*

# 7

Kurt's eyes snapped open to the dark ruins with people sleeping nearby. A cold breeze blowing by coupled with the dream he felt chilled him to his core.

"You alright Commander?" Lief asked, she had been standing nearby keeping watch and had noticed Kurt jump awake.

"Yes. Just a bad dream," Kurt replied without any hesitation, which shocked him. He wanted to tell the truth, but his mind just felt stuck when he tried to talk about Orlan.

Lief smiled and gave him a reassuring pat on the shoulder as she walked across the camp. Sat in the dark, Kurt tried to speak aloud about Orlan and his dream, but found the words wouldn't form. Kurt shook his head and pushed the thoughts away.

*It was just a dream,* he thought to himself. He sat in the dark repeating that thought until the first glimmer of light started to appear above him. Dawn eventually broke through in full and chased away the cold night. Kurt was tired but found the energy to get up and stretch, pushing the dream to the back of his mind for now. The rest of the group also started to wake up and get breakfast for themselves while a few of the recruits started to wander around the ruins to see what they could find. Peyton and Lief approached Kurt with a bowl of porridge.

"Eat up," ordered Peyton. "We're gonna search this place and hopefully leave as soon as we can."

"Good thinking," Kurt replied. "The sooner we get back to Bismurr, the better."

Peyton nodded and walked away to search the place with his squad. Lief waited until Kurt had finished his breakfast before snatching the bowl from his hands and walked back to the campfire to get some food for herself. Left alone with his thoughts once more, Kurt left the camp and started walking around the ruins. Any hint of fear he had about his dreams faded as he realised one thing. Ever since he had started to fight for the town, he had beaten everything that came his way. These dream incursions were just another front to to fight on. Kurt steeled himself as he continued his walk, his new-found confidence driving him forward. He managed to walk around the entirety of the ruins before he saw everyone starting to gather, Kurt joined them and walked up to Peyton who was standing near a sack of their spoils.

"Find anything?" Kurt asked.

"Some books that look like diaries which we'll take back with us," replied Peyton. "Apart from those, just bones and broken things."

"Well if that's everything we'd better get moving." Kurt looked around to see many eyes were on him. "Get your things together, we're moving out."

Almost in unison the squads gathered up their equipment and dismantled the camp. The group then began their journey back home. Kurt looked back at the ruins one last time, curious as to who might have dwelled here before. His gaze then fell onto the burnt monster corpses and his blood ran cold. Six bodies were still smouldering but there was only a small pile of ash where the seventh should have been. Kurt turned back to shout but was immediately thrown back as the body of a human recruit was flung into him.

As the pair tumbled down the small hill, Kurt caught a glimpse of the creature amongst the large group. Somehow it had buried itself in the dirt and had burst forth right in the middle of both squads. Its monstrous body had also somehow grown larger than the night before. While the creature's flesh was still burned, the wounds inflicted from either axe or arrow had managed to heal. Kurt stopped tumbling and pushed the heavy body off himself. He quickly checked to see if the recruit was alive and thankfully the young man was still breathing, just knocked out. Kurt dashed back up the hill to reach the fight. The creature was flailing its long limbs back and forth which was knocking some people down and keeping others back. As he approached Kurt looked over everyone that had been scattered by the creature's swinging attacks. Everyone seemed to only have minor injuries, except for one young woman who had several gashes across her arm. It wasn't until he reached the inner circle that he saw the first casualty, a dwarven man whose head was turned to an unnatural angle, lying lifeless at the monster's clawed feet.

Rage flooded through Kurt as he drew his axe. He gripped it with both hands and flung it forward. The weapon embedded itself into the arm of the creature, which fell limp to its side. A few arrows launched from nearby struck into the monster's back. Not letting up, Kurt rushed forward and leapt upwards, using the handle of his stuck weapon to steady himself. The monster roared and raised its other arm to strike the small human. Kurt then shoved his wrist weapon in the mouth of the creature. With a quick twist against its fangs he pulled the trigger and with a muffled bang, the back of the monster's head exploded, spraying blood and meaty chunks upward. As the lifeless body of the monster fell back, Kurt dislodged his axe and raised it above his head. With a scream of rage he slammed it down into the creature's chest. Everyone looked on in silence for a few moments, before some of the recruits came to their senses and started to help the wounded.

"That thing was dead," said Peyton, mostly to himself.

"Well it's definitely dead now," Lief said, clutching a large scratch on her arm as she approached.

Kurt was barely listening. He stepped away from the carcass, ripped his axe free and walked towards the remaining burnt monster corpses. The crowd watched as one by one, Kurt raised his axe up and brought it down onto the heads of each creature until nothing remained of their heads but a large puddle of charred meat. While catching his breath he froze and remembered why they had come here. Kurt looked up to Peyton who was clearly having the same thought, as a terrified expression spread across both of their faces.

"They dragged one of these back to town," said Kurt, causing Lief's eyes to widen in realisation. "We have to get back there right now."

"Even if we travel as fast as we can, it'll be at least a day before we can get there," Peyton replied, worry in his voice. His eyes then fell on his fallen squad member. "We need to take Hector's body with us as well."

"Do what you need to do," Kurt said, struggling to contain his anger. "I'm heading back now. We don't have time to wait."

Kurt didn't wait for a response. He just started jogging towards the tree line to begin the journey back to town. There were raised voices calling from behind him that he ignored. His rage drove him forward and he knew the longer he waited, the worse things would be. Kurt couldn't explain it, but the feeling that the creature back at town had risen was not leaving him. He hadn't gotten far into the woods before Kurt heard hurried footsteps approaching him. Looking back he saw Lief running toward him, her arm hastily wrapped into a sling.

"Slow down ya big idiot," she called out. Kurt obliged and waited for her to catch up.

"I'm not waiting," Kurt said, matter-of-factly. "If there is a even a chance we can get back in time to help, then we need to move."

"I'm not questioning that," Lief replied. "I just thought the whole point of this was that we learn to work together. I left everyone else behind, figured we'd be quicker just the two of us."

"What about your arm?" Kurt asked.

"This?" she replied, raising her sling. "That thing got my wrist pretty good when it first appeared, but I'll be good to fire a bow when we get back to town, don't you worry."

Kurt nodded and broke into a run again. Lief quickened her pace to be ahead of him and together they started the race back to town.

* * *

It was sunset before another word was said between the travelling pair. Kurt and Lief had spent the whole day either running or walking, stopping only to drink water. They were both exhausted but knew they had to stop for rest or they'd be in no fit state to do anything to help anyone. Sitting down under a large tree the pair finally took some time to eat some food and finish off the last of their water.

"Well that's that then," said Lief, letting the last few drops from the flask drip onto the ground. "But if we can keep this pace up, we should reach Bismurr in the middle of the night."

"Good," Kurt replied. "We'll leave in a few minutes."

Lief nodded and resumed eating a small hunk of bread, struggling to finish the last bite without anything to drink. Kurt meanwhile was rubbing his ankles, he knew that there were blisters on his feet and blood in his shoes, but the pain didn't bother him. His thoughts were only of the town, concerned that they were already too late. He also cursed the fact he didn't know enough about what he was fighting, every time he was sure of something a new challenge presented itself.

"Shall we get going?" Lief said, breaking the silence. She was already up and ready before Kurt could reply.

He didn't respond, he just got up and started running once more. Lief soon overtook him, she'd even let her arm free of the sling. If she was in any kind of discomfort, Kurt couldn't see it. The sun set as they moved onwards; clouds blocked the moon, sinking the pair into pitch darkness. They didn't talk as they crested the last hill of their journey. Looking down, Bismurr seemed the same as they had left it. The defensive structures were untouched, there were even a few figures patrolling the outskirts of the town with torches. Lief and Kurt picked up their speed until they were sprinting towards the nearest patrol. They were soon spotted and someone ran out to meet them. As they drew closer, Kurt recognised the figure as Garet.

"What happened?" the dwarf asked, struggling to catch his breath.

"The creature Pete and the others dragged back here. It might not be fully dead." Lief said before Kurt could even take a breath to talk.

"What?" asked Garet, confused.

"Where did they take its body?" Kurt asked, finally able to talk.

"Over the other side of town, near the livestock. We already burned it so we just buried it with others from before." replied Garet, panic starting to enter his voice.

Lief shot Kurt a look and the pair moved past Garet and started running towards the other side of town. The townsfolk they passed looked confused but moved aside as they approached. Garet caught up with them as they ran and had even managed to grab a few recruits as they drew closer to where the creature was buried. Kurt didn't feel relief that the town was safe as he was dreading what they might find at the creature's grave.

The large group arrived just outside of town, scaring off the cows grazing nearby. They were presented with a large mound of disturbed soil where the monsters' bodies were buried. Thankfully, a few of the recruits had the sense to grab some shovels and with a quick order from Garet two dwarven men started digging. A nervous silence fell over everyone, broken only by the rhythmic sound of metal scraping against soil while the two recruits dug downward. There were a few minutes of digging before the recruits stopped and climbed out the hole. Everyone froze in place when they looked down into what was supposed to be a grave. There was nothing in the hole except several half-chewed bones. Kurt took his axe, jumped down and with his free hand started to move some of the dirt. He soon found a small dug out section that looked like the start of a tunnel, some of which had collapsed.

"See anything?" Garet asked, tightening his grip on his own weapon.

"No," Kurt replied. "But there's some kind of tunnel. Looks fresh, so that thing can't have travelled far."

"So we have no idea where it could be," said Lief angrily. "It's not like we can track it down now."

"That..... might not be true," Garet replied, causing a few heads to turn in his direction.

"You have an idea?" Kurt asked.

"I was talking with Pete yesterday, and I remember the night when Orlan set his men on us," Garet explained. "Each time, the creatures attacked the largest groups they could find. So if we could gather the recruits and make some noise nearby, it might come out to attack us?"

"Good idea," Kurt replied. "Get everyone who's ready to fight into the centre of town, and make sure the rest of the town get into their homes."

The gathered recruits nearby started to disperse following Kurt's orders. Garet offered a hand to help Kurt out of the hole then the two of them, along with Lief, made their way to the town centre. By the time they arrived, the area was pretty clear with only a few stragglers hurrying away to their homes. Nearby, several recruits started to block the paths while a dozen more stood in a large circle, awaiting orders.

"This all we've got?" Lief asked.

"We've still got people patrolling the town, so this will have to do," said Garet. "What's next?"

"It's your plan Garet," Kurt replied. "Take the lead."

"Alright then Commander," said Garet. He took one last look around before coming to a decision. "Alright everyone, start making noise, as much as you can. Then when that son of bitch comes out, chop it to pieces!"

Mere moments later, the recruits started shouting and jumping up and down. For a short time they looked like an unintelligent mob, but their efforts were soon rewarded. Nearby a small portion of dirt started to shake before swiftly sinking. The now familiar face of the monster then burst forth, using its large clawed arms to drag itself free of the soil. Before the creature could fully emerge, Garet and his squad jumped forward to attack, ripping into the flesh of the monster with their axes. Kurt felt no remorse for the creature as it roared in pain before falling silent. Once they were satisfied that the creature was definitely dead this time, the recruits started to look around, some even started to smile.

"Well done," said Kurt, impressed. "All of you, well done."

"You three, take those pieces and burn them. Separately," ordered Lief. The recruits didn't question anything, a few of them simply started picking up the bloody chunks and taking them away.

"Alright you two. What happened out there? Where is everyone else?" Garet asked, frustration in his voice.

Between the two of them, Kurt and Lief explained what had happened outside the town. Garet listened and sighed with relief when he heard that almost everyone was fine. As they told the tale, the recruits finished cleaning up the monster carcass and some of the townsfolk even started to leave their homes to see if they could resume their daily chores.

"I think the others will get back here within a day or two. What do you want us to do in the meantime Commander?" asked Lief.

"Now that we have room to think, have some of the recruits dig up the rest of the creatures, make sure they're all accounted for and make sure they'll stay dead," Kurt replied. As he was talking he started to feel how pained his feet were, but that feeling was dwarfed by the exhaustion that had finally begun to catch up with him. "You need to get your arm seen to and I need to sleep, so we'll meet again tomorrow morning."

Lief gave him a half-hearted smile and turned away to hobble out of sight. Garet gave Kurt a small thump on the arm before walking over to a few members of his squad still milling around the town centre to relay Kurt's orders. Tired yet satisfied, Kurt started to make his way home. He had wanted to visit Cali and Melrose but his exhaustion had other plans. He limped away from the town, refusing to acknowledge anyone as he struggled to get back to his cabin.

It took almost twice as long to get there, but eventually Kurt arrived at his home. He peeled off his boots and socks to reveal his painful blood-coated feet. He managed to pour out some water into a basin and sat down in his chair, wincing as he placed his feet in the cold liquid. Kurt had intended only to soak for a few minutes before washing up, but a creeping blackness fell over his vision and he drifted unwillingly to sleep. He awoke in the night briefly to find he kicked over the basin and water had spilled over the floor. Kurt sighed in exasperation but despite his need to sleep, he found a rag to wipe away the spill whilst ignoring the pain with each step he took. Once most of the floor was dry, he tossed the damp rag aside and stumbled over to his bed. Kurt made no effort to stop himself as he fell face first into his pillow, slipping back into unconsciousness instantly.

* * *

Kurt didn't wake up until the morning light shone through his window onto his face. As he woke, his feet complained about the state they were in before he even started to move. Ignoring the pain, he hobbled over to his kitchen to make a small breakfast with his dwindling supplies. Kurt then set about wrapping his wounds. His feet were the priority so he first applied a dark green salve he had acquired some time ago from Cali; she'd said it would help with scrapes and burns. The smell from the jar was horrendous, but as he put the salve on his blistered skin, the pain started to fade away. After wrapping his feet in the last of his bandages, Kurt made a mental note that he needed to restock most of his supplies. After getting dressed into fresh clothes, tossing his old ones into an ever growing dirty pile, he turned to leave but his gaze fell onto the chest at his bedside.

The gnawing chill in his spine returned once more, but Kurt expected it this time. He walked over to the chest and rested his hand on top of it. A strange urge to open the chest started to form and he very nearly reached for the latch. He stopped when he realised what he was doing. Kurt shoved the box away so that it was out of sight and hurried out of his home.

Outside, a layer of frost had coated the grass and trees. Rubbing his hands together for warmth while he moved, Kurt made his way back into town, taking care to go easy on his feet after the abuse he had put them through in recent days.

Once he reached the outskirts of town he thought about where to go first and quickly decided that he wanted to see Cali. Whether it was the chill of the early hours or the drama from the day before, the streets were mostly empty. Kurt only saw a few faces tending their duties as he walked through town. The sight of Cali's bakery and its ever-active chimney sent a warm feeling through Kurty before he even stepped inside. Upon entering he was tackled into a hug around his midriff from his short friend.

"Ah you silly boy," she mumbled into his shirt before slapping him on the arm as she parted. "Why didn't you come and see me yesterday?!"

"I'm sorry," Kurt said. "After the threat was over, I really needed to sleep. I did run a long way to get back here."

"Well, even so," Cali said, the worry in her voice fading now that she could see Kurt was fine. "Now come here. Drink some tea."

She poured a second mug of tea and they sat down while Kurt shared his recent adventure. Cali was a fantastic audience; gasping in shock, gripping her knees and all but applauded towards the end. Kurt then listened while she shared what she'd been up to over the past few days. It was pleasant to hear that some people were still having normal and peaceful days, despite all that was going on. A comfortable silence fell between them as Cali poured out a second drink for the two of them. The mood was so warm and nice that Kurt felt comfortable enough asking a question that had bothered him since he had first met this kind woman.

"Cali?" He paused for a moment unsure if he wanted the answer to his next question, but his curiosity got the better of him. "You've been my friend basically since I arrived here. Given me so much. I know you don't treat everyone this way, why have you always been so kind to me?"

"Oh Kurt. Only you would ask someone why they are kind to you," she replied. She sat down and took a deep breath before continuing. "Years ago I was married. Lovely man, we didn't have much but together we managed. He used to work the mines." She paused as tears began to form, wiping them away before continuing. "One day there was an accident and to be blunt, he didn't come home. I was sad for a time but life only moves onwards." Cali stopped talking and stared down at her knees for a short while. Kurt poured her another cup of tea, and she continued: "Once a year, I take a day to think of him and what might have been. We'd planned on having children you see. But on one of those days, a strange young man stumbled his way into town. Not speaking a word of sense, wearing strange clothes."

"That sounds familiar," Kurt said with a smile.

"Now, I'm not a superstitious woman but when you think of a child you may have wanted some day and suddenly someone who would be about the right age turns up on your doorstep? You don't ignore that kinda thing." She walked over and gave Kurt a hug. He almost fell off the stool as she gripped him tightly. "I know I'm not your mother," she muttered through a few tears, "but I think of you a bit like a son."

Kurt was at a loss for words. From the first day he arrived in Bismurr over a year ago, Cali had helped him. She'd always been so kind and now that he knew why, Kurt didn't know how to respond. He still hugged her back, knowing that anything he said wouldn't be enough to convey his gratitude.

When the pair separated, Cali put on her regular smile. The conversation turned back to the mundane until the hot drinks were spent and a silence drifted through the room again. With one last warm hug, Kurt said his goodbyes and left. The chill wind of the day didn't phase him while he walked through the streets. Kurt was smiling all the way to the tent where the squad leaders should be gathered. When he arrived he only saw Garet and Meredith talking to each other. They both went quiet when Kurt entered the tent.

"Commander," Meredith greeted with a small nod. "How're you feeling?"

"You certainly look better," said Garet.

"My feet are a little ruined, but other than that I'm good," Kurt replied. "What were you talking about?"

"Just trying to decide where we want to place the last few towers," Meredith said, indicating on a map where she meant. "We've only got enough time and wood to construct about four more."

"Only four?" Kurt asked.

"Well, we could have more, but they wouldn't be sturdy," Meredith replied with a small chuckle. "Garet thinks they should be further away, but then we might not see a warning in time."

"Then we just have more patrols around to keep an eye on everything the towers could miss," Garet blurted out exasperated, as though he had repeated this point already.

"Commander?" Meredith looked to Kurt to cast the deciding vote.

"Let me see that map." Kurt looked over their markings and quickly made a decision. "Place the eastern tower as far as possible, since that's likely to be where the enemy comes from. Keep the rest close, that way we can keep excess patrols to a minimum."

"That's...." Garet looked like he was going to complain until he looked at where Kurt was pointing on the map, "...a good idea."

"That's sorted then," said Meredith, pleased with herself. She marked the spots Kurt mentioned and rolled up the map. "I'll get those built then, see you both later."

Meredith marched away, grabbing a passing recruit with her. Garet gave a quick nod and also walked away. Kurt watched them both leave and looked over the map one more time before also making a move. He headed back into town and made his way to Melrose's home. Kurt took his time while he walked, partially because he was enjoying the day, but also because his feet were starting to complain again. Eventually he arrived at Melrose's house and knocked on the door.

“Come in dear,” an unfamiliar woman's voice called out.

“Hello,” said Kurt as he stepped inside.

“Ah Kurt. I'll grab the old man.” She left before Kurt could respond.

He looked around the shop and saw piles upon piles of the leather armour pieces that he'd recently worn himself. Melrose and his new workers had outdone themselves, there was more than enough for all the recruits - in fact there looked like there was almost enough to protect everyone in town. While Kurt looked around in awe, Melrose made his appearance, looking a little dishevelled as he walked between the towering piles of fabrics.

“You woke me,” the old dwarf said, not hiding his frustration. “How're you doing lad?”

“I've had better days,” Kurt replied. “Things been alright here? I see you've been busy.”

“Yes yes. It's why I've taken to napping at all hours,” Melrose said, yawning with a weak smile. “Things here are the same as ever, despite the excitement yesterday. Speaking of which, Cole was looking to speak to you.”

“I'll go see him soon,” Kurt said. He then looked down at the floor as shame crept through him. “We lost someone out there.”

"Probably won't be the first time that'll happen," said Melrose, unsurprised. "I presume that's how you learned these things don't always stay dead?"

Kurt nodded in response but kept his gaze downwards. Melrose put a weathered hand on his shoulder.

"I think everyone knew what might happen if they chose to fight," said the old man. "I know this might sound harsh or cold but you can't feel this way right now. Others are looking to you for some form of strength."

"I know," Kurt said, almost spitting the words out. "It's just that I didn't think we'd be losing people so soon. I truly believed we had time. Whatever might be coming for us is probably going to be worse than what we've faced already, and if we're struggling now? I don't think I can prepare any of us in time."

"Enough of that now," Melrose said, tightening his grip a little. "Remember one thing about all of this. We all chose this path. You may have taken the first steps, but we all agreed to walk that path, with or without you."

"I just don't know if I can be enough to help everyone," Kurt replied, looking up at the old man. In the light, the overwork and lack of rest had caught up with him, and he seemed to have aged in the last couple of days. "I want to be though."

"Then that's all anyone can ask," Melrose replied with a smile. He gave Kurt a single reassuring pat on his shoulder before walking back to his own chair. "Now sort yourself out, we've still got a lot to be getting on with."

Kurt did his best to force a small smile. He stayed for a few moments longer until his head cleared. As he turned to say goodbye, Melrose had already fallen back to sleep and was snoring. With a more genuine smile on his face, Kurt left as quietly, closing the door gently on his way out. Kurt felt a little better but found himself wandering aimlessly down the street, lost in his thoughts. After a while he decided to stop delaying and go to Cole's. Kurt did his best to remain unnoticed by anyone as he made his way through the town. He managed to get to the blacksmiths without being stopped. When he arrived, Cole was resting on a stool, wiping sweat from his brow with a rag.

"Hello there," said Cole, tossing the rag to one side. "How're you doing Kurt?"

"Tired," sighed Kurt. "I hear everyone in town has been busy, especially Melrose, he's outdone himself."

"That he has, that he has," Cole said, he then turned to Kurt with an intense stare. "How'd your new weapon work out for you?"

"It was great. Worked better than I thought," Kurt replied. "Do you think you could make more like it?"

"Similar maybe," Cole said, tilting his head in thought. "Yours was unique, if I was going to make some more I'd probably make them a tad smaller, single shot. To be honest, knowing that it works I'll probably focus my efforts on making some substantially larger versions."

"Good idea, could be more useful on top of those towers that people are building all over town," said Kurt, struggling to hold back a yawn.

"You are tired," Cole laughed. "I know it's been a rough few days, but do your best to get a good night's sleep soon."

"Not so easy these days," Kurt muttered. "I'll get some rest soon, I promise."

"Good lad," Cole replied. "You'd best be off, I've got another long afternoon of work ahead of me. New designs to work on."

"Understood," Kurt said before turning to leave. "See you soon."

Cole grunted in reply as the younger man walked away. Kurt's feet didn't stop complaining for the rest of his journey back through the town, but he pushed the pain aside as he set about the chores he'd been ignoring for weeks. He made his way between a few stalls people set up outside their homes and gathered some fresh food for his home, even managing to grab some extra pots of the salve he'd used up.

Kurt was making way back through town with his haul draped over his shoulder when he heard shouting nearby. Looking around, he saw townsfolk were gathering towards the south of town. He struggled to quicken his pace, but managed to keep up with those around him. What had drawn everyone's attention was the return of Peyton and the two squads. Some people even started cheering while others ran to embrace their family members. Kurt watched as one by one each recruit was reunited with their loved ones. He didn't smile however, his gut tightened as he knew what was to come. Soon enough, Peyton approached an old dwarven woman who was looking around the arrivals, waiting to see someone who wasn't there. Peyton whispered to her and once he'd finished speaking she broke down into his arms. Before Kurt could do anything he was spotted by the old woman. She pushed Peyton away and hurried over to Kurt, her expression turning from grief to anger as tears streamed down her face. Stopping just in front of Kurt, he met her gaze and was about to speak before she raised a hand to stop him.

"My boy..." she struggled to talk through tears, but she maintained some composure to get the words out. "He died because of you. I want you to know that."

"I didn't..." Kurt tried to speak but before he could reply, the woman slapped him.

"How many more of our sons and daughters are going to die because of you?" The old woman was then grabbed gently on the shoulders by Peyton and steered away into the crowd.

Hushed conversation broke out, some of the townsfolk started to look at Kurt with disdain on their faces while others carried on talking with their returned family. He ignored it all and hurried past everyone to get home. He heard some people start calling his name but he walked on. Whether it was the noise, the judgmental gazes or just hearing his name from many places, Kurt found himself struggling to breathe as his lungs seemed to tighten. Kurt managed to get away, hidden amongst the trees on the outskirts of the town, he hunched over and leant against a tree. It was a struggle, but eventually he calmed down and started to breathe again. With a shaky hand he wiped sweat from his brow before continuing his journey back to the cabin.

Once he got back inside, he threw his supplies into the kitchen before collapsing into a chair. As Kurt closed his eyes and tried to think, the old woman's words burned a hole in his mind.

*"Guilt plaguing you?" A familiar voice spoke from behind him, making no attempt to hide his amusement.*

*"Not now Orlan." Kurt spat. "Just leave me alone."*

*"You and I both know that's not going to happen," the elf replied. "So just be quiet while I get what I need."*

*Kurt opened his eyes to see the surrounding fog with Orlan standing ahead of him. His rage got the better of him once more and he rushed forward to tackle the elf. His intent was to throw him to the ground but the moment his hands touched the elf's form, Kurt fell forward. A strange spinning sensation overwhelmed him and as the dizziness faded, the scene around him warped and shifted into something he didn't recognize.*

*Kurt found himself in an ornate stone chamber, with what seemed like hundreds of candles lighting the room. A large wooden door ahead of him seemed to be the only way in or out, and in the centre of the room was a glowing green pool with two figures sat in it, their faces obscured by shadows. He moved closer and saw that both of them were elves, one looking down whilst muttering, but the sight of the other made Kurt's blood boil. It was Orlan, difficult to recognise at first as his face was covered with bandages.*

*The elf Kurt didn't know was sitting behind Orlan, resting one hand on his back and whispering under his breath, his eyes closed the whole time. Orlan himself seemed to also be in a strange meditative state. It dawned on Kurt what was happening - while he wasn't sure of the exact details, he felt that this was how Orlan was infiltrating his dreams. He walked up to the elves, his footsteps echoing in the small stone room. Neither of the pair reacted to the noise, which emboldened Kurt as he approached. He leant down and brushed his hand against the surface of the pool. The liquid was cold and thick, but when he lifted his hand, every drop moved back into the pool, leaving his hand dry. Kurt walked around the pool until he was behind the two elves. He carefully lowered himself into the pool and waded around until he was stood in front of Orlan. Looking down at his foe's injured body and the fact he was hiding his true nature gave Kurt a sense of satisfaction about what he was about to do.*

*He leant back and threw a punch with all the rage he could summon in that moment. The hit echoed throughout the chamber as the elf was flung down into the pool. Orlan woke up, coughing and flailing as he tried to get back his feet, splashing the green liquid everywhere. The other elf didn't react at all, his hand still held up as though nothing had happened. Kurt then reached down and picked up the frail body of his foe.*

*"I don't know how this is possible and frankly I don't care," Kurt said, punching Orlan down once more. "So I'm going to make the most of this."*

*Orlan looked furious and was about to speak, but Kurt was in no mood to listen. He threw punch after punch at the elf, not letting up until his fists were numb and bloody. Eventually, either the pain in his hands or the need to breathe made Kurt stop. He tossed the barely-breathing Orlan across the pool before taking a few short steps over to the other elf. He shot Orlan one more glance.*

*"Stay. Out. Of. My. Mind." He punched the elf again. As the blow landed there was a sound of shattering glass that echoed throughout the chamber and into Kurt's mind. With a forceful tug at the back of the neck, Kurt felt himself ripped backwards. The chamber faded to darkness as he tumbled backward. As Kurt fell through this strange void, he felt an odd falling sensation before sitting bold upright in his chair.*

# 8

Night had fallen while he was asleep. Looking down at his hands, Kurt saw they were still bloody and raw but despite the pain, he smiled. He got up to wash his hands and tend to the wounds, smiling all the while. He had beaten Orlan. Beaten him in a way the elf hadn't expected.

Kurt's thoughts raced, while he set about preparing some food and starting a fire. He thought about what was on his mind when he struck out in the dream. His thoughts were of the town, his recruits, his friends and Cali. His family.

Kurt realised that when he fought back, he'd only been thinking of where he was and where he was going. For the first time in over a year he hadn't spent one moment of his dream remembering the past. He looked over at his bed and saw the edge of the chest stashed there, and he made a decision.

He walked across the room and dragged it over to the light of the fire. Kurt took his time as he opened the latch and as the metal hinges creaked open for the first time in over a year, he looked upon the contents.

A pile of dark grey clothes lay one side of the chest, with a thin layer of dust sprinkled on top of them all. His old uniform. He lifted the jacket and trousers out carefully and looked them over. They were what he was wearing when he first arrived here all that time ago. They felt heavier than he remembered.

Kurt bundled them up and threw them into the fire. He watched them burn for a while, using a fire poker to keep them burning safely at the back of the fire. Kurt felt calm as he watched one of the few things that tied him to his past burn away.

Once there was nothing but ashes remaining, he turned back to the chest. The uniform had taken up most of the space so only two things remained: a small metal canteen that had not been used for some time even before Kurt had arrived in Bismurr, which he took out of the chest and stared at for a moment before placing on the floor; and a small brown leather bound book. His diary. He picked it up and blew away the dust that had gathered on the cover. This too, was heavier than he remembered. Kurt untied the string that kept the diary bound shut and, with some slight hesitation, opened it. As he started flicking through the pages, a mix of memories flooded through him. Some of the early entries bought a smile to face and even a few happy tears. Yet as he went through each entry in the diary, his mood soured. His fingers stopped when he reached the final pages and shame started to flood through his thoughts.

Kurt didn't need to read those final words, he could remember vividly everything he'd written in there. Tears silently rolled down his face as he tossed the book into the fire. He looked into the flames once more, hoping that he'd feel some sense of relief as the pages burned. As Kurt watched the paper turn to ash however, he just felt hollow. He didn't move for a time, he simply watched the fire dance around the ashen remnants of his past. The flames started to die before Kurt came back to his senses. After drying his face on his sleeve, he got up and grabbed the canteen from the floor before walking outside.

The cold night air bit at his skin but Kurt ignored it as he walked into the forest. He didn't travel far, he just wanted to make sure he couldn't see his home any more. He knew the metal wouldn't burn in his measly fire but he wasn't going to give the canteen to anyone else. Something in his gut told him that this was something he had to deal with himself. Kurt used his free hand to dig a small hole in the ground and placed the canteen down. He buried it with dirt and made sure to hide the spot with a few handfuls of leaves from nearby. Once he was sure it was hidden, Kurt returned to his home. Despite the dirt on skin and his bloodied bandages, he felt clean, refreshed. He took the time to wash up and eat some food before going to bed.

The sheets felt softer than they ever had before and as a sense of comfort and safety embraced him, Kurt drifted happily into a dreamless slumber.

* * *

The next morning he felt reinvigorated after the night's events and was eager to get started on the day ahead. A quick breakfast later and he was on the road to town. As he travelled he remembered he should address his recruits; he had trained them how to defend themselves, how to follow orders, but after what happened at the ruins, it became clear he should ready them for loss. It was something he had hoped not to deal with so soon, if at all, but he steeled himself. With each step he took, Kurt felt more sure of himself now that he'd finally made a decision about his place in Bismurr.

Kurt strolled past a few other early risers and approached the squad leaders' tent. For the moment he was alone, so he looked out over the fields they had been using for training. He thought about what they had fought so far and tried to make sense of everything they had learned about their enemy. At first, Kurt thought about the magic the elves wielded but soon gave up - there didn't seem to be any rules to it as far as he could see. The creatures however, they were starting to understand. While he was thinking, a few familiar faces started to gather nearby. Lief and Peyton appeared first and were whispering between themselves as they approached. Garet followed soon after walking alone, hunched over and deep in thought. Meredith also appeared from around a corner but slowed down a ways off as she looked around for the remaining squad leaders. She didn't have to wait long, as Soren, Yvette and Sig soon appeared from between two buildings, chatting amongst themselves. Everyone approached the central table, falling silent as they waited.

"Before we start there's something I'd like to say," Kurt said, taking the time to look at each squad leader in turn before continuing. "Since I agreed to help you all and train people to be ready, I thought I could use my past as a weapon to try and protect this place. But I was so focused on the past that I wasn't thinking of the present, let alone the future. That was wrong. I was wrong."

"We don't think you've done wrong so far Commander," said Yvette, prompting a wave of murmuring agreement from the others.

"That's kind of you, of all of you," continued Kurt, "but I swear to you all that I'm not letting the past, what I was and what I did, define what I do here. This place is my home now. We're not just going to survive one attack, if it comes. We are going to win it and we're going to keep winning, whatever it takes."

When Kurt had finished, Peyton let out a loud cheer which was followed by an awkward silence. After a few moments, everyone in the tent burst out laughing. Even Peyton, who had turned a shade of pink, couldn't help himself from smiling.

"So what comes next?" Sig asked, once the laughter had died down.

"Next? Next we work out a plan, with no holes in it," Kurt replied. "We go over everything we know about the creatures we've fought already. Then everything we know Orlan can do. Finally, every rumour anyone knows about what magic the elves wield? We think of ways to counter all of it."

"All? That's a lot," Garet said, sighing to himself. "You'd be surprised how many stories have spread over the years. It's hard to know what might be the truth or just some childhood nightmare."

"Even so, we can't take any chances," Kurt said. "We've already had too many people hurt because we didn't think about everything our enemy could be capable of. Even those creatures have surprised us far more than they should have."

"Speaking about the creatures. We should really start naming them," said Meredith.

"Well Orlan always treats those soldiers like they are his lesser, plus they're not nearly as powerful as him," Lief said. "Since the monsters are from the lowest of the elven ranks that we know of, let's call them 'Dregs'. Seems appropriate."

"Dregs it is," Kurt agreed. "What about the bigger ones?"

"They seem to be like pack leaders right?" Garet asked. "How about we just call any of the larger ones that we might see, an Alpha?

"Done," Kurt said. "Now, onto Orlan. What do we know?"

"Well he could turn his soldiers into Dregs, create fire from nothing and move things with his mind," said Soren.

"That's not accurate," Meredith countered. "He raised his hands when he moved things, like he was using an unseen force."

"That seems to fall in line with what I experienced when I faced him," said Kurt. He was about to mention his dreams, but he decided to keep his focus on the task at hand. "I do remember that his grip on me weakened when he started creating that ball of fire."

"Right, he didn't seem to be able to focus on too much at once," said Lief. "We could probably overwhelm him with numbers if enough of us got close."

"That might be dangerous, but probably our only option," Kurt replied. "We'll need to be faster at dealing with any Dregs he brings before trying to deal with him."

"We're all in agreement on that, especially after the past few days," Soren said, his brow furrowing in thought. "I think I can come up with a few more useful training routines, now that we've seen more of those things, Dregs, in action."

"I think the main thing would be to focus on our archery and getting used to using those new weapons Cole is building. My squad will take that lead on that," said Sig.

"Good plan," Kurt replied, giving Sig a quick nod. "Now, what else do we think these elves can do?"

The group spent the rest of the morning, and some of the afternoon talking back and forth about what they thought the elves might be capable of. From the things they had seen to the more outlandish rumours, they discussed it all. Breaking only to grab some food, it was almost the evening before they finished. As everyone went their separate ways, Kurt made his way to Cali's bakery. He took a shortcut down an alley and as he walked into the shadows, felt a strange wave of dizziness come over him.

The spinning sensation threatened to overwhelm Kurt, forcing him to grip onto a nearby barrel to try and steady himself. For a moment, he thought he'd recovered until he tried to take another step forward. The wave of dizziness struck again, faster this time. Kurt stumbled and fell down to his knees. Darkness poured around the edges of his vision and before he could make a noise, Kurt collapsed into the dirt, unconscious.

*Kurt found himself surrounded by fog and the familiar icy chill crept through him. He stood and saw a hooded figure hunched over nearby. Shadows obscured the figure's face under the hood, but there was something instantly recognisable about it.. Frustration started to fill Kurt, but he pushed the feeling down as he squared up to the figure.*

*"Orlan," Kurt muttered.*

*"Human," spat the elf in response.*

*"I would have thought you would have avoided another meeting so soon," Kurt said with a smirk.*

*"You will be silent," Orlan hissed. "I suspect your otherworldly nature corrupted my last attempt to look into your mind, but we won't be repeating what happened last time."*

*Kurt tried to reply, but his mouth wouldn't form words. He tried to rush forward, but with a raised hand from Orlan, his body froze in place. Kurt looked up and struggled furiously but found himself completely powerless. As Kurt's gaze fell back onto his foe he noticed two strange shadows floating behind the elf, with their arms outstretched.*

*"I acquired an extra weaver, just for you," Orlan said, as he stepped towards Kurt. "You have proven yourself to be more trouble than my superiors think you are worth, but they granted me one last chance to see your mind. An opportunity I most definitely wasn't going to squander."*

*Kurt tried again to break free but found the strange grip on his body tightened even more, causing him pain until he fell limp.*
*"Do you have any idea what you cost me?" Orlan said, not even attempting to hide his rage. "Not once but twice you have humiliated me. I have lost all credibility with my superiors, my family, all because you and your pathetic misplaced guilt."*

*The elf then leant down and grabbed Kurt's hair, pulling his face up to look into the fog. With a wave of his free hand, Orlan parted the grey clouds that surrounded them. Unveiled were Dregs, hundreds of them, Kurt couldn't guess how many, as their numbers disappeared further into the fog.*

*"I've been granted an army, five hundred strong to wipe away the stain of your pathetic resistance," Orlan whispered into Kurt's ear. "I will walk upon the corpses of your disgusting friends and make you watch as I burn down everything you've tried to build. Then when it's all done, I will drag you back to the capital and rip apart your mind until you are nothing more than a husk."*

*Orlan threw Kurt downward into the dirt. Darkness flooded his vision as he tumbled through the void again.*

# 9

Kurt jumped up in a panic and almost fell over, head still spinning. He leant against a wall for support and took some deep breaths. Kurt's first thought was to run to anyone he could find and scream about what had just happened, but when he opened his mouth to talk, nothing happened. The strange effect that was blocking him from speaking had made itself known. He tried again to scream out about his dream but this time as he tried to force the words out, his body reacted violently against the act and Kurt started to vomit, profusely.

Once he had finished, Kurt considered staying in town, but opted instead to head back to his cabin. The dream continued to pester his thoughts as he walked past the townsfolk, but despite the panic and dread he was starting to feel, Kurt found himself being filled with a strange confidence. Orlan had shown his hand and though the number of Dregs coming was overwhelming, he now knew what the town had to deal with. No more unknowns, just facts, which was something Kurt found very comforting. He didn't find rest that night, he found himself pacing across his home trying to think up ways to fight a force so much larger than the fighters Bismurr had gathered. As the night went on and dawn approached, Kurt spent most of his time sat down staring at the floor. Even with his lack of sleep, he didn't feel tired, too many ideas were rushing around his mind.

By the time the sun had fully risen, Kurt was already walking into town. He took his time, making mental notes as he passed the various defences that were almost finished being built. As he passed the buildings on the outer edge of town, he started thinking about what else could be done to counter the huge numbers coming. As he was making his way to the smithy to talk with Cole, people he walked near gave him a wide berth, a few started tutting and whispering about him. Kurt didn't mind their

judgmental looks; he wasn't looking for anyone's approval, not any more. Before he reached the smithy, he spotted Cole walking ahead of him, the older man also deep in thoughts of his own.
"Cole!" Kurt called out.

"Oh Kurt! Good morning," he replied, a little startled. "You're looking even worse for wear than the last time I saw you. What did I tell you about getting some sleep?"

"Yes, I remember, but this is important," Kurt replied. "Those new weapons you're building, the cannons? How many do you think you'll have ready in the next few weeks?"

"Hmm. Hard to say at this stage," Cole said thoughtfully. "If I was to guess, maybe twelve?"

"That's enough to work with, thank you," said Kurt. "When you complete each one, send them to our command tent. The squad leaders will make sure they're placed where they need to be."

"Alright, not a problem. We'll send the ammunition for them there as well," Cole replied. "I'd best be going, Lots to be getting on with as usual." He looked Kurt up and down one last time. "And get yourself some sleep, you're no use to anyone if you're dead on your feet."

The pair then parted ways and once he was out of sight, Kurt took a moment to think about his next stop. Moments later he was striding towards the eastern edge of town with some ideas in mind. Once he arrived at the field he spotted a new watchtower, still under construction, with a few people gathered around it, Garet among them. The dwarf spotted Kurt and jogged to meet him halfway across the field.

"Commander!" Garet called out as he skidded to a halt. "How're you doing?"

"I'm fine, a little tired," Kurt replied, stifling a small yawn. "How are the towers coming? No problems I hope."

"Nah, all good here. Though making them ready for weapons we haven't got yet is a little strange," Garet replied. "I do have some good news though! We've got just two days of work left before we finish reinforcing the homes of everyone who isn't fighting."

"We're not building defences in all the buildings?" Kurt asked, confused.

"Ah yeah, the rest of the townsfolk wanted to help how they could. So everyone who isn't fighting will hide in the houses we've reinforced, leaving some places empty. We figured they'd still be useful as a distraction, since we're likely to have a few of those Dregs slip past," said Garet.

"That's smart. At least that's one problem solved," Kurt said, looking out past Garet to the open space leading to a large hill. "We need to do something else with this space, maybe some traps."

"Good idea Commander. I'll see if the hunters can help us out," replied Garet. "Me and the others have been thinking about how many Dregs might be coming. We think it might be best if we assume they'll try to overwhelm us. Orlan seems like the type to take things too far."

"That's..." Kurt's words couldn't form the way he wanted, but he managed to force out a sentence regardless, "...possibly a good idea. Whatever you and the others think is the best. That's why you're the squad leaders after all."

"Fair point," Garet said with a laugh. "You're looking a little tired by the way. You wanna grab some food?"

"Thank you, but I'll pass," said Kurt before turning away. "See you soon."

The dwarf jogged away leaving Kurt to walk back into town. His feet were starting to hurt once more so he walked his way to the centre of town and sat down on a bench to rest. Kurt stayed there for a long while, watching people going back and forth. As he was sitting, images from his dream flashed through his mind over and over again. He felt like he was missing something but couldn't figure out what.

While he was thinking, Kurt ended up staring at a few people heading towards the mine with pickaxes slung over their shoulders. He watched them until they disappeared from sight and as they did so, an idea started to form in his head. He stood up and rushed toward the training grounds where some of the squad leaders should be working. When he neared the command tent, Kurt could hear muffled voices coming from inside. He hurried inside to discover Peyton and Lief stood over the map of the town, their conversation ending as Kurt entered the tent.

"Ah, we were hoping to talk with you," Peyton said with a smile. "We have some news about the books we found in those ruins."

"Yeah, a lot of interesting reading apparently," Lief said with a smile.

"Oh?" said Kurt, briefly distracted from his own idea.

"That's right!" Peyton replied. "We've only just started going through it all, but it seems to be a lot of history from before the elves arrived. No idea how long it'll take to read it all but I think that trip is turning out more useful than we first thought."

"That's good, worth looking into whatever we can find if it could teach us more about elves and what they've been doing all these years," said Kurt. He took a deep breath to order his thoughts. "I've been trying to figure out our plan for the coming attack. Every idea that I came up with, we failed. Each and every time. There's so much open space surrounding Bismurr and I think when it comes down to it, we'll get overwhelmed too easily."

"You don't sound upset about that. I take it you have a plan?" Lief asked, confused.

"The start of one, maybe," replied Kurt. "I think we need to find a way to make our enemies only come from one direction, funnel them."

"And how exactly do we do that?" asked Peyton.

"We need to get everyone into the mines and keep the fighting at the entrance," Kurt answered. Lief and Peyton looked at each other, their expressions grave.

"That's not possible Commander," said Peyton. "That many people moving in there, we'd have to go deep into the mine and that's going to attract the wrong kind of attention."

"He means the orcs," Lief interjected. "They live in tunnels that run deeper than the mines. I mean half of what we've been made to use down there was just their tunnels. The elves may be the ones that forced them deeper into the ground, but we're the ones that have been down there most of the time. I agree with Peyton, if we move the town in there, we'll just have people killing us from both sides."

"Well we won't survive out here. As far as I can tell the mine is the only option to give us the edge we need," argued Kurt. "These orcs, can't we try talking to them? Surely they'd want to help make sure the elves stay gone?"

"It'll probably be a waste of time, but we won't know for sure unless we send someone to check," Peyton replied.

"No!" Lief said, slamming her fist onto the table. "They are bloodthirsty and dangerous, probably just as dangerous as Dregs. If we send someone down there, they'll be killed and just get attention that we don't need right now."

"Well that's just going too far," Peyton said, glaring at Lief. "They've suffered at the hands of the elves as well, there's a chance they might listen to us."

"It's a suicide mission!" she spat, before storming out of the tent.

"I truly believe it's the only option we have," said Kurt.

"Not arguing there Commander," Peyton replied. "But she is right to be angry, the orcs are very likely to kill us if we delve into their territory."

"In that case I'll go myself. I'm not risking anyone else," Kurt said. "I'll need a guide to get me through the mine though. Then once I'm in their territory I'll take my chances on my own."

"I'm sure I can find you one, but I think we need to move quickly. If too many people hear about this, you're likely to cause a small riot," Peyton said. "We can meet at the mine entrance at sundown. I'll talk with Lief as well, make her understand. She'll keep quiet I'm sure, until we make it out or get killed anyway."

"We?" Kurt shook his head. "I don't thin-"

"Yes. We." Peyton interrupted with a pointed stare, as though demanding his answer be challenged. "You're right. We shouldn't send many people down there, but there's a better chance we'll make it out alive if there's two of us."

"Alright," Kurt relented. "I'll see you at sundown then."

Peyton nodded in reply and hurried out of the tent. Kurt did the same and headed straight to his cabin, to get himself ready. The first thing Kurt reached for was his weapons but he decided to leave them behind, if this was to be an attempt at being peaceful he thought it best to present himself as non-threatening as possible. He changed into some warmer clothes and made himself some food. The remaining few hours of the day seem to fly by after he eats his meal, all the while thinking about what to say to these people he'd never even seen before.

As dusk was settling Kurt left his cabin and made his way around the outskirts of town with his collar pulled high to avoid being recognised by anyone. Soon enough, he found himself at the entrance of the mine, staring down at the town. As the last slivers of orange light disappeared, Peyton and a young male dwarf appeared at the bottom of the hill leading toward the mine, both moving quickly despite being laden with large packs as darkness fell around them.

"Kurt," Peyton greeted as he approached. "This here is Belorn, he's going to guide us into the mine."

"Though I ain't going all the way into their territory," said Belorn. "I'll take you down there to the last part of our mine and wait for you, but no way am I going any further than that."

"Fair," said Kurt, looking around to make sure no one else was nearby. "Shall we get going?"

"Lead the way," Peyton gestured to Belorn. The young dwarf walked ahead and the three began their venture into the mine.

Once they had passed over the opening's threshold, Belorn took a torch from his pack and lit it to light the way. Kurt couldn't help but stare nervously at each of the wooden beams that lined the walls and ceiling as they marched into darkness. He took a deep breath of the musty air, trying in vain to calm himself as they moved onward. The mine tunnels were narrow, but there was just enough space for the three men to walk side by side.

The trio travelled in silence for hours, the only sound they heard was the soft crackle of the torch and the crunching of stone beneath their feet echoing down the tunnel. They huddled close to the dim torchlight as the pitch black darkness threatened to

engulf them. Kurt became very aware of how lost he would've become if he wasn't with others, each twist and turn they took only served to further confuse his sense of direction. The group reached a large opening, the beams of wood and carved rock ending at a gaping maw of uninviting shadows. As they stepped forward the light revealed a far more wild-looking tunnel with moss-covered jagged rocks littering the roof of the path ahead. Before they crossed the threshold into unknown territory, Belorn stopped to ignite a second torch which he handed to Peyton.
"This is as far as I go," said the young dwarf as he took out a large roll of string wrapped in a tight bundle. "I'll tie this off here, keep track of it as you go forward, otherwise the orcs will be the least of your problems."

"Understood," whispered Peyton, doing his best to hide his nervousness, but still worried. "We'll try to be back soon, but don't wait too long for us."

"I don't plan to," laughed Belorn. "Get going, I don't wanna be here longer than I need to be."

"Thank you." Said Kurt taking the bundled string before following Peyton into the tunnel.

After only a few dozen steps the light from Belorn's torch had completely vanished. The pair kept quiet as they travelled onwards and downwards, Kurt slowly unravelling the string while they walked. Their pace slowed as they found themselves starting to climb over rocks and stoop to avoid the ever-lowering ceiling. Despite not knowing exactly how these tunnels had been dug out, Kurt noted that they seemed incredibly stable as only a few loose stones shifted while they moved through the darkness, though the stability of the tunnel didn't do much to put the two men at ease.

After a short while Peyton stopped in his tracks causing Kurt to almost bump into him. Ahead of them the tunnel had opened up into a huge cavern, so large that there was no telling where the ceiling was amongst the shadows. Moss and mushrooms seemed to cover most of the rocks and the sound of rushing water could be heard in the darkness. There were no other lights to be seen but their own torch gave them more light in such an open space. They walked for a short distance before Kurt felt the string become taut.

"Well that's the end of the easy way back," said Kurt, showing Peyton the string.

"Shouldn't be too much of a problem," replied the older man, nodding towards something in the dark behind them. Kurt turned just in time to see a figure dash behind some rocks and vanish into the shadows.
"So they know we're here," Kurt said, swallowing his nervousness away. "How should we approach them?"

"Carefully," said Peyton with a weak laugh. "I think we should tie the string off here and walk on a short way. They can hear us, so I think we should just say what we're here for and see how they react."

Kurt nodded and found a rock nearby to tie the string to. After it was secure, the pair walked forward a little further and came to halt, the light from the torch looking a little less bright all of a sudden. They also heard scuffling coming from almost all directions so it was a certainty that they weren't alone. Peyton found a small patch of earth to stand the torch and then he turned to Kurt and gave him a reassuring pat on the shoulder. Taking one last deep breath to steady himself, Kurt stared out into the blackness, focusing on a point he thought he could hear movement from.

"We're here in peace," Kurt said, his voice calm but loud. "Things have changed on the surface and we're fighting back against the elves. The battle to come isn't going to be easy and we need your help. I know you haven't seen the surface people as allies in the past but surely even your kind has issues with the elves."

There was silence for what felt like an eternity as many unseen eyes glared at the pair. Before the two humans were about to turn around, a solitary figure stepped into the circle of light. A large male orc, he stood a full head taller than Kurt and was wearing simple brown leathers across his muscular frame. For a short moment he simply looked at the two humans with green eyes which almost seemed to glow in the dark.

"Follow me," said the orc before turning back into the darkness. His heavy footfalls echoed as he disappeared from sight.

Peyton grabbed the torch and together with Kurt they hurried to catch up with their new guide. As they journeyed further downward, the number of noises from the shadows increased. Footsteps and unintelligible whispers accompanied the three while they walked. After a short while Kurt had completely lost track of where they'd come from and was glad when he finally saw some more light ahead. Lining the floor to light a path were glowing yellow stones, darkness still surrounded them but the strange stones provided an easy route to follow. Further ahead was what looked like a huge dome made of rock, its edges stretching so far out that most of the structure was hidden in shadow.

As they drew closer, more grey-skinned figures moved from the darkness into the light. The orcs that were stepping forward seemed more curious than aggressive about the strangers in their midst. Kurt looked around but tried to keep himself from staring. He did manage to notice that everyone he saw seemed scarred and muscular, more than anyone he'd ever met above ground. These people were fighters, warriors.

Their orc guide took them right up to a large archway that acted as entrance to the stone structure. He stepped to one side and gestured for the two humans to walk inside. They obliged and upon entering the large chamber, the pair were almost blinded by the bright light emanating within. Glowing stones were littered all over the walls of the circular chamber; while it wasn't too bright compared to the surface, after spending time in the dark tunnels it was like stepping into a sunlit day. Once his eyes adjusted to the light, Kurt realised the chamber was filled with dozens of orcs, all of them staring intently at the two trespassers. The crowd parted to create a path forward, leading to a large stone throne with a female orc sitting upon it. She was adorned in what looked like fur-trimmed silk robes and grasping a staff with a large skull of a creature that Kurt didn't recognize. As they approached, her gaze on them was intense, like there was something about their very presence she was measuring. Standing on either side of her were two more female orcs wearing dark hooded capes. Judging by the stance and the large spears at their sides, these were her personal guards. Peyton leaned over to speak to Kurt as the pair walked through the crowd to approach the throne.

"That's the Matriarch," Peyton whispered. "Other than her title, I don't know anything else about her. Be respectful and honest."

"Understood," replied Kurt. The pair stopped a short distance from her and they heard the crowd shift behind them to block the exit. Silence fell over the crowd as all eyes fell upon the Matriarch.

"Humans. Surface dwellers." Her voice was strangely amplified throughout the chamber and her eyes started to glow a brighter green than any of the other orcs in the room. The green glow even shone through her thick black hair that hung loosely over one side of her face. "I'm informed you came here unarmed, wanting to talk? Wanting our help? What makes you think you have the right, why should we not slaughter you where you stand?"

"If you weren't willing to listen, we'd be dead already," said Kurt, unsure of where he was pulling his confidence. He took a step forward while Peyton stood silent. "As for the right? I've lived here for only a year, as such you are strangers to me. You and I have no history and no animosity, I think that gives me a neutral standing."

"Neutral?!" the Matriarch hissed. She then leaned forward and sniffed the air, smirking afterwards as though she had proven something to herself. "You've been influenced by a weaver, your words could be lies or simply poison to our ears."

"Weaver?" Peyton asked, not trying to hide his confusion.

"You don't even know what your enemies can do and you think we'd help you?" The Matriarch laughed. "The elves have many weapons they use. One of which are the 'dream weavers'. They delve into your mind while you sleep and change your thoughts, make you a slave to their will and whim."

"Kurt?" Peyton turned to look at the younger man in disbelief. But when Kurt wanted to say something to defend himself, the words got stuck in his throat. Peyton started to back away a little, fear spreading across his face.

"What can I do to prove myself?" Kurt asked, trying to change the subject "Whatever you think of me, the elves are the real enemy. There must be something I can do to make you see that."

"Prove yourself?" the Matriarch said to herself, a smile spreading across her face. "I speak for my people, but in most things what I respect most is personal strength. You, Kurt, choose from among my people. Beat them in combat and I'll consider listening to your request."

"I have to choose?" asked Kurt confused, as his eyes darted around the room, looking for someone he believed he could defeat.

"You are the trespassers here, the challengers, it's only fitting you have a fair chance." She continued to smirk as she leant back in her throne.

"Then I pick her," Kurt pointed at the orc woman standing to the left of the throne. She was smaller than him and despite her athletic frame, he was confident that the size advantage would make the fight easier.

Various orcs in the chamber started to laugh and even the Matriarch covered her mouth as she chuckled to herself. Peyton was dragged to one side before he could speak any further. The woman Kurt had pointed to stepped forward and threw her cape to one side, before looking to the Matriarch for instruction. Kurt took a few steps back and dumped his heavy jacket on the floor.

"Begin," said the Matriarch, the singular word causing the crowd to cheer and stamp their feet. Looking over to Peyton, Kurt could see the older man was trying to shout something to him but the words were drowned by the noise.

Before Kurt could turn to face his foe, the orc had already dashed forward and slammed an elbow into his midriff. The sheer force of the blow flung him into the air. Kurt's body crumpled as he landed heavily on the stone floor. Winded, he tried to start rising to his feet. The orc woman sprinted across the room with blinding speed and before Kurt was even standing again she threw a punch that sent him sprawling back to the floor. He managed to roll away just in time to dodge another blow, and her fist slammed into the ground below, cracking the stone floor. Kurt kicked out her legs to send her to the ground, but before he could attack again she kicked him in the chest with such force that he was sent flying across the chamber. After crashing onto the stone floor, he skidded to a halt with the wind completely out of him. Kurt rolled over just in time to see the orc's small fist slam into his face and knock him unconscious.

# 10

Kurt felt a strange swimming sensation as he drifted back to consciousness. His head and chest were aching, but much less than he would have expected. Opening his eyes to look down at his chest he saw that his body had been wrapped in bandages in every place the orc had struck him.

"You should move slowly," a soft voice said from his right. He turned to see the same orc that pummelled him, sitting by his bedside, holding a wet cloth which she placed into a bowl at her feet.

"You're helping me?" Kurt asked with a small cough, a dry throat making his voice hoarse. She leaned away and handed him a cup of water which he drank.

"Indeed she is," said a familiar voice from the other side of the room. Kurt winced as he sat up to see Peyton leaning back against a wall. "Quite kind of her considering the beating she gave you."

"I guess I failed the trial?" Kurt said, still trying to think through the pounding sensation in his head.

"Not exactly," replied Peyton, "but we'll get to that. Get yourself ready, the Matriarch wanted to see us the moment you woke up."

"What?" Kurt asked, rubbing his aching jaw.

"She made you fight to prove something - she never said you had to win," laughed Peyton as he walked out of the room.

"Thank you for tending my wounds," Kurt said to the orc woman.

"Seems fair that I help you, considering how easy you were to beat down," she said with a smirk. "I am surprised you chose to fight me though."

"I thought I could win," Kurt replied. "Guess I underestimated how strong you were."

"You really are a stranger here aren't you?" she asked, staring at him with confusion on her face.

"Yes. I thought telling the truth was the smart thing to do," Kurt replied, meeting her gaze. Unlike the other orcs she didn't seem to have as many scars, her grey skin unblemished. Like most of the orcs Kurt had seen, she also had green eyes that glowed softly in the dim light.

"Well that was smart," she said, leaning over him to check on his bandages, her long dark hair brushing his chest. "Fighting me though? Not so smart. Our women are much stronger than the men. Your friend tried to warn you, didn't you hear?"

"I think I was a little distracted by the shouting and having my skull smash against the floor," Kurt said. The orc laughed, revealing her fang-like teeth. "What's your name by the way? You may have heard from my friend, but I'm Kurt."

"My name?" she asked, still smiling. "You can call me Nul. Now get dressed and join us when you're ready."

Nul then left him alone in the room, looking back only once as she left. Doing his best to ignore the pains across his body, Kurt got out of the bed and saw that his shirt was neatly folded on the floor next to him, laid next to his boots. With some difficulty he pulled it on and despite struggling to breathe when he leant forward, Kurt managed to get his boots on as well. Standing up wasn't much of a struggle but he had to take several deep breaths before he started to walk as his chest felt tight and painful. Slowly but surely he made his way out of the room and into the hallway where Peyton was waiting for him a short distance away.

"Good to see you up," said Peyton. "It's only been a few hours, but after that beating I thought I'd be waiting 'til morning."

"So what happened after Nul knocked me out?" Kurt asked as the pair walked down the stone corridor.

"Nul?" Peyton raised an eyebrow, before moving on. "Well, once you were out, the Matriarch said she'd listen to us. I spoke with her alone for a short time and she agreed to let everyone in town come into the mines as long as we don't delve too deep."

"That's great!" Kurt replied. "That's at least one less worry for the time being."

"True, though the fact she still wants to talk with us makes me a little worried," replied Peyton. "We need to get back soon, hard to tell down here but I think it'll be dawn soon."

"Well if it takes too long, you head back to the surface and I'll stay behind for a time," said Kurt, slowing down as Peyton stopped at the edge of a doorway.

"You ready?" Peyton asked. Kurt nodded in response and the pair walked through the doorway into a small chamber. Sitting in one of four identical wooden chairs at the edge of a square table was the Matriarch, while standing behind her was Nul and the other female orc from the throne room. As the humans drew closer, two large orcs appeared from nowhere and grabbed Kurt, pushing him down to his knees easily.

"Don't fight back," said Nul, a look of sadness flickering briefly on her face. Kurt looked back and saw that Peyton was watching, making no motions to intervene.

"Peyton?!" Kurt struggled to break free as he looked to his friend for help.

"Sorry Commander," Peyton said as he stepped forward to take a seat at the table. Before Kurt could respond, one of the orcs tied a gag around his mouth.

"So before we continue, what are we going to do about this man?" asked the Matriarch. "We can't know if anything he says can be trusted while he's under the effects of a weaver."

"Agreed," replied Peyton. "I still think the idea of using the mine to funnel our enemies will work in our favour. I'll need to look over our other weapons and plans before we can be certain of our safety."

"I'll provide some of our warriors for your front line," said the Matriarch. "However, if your people fall, you know I won't put my own at risk to provide more shelter."

"Of course," Peyton replied. "Now for Kurt, what would you suggest?"

"Hmm?" The Matriarch looked down at the struggling human and regarded him slowly. "We can keep him here for now. We will see the amount of influence upon him and we could see to his release soon enough, assuming it's possible to free him."

"Matriarch?" Nul stepped forward, her eyes locking with Kurt's before turning back to the Matriarch. "May I take charge of that? I'm not done treating his injuries."

"If Peyton here agrees to have him stay here, you may," the Matriarch replied.

"I think that might be for the best," said Peyton, turning his attention to Kurt. "There'll be less arguments if the decision has already been made. I presume you'll return him to us if you can solve this weaver problem?"

"Of course," replied the Matriarch. "Now before we discuss details, You two, take the human back to his room, we'll see to him later."

The two large orcs dragged Kurt out of the room. Peyton averted his gaze in shame as his young friend was taken away. Kurt gave up struggling once he was taken out into the corridor as the pain throughout his body was forcing his strength to fade. He soon found himself back in the room he had awoken in and once they removed his gag, the two orcs left, locking the door behind them. Kurt crossed the room and sat on the edge of the bed. While he understood the decision, it didn't make him any less enraged that Peyton had betrayed him like this. Looking around he tried to see if there was anything he could use to attempt an escape. Other than the sheets on the bed, the room was completely bare. The dim glow of the rock in the ceiling was oddly soothing and gradually Kurt found a small sense of calm. As his frustration ebbed away, a tiredness started to fill him. Knowing he could do nothing for the moment, he decided to get some rest and lay back on the bed. As Kurt stared upward at the ceiling, his eyes were soon closed as sleep began to take hold.

*Kurt opened his eyes to find himself standing in a familiar fog and a chill snaked its way up his spine. The stench of burning filled his nostrils and he found himself almost wishing for Orlan to appear. Terror gripped him as he felt a cold hand touch his shoulder and when he turned he saw the face of a woman, burned beyond any recognition, whispering words he couldn't make out. The moment he tried to move, the woman walked away into the fog. His vision slowly faded back into darkness as Kurt came back to consciousness.*

# 11

Kurt's chest felt tight and painful again, but less so than before. The glow from the ceiling was unchanging, leaving him at a loss as to how much time had passed, though he felt like he'd slept for a long while. He sat up against the wall and sighed, thinking about the strange situation he found himself in. While being taken captive wasn't the best outcome, part of him felt like he deserved this, and Kurt took comfort in the fact that he had accomplished what he set out to do. Almost as though someone was listening outside for him to awaken, the door opened and Nul entered. She was carrying a tray with fresh bandages and some food, a bowl of soup so hot it left a trail of steam as Nul made her way across the room. She placed the tray on the small table at his bedside and took a step back.

"Did you get some rest?" Nul asked, breaking the awkward silence.

"Despite being held against my will? Yes I got some sleep," Kurt replied with a glare.

"It may seem cruel, but even you can't know what control has been taken from you," Nul replied, sitting down at the end of his bed. "You have to understand that this is for the best? What's inside you could be dangerous to our people, your own people even."

"My people," Kurt said with a small amused grunt. "I don't think that's appropriate any more."

"Your friend wasn't happy with our deception at first," Nul said, tilting her head to try to meet Kurt's gaze. "But the effect of the weaver on you was something most of us could sense the moment you came close. It's why the Matriarch suggested that trial so quickly."

"So everything here has been a lie?" Kurt asked.
"Not everything," Nul replied. "Besides, the fact you can't even deny that you're under the effects of the weaver doesn't help you."

"That's...." Kurt tried to speak but yet again found himself unable to form the words he wanted. He leant back against the cold stone wall and stared at the ceiling.

"But we'll see to that," Nul said as a smile spread across her face. "We could even start today if you'd like?"

"I have a choice?" Kurt asked, confused. "I thought I was your prisoner."

"Well that's to be decided," Nul explained. "The effects on you are completely unknown; you might just have had some dreams you can't explain, but you may try and kill everyone when you hear a certain word. When we know what the weavers have done to your mind, we can spend time trying to make you right again. While we do that you will be free to move around as you please."

"Surprising," Kurt muttered to himself. "But I still won't be allowed to leave?"

"The other human, Peyton? He and the Matriarch spoke for a while before he left. She made it clear that you won't be returned to the surface until you are made 'clean' - her words," Nul said, rolling her eyes. "She can be a bit heavy on speeches sometimes, but she does stick to her word."

"I can respect that," Kurt responded, before his stomach growled loud enough to make Nul smirk. "I guess I should eat something before we get on with the day?"

"You should," she replied with a smile, she stood up leaving the tray on the bed.

"Change your bandages as well. Call for me when you're ready and we'll get going."

Once Nul had left the chamber, Kurt started to eat the hot soup. It was bitter, being made of mushrooms but it was pleasant enough that he ate it all it quickly. Changing the bandages was a more troublesome affair but he managed to get himself ready for the day ahead. The pain in his chest faded a little more once the clean bandages were on, but it still slowed him down as he pulled his boots on. Leaving the tray and its now-dirty contents on the bed, he knocked on his locked door and called out for Nul. He heard the shifting of a lock and the door drifted ajar. A large orc standing guard gestured for Kurt to step out and once he did, closed the door behind him. Nul was a short way down the hall and upon seeing Kurt, nodded down the hall and started walking away. He caught up to walk at her side.

"So where are we going?" Kurt asked.

"We have a few people who can look you over. They can see how much influence the weavers have placed on you. It's not too far," replied Nul.

"What are they going to do? I'm not going to get beaten again am I?" Kurt asked with a half-hearted chuckle.

"You did bring that on yourself," she replied with a laugh. "And no. They'll sit with you for a time and get a feel for you, like how the Matriarch could sense it on you before."

"Does she have a name other than 'The Matriarch'?" Kurt asked out of curiosity.

"She did," Nul replied. "But when one of us takes the mantle they forsake their name. It's supposed to show how you've left behind your old self and given yourself fully to lead us all. Small warning, it's a little disrespectful to use her old name, so probably best that you don't hear it. Avoid the temptation."

"Of course. I'd hate to be disrespectful to my captors," he said with a smirk.

"We're nearly there," Nul replied, grunting with annoyance as they rounded a corner.

Kurt had been struggling to remember the route but almost all the stone corridors in the place looked the same with the glowing rocks above them and similar unmarked doors all over the place. When they reached their destination, the door was already open, Kurt got a strange sense that something was inviting them in. Inside was a large circular chamber with dozens of lit candles filling the room, giving the whole place a comforting warm glow. Three older female orcs sat on large stone blocks all facing inwards where a small pile of furs had been placed. Nul gestured for Kurt to walk forward to the centre and as he did, the three other orcs followed his movements, already judging his every action.

"Make yourself comfortable," said Nul as she stepped back to lean against a nearby wall. The candlelight stretched the shadows nearby to almost completely shroud her in darkness.

Kurt sat down and looked between the three women staring at him. Each one was looking over him with an intensity that made him uncomfortable, but he did his best to be patient. One of the women finally broke the silence with a throat-clearing cough and started to speak.

"What is your name?" she asked, her voice seemed grave and cold as though the answer to the question could be wrong. Kurt looked over at Nul who gave him an encouraging nod.

"Kurt Bauer," he replied.

"Why did you come into our home?" asked another of the women, her tone colder than the first.

"I was looking for your help, trying to help protect the people who live above you," Kurt stated.

"You said to the Matriarch that you were a stranger to those people. If that's true, why help them?" asked the first woman.

"They took me in," replied Kurt. "They're my friends and family."

"Where did you come from before you settled in Bismurr?" The third woman spoke up, just as cold as the other two.

"Somewhere far from here. I'm not exactly sure where." Kurt tried to be honest, but didn't want to delve into this past with these strangers, not if he wanted them to trust him. "It was a different place that I left behind. I have no ties with it any more."

"What do you know about the Elvish dream weavers?" asked the first woman.

Kurt froze, trying to speak but found his throat had closed up. Struggling to breathe, he kept pushing until he was red in the face. Kurt stopped trying and he was able to take a long deep breath. All the while the three orc women stared at him, watching his struggle. Once he had settled down, they resumed their questioning.

"Moving on, why did you choose to fight an enemy more powerful than yourself?" The second orc woman leaned forward slightly as she spoke.

"People were getting hurt. I had to do something," Kurt replied, trying to meet the gaze of each woman.

"Elves hurt people constantly. Why did you choose now of all times to do something?" the first woman pressed.

"I wasn't there to do anything before. When I was present, I couldn't just stand by and do nothing. Not again," Kurt responded.

"Again? You said you were a stranger here," said the first orc. "You allowed people to suffer before? Perhaps in the place you are truly from?"

"I..." Kurt paused and didn't know how to respond.

"Or are you the one who caused the suffering?" the second woman asked.

"No, I didn't cause it. I just didn't..." Again he trailed off as memories began to flood in.

"Didn't what? You didn't think people were suffering?" The first orc pressed again. "Do you think yourself innocent?"

"I'm not innocent," Kurt admitted. He met the gaze of the woman staring at him, awaiting his answer. "But I'm not going to let that happen again, I refuse to. This place is my home now and I'm going to fight for it. If you'll let me."

The orc women looked away from Kurt as they started to whisper amongst themselves. After a while, the three women fell quiet but continued to stare at one another. There was silence for a time and unsure what he should do, Kurt looked over at Nul, who didn't react, she just stood waiting for the three women to pass their judgement.

"We have reached an understanding," said the first woman, her tone much warmer than before. "While the effects of the weaver on you aren't strong, it is still unique."

"Indeed," joined the second, whose tone remained cold. "It would seem your mind was open for a time but rather than place things there, someone would rather simply look inside. A curious change."

"Nulkala," called the third woman, causing Nul to step forward into the light. "We need to meditate further on how to purge these unique weaver effects on him but he is safe enough to walk around as long as he's accompanied."

"Good to hear," Nul said with a smile.

"Now we need to decide how to proceed further," said the first woman. "You're free to go for now, young man, but ready yourself to be called on again."

Kurt nodded and before he could speak further, Nul grabbed his arm and pulled him towards the door and back out into the hallway.
"Nulkala?" Kurt asked as soon as they were alone.

"My full name," she sighed before an excited smile spread across her face. "But at least you're free to move around now!"

"True. Nice to know I'm still in control of my mind," said Kurt, feeling a little relieved.

"Strange how the elves wanted to look inside rather than make you do something," Nul said as she furrowed her brow in thought. "You really are a strange human."

"I did say I was," Kurt laughed. "So what can I do now? I've no idea where to go."

"I've got some ideas," said Nul with a smile. "Come with me."

She didn't wait for Kurt to reply and started walking down the stone corridor. He ran to catch up and the pair walked for a time before they rounded a corner to a large archway. There were several more orcs passing through, turning down more identical corridors. Nul gave a few of them friendly nods and waves as they passed, which everyone reciprocated. Once they passed through the archway Kurt stopped in place and gasped at the sight before him.

The corridor they had walked down had opened up into a huge sprawling valley. A large waterfall in the distance was cascading from the darkness above to form a river that flowed through a small forest. The glowing orange rocks were scattered everywhere above and below, causing everything to be bathed in soft, warm light. At the edge of the valley Kurt could make out dozens of smaller stone domes which had many people walking around near them. Kurt walked ahead quickly and looked back in wonder at the stone structure they had come from. Before he had thought of it as a building but from this side it looked like a huge fortified gate. Nul was smiling at Kurt's reaction as she caught up.

"This is amazing," said Kurt, still staring out over the valley.

"Our home," Nul said, smiling with pride. "We call it Shadehill."

"All of this has to be at least twice the size of Bismurr," Kurt said while he started to walk down the path.

"Oh, easily. Why do you think the Matriarch didn't want you returning to the surface without being dealt with?" Nul caught up and again led Kurt as they made their way down the winding path that soon became surrounded by the tall trees. "Are you hungry?"

"I could eat," Kurt replied without thinking as his attention darted around the undergrowth and the canopy of leaves. There was something more wild and lush about everything here than the surface, which seemed so controlled and docile in comparison.

The pair walked for a time, as Kurt just stared in wonder at this strange world that had been hidden beneath him for a year. Nul was a fantastic guide, waiting every time Kurt stopped to look at something. She even took the time to point out some of the small squirrel-like creatures that darted between the undergrowth and the trees. As the path opened up to the settlement and more orcs seemed to be walking back and forth, the two of them walked a little quicker to keep out of anyone's way. Kurt was surprised that everyone they passed greeted both Nul and himself. No one seemed to be upset by his presence; in fact they all seemed very welcoming to the human amongst them. After a short walk, Nul pulled Kurt down a path that led away from the main route into the orc settlement. The pair were soon standing outside a small grey dome at the edge of the treeline. Outside was a large stone table with sawn-off tree trunks as makeshift seats.

"Wait here. I'll get us something to eat," said Nul, walking inside.

Kurt sat down and looked around. The few orcs that were nearby didn't seem to notice him while they walked on by. His gaze fell back on the stone hut and through a carved window he could see Nul moving around what looked like a kitchen, putting together a small plate of fruits and filling a large jug with water from a barrel. She returned with everything on a large tray that she placed on the table between them and took a seat opposite Kurt. Together they ate and drank in silence for time until curiosity got the better of him.

"Those glowing rocks that are all over the place, how do they work?" he asked.

"The glowstones?" Nul looked upward at the lights dotted throughout the darkness. "I'm not quite sure. We do know that if they are exposed to sunlight they fade. It's like they only provide light for the darkness."

"That's fascinating," said Kurt, looking up into the darkness as well. "They look like stars."

"Stars..." said Nul, looking upward. "I've never seen them."

"You've never been above the mine?" Kurt asked, looking at Nul.

"No," she replied, meeting his gaze with a serious expression. "There are only a handful of us that have. The rest of us have spent our entire lives underground, though I expect that's about to change if the Matriarch sends some people to join your friends."

"I'd heard you've had some conflicts with the miners from Bismurr before," said Kurt. "Why didn't you try to talk to each other in the past?"

"That's a little complicated," Nul replied. "For the longest time we were content here. Then the elves kept forcing the town above to dig deeper and take more. As the stone fell away, the path to our home became open. The Matriarch made the choice to only attack those who came close to our tunnels, to steer people away to other parts of the mountain. Some of us maybe got a bit too aggressive during those raids but I think we did the right thing in the end."

"We? You took part in some of the raids?" Kurt asked. Nul froze for a second, and for the briefest moment there was a flicker of regret on her face.

"Some,"she replied, her expression shifting back to a smile. "Not for a while now though. Me and the Matriarch got closer over the past few years so I've been busy attending to her."

"I see," was all Kurt said, not wanting to pry any further. "I have to say this place, your home? It's amazing, truly. I was angry before, but I can see why you would want to protect all of this."

"Thank you," Nul replied with a smile. "When you're ready I have one last place to show you today."

Kurt gave a nod and once Nul put the plate and cups back inside, the pair started walking away from her home and into the forest. They walked without talking for a long time, only breaking the silence when they needed to move around tough parts of the undergrowth. While they journeyed, the sound of rushing water became louder and Kurt realised they were heading to the large waterfall he'd spotted earlier. Sure enough as they drew closer a light mist began pouring through the area. The water itself was warm and despite their obscured vision, the pair pushed forward until they broke through the edge of the forest. Before them was the bottom of the waterfall: several huge rocks with the rushing water crashing onto them, spreading the mist everywhere around. The rest of the water pooled at the bottom and became a large river that flowed away back through the trees. Nul came to a stop just before the grass fell away to the rocks and turned to face Kurt.

"This is the Vastep," she said, raising her voice to be heard over the sound of crashing water. "I think it means 'the one river', but I don't really know our old language that well."

"Where does the waterfall come from?" Kurt asked, looking up into the darkness.

"Flows from deep within the mountain," replied Nul. "We think it comes from as far as the opposite side, miles away!"

"That's impressive," said Kurt, turning his gaze back to Nul. She smiled at him as she began to walk back through the forest, away from the waterfall.

"I like it there," Nul said, talking at a normal volume once they had walked away. "It's where most of our water comes from but it's also a good place to think, or at least drown out your thoughts."

"This place, your home, it's something else. So peaceful," Kurt said. He stopped walking and took a breath. "But I have to ask, why are you sharing this with me? I know you're trying to make sure I don't feel like a prisoner here, but you don't have to go out of your way this much."

"Before I answer that, answer me this." Nul also stopped and turned to face Kurt. "Would you say I've been anything other than fair to you?"

"No. You've been more than reasonable, kind even," Kurt answered.

"So why disrespect me by asking why I want to help you?" Nul asked. She folded her arms, waiting for an answer while Kurt stood still for a few moments, trying to think of what to say.

"I'm sorry. I just don't see why you'd think I deserve your help," Kurt replied.

"What you deserve? How does what you deserve change what I want to do?" Nul asked, but she didn't wait for Kurt to answer. "Life isn't so simple that you can just decide what others should or shouldn't do. Whatever you think should happen to you isn't going to change what I'm going to do, understood?"

"Understood," Kurt said. He wanted to argue back, but it looked like Nul was starting to get angry.

"I think that's enough for today," Nul sighed. "Come on, I'll walk you back."

They stayed in an awkward silence as they made their way back through the forest. Once they reached the giant stone gate, Nul had warmed a little more and smiled when Kurt caught her gaze. Soon enough, they were walking back through the stone corridors winding their way back to Kurt's room. Once they reached an identical corridor to the last few they had walked down, they stopped just outside his door. Kurt looked around and Nul noticed that he was looking for a guard that was no longer around.

"You don't need to be guarded any more," she said. "You're free to roam around as you like now."

"Thank you," Kurt replied as he stepped into his room. "Sorry if I upset you today. Your people are not at all what I expected."

"And neither are you," Nul said with a small laugh. "I'll see you tomorrow morning."

She left Kurt alone and walked away down the corridor. Kurt watched her until she rounded the corner and then went into his room. He felt tired enough to lay down and sleep, but he kept himself awake for a time to think about the day.

Knowing that whatever effect Orlan had placed on him was going to be removed gave Kurt some patience about staying here for a time. He knew that an army was coming for Bismurr, but they had time and everyone in the town was pulling together better than he could have hoped. He drifted into sleep thinking about what his place in town should be now.

*Slipping once more into the fog, a chill gripping his entire body, Kurt kept his eyes closed. The stench of burning flooded around him and despite how much he wanted to, Kurt couldn't block it out. A rough hand touched his back. His eyes snapped open.*

# 12

As Kurt sat upright in a panic, it took a few moments to realise where he was. He fell back into the bed and stared at the ceiling for a while, calmed by the dim light of the glowstones. Now that Orlan was no longer invading his dreams, his familiar nightmare had returned in full force. Not wanting to return to sleep, he decided to get up and go for a walk. It was difficult to navigate the stone corridors but Kurt managed to make his way back out of the gate fort. There were a few orcs going about their own jobs but the few that passed by Kurt gave him space and left him about his own business. There was something about this forest that he noticed earlier and it was still present this time, the air had an inviting quality to it. Kurt lost track of time as he walked between the trees, letting his fingertips brush over leaves sprouting around the undergrowth. The constant soft orange glow made it impossible to know whether it was day or night, but something about the low light was relaxing enough that Kurt found himself not caring.

He ended up walking into a glade filled with vibrant green grass and bright white flowers. The place was so serene that Kurt felt compelled to lay down and was soon staring into the inky shadows, letting his eyes fall on each distant glowing rock, and tracing shapes in his mind. For a time he felt his worries slip away and lost himself to this unexpected paradise.

"You've made yourself comfortable," said a voice, startling Kurt enough to sit bolt upright. On the other side of the glade Nul was leaning against a tree, staring down at Kurt.

"Sorry," said Kurt, standing up and dusting off the dirt from his clothes.

"Don't panic yourself." Nul smiled as she approached. "I wasn't expecting you to be up so early. Didn't you sleep well?"

"I.." Kurt paused, he felt a compulsion to tell her the truth but decided against it. "I don't sleep well sometimes, especially when I've got a lot on my mind."

"That's fair," Nul replied. She stopped in front of Kurt and looked upward to see where he had been staring. "Do the glowstones really look like stars?"

"They do, mostly," Kurt replied, happy to change the subject. "If you look at the sky outside on a clear night, you might see thousands of them."

"That sounds pretty," said Nul as she turned her gaze back to Kurt. "Since you're up, do you want to help me with my morning duties?"

"I'll have to check in with my jailer, but I'm happy to come along," said Kurt. Nul laughed a little and punched his arm.

"Come on," she said with a grin before turning away.

Kurt followed her as she made her way back through the woods to the path. They headed toward the orc settlement in the valley in good spirits. The path grew busy with orcs travelling back and forth as they walked on. Despite his lack of sleep, Kurt felt energetic; something about this place seemed to invigorate him.

"So what sort of morning duties are we doing?" Kurt asked, walking close to Nul to avoid straying too close to the other orcs travelling up and down the path.

"Nothing interesting," Nul replied, stifling a yawn. "I just need to gather some food for myself and check on a few things for the Matriarch. She likes to keep a close eye on what we grow and make sure we harvest as much as we can without taking too much. But when that's done I'll be free for the day."

"Any plans for me?" Kurt asked, ever curious about his situation in this place.

"A few," Nul said coyly. "We'll get to you later though."

The pair then spent their morning walking through a variety of farmland that Kurt hadn't spotted earlier. Nul gathered a large basket of fruits, vegetables and mushrooms. She held it with ease and laughed when Kurt offered to carry it, yet struggled to lift it. Not wanting to be a burden, he did manage to keep the basket off the ground while Nul went about checking the fields, making mental notes on their state. Kurt barely managed to get the food to her home and was going to put it down at the threshold before she stopped him.

"Bring it inside, leave it in there," Nul said as she walked inside, pointing to her kitchen.

She strolled off into another room of the small abode, leaving Kurt outside. He entered and dropped the heavy basket on the stone floor of the kitchen. Looking around, he realised that this place seemed strangely similar to his own, not in design but because the small amount of furniture, utensils and food supplies showed that only one person lived here. He stepped back into the cosy hallway and heard Nul moving around another room; he chose to be polite and not open the door.

"That was a lot of food for one person," Kurt said, trying to sound casual. "Planning some family meal?"

"Hah! Family? No it's just me here," Nul said, her voice muffled through the thin wooden door. She paused for a moment before continuing. "Some of that will be for you. I spoke to Jaskor, he was guarding your room before - he was going to be responsible for your meals, but I offered to take over for him."

"Oh," said Kurt, feeling a little more awkward standing in the hall. "Thank you, but you didn't have to do that."

"Did you not like the food yesterday?" Nul asked, her voice suddenly clearer as she was nearing the door.

"No no, it was delicious," Kurt said, backtracking down the hall. "I just don't want to make you busier than you need to be."

Nul then stepped into the hall with a look of frustration across her face.

"Sounds an awful lot like you're trying to tell me what you think you deserve again," she said as she stepped up to Kurt, stopping close enough that he could feel her breath on his face. "Remember what happened last time you had an expectation about me?"

"I remember," said Kurt while rubbing his still-aching chest.

"Good," Nul said with a smile. "Now let's get going. You really don't want to keep the Matriarch waiting for too long."

She then pushed him back outside and the pair made their way back to the gate fort. Kurt waited outside as she rushed in to deliver her report; he wasn't waiting long before she rejoined him.

"So," she started while steering him back onto the path. "I was talking with the matrons last night--"

"The Matrons?" Kurt interrupted.

"The women from yesterday? Did I not tell you who they were?" Nul tilted her head while trying to remember. "Well anyway, they really thought about your unique problem and decided that pressing the issue might be more damaging than they first assumed... but they did have one idea. We could maybe - and this is a big maybe - try to strengthen you to purge the effects of the weavers yourself."

"Well I'd not risk hurting myself so that certainly sounds like a better idea," Kurt said with a sigh of relief. "But how are we going to do that?"

"Simple, I'm going to teach you," Nul said with a smug grin. "And I know that you're worried about time but if this works? You'll be free to leave in just a few weeks."

"That sounds a little too good to be true," said Kurt, doubt replacing his relief.

"Well I said simple, not easy. It'll be down to you and how quickly you can do this," Nul explained. "But I think you can do it. You had the guts to come here and face us with no idea what we would do, so I think you have the strength for this."

"So what will we need to do?" asked Kurt, feeling a little more emboldened.

"First, we have to go somewhere quiet," replied Nul. "And I have the perfect place in mind."

She then took off down the path with Kurt in tow. The pair didn't walk very far before they turned off the main road and walked down a thin footpath that was hidden enough that Kurt would have missed it without a guide. This secluded place was lined with hundreds of bright blue flowers that glowed under the shade of the trees. They heard some quiet voices ahead of them. Nul turned back to Kurt, holding a finger to her lips. She stopped just shy of a clearing, stepping off the beaten path and waved Kurt to join her by a tree to look inside.

A large glade lay before them with flowered bushes forming a barrier from the rest of the forest. A circle of glowstones littered the edges, so despite the thick tree canopy, the entire place was illuminated with a soft orange glow. The glade itself was covered with short grass with several orcs sitting in random places all over the clearing. Each of them had their eyes closed and mumbled under their breath. After watching for a short time Nul grabbed Kurt by the arm and pulled him out of earshot of the meditating orcs.

"This is a special place to us," she whispered. "There's a few of them hidden away in this valley, it's busier today than I thought but it should be perfect for what we need."

"Why is it special?" Kurt asked, also whispering.
"Hard to say exactly, but this place has a strong effect on people who rest here," Nul whispered. "If you just relax here you'll find yourself feeling healthier and sometimes stronger. We've learned over the years that if you focus your thoughts in a place like this, you can control its power over you. It can help you heal wounds, get stronger and cure any kind of illness."

"And you think this place could help me... would it even work on me? I mean only your kind has used it I imagine?" asked Kurt, carefully choosing his words so as to not trigger the weaver's effects.

"It's worked on some of our animals, so I'm sure it'll be fine for you," Nul said with a smile. "Now, when we go in, do not talk to anyone. I'll lead us to a spot for ourselves, but it's incredibly rude to disturb someone here."

Kurt nodded in reply and Nul grabbed him by the hand to lead him into the glade. They did their best to be quiet as they walked around the others there to find an empty space for themselves. As they walked, Kurt became very aware of every inch of his body. Every breath he took in the glade sent a wave of warmth through his muscles and across his skin. He could feel all his hair standing on end as though electricity was flowing through him, each wave only ending when it reached the tips of his fingers. Kurt became very aware of Nul's hand gripping his own. As he found himself focusing on the feeling of her soft skin touching his own, the strange waves of warmth continued through his hand and started to flow into hers. She stopped in her tracks and turned around. As she released his hand, the waves of warmth felt like they were flowing straight into the air. Nul sat down and motioned for Kurt to do the same. He situated himself opposite her, and once he was settled she leaned forward to whisper to him.

"I take it you can already feel the power here?" Nul asked as she raised the hand he had just been holding, gesturing at the glade.

"I've never felt anything like it," Kurt said, each breath still sending the waves throughout his body. "You said this place had power but I didn't think I'd feel anything quite like this."

"It's good that you can feel it so well, that was going to be the first lesson," Nul said. She closed her eyes and took several slow deep breaths, keeping her eyes closed while she talked. "The next step is to try to focus on a single point, get this place and its power to only affect what you want. So for now just do what I do, breathe with me. Keep your eyes closed and focus your mind on your injuries."

Kurt closed his eyes and started to breathe in time with Nul, and with each intake of air he found it was easy to start mimicking her perfectly. Soon enough he couldn't hear anything but his own breathing as each wave of strange energy flowed through him. He focused on his aching chest and as he did so the waves grew slower. Each wave of energy timed itself with the beat of his heart. The sensation reversed when the energy reached the tips of his fingers, pulsing through his skin back to his heart. This continued for a time, never changing in speed, just a simple, rhythmic pulse. Kurt lost focus and just sat for a while, feeling the steady pulse of his own heartbeat. After a few minutes he felt a warm hand touch his shoulder and when he opened his eyes, Nul was crouched in front of him, shaking him out of his self-induced stupor.

"I think that'll do for today," she whispered.

"Oh, are you sure?" Kurt asked as he stood up. "I feel fine. I could do this for longer, I think."

"Probably not a good idea," Nul said as she started to walk out of the glade. "You've been here for most of the day already. I think we can try again tomorrow."

"The day? How is that possible? I relaxed, but it can't have been that long." Kurt replied, confused.

"This place is powerful," Nul said, as the pair stepped outside into the surrounding forest. "You did well today though. After we eat tonight we'll talk about what's planned for tomorrow."

As Kurt left the glade its effect wore off instantly, yet he didn't feel like something had left him. If anything he felt nourished, as though he'd just eaten a large meal. He caught up with Nul and the pair had only walked a short distance down the path when they noticed a small gathering of orcs approaching. Nul's face lit up when she saw the pair leading the group, an orc woman arm in arm with an orc man.

"Wait here," she muttered before running to the group with a huge smile on her face.

Nul pounced on the couple leading the others and pulled both of them into a hug. When they broke apart they had a quick conversation that Kurt couldn't quite hear; his ears only prickled when he heard his own name and Nul briefly looked over in his direction. The pair agreed to something Nul said before she ran over back to Kurt.

"We're not going to head out just yet," she said, with a wide grin. "My two friends Krayte and Del, they're going to perform a Vastupa!"

"A Vastupa?" Kurt asked, as they joined the back of the group walking into the glade.

"It's a joining ceremony, they're bonding to each other for the rest of their lives,"

Nul explained, "and before you complain, they are perfectly happy for you to be here with me."

"That sounds like a wedding," said Kurt. "Is the glade a part of it?"

"Clever boy," Nul said with a smile, as the group came to a stop. "Hush now though, they're starting."

Kurt and Nul joined a dozen orcs in a circle around the couple. The effects of the glade flooded over Kurt once more, but he ignored it to pay attention to the ceremony. The orc couple knelt down and started holding each other's hands, smiling at each other as they closed their eyes. Kurt looked around the circle and saw that all eyes were on the couple - everyone was waiting, and after a few moments Kurt could see why. Krayte and Del had started to glow, dimly at first, but soon they were lighting up the whole glade with a blue light. The light kept growing until it was almost too bright to look at and then, just as Kurt was about to look away, it began to fade. Once the light was gone the couple opened their eyes, each of them beaming at the other.

"I know you," said Krayte, raising his hand to touch Del's cheek.

"And I know you," Del replied, touching Krayte's cheek the same way.

The gathered crowd cheered and rushed forward to the couple, sharing congratulations as they embraced the pair. Nul grabbed Kurt by the shoulder and pulled him away.

"You don't want to talk to your friends?" Kurt asked, confused as they walked back down the path.

"I'll see them later, they've got their families to talk things over with. But wasn't that beautiful?" Nul said, letting out a contented sigh.

“I'm not exactly sure what I just saw,” said Kurt. “I thought someone would have said something, shared some words? Where I'm from if you promise to share your life with someone, usually they say that aloud. Not to mention that it seemed so quick for such an important thing?”

“Let me explain,” Nul said, coming to a stop. “I said the Vastupa was a joining ceremony. You saw how they sat in the glade, focusing on each other and then lit up? Beautifully I might add. Well, they became joined, they shared their lives with each other, letting their memories flow between each other. Not everyone wants to do it - letting someone see the entirety of your life? It can be overwhelming to some. But those that do it are always closer for it.”

“I can't imagine sharing some parts of my own life,” Kurt replied. “Some things in life are best left behind you.”

“As much as I love it for my friends, I'm tempted to agree with you there,” Nul said, turning away to continue walking. She fell silent for a brief time as the two of them made their way through the forest.

The mood shifted to a more positive note once they sat down to eat outside Nul's home. By the time they finished their meal of fruits and a strange biscuit that Kurt struggled to bite through, the pair were laughing.

“So what's the plan for tomorrow?” Kurt asked once there was a lull in the laughter. “Sorry that I completely lost track of time today.”

“Oh don't be sorry!” Nul said, touching his arm to comfort him. “You did great today, especially for your first time trying to use the glade. We just need to make sure you stay in the moment, keep your focus on the physical.”

“Any advice?” Kurt asked, as he thought back on the glade's power being so overwhelming.

"I've got a few things I can try when we're there, but advice for you?" Nul sat in silence for a few moments whilst in thought. "One thing you could try is to think of yourself in a circle, and the glade's power is outside that circle. That might help you a little."

"I'll keep that in mind," said Kurt as he finished the last of his meal. "Anything else planned for the evening? After today I don't think I'm going to rest any time soon."

"I have something in mind, don't you worry," she replied as she collected their plates and cups. "Let me tidy these away and we'll get going."

After she had stashed their dirtied plates inside, Nul grabbed Kurt and led him into the woods behind her home. The undergrowth was wild here, this wasn't a path beaten down by years of use. Kurt did his best to follow but found himself struggling. If Nul wasn't dragging him through the thick wall of plants, he would have gotten stuck a short distance into the walk. After a brief but difficult time, they broke through into a tiny clearing. Glowstones were scattered nearby to light a small pool that had been carved into the rocky ground, with the water filling it hot enough to spread steam across the floor of the entire clearing.

"A hot spring?" asked Kurt as Nul released his arm to walk around the pool.

"My hot spring," Nul replied. She looked around the clearing and let out a contented sigh. "I made it myself. If we're going to purify your mind, you definitely have to do the same to your body."

"Makes sense," Kurt replied, stepping forward to test the water with his hand. "Where does the water come from? And the heat?"

"I fill it with fresh water myself, straight from the river," Nul explained. "The heat was tricky, but there are these vents of steam underneath us. With a little bit of work I managed to tap into one. It takes a while but eventually all the water disappears, so

I don't even have to empty the thing."

"That's impressive. You did this by yourself?" Kurt asked, staring at this woman who kept surprising him.

"Yes I did," she replied. "So are you getting in or what?"

"Uhh..." Kurt became red in the face as Nul watched him. After an awkward few moments she burst into laughter.

"Alright, I'll leave you to it," she said as she stepped past him. "I'm going to go see Krayte and Del anyway. Wait around here when you're done if you like."

She then started to climb her way back out of the clearing, though Kurt noticed Nul kept looking back at him, laughing to herself as he stared back at her with a blank expression. Once she was out of sight and he couldn't hear footsteps any more, he let out a sigh of relief. He stripped off and lowered himself into the pool of hot water. The temperature was perfect, the heat washed over and through him. Kurt felt himself melt as he leaned back against the rocks. He couldn't remember the last time he'd even had a decent bath, let alone something as luxurious as this. As he soaked in the hot water, he realised just how much his joints were aching, but allowing his body to relax in the heat filled him with a small sense of euphoria.

He sat for a long while, with his eyes closed, letting his thoughts drift. His small sliver of peace was broken when he heard some branches creaked above him, snapping his attention back to reality. Kurt then got out and noticed a large towel hanging from a branch that Nul had left behind without him noticing. After drying and dressing himself, he made his way back through the thick barrier of plants to return to Nul's home. Arriving back at her front door, he was surprised to see her sitting at the bench drinking from a small metal cup. Nul had a sombre look on her face until she heard him approach, quickly shifting her expression back to her usual smile.

"I thought you'd be spending the evening with your friends?" Kurt asked as he sat down opposite her.

"I just wanted to congratulate them. I'm not one for parties," Nul replied. She then took a quick sip of her drink before offering it to Kurt. "Careful, might be a little strong for a human."

"Thank you," Kurt said before drinking. The fruit-flavoured liquid tingled in a familiar way and Kurt was astounded that he recognised it. "This is schnapps!"

"Schnapps?" Nul asked with a confused look, while still smiling. "No, that's called Finka. Berry-Finka to be accurate. It's my favourite drink, a little difficult to make down here, so we don't have much."

"Then, thank you even more for sharing it with me," said Kurt as he slid the cup back across the table. "It tastes exactly like a drink from my home, my first home. It's been years since I had anything like that."

"Do you miss it? Your home I mean. I know you said it wasn't just above-ground." Nul took another sip as she waited for an answer.

"Parts of it I miss." Kurt said. He thought for a moment and whether it was all the kindness Nul had shared with him or the drink going straight to his head, he decided to share some of the truth with her. "My home changed though, even while I lived there. Whatever it's become now, I know I never want to see again."

Silence fell between them and Nul slid over the drink again, which Kurt took, nodding his gratitude. The pair shared the rest of the contents for the evening, only breaking the silence when Nul finished the last few drops.

"Suppose I'd better be going," said Kurt. He was a little light-headed from the drink but steadied himself with the table.

“For the best,” Nul replied. “Want me to walk you back?”

“No need, I think I can find my way back now,” Kurt said, but after noticing her expression sadden a little he continued. “But I'd appreciate the company.”

She jumped out of her seat and despite being a little unsteady on her feet as well, managed to walk side by side with Kurt. They made their way back to the gate fort, stumbling and laughing a little as they did so. Once they reached its large entrance, Nul stopped and with one last smile gave Kurt a small kiss on the cheek, causing the young man to turn bright red.

“Sleep well,” she said before walking away.

Kurt grabbed his face in shock and stood still watching her leave. He walked back to his room baffled but happy nonetheless. As he drifted off to sleep that night he felt content. Nul's approval was important to him leaving this place, but something about her affection felt fulfilling in a way he didn't expect.

# 13

Over the next few weeks, Kurt fell into a routine. Sharing meals with Nul, meditating in the glade and occasional nights relaxing at Nul's hot spring. He also found himself making gradual progress in learning how to use the glade's power, but still couldn't push the strange weaver influence out of his mind. Kurt's frustration in his failure had built up to a point when he stopped in his tracks on the way to the glade.

"Something wrong?" Nul asked when she noticed he wasn't following her.

"We've been at this for weeks now. I'm beginning to think this might be a wasted effort," Kurt said, trying to keep his anger under control. "If we're wasting our time trying to teach me something that might be impossible for me to learn, then we should try something else otherwise I'm never going to get back above-ground in time."

"Don't look down on our progress," Nul replied, stepping up to Kurt to stand right in front of him. "Giving up now would make all our work pointless and I refuse to believe we've wasted our time. I understand your frustration, I do, but we can't stop now."

"This isn't about your help. This is about me not being strong enough to get through this," Kurt said, squaring up to the smaller frame of Nul. "I can't stand the idea of staying here if all I'm going to do is fail."

"You're not going to fail," Nul replied. "But I think you need to take a step away from things for today."

She then started walking away from the glade, leaving Kurt standing alone. She stopped at the end of the path, waiting for him to catch up and after a few moments, he begrudgingly followed her.

"So what now?" he asked, not trying to hide his frustration.

"First? We take a walk." Nul grabbed Kurt's hand and dragged him forward through the forest, heading towards the orc settlement. "Second? You leave your anger behind before I beat it out of you."

"Sorry," Kurt muttered, pulling his hand free as he walked alongside Nul.

Despite Kurt's mood, Nul returned to her usual sunny disposition, ignoring his attitude altogether. While they travelled, Kurt noticed there seemed to be fewer orcs around than normal. He hadn't been there long, but he knew that the orcs stuck to their routines. He looked to Nul, who wasn't reacting to the change, which put him somewhat at ease, but suspicion started to nest in the back of his mind. The pair veered away from the path before they got too close to the stone homes on the outer edge of the settlement and walked down a side path that led into an area obscured by trees. Stepping around a large tree that obscured the path, Kurt arrived at the top of a set of stone stairs. The staircase led down into a large open area that had been dug out to form a pit. Stones lined the walls of the pit while its floor was flattened dirt that had been disturbed in random places.

"What is this place?" Kurt asked as he stepped down into the pit, following Nul to its centre.

"This.." Nul spun around with her arms raised, gesturing all around. "This is the fighting pit. We use it all the time, to settle arguments, for fun and any reason we want really. I think we need it today."

"Why?" Kurt scratched at his chest as a dull ache that he'd forgotten made itself known again, causing Nul to laugh.

"You're frustrated. I know you feel stuck, so we're going to take your mind off it." She walked around him, like an animal stalking its prey.

"I really don't want you to beat me into the dirt again," Kurt said, following Nul with his eyes, trying to ready himself for her to attack.

"Oh you can't beat me outright," she said with a smirk. "So we'll have a few rules that we're going to follow."

"What rules?" Kurt asked, starting to walk in a circle as well, mirroring Nul while keeping her in sight.

"I've known you for a short time now and whether you believe it or not, I can tell when you're lying," she said. "So here's the rules. We take turns asking questions and the other has to answer. If someone tells a lie, they get hit - and they have to let it happen. If someone tells the truth and the other doubts them and tries to attack, they're allowed to block and hit back."

"Seems a little unfair, how will I know if you're lying?" Kurt asked.

"Simple," she replied with a smile. "I don't plan on lying to you."

Kurt lunged forward and swung a punch at her that Nul caught with ease. She tapped him on the forehead with her free hand and pushed him away. He stumbled back and landed on the ground.

"Your turn," Kurt grunted as he picked himself up.

"Hmm..." She thought for a moment, deciding her question. "You're eager to get back to your friends, but you've not once tried to escape, why?"

"You know why. I decided to defend the town and I can't stand not being part of that fight," Kurt replied. Nul dashed forward and kicked out his feet, causing him to fall onto his back.

"Anyone with some morals would feel that way, what's the real reason?" Nul asked as she offered a hand to pick him up.

"Responsibility. I promised that I would help them." As he took her hand, she let him go, making him fall back onto the dirt.

"Why?" she asked. Anger had been bubbling inside Kurt from the start of this and being thrown onto the ground repeatedly had sent him to a melting point.

"Because I deserve it. I deserve to be trapped down here," he muttered, rising onto his knees. Nul took a step back and let him return to his feet.

"Ask away," Nul said. Seemingly satisfied with his answer, she resumed her predator-like circling. Kurt thought for a moment and tried to let his frustration simmer a little before asking his question.

"Why are you so keen on helping me?" Kurt asked. Nul seemed a little stunned at the question as she stopped moving.

"I find you curious and wanted to help you," she averted her gaze as she spoke, and Kurt knew what to do. He rushed forward and with both hands pushed her. She didn't fall as she stumbled backwards, managing to keep her balance after a few awkward steps.

"I thought you didn't plan on lying?" Kurt said with a smug grin. Nul grunted in response before Kurt continued. "So why do you want to help me?"

"Fine." She closed her eyes briefly and took a breath. "A few years back I did my

duty to protect our home, and I hurt people. I didn't enjoy it, I hated it and did everything I could to forget what I did. So when a strange human appeared one day asking for help, I felt that it was a chance to make things right."
"I see," was all Kurt could think to say. He believed she was telling the truth so he started circling her again. "Ask your next question."

"Alright." She thought for a moment. "You've spent almost a month with us now. What do you think of our people? Are we the animals the Bismurr folk think we are?"

"Not at all," Kurt replied. "I didn't know what to expect, but in the short time I've spent here you've been nothing but fair to me. And you in particular have been more than kind to me. So I'd say no, you're not animals."

"Good." Nul said with a weak smile.

"My turn," said Kurt. He took a breath to prepare himself for his next question. "If I can't be helped, will I be allowed to leave in time to join the fight that's coming?"

"If it gets to that time and we still haven't gotten rid of that weaver influence? I'll take you above-ground myself, regardless of what my people say." Nul replied.

Kurt moved forward and tried to throw a kick, only to have his leg caught in the air. Nul then spun him around and with almost no effort, threw his body across the pit. He managed to break his fall and roll back to his feet, but found himself more stunned at Nul's answer.

"Thank you," he said after a few moments of silence and Nul shrugged in response.

"I've only got one question left," she said, walking up to Kurt. "Do you feel better?"

"That's it?" He stared at her, confused.

"Answer honestly now," she clenched a fist and took a stance just in front of Kurt.

"I think I do," Kurt replied and after a few seconds of thought with Nul's menacing fist waiting above his head, he continued: "Yes, I feel better. This helped."

"Good," she said with a smile as she lowered her fist. "Let's go eat."

She marched off towards the stairs, leaving Kurt dumbfounded that this was over so easily. He did feel better, knowing that Nul would let him leave if the time came. He followed her out of the pit, rubbing some fresh bruises on his back and the two of them made their way back to her home for a meal. By the time they were finished, the pair were back in high spirits again.

"So, do you wanna try meditating again for a while?" Nul asked when she returned from cleaning up their plates.

"I'm in a better mood now," said Kurt as he stood up. "Let's go."

As they walked to the glade, Kurt noticed again that there were far fewer orcs around but Nul caught him looking around this time.

"Something wrong?" she asked.

"Just noticing a lot less of your people around," he replied. "Does that have anything to do with the town above?"

"It does," Nul replied, walking ahead of Kurt so he couldn't see her face. "Your friends and the Matriarch have been in several talks over the past few days and she's decided some changes in the deal were for the best."

"Changes that involve your people getting involved with our fight even more?" Kurt felt a slight pang of guilt.

"That's right," she replied, turning back with a small smile on her face. "It's a good thing. There hasn't been this much talking between us and the surface for as far back as any of us can remember. So take that look off your face, don't go thinking we're putting ourselves in harm's way needlessly."
"Sorry. It's just when I first came down here, it wasn't my plan to get you involved. Knowing that your people are choosing to go and fight for us is just a little hard to hear," said Kurt.

"If we have time, we should try to teach you not to hold yourself to be so responsible for other people's choices," Nul said with a laugh.

Kurt managed a weak smile before they turned off the main road to walk down the quiet path to the glade. When they did arrive at the glade proper, Kurt realised they were alone, it was the first time he had seen the place empty since he started meditating here. Nul took this as an invitation to walk to the very centre as their spot of choice. Kurt joined her, feeling the familiar wave of energy wash through him as crossed the flower-covered threshold. He sat down facing Nul, closing his eyes as they both began to breathe together. Soon enough he slipped into the warm and ethereal sensation that he'd spent most of his recent days in. Before, he had struggled to make the power move towards his mind but now, when he started to think on it, a sense of control seemed to manifest itself. A feeling of calm that seemed to flow between himself and the glade's power, like two strands of string spinning together to form something stronger. Tentatively he tried to get a feel for this new sensation but the moment he reached out he was pushed free of the meditation. His eyes snapped open and he saw Nul sitting in front of him with a large grin.

"You felt it didn't you?" she asked, standing up.

"I'm not sure what I felt, but I think I'm getting better at this." Kurt said, but as he stood up a wave of dizziness flooded over him and he stumbled forward.

"Easy there," said Nul, grabbing him by the shoulders before he fell. "I think maybe we pushed a little too hard today."

"Maybe," said Kurt, still struggling to get his balance. "Thank you though, I think I'm good."

He tried to move away, but Nul didn't release her grip. She did however, step closer until she was stood just inches away; only then did she let her hands slip away. Kurt stared into her green eyes that were glowing brighter than normal. She slowly moved closer and pressed her lips gently against Kurt's. He stood frozen for a moment, but was soon kissing her back. They broke apart and Nul pulled Kurt into a hug. He gripped her back and as they stood there holding each other, for a few moments Kurt forgot about the world around him.

"That was unexpected," said Kurt, breaking the silence. Nul took a step back and reached out a hand, which he took into his.

"I probably shouldn't have done that," she said, but didn't release his hand. Kurt tried to pull his hand away, but she tightened her grip. "I don't want to leave just yet."

"Neither do I," Kurt whispered. Nul let out a small sigh of relief and smiled at him. She then pulled him close and gave him a small kiss on the cheek. As Kurt leaned forward to kiss her again, they heard footsteps coming towards the glade.

"Come on," Nul said, stepping away from Kurt as an older orc man appeared and sat down at the edge of the glade. The pair left as a few more orcs started to enter the glade and walked back the main path. Nul was the first to stop walking, looking around to make sure they were alone. Once satisfied, she pulled Kurt in for another quick hug. "You should go and get some rest."

"That's for the best," Kurt said as he freed himself from her. "See you tomorrow?"

"Oh definitely," she said with a smile. Nul was the first to leave, stepping backwards into the forest and disappearing into the trees as she made her way home.

Kurt stood still for a time, pondering over what just happened. A part of him was whispering in the back of his mind that this was a bad idea, but as he dwelled on the kiss, all other thoughts faded away. He couldn't help but smile as he eventually began walking back to the gate fort. He tried to think on the day, his progress with his meditation, knowing he'd be able to get back to the surface soon, but his thoughts kept drifting back to Nul.

Kurt was so preoccupied that he barely noticed the journey back to his room. He touched his lips as he remembered the kiss and couldn't help but smile. Kurt laid back onto his bed and let the warm feeling surrounding his mind carry him into a dreamless yet blissful sleep.

* * *

Kurt wasn't sure how long he'd slept for, but when he did wake he felt rejuvenated. Springing out of bed, he got dressed as quick as he could and rushed out of the room. He wasn't sure how, but Kurt had learned to navigate the identical stone corridors without issue, almost as though wanting to get to a destination was enough of a guide to get around the fort.

He hurried past the few orcs who were walking around performing their usual morning duties, stopping a short distance from Nul's home. Kurt tidied himself up and made himself more presentable, difficult considering how worn down his clothes since he'd first arrived, but he managed to make his clothes look a little less wrinkled at the very least. Taking a few deep breaths to calm his nerves, he resumed walking. As he approached her stone home, Kurt could see through the trees that she was already outside. She had prepared a slightly larger looking breakfast than he'd grown used to in the days past. Bread rolls, sliced meats and the usual collection of fruits. As soon as she heard him approaching, Nul's attention was drawn upward from the table of food and she gave him a warm smile. An awkward silence fell between them, neither of them sat down or made any move toward the other.

"We should eat," Nul said, breaking the silence.

"Yes. Yes we should," Kurt replied. He looked over the large amount of food on display, trying to decide where to start. "This all looks so good."

"Ruuuhht?" Nul had taken a huge bite of a roll.

Kurt laughed as she struggled to chew the chunk of bread that made her cheek swell up like a large rodent. Nul started to laugh as well, once she managed to swallow the food. Soon enough the pair set about eating the meal properly, exchanging smiles and chuckles. After eating their fill, the pair looked at each other, waiting for the other to say something. Kurt was the one to speak first.

"So I'm thinking we should talk about what happened yesterday," he said, leaning back, as Nul leaned forward to rest her arms on the stone table.

"Alright," she replied, waiting for him to continue with an indecipherable look on her face.

"Well this is going to sound very formal, but please let me finish before you say anything," Kurt said. Nul nodded in response and stared at him. "I spent some of last night thinking about this, mostly reasons why it might be a bad idea, but I kept coming back around to one thing. Despite the circumstances of why I'm here, I was flattered when you kissed me, happy even." He took a moment and reached out for Nul's hand. She grabbed his in return, and squeezed it tightly as he continued. "If I'm honest, I feel like I don't deserve this, you or any affection really. But you've been very clear about how what I think I deserve has no control over what you want to do. So if you'd like to, I would very much like to continue whatever this is between us."

“You're right, that was a bit too formal,” Nul said, pulling her hand away. She walked around the table and dragged Kurt up to his feet to kiss him again. They pulled apart and hugged for a time but as Nul stepped away, she took Kurt's hands into her own. “We'll need to keep this a secret from my people.”

“Because I'm a human?” he asked, no small amount of disappointment in his voice.

“Maybe a little,” Nul replied, touching his cheek with one hand. “Though most of us have no real opinion on who we choose to be with. The main problem is that I'm supposed to be looking after you. People will think my judgement is flawed.”

“I mean... it is a little bit,” said Kurt with a laugh. Nul pulled away and hit him on the arm.

“Rude,” she replied with a smile. “But for now we have to go about our day as normal. We'll pick this up later.”

With one final quick kiss, she left Kurt outside as she packed away the empty plates. Once she was done cleaning up, she grabbed him by the arm and led him away from her home. Just before they reached the road she rested her head on his shoulder and gave his hand one last squeeze, releasing him just as they reached the road, and led him to glade just as they had done every other day.

They spent the day trying to meditate and strengthen Kurt's mind but found themselves a little distracted. For the first time since he had arrived here Kurt didn't mind the lack of progress. After a few short hours of exchanging glances and smirks in secret while other orcs came and went, the pair decided to leave. They hurried back through the forest, Nul took Kurt's hand and their pace slowed. They'd made this journey countless times over the past week but this time was much more enjoyable. When they got back to Nul's home, she pulled away from Kurt and gestured for him to sit down. She gave him a kiss on the cheek before sitting down opposite him.

"I'm going to have to go see the Matriarch soon. She asked me to tell her of whatever growth you make," said Nul. "I was going to ask about the surface, if there is anything you'd like me to find out for you?"

"I'd like to know that everyone's doing alright," Kurt said, looking up into the darkness. "Wouldn't mind knowing about the defences as well, I know I'm not in any position to help but I'd like to at least know what they're doing up there."

"No one specific you'd like to ask after?" Nul asked, her tone shifting as though she was fishing for something specific.

"Well if you can get a message out, I'd like Cali to know that I'm doing fine." Kurt hoped she hadn't worried herself too much during his absence.

"Your baker friend? I'll see what I can do," Nul smiled, taking his hands into her own. "Will you wait for me here?"

"Of course," Kurt replied.

Nul stood up and ran her fingers up his arm as she walked past, sending pleasant chills up Kurt's spine. She parted with a kiss and left Kurt outside her home. He watched as she left, until he was just staring at the tree line. For a time he just sat at the table, but after a while he decided to make himself useful. He hurried around Nul's home and grabbed the large bucket that she left outside. Kurt entered the forest and headed to the small river that flowed nearby to fill the bucket with the clear water. Taking care not to spill as he passed back through the thick undergrowth, he made his way to the hot spring. After emptying the bucket into the empty stone pool, he returned to the river. It took many repeated trips but eventually the pool was filled and Kurt took a moment to enjoy the sight of the steam rising up to the leafy canopy above. Satisfied, he went back to Nul's home and walked inside. He was a little curious to explore the place, but decided to be respectful and went straight to the kitchen. Over the time spent here through the window he'd seen Nul make tea for the two of them before.

He set about brewing a pot of the bitter brew that she seemed to prefer, struggling briefly with the fire, but soon enough the smell of the tea was filling the kitchen. It took the pot and some cups outside to wait for Nul's return.

He wasn't waiting long as she appeared from between the trees a few minutes later. Kurt poured out two cups of tea as she sat down with him. She seemed a little tired, but brightened up when Kurt slid a cup of tea across the table for her. She took a sip and let out a breath of relief.

“That was a tense time,” Nul said, taking another sip from her cup. “The Matriarch wasn't in the best of moods. Things are getting a little disagreeable with the Bismurr folk - nothing severe, but people are arguing more than doing anything else.”

“Are they at least preparing the mine entrance?” asked Kurt.

“A bit. Lots to be done, but people are pulling together for that part at least. It's just slow going with people not agreeing with every other little thing that comes up.” She sounded exasperated as though she had heard each and every complaint.

“That's better than I would have thought. I expected some more fighting at least,” Kurt said, taking a sip of his own drink. “Any word on how they feel about my situation?”

“Your friend Peyton managed to convince almost everyone that your being here was for the best. Though I heard he had a few issues with certain people. Those other squad leaders didn't accept it easily - and your friend Cali? She broke his nose!” Nul laughed. “The town is asking after you though, it seems like everyone wants to know when you'll be back.”

“Well we're working on that aren't we?” Kurt held up his tea and Nul tapped her cup against his.

"Speaking on that, the Matriarch wanted me to ask you something," said Nul before finishing the last of her drink in one gulp. "She's been informed about how you helped shape the training of your friends in town and after conferring with the matrons she trusts your intentions a bit more. I've been keeping her up to date with your progress with me as well. So she wanted to know if you'd come see some of our people training tomorrow, maybe even share what you know with us. Only if you want to of course."

"Considering that we all need to work together, I probably should say yes," Kurt said, thinking to himself for a moment. "I don't know how much I could teach you all though."

"Well I'd very much like you to do it," Nul replied. "It will mean your time here will be a little busier but you'll have spend more of it with me."

"Ah, well then I'm definitely going to say yes," said Kurt with a smile.

"Smart choice," Nul walked over to his side of the table and sat on his lap, wrapping her arms around his shoulders. Letting her head rest against his, they sat for a while, enjoying each other's company.

"I'd better go get some sleep," Kurt said after what must have been at least an hour. "I imagine tomorrow is going to be exhausting?"

"Oh, no doubt," Nul said. She got up, allowing Kurt to stand. "I'll come and get you first thing."

She kissed his cheek and walked by him to head into her home, turning at the door frame to watch him leave. He gave her a wave as he walked backwards into the woods. The walk back to his room was quiet which left Kurt feeling contemplative. Knowing that people were arguing back at the surface was troubling, but he still found himself hopeful for the fight ahead with the orcs involved. When Kurt did reach his room, he didn't quite feel tired enough to sleep but knew there was nothing else to be done for the day. With a contented sigh he sat down and started to remove his shoes. As Kurt was sitting on his bed thinking about what might be in store for tomorrow, there was a knock on his door.

"Hello?" he called out.

The door opened and Nul stepped inside, closing it behind her. Saying nothing, she crossed the room and sat beside him. Kurt was about to say something, but his mind went blank as he found himself moving closer to her. Nul placed a hand on his chest and looked up to meet his gaze. He stared into her bright green eyes and leaned down to kiss her. Nul kissed him back and the pair started to rip each other's clothes off as they tumbled back onto the bed.

# 14

Kurt drifted to consciousness as a feeling of warmth suddenly left him. Opening his eyes, he saw Nul gathering her discarded clothes. While getting dressed, she spotted him staring and completely unabashed about her nakedness, walked over to give him a kiss.

"Good morning," she said. "You sleep alright?"

"Eventually," said Kurt with a smile as he replayed the night in his mind. He ran his hand down the bare skin of her back and for a few moments Nul closed her eyes, enjoying the attention. She shook his hand off however and moved away to continue getting dressed.

"I need to get going if I'm going to sneak out of here," Nul said. Taking a deep breath she calmed herself before looking over to Kurt. "Take your time getting ready, I'll get some breakfast for us and we'll get going to the training."

"I'll see you soon." Kurt said. Nul dashed across the room to plant one more kiss on him before leaving.

Once she shut the door behind her, Kurt got out of bed and let out a yawn. He wasn't too tired, but it had been a long time since he'd had a night quite like that. Once Kurt got himself dressed, he paced around his room trying to waste time. It wasn't long before he got bored but he managed to wait long enough for Nul to get back to her home. Satisfied that he'd waited long enough, he left his room to begin the day. Kurt didn't rush as he walked past the few people that he passed by on his way to Nul's. When he reached the treeline, out of sight of any onlookers, he sprinted until he reached the clearing of her home. He was greeted with the smell of cooking meat as he arrived and when he got closer, Nul emerged from her home carrying two plates of food. Spotting him, she dropped off the breakfast and the pair met each other halfway. After a brief embrace they sat down to eat breakfast together, not breaking eye contact as they did so.

"So..." said Kurt, looking away to try to shift the mood. "We should talk about last night."

"Oh?" Nul replied, a coy smile on her face as she ran a finger across the back of Kurt's hand. "Something wrong?"

"No, no. It was wonderful." Kurt said. "I just think we should probably be careful if we do that again."

"Careful?" Nul asked with a raised eyebrow.

"Yes. We don't want..." Kurt paused as he tried to find the right words. "...a little problem to start worrying about."

"Ah I understand," said Nul, struggling to hold back a laugh. "You're sweet, but you and me? We can't make that little problem, so you don't need to worry yourself."

"You're sure?" Kurt asked, feeling a little relieved.

"Very," Nul replied, letting out her laughter.

"Alright, alright," said an embarrassed Kurt. He waited for her laughter to die down before changing the subject. "So what's the plan for today?"

"Today? I imagine it'll mostly be a demonstration of how we fight," Nul said. "You'll probably be given a day or so then you'll be expected to share some insights that could be of use to us. Don't worry much about that though, with the way things have been going with the surface, I think any suggestions will be good."

"And we'll still find time to visit the glade to keep my training moving forward?" Kurt asked, reaching out a hand to Nul.

"Of course," she said, tracing her finger over the lines across his palm. "I made it clear to the Matriarch that helping you get rid of the weaver influence should still be our top priority."

"Thank you," Kurt replied.

"Speaking of that, I wanted to ask you something." Nul grew still and tense and took a deep breath. "I do believe we're going to get your mind free and I know when we do you're going to want to return to the surface as soon as you can. When you do leave I'd like to join you, at least for a while. If you'd have me up there with you?"

"At the moment, I really don't want to be apart from you. I assumed that was the same for you," Kurt said, squeezing Nul's hand to comfort her.

"It is," Nul replied. "I've never thought about going to the surface before and now that I have a reason to go, I guess I'm worried about it since we've only just started this..." Her gaze fell over their now intertwined fingers. "And I know you need to leave, but this is something I want to keep."

"Then let's be clear." Kurt placed his other hand in front of him and Nul reached for it. "Whatever the next few weeks hold for me or you. Let's face it together."

"I'd like that," Nul said with a smile.

"Good," said Kurt. "I imagine we need to get moving soon?"

Nul nodded in response as she finished the last scraps of food on her plate. After Kurt helped her clear the table, the pair made their way to the orc settlement. They walked past the stone structures to an area Kurt hadn't seen before, an open field with a dozen humanoid figures made out of rocks in a row. Nul looked back and gave Kurt an encouraging smile as she led him by a few other orcs who were already gathered. At the head of the small crowd stood the Matriarch, speaking to a burly male orc leaning on a wooden staff. They finished their conversation before Kurt and Nul came within earshot, both turning to greet them.

"Nulkala. Kurt." The Matriarch looked at the two of them in turn. "I trust you're both prepared?"

"We are," Nul replied with Kurt nodding in agreement.

"Excellent. If you'll excuse me, I have other matters to attend to." The Matriarch turned to leave, but looked back briefly. "Baku, come see me when you're done here."

The large orc gave a bow as the Matriarch left through the crowd. Once she had left, everyone who had gathered started to form rows, stretching and readying themselves. Baku looked out to everyone judging each person in turn as his eyes moved over them all.

"I'm told you've fought a few elves. Killed them even," said Baku as he turned to face Kurt, standing a full head taller than the human.

"With some help, yes," Kurt replied. "Though we only fought them in a strange monstrous form. Dregs, we call them."

"Dregs? Hah! I like that." Baku let out a hearty laugh. "Still, whatever form they took, you surface folk have managed to take out a few more than us. We've got some catching up to do!"

"Well I'm sure you'll get your chance soon," said Kurt, turning to the crowd. "So what happens next? The thirty or so you've got here look ready."

"I'll get them started," said Baku with a grin. He then raised his voice to speak to everyone. "Alright you lot - listen up! Form up, take your strikes, I want fifty from each of you and then run to the gate."

The large group assembled in front of the rock formations and began to strike them with kicks and punches, yelling as they did so. Kurt watched as they each took turns, offering advice about stance and balance to one another as they struck the stones. While he was looking on, Nul and Baku walked away, towards the path back to the gate. When Kurt noticed that they'd moved away he hurried to catch up to them.

"So how often do you do this training?" Kurt asked, out of breath.

"Maybe once a week? After the run we'll get them doing weapons practice, our people do that almost every day when they choose to become fighters," Baku replied. "Though we tend to use clubs and slings down here, we're going to need practice with some of the stuff your surface friends have been cooking up."

"Well I have no say in that. At least for the moment," Kurt said as he turned to Nul, who shrugged in reply. "I don't know if I'm going to be able to suggest anything useful to you. The only reason I've been able to help the people on the surface is because they had no training at all."

"Don't undermine yourself," said Nul, nudging him as they walked. "You helped build something up there. Not to mention convincing the Matriarch to start talking to the surface."

"And she doesn't change her mind that much," Baku chimed in.

"Exactly." Nul said, giving Kurt a comforting pat on the shoulder. "You've helped a lot more than you think."

Kurt gave a small smile as the three of them finished their walk, having now arrived outside the gate fort. Near the entrance someone had set up a large wooden rack filled with wooden staffs and clubs, which Baku set about inspecting.

"So these Dregs, what can you tell us about them?" he called out, without looking away from the weapon rack.

"They're big, strong and fast," Kurt thought for a moment. "They seem feral, but still follow whatever order they were given. We found some living out of some ruins, not sure exactly how long for, they could have easily made their way to Bismurr but they didn't. If I had to guess, I also doubt they can turn back to normal, not without help at least. I would have thought you'd know some of this already, haven't you had a few run-ins with some elves in the past?"

"Not exactly," said Baku as he finished his inspection. "They usually just cause the tunnels to collapse and crush any of our people in the area. We've hardly had any physical encounters with them."

"I was always curious why they've avoided fighting us openly," Nul said as she twirled her long hair between her fingers. "Guess they were worried they wouldn't win."

"Well they ain't stupid, I think we've always known that," Baku said with a chuckle.

The sound of heavy footfalls started to echo from nearby and shortly the orc fighters began to pour in from back along the path. Each of them ran up to the rack, grabbed a weapon and started to form up in front of the gate fort. Before the last of them trickled in, Baku stepped up to Kurt to speak.

"When they're all settled, tell them about the Dregs, then I'll tell them how to do their practice," he said in a hushed voice. Kurt nodded and waited for the last few to appear from the treeline.

"Hello everyone," said Kurt, making sure he had everyone's attention before continuing. "Firstly, I want to thank you all for letting me speak about what I know." He paused for a moment and thought about everything he wanted to share. "The creatures the elves made us fight, the Dregs, are dangerous monsters. They're fast, strong and fight more like animals than people. They don't do well against multiple opponents though, and despite their strength, they can still be cut and beaten down with enough force. The real danger that we struggled to fight was Orlan, the elf who led them. Even with the powers he can wield, his ability to give the Dregs orders can make them much more dangerous."

"Thank you," Baku said before turning to address the fighters. "Now you lot: fall into groups, practise heavy hits and blocking. These things will hit hard, so you all need to hit harder. I want to see you knocking each other to the ground!"

The burly orc walked away to help his warriors as they began their practice strikes. Kurt marvelled at their discipline, obeying the orders to strike one another without question but still taking the time to help each other up. He caught Nul smiling at him as he was staring into the crowd.

"Something wrong?" he asked, turning a little red from the attention.

"Not a thing," she replied, stepping closer so no one could overhear them. "You've been pulling that face constantly since you came down here. Like everything we do amazes you. I think it's adorable."

"Oh," was all Kurt had time to say as Baku marched over to them.

"I'll have them working on this for a while, a few days to get them in good shape. You can check in with us then. I'll try to think of ways we can fight back against

Orlan's magic as well," he said, keeping his gaze on the other orcs clashing in mock combat. "You two are free to leave if you like."

Baku then hurried away when he saw one orc smash a club into the face of another. The injury seemed small as the orc, who was now bleeding from the nose, was laughing. Nul tapped Kurt on the shoulder and pointed towards the woods, in the direction of her home. With a nod, the pair then made their way through the fighters, giving encouraging looks to each person they neared. This was the most attention Kurt had received since arriving here and it felt good to be welcomed by these strangers, despite the circumstances. After he and Nul had moved away from the crowd, getting back to her home was a brief journey.

"Wait here," she said, strolling inside. Kurt was left waiting for a few moments before Nul returned holding a wooden staff in each hand. She tossed one to him and used the other to carve a wide circle in the dirt around him.

"Weapons training?" Kurt raised an eyebrow. "A staff isn't really something I'm used to."

"Well that's why we train," Nul said. "Besides, this is less about the weapon and more about you, your reflexes and trying to make you think clearly while you fight."

"I already know how to fight," Kurt replied, taking the staff into both hands.

"Hardly," said Nul with a smirk.

"Well you have a small strength advantage," he said as his chest began to ache defensively.

"Firstly, not small. Secondly, fighting is more than often an unfair thing." She twirled her staff with one hand, bringing it to a stop by sticking it into the ground. "But I do take your point. While we train, I'll use just one hand, sound good?"

"Not sure that makes things exactly even, but let's see how it goes," Kurt said. He tightened his grip on the staff and slid one foot back, taking a more balanced stance.

"Ready?" Nul asked as she placed one arm behind her back and grabbed her staff with the other.

Kurt nodded, not taking his eyes off of Nul - something he found much easier of late, but he did his best to keep focused. Meanwhile, she had started to circle him, once again resuming the role of a predator. Kurt wasn't intimidated, he'd seen her do this before and was ready for her next move. Almost on cue, she rushed forward, raising her staff up to strike him from above. Kurt moved his weapon over his head, bracing himself as she swung downwards. He'd expected the blow to be strong, but he was still brought to his knees as Nul's staff slammed into his. With a quick shove, he managed to push her back to gain a little breathing room. Knowing she would recover quickly, Kurt lunged forward and swiped his staff at her legs, trying to trip her. Nul jumped to dodge the attack and spun around in the air, using the momentum to strike Kurt in the side with a kick. He tumbled over but hurried back onto his feet, even with his ribs now throbbing with pain. Nul moved in to attack again but Kurt was ready for her, using all of his strength to throw his staff like a spear at her. She blocked the attack but while her attention was diverted, Kurt had run forward and leapt into the air toward her, tackling her to the ground. As the pair rolled across the dirt, Nul let go of her own staff and pushed Kurt away with her one free hand as they skidded to a halt.

They both scrambled back their feet and barely a breath later were charging at one another once more. Nul flung a kick at Kurt's head which he avoided. He tried to throw a punch but Nul caught his fist and pulled him off balance. She let go and in the blink of an eye stepped forward and grabbed his throat. Kurt tensed up, expecting to be throttled, but found her grip loosening. The couple locked eyes for a few moments, the only sound shared between them their panting breaths. Nul shifted her hand to the back of his neck and pulled Kurt forward into a kiss. Once she pulled away and released him, Kurt opened his eyes and was greeted to the sight of her smile.

"I win," Nul said, raising her other hand to embrace Kurt.

"Matter of perspective," he replied with a smug smile of his own. He then leaned forward for another kiss, but Nul placed a finger on his lips and gently stopped him.

"Not now. As much as I'd like to, we still have meditation to do," Nul then peeled herself out of his grip.

"You're right," Kurt sighed, not trying to hide his disappointment. He waited as Nul collected their discarded weapons and stashed them back inside her home.

"We'll pick this up later, I promise." As she walked past Kurt she ran her hand across his shoulders, her fingers brushing his neck, sending a pleasurable shiver down his spine.

Kurt stood there for a few seconds, catching up with her when he came back to his senses.

* * *

Once they were at the glade, Kurt and Nul sat amongst a few others to continue his training. The pair were still attempting to concentrate on strengthening Kurt's mind. It was slow going at first; Kurt kept being distracted by the new bruises he'd received. The pain made him smile as his thoughts drifted to Nul.

"Don't lose focus," her voice whispered.

He didn't open his eyes, but Kurt did take a deep breath and let the smile fall away as the power of the glade washed over him. Ignoring the small wounds across his body he sent the flowing power to his mind, weaving around the strange block that wrapped around a portion of his thoughts. He tried to move the power forward, but found himself still being pushed back by a force he couldn't quite get a grasp on. Kurt tried again, this time allowing more of the glade's power to flow through him. The block resisted again but this time it did so violently and a sharp pain pierced Kurt's mind.

He slumped forward, coming out of his meditative stupor with blood dripping from his nose. As Kurt opened his eyes the pain quickly faded to nothing. He Looked up and saw that Nul still had her eyes closed. Being careful not to disturb her, Kurt used his sleeve to wipe away the blood on his face and rolled it up to hide the stain. Before he had time to try again, she opened her eyes with a look of concern.

"Are you alright?" Nul asked.

"I'm fine," Kurt replied, careful not to mention the block. "Just feeling the same."

"Let's finish for today," Nul stood up.

Kurt got up and the pair left the glade, doing their best not to disturb the others that were sitting around, busy with their own meditations. They went back to Nul's home and while she set about preparing some food for them, Kurt stared into the darkness above, losing himself in his drifting thoughts. It wasn't until Nul came back with two bowls of soup, their delicious smell wafting into the air, that he snapped his attention back to reality.

"You seem a little distracted," Nul said, breaking the silence. "Are you sure you're fine?"

"Sorry," Kurt replied, making sure his sleeve was still hidden. "I think you just knocked my head a bit too hard earlier."

"Hmm." Nul stared at him, clearly doubting his words.

"I'll be fine," Kurt said, offering a hand to reassure her. "I promise."

"Alright then," she said, taking his hand into her own.

They sat for a while, enjoying the meal. When they were finished, Nul gestured for Kurt to follow her and she led him to the hot spring. In a matter of moments, the couple had stripped off and were sitting down in the small pool. The water was soothing to his skin as Kurt let its heat sink through his flesh and into his bones. As he became more relaxed leaning against the warm stones, he started to feel tiredness creep over him. Kurt lay his head back, only intending to rest for a minute but within a few moments he was asleep.

He woke briefly when he heard the water splash a little as Nul waded over to him, sitting beside him to rest her head on his shoulder.

Some time later he felt Nul shaking him awake, she was speaking but his exhaustion was making her words confusing. Despite his sleepy haze, she managed to drag him out of the hot spring and take him back through the woods. Sliding in and out of consciousness the rest of the evening was a blur to Kurt. Being taken back to Nul's home, getting placed onto a soft bed and Nul herself lying down next to him, pulling several blankets over them as she went to sleep herself. Kurt woke one final time to feel Nul's heavy breathing next to him and he felt a sense of bliss as he settled into a deep dreamless slumber.

* * *

When Kurt awoke he felt recovered. Nul was still asleep at his side, her dark hair covering her face. Not wanting to wake her just yet, he kept still as he looked around the darkened room. Despite their time together, Kurt hadn't spent much time inside Nul's home and his curiosity was grateful for the chance to explore. A singular glowstone placed in the wall, its dim orange light illuminating everything in the room. Hanging on the wall by the door was a small assortment of clubs and staffs that he recognised from the day just gone. By the bedside was a pile of Nul's neatly folded clothes and draped atop them were Kurt's own worn-out garments. A large collection of blankets were scattered over the stone floor, acting a carpet of sorts. Even though Kurt wanted to start the day, he felt so comfortable that he was happy to lay still while waiting for Nul to awaken. It wasn't long before she started to stir, and as she did so Kurt leaned down and kissed the top of her head. Nul rolled over and looked up, blinded by her tousled hair, but still smiled when she sensed Kurt was staring at her.

"Good morning," he said. She mumbled in response, sliding over to put her arm across him in an awkward hug. "Want me to get you some breakfast?"

She didn't say anything, but she did pull the blankets off of him and pushed him with one hand until he fell out of the warm bed.

"Understood," Kurt said with a laugh.

Grabbing his clothes as he left the room, he got dressed in the hall and went into the kitchen. As he plated up some fruits and dried meat, he heard Nul get up. Kurt finished preparing the meal and took the plates outside and by the time he turned back, Nul was standing in the door frame. Her hair was still a giant tangled mess as she walked over and sat at the table. She seemed to transform as she ate, and by the time the plates were clear, Nul was back to her normal smiling self. Once they'd both finished eating, Kurt tidied up. When he got back outside, Nul grabbed Kurt's hand and led him into the woods to start another day.

# 15

The routine of weapons training in the morning and meditation in the afternoon became the new normal for Kurt over the next couple of days. While challenging and tiring, the time he spent with Nul in secret made everything seem easier. Kurt thought about this with a smile as the couple made their way to the gate fort to see Baku and his warriors. Kurt had seen the warriors training a few times since his first meeting with them and they seemed like they'd grown into a stronger force than they were before.

"Today's going to be interesting," Nul said as they left the forest behind them. "Do you feel ready? Good chance people might ask you to show them how you'd fight."

"I think I'll be alright. I might even have picked up a few things from you," replied Kurt, scratching at his new bruises his chest had acquired in his training sessions.

"Well I hope so. I've been putting a lot of effort into your training," Nul said, looking Kurt up and down. "Among other things."

"And I'm very grateful for everything you do," Kurt whispered as they drew closer to the gathering crowd.

As they arrived at the training field, Kurt and Nul soon discovered that most of the fighters had already gathered. The couple made their way through the huddled group to get to the front. At the head of the crowd stood Baku, looking out over everyone and muttering to himself. When he spotted Kurt and Nul approaching, he waved for them to come forward. The crowd of warriors stepped aside to clear the way for the pair.

"Morning," Baku said when they reached him. "I hope you're both rested."

"Pretty much," said Nul, shooting a knowing glance at Kurt. "Well-fed anyway."

"Good, good," replied Baku. "I've heard a few rumblings here and there. People are questioning whether this human who's been living with us can actually fight. Some of the whispers starting to spread say that you probably haven't fought any kind of monster."

"I'm guessing this means I'll be first up to spar with someone?" Kurt asked.

"It'd certainly put a few people at ease. I'll let you pick whoever you want," Baku replied, a grin spreading across his face.

"Careful who you choose now, that didn't go so well for you last time," Nul laughed.

"I completely disagree with you there," Kurt countered, smiling at her. "But maybe things would be easier if you pick someone for me."

"Easily done," Nul said. She looked over the crowd and after a few moments her eyes locked on a muscular orc standing at the front. "Him."

"Poda," Baku said. "Yes he'll do fine. Quite strong, no one will think we're taking it easy on you. Remember that you don't need to beat him, just don't lose too quickly."

"I appreciate the confidence," Kurt muttered.

"You'll do fine," Nul said, patting Kurt's back. "I think you might even beat him."

"Hah! Well we'll find out soon enough," Baku said, looking out to the crowd. "Last of the stragglers are nearly here."

Kurt and Nul looked past the crowd and watched the last few people arrive. Once they joined the others and the conversation died down, Baku cleared his throat to get everyone's attention.

"Good to see everyone." As Baku spoke, he began to pace in front of the crowd. "You've all done good these past few days and I think our guest will be satisfied. He's also been training so I think we'll have him spar one of our own. Poda, grab a weapon."

Murmurs of agreement broke out throughout the crowd. Poda marched forward and cracked his knuckles before grabbing a staff from the weapon rack. Baku looked over to Kurt and gestured for him to do the same. The lone human walked forward and grabbed a staff of his own. The crowd moved back to give the combatants some room as the two fighters walked over to the centre of the space. Kurt's gaze fell onto Nul, who gave him an encouraging nod. He turned his attention back to the large orc in front of him and after one long and deep breath, Kurt raised his weapon.

"Whenever you're both ready," said Baku.

Poda gripped his own staff with both hands and began inching forward. Kurt relaxed his grip on his weapon and rushed forward. As Poda tensed up to defend himself, Kurt raised his staff over his head and brought it down with all his might. Poda managed to block the attack but his staff cracked under the blow. Kurt knew he had to land a solid blow so he tightened his grip and pulled his staff back. Poda took the bait and tried to move forward, giving Kurt the opportunity to thrust his staff forward into the orc's gut. Poda doubled over, winded, and dropped his staff. Knowing he didn't have much time, Kurt swung his weapon in a wide arc at his opponent's legs. The blow knocked Poda to the ground and before he could even try to roll away, Kurt moved in and held his staff at his throat.

"I think that's enough," Baku declared to the crowd.

Kurt stepped back and placed his staff on the ground. He reached down a hand to help Poda up, which the orc accepted. The crowd around them started to murmur with approval as Poda rejoined their ranks. Kurt put the staff back on the rack and then walked back to stand with Baku.

"You did good," the large orc said. "I didn't think it was gonna end so quickly."
"Well Nul's a great teacher," Kurt replied, trying not to sound too smug. "We still need to see if the rest of them are ready though."

"I'll handle that," Nul said. Before anyone could say anything in response, she marched up to the crowd. "Three of you, grab some weapons and try to bring me down."

She then waited for three volunteers to come forward. It wasn't long before three men stepped up to the weapons rack to arm themselves. Each of them looked calm as they surrounded her and began to walk around in a circle to keep her between them. They didn't pace for long, as one behind Nul ran up and tried to bring his staff down on her head. Nul crouched to dodge the blow but grabbed the staff with one hand as she moved. With a hard pull, she sent the large orc sprawling face-first to the ground at her feet.

The two left standing both sprinted forward and swung their weapons at her chest. Nul spun round and with a few quick steps moved right up to one of her attackers, landing an elbow to his gut. As he was reeling from the attack she kicked out his legs to send him to the ground as well. While Nul had been busy, the third attacker had rushed forward to grab his fallen partner's staff. In one fluid motion he rolled forward to grab it while throwing his original weapon at Nul. She dodged the staff and dashed forward faster than Kurt had seen her move before. Her attacker swung his new staff hard at her head before she could get too close, but once again Nul caught the staff with one hand. The orc struggled to pull his weapon free for a moment, before Nul pulled herself closer to him. With a single punch to his gut, Nul sent the last man standing flying backwards. Behind her, the first orc she'd knocked down was getting back to his feet. She turned and threw the staff at his head, knocking him down again. As each of the three were now groaning with pain and refusing to get back up, the nearby crowd took the fight to be over and erupted into cheers.

"I think they did pretty good," Nul said as she walked over to Kurt and Baku. "Kurt? Anything to add?"

"Still a little hard to judge," Kurt said. "They seem pretty organised though, attacking quickly without discussing a plan. I'd say if all of them can fight like that, you'll do just fine with the surface folk."

"Good to hear," said Baku before turning to the crowd. "Alright everyone, good work. Grab yourselves some weapons and get some practice in. We'll be sending you to the surface soon."

The crowd then began to arm themselves, a few people picked up the three injured orcs still lying on the ground. As they formed up into small groups to start trading blows, Kurt walked up to Nul.

"You really think they're ready? she asked him, concern in her voice.

"If I'm honest, I think all of you were more than ready before I came here," Kurt replied. "But I'm happy to help them be better prepared."

"Thank you," Nul said, relieved.

"Though watching you back there has left me curious about one thing," Kurt said, turning to face her. "Every fight I've seen you in, you never seem like you've pushed yourself. How strong are you exactly?"

"To tell the truth? I don't know," said Nul. "I remember struggling when I was younger, I can only think of a handful of people who are stronger and they're all bodyguards for the Matriarch. Thinking about it though, it's been years since someone could beat me."

"I'm glad you're on my side," Kurt said as he felt a small tickle of fear in the back of his mind.

Nul smiled but before anyone else could speak, an orc came sprinting from the gate fort, shouting for Baku. The man was so out of breath by the time he reached the front of the crowd that he fell to his knees for a few moments before he could breathe again. Baku hurried over to him and after a brief exchange sent the young man back to the gate fort.

"Everyone, form up!" Baku called out as the young orc jogged away. "Gather what you need, we're heading topside right now."

The crowd began to disperse while Nul and Kurt moved over to Baku.

"What's happening?" Nul asked.

"Surface folk spotted what looks like a scouting party," Baku explained. "Looks to be a few dozen of those Dregs. They've called on us to help reinforce the town since they're not ready to move into the tunnels just yet. Those things will be in town in a day or so."

"We need to get up there," said Kurt. He looked to Nul who shook her head. "This is just the start. If their attacks are beginning then I need to get back."

"Been no sign of anything more just yet. No sign of Orlan or his army," Baku said, as he began to leave. "I need to get ready as well. See you."

"You're not ready," Nul said, meeting Kurt's gaze. "I said when the time came I would take you back. It isn't time yet."

"This is the time!" Kurt said, his anger beginning to boil over. "If they're starting to arrive, more will come soon. Don't break your promise Nul, not after all this time, please."

"Kurt." Nul stepped forward and grabbed his hand. "You need to listen. I know what this means to you, but it's not time yet. We still have a few days left to help you."

"No, we don't," Kurt said. He pulled away from Nul and let his anger evaporate, leaving only disappointment in its place. "And if there's only one way out of here, then I'm leaving today. Whatever it takes."

He stormed forward towards the glade. Nul called after him and though it pained him to do so, Kurt ignored her. A few passers-by turned their heads, giving looks of annoyance towards him. Kurt didn't care. A part of him was screaming to turn back and apologise to Nul, but he squashed those feelings as soon as they bubbled to the surface.

Once he arrived at the glade, thankfully finding it empty, Kurt sat down near the entrance and started to take slow deep breaths. He let the strange energy of the glade flow over him, pushing it towards his mind. Just like each time he tried before, he felt the power become tentative as it snaked around the weavers magic. As he tried to push past the block in his mind, he felt the resistance build. His pain and frustration grew the more he pushed. Kurt gritted his teeth and kept trying to break through even as blood started to trickle from his nose. The piercing pain grew until Kurt tasted blood pooling in his mouth, forcing him to stop.

He slumped forward panting, and as he opened his eyes he realised his vision had become blurred. Kurt wiped away the blood and waited for the pain to recede before trying again. As it left, his vision returned but before he could try again, the sound of footsteps drew his attention. Even though he couldn't see properly, he recognised Nul as she approached and sat down in front of him. She didn't say anything but she did reach out a hand to Kurt. He was about to reach for her but despite knowing that her touch would make him feel better, he stopped himself.

"I'm not going to stop until I can leave," he said, wiping away the last of the blood off his face.

"Even if it kills you?" Nul replied as she lowered her hand. "Look at yourself. I've watched you try harder over the past few days. Every time you push against the weaver's hold on you, it fights back. I think breaking it would mean breaking you."

"What else am I supposed to do?" Kurt snapped. "I care about you, I truly do. But I'd rather kill myself trying to do the right thing then hide down here."

"I see," Nul whispered.

The pair sat there in silence for a short while, neither one reaching to the other or moving away. Kurt relented as guilt festered inside him.

"I'm sorry," was all he could think to say. He wanted to speak more but Nul raised a hand to his mouth, silencing him.

"We both said we'd face what's to come together. Do you still want that?" Nul asked, only moving her hand away once Kurt had nodded. "Alright then. One last thing to try."

"I thought this was the only plan we had?" Kurt asked.

"It still is. Just trust me," replied Nul. She took a deep breath and started to breathe steady and slow. "Close your eyes. Concentrate on breathing with me."

Kurt did as he was told without question. Together they began to breathe in unison and Kurt felt the glade's power begin to move between them. He heard Nul move and as though by instinct he raised a hand. As he reached out he felt Nul's hand meet his and when they pressed against each other the glade's power started to flow stronger between them.

"The weaver's grip on you is stronger than you are able to break," said Nul, her words echoing in Kurt's mind and across the glade, though he wasn't sure if she was speaking aloud at all. "If for just a moment your mind wasn't alone, I think you could break free."

Keeping his eyes closed, Kurt nodded. There were a few moments where he felt the rhythmic pulse of energy from the glade flowing between the two of them before it seemed to stop. A moment of silence passed. Kurt opened his eyes to see Nul sitting in front of him. Her green eyes started to shine brighter than normal as she reached forward with her other hand. Nul placed her soft palm against his cheek and as she touched his skin his vision fell to darkness and a sensation of falling swallowed him.

Kurt tried to yell into the black void but no sound came. Just as suddenly as this started, there was an explosion of light below him and as he fell closer a deafening noise blasted around him. The light and the noise combined forced Kurt to grab his head and close his eyes, but before it became unbearable, it stopped. He opened his eyes and the sight that greeted him caused tears to form. Sitting on a wooden chair was an older woman sewing a patch of fabric to a torn pair of child's trousers. Kurt looked around and recognised where he was. The worn-out furniture, the empty bookshelf and tiny fire struggling in the hearth. This was his home. He heard scuffling from behind him and he turned around. Sitting on the floor, playing with wooden toy soldier, was a small boy. Kurt knew who it was because he remembered playing with that toy while waiting for his father to come home. He remembered that he hadn't eaten anything but stale or rotten bread for a few days and in a few moments his father would come back with the tiniest portion of beef to share between them.

The memory didn't last however, as without warning Kurt was flung back and once again found himself falling through the darkness. With another rush of blinding light and deafening sound he landed in a new place. This time he was in a dimly lit stone room he didn't recognize. Kurt looked around and as he struggled to see into the dark, he heard a loud damp thud over and over again. In the shadows over by the wall he saw a young girl, an orc girl. She looked so much younger but Kurt could see that this was Nul, no older than he was in the vision before. Somehow he knew that she'd been crying earlier but right now she looked angry as she punched the wall in front of her. The grey stone surface was littered with tiny circular bloodstains and small cracks.

"Again," a voice called out from the dark.

Kurt looked around but still couldn't see where it came from. The young Nul punched the wall, leaving more blood across the stone. She was silent as fresh tears fell down her face, her hand trembling with pain. Kurt winced as his own hand started to hurt like this was his own memory.

"Again," commanded the voice. Nul punched the wall, this time the stone cracked where her blow landed and a little dust sprinkled down from the ceiling as more pained tears streamed down her face.

"Again!" the voice called out.

Kurt turned around and out of the shadows he could make out the form of an elderly orc standing nearby, staring down at the young girl before him. Kurt couldn't explain how he knew, but he was certain this man was Nul's father. He wasn't sure why but Kurt felt afraid of him, as images flashed through his mind of beatings he couldn't remember, memories of being starved and locked away in a darkened room. While Kurt was reeling from the sudden wave of fear, he was again wrenched away into the darkness.

The next memory that Kurt landed in was a familiar one. He was a young boy again, sitting at a table with his father and mother along with a fourth person. A young but haggard man, one of Kurt's brothers, Karl. The family was talking about a meeting Karl had attended the night before. Kurt couldn't make out the specific words, but he remembered what was coming. He remembered Karl was suggesting the family should come to the next meeting, that it would help them put food on the table and new clothes on their backs. Kurt knew where this was going to lead and closed his eyes. He didn't want to see the rest of this memory. He knew his parents would look at their youngest son and make their decision for his sake. After a few moments, Kurt was relieved to find himself tumbling back into the darkness.

With another explosion of colour and noise, Kurt was slammed down into dirt. He stood up and saw that he was standing in front of many orcs on their knees, each holding a small glowstone. The crowd was surrounding a large wooden pyre with a body on top. The body was that of Nul's father, now much older than the last time Kurt had seen him. This was his funeral. Kurt turned around and saw the young Nul walking towards the pyre holding a lit torch. She couldn't have been more than a few years older than the memory before but even Kurt could see that something was different about this Nul. Each person she passed in the crowd whispered condolences and sympathies to her, each one telling her that they'd miss her father in some way. With each word she struggled to stay calm and as she got closer to her father's body, Kurt felt his own rage grow to match hers. It wasn't until she reached the body that the crowd became quiet. Nul tossed the torch onto the pyre and watched as the whole thing went up in flames. Despite the rage that no one here knew the truth about this dead man, a feeling of satisfaction washed over Nul and Kurt could feel it too. Knowing that this man was gone gave both of them a sense of comfort. Kurt then felt himself being pulled away again.

He then fell between other places and different times. Rushing through his own life moment by moment, but with his own memories Kurt was thrown into Nul's life as well. He didn't stay still for very long in each place. One moment he saw children playing in a park, throwing rocks at peoples houses. The next he watched a teenage

Nul sparring with a much younger Matriarch. Kurt saw friends of his come into his life and friends of Nul's leave hers. He lived through romances that had been long since forgotten, his pain and Nul's joy. Kurt struggled to make sense of where his thoughts and feelings were, as a whole other lifetime was shunted into his head. Most of what he saw was random flashes like he was going through a child's storybook. Some of the memories lasted longer than the others and while Kurt wasn't sure of the importance of any of them, he still found himself witnessing a multitude of specific events throughout his and Nul's lives.

Kurt's journey through the void slowed again and he landed into the midst of a panicked crowd. His stomach dropped when he recognised what memory he was in. Kurt watched entire families being forced onto a train, some of them struggling to keep their children close while others tried in vain to hold onto their belongings as they were pushed forward. Standing at the centre of it all was a younger Kurt, dressed in the same grey uniform as his fellow soldiers, pushing everyone who came close to him onto the already full carriage. The various men, women and children were fearful but did as they were told. One woman surged past the others, clutching a small child. She approached Kurt and started to speak in a language he didn't know but her meaning was clear. The panic in her face as she gripped her child made the younger Kurt uncomfortable and he pushed her onto the train with the others. The older Kurt felt sick. Knowing where the train was going and what was going to happen filled him with guilt. A guilt that felt like it wanted to rip its way out of his gut and scream out to the world what he had done. The memory lingered for a few moments as Kurt watched his younger self continuing to shove people away, choosing to remain ignorant of their eventual grim fate.

Once he was ripped back into the silent darkness, a huge sense of relief washed through him. Kurt was so happy to be free of that memory and be taken somewhere else. His relief was short-lived as he was soon thrust into yet another place and time. As Kurt looked around, he saw that he was standing in the dark, but he recognised the walls and rocks around him. He was in one of the many tunnels that made up the mine he had traversed weeks ago. Looking around, he soon spotted Nul crouching in the shadows trying to remain hidden. Nearby, a light started to shine as someone with a torch was making their way through the tunnel. Now that Kurt could see better, he saw that this Nul looked much older than any of the past memories but still a few years younger than when they'd first met. The light grew brighter as a figure emerged from around a corner. A young human man, looking worried and lost as he squinted into the shadows of the tunnel. Without warning, Nul rushed forward and kicked the man in the chest with enough force to send him flying. The man slammed against the rough wall of the mine and slid down into the dirt, leaving a dark splash of blood dripping down the stones. The man was still for a few seconds before he started to get his bearings and got back to his feet.

"These tunnels aren't yours. Leave," Nul hissed, creeping forward into the light.

The man didn't respond. He reached down to grab a rock and with a shout of rage he threw it at Nul. She caught it with ease and in a fluid motion spun round to throw it back. The rock smashed into his gut and as he doubled over in pain his face collided with Nul's rising knee. Before the young man could do anything to retaliate, Nul punched him back down to the ground with a sickening crack.

"Get up," she said. He didn't move. Nul grabbed his shoulder and rolled him onto his front to reveal a large wound on his head.

Her cold demeanour dropped when she saw blood dripping down his lifeless face. Just as she was about to reach down, footsteps started to echo from further up the tunnel. More light started to pour in as the people from Bismurr began to draw closer. A panicked Nul stepped away and retreated into the darkness. She stayed hidden as two more humans appeared and saw their fallen friend. Just as Nul was about to disappear around a bend, one man raised his torch and the light revealed her. One of the men rushed forward but before Kurt could see any more he was once again wrenched back into the dark void.

As he fell, the image of the man's lifeless body burned his mind. He wasn't disturbed by it, Kurt had assumed Nul had hurt people while defending her home, but that memory was something she had held onto and now it had burrowed into his mind as well. Kurt drifted in the dark for a time and as he floated through the void, a chill began spreading up his spine. He already knew what was coming. Nightmares had been plaguing him ever since he'd first lived through it. On cue, light and sound rushed toward him and Kurt landed in the memory that he'd dreaded thinking about.

He was standing in a field surrounded by tall fences, spiked metal wire preventing the idea of escape. Nearby were several large buildings, the base Kurt had been assigned to. Many of his fellow soldiers were busy with their own duties. He'd arrived only a few hours ago and he'd decided to take a walk around the place that was to be his home for the coming months. If it hadn't been for the rain, he might have smelled the stench of what he was about to see. As the young Kurt stopped in his tracks, the older Kurt knew what image was burning into his memories.

A long trench had been dug out and inside, maliciously discarded, were piles upon piles of innumerable human bodies. Men, women, and children had been thrown into the mud, creating a tangled mass of rotted flesh. So many of the bodies were beaten, torn, burned and scarred while others seemed untouched, like they had dropped dead for no reason. The younger Kurt vomited at the sight of it all, causing a pair of his patrolling comrades to laugh. As he struggled to breathe, it dawned on Kurt what he'd been a part of. He had sent people here. He was the one who put so many of them onto trains and forced them out of his sight because he'd been following orders. Being a good soldier. He looked to the bodies and his eyes locked with the glassy lifeless stare of a woman covered in burns, the image of her face burrowed its way into his mind and future nightmares. While the two Kurts looked on, more bodies were dumped on top of her, obscuring her from their view. Kurt then watched as his past self turned and walked away, quickening his pace with each step until he broke into a run. Other people began to shout, but their words slipped away into silence as Kurt felt himself being yanked back into the darkness.

There was nothing left for Kurt to see. All that remained was the past year of his life. The images of his arrival in Bismurr and being found by Cali began to play out in his mind. Despite the kindnesses he'd been treated to, he watched as a man he barely recognised lived a half life. A man with no hope or desires, just living day to day, doing the minimum to keep himself alive. Kurt had no pity or shame left for that person, just anger for them, for himself. Before this rage began to build up inside him, the darkness spat him back out into another memory that was not his own.

He saw Nul, looking the same as she had when he'd first met her. She was sitting in the glade he had spent so much time meditating in over the past few weeks. Looking around, he could see she was alone. Kurt watched as she pulled out a knife and dragged it across her open palm. She then closed her eyes and after a few deep breaths, Kurt watched the cut heal itself. Once her hand was restored Nul opened her eyes and stared at where the cut should have been.

"Why didn't you just leave?" she muttered to herself.

She then cut her hand again, this time letting it bleed a little before healing it with the glade's power. Kurt saw the image of the young man from the tunnels flash across his own mind and knew that was what Nul was thinking of as well. He watched as she cut and healed herself over and over again, each time Kurt felt his own hand burn in the same place. She looked like she had no intention of stopping but the sound of footsteps crunching over branches nearby drew her attention. Nul hid the knife in her clothes and stood up. An orc man appeared and gave Nul a wave.

"The Matriarch is calling a gathering," he said. He waited a moment for Nul to get back to her feet and the two of them started to make their way out of the glade.

"What's happening?" Nul asked.

"Two humans came wandering into our territory. The idiots want to talk or something. I think she wants to make an example out of them," he replied with a chuckle.

"You'd think they'd know better than to try and take more from us." Nul said with a sigh. Kurt watched as they walked away. A small smile started to form as he knew that she was about to head to their first meeting.

Just as Nul took her final step out of the glade, Kurt slipped back into the tumbling dark void. The last of Nul's memories settled in his mind and as they did, the darkness slowly began to shift into soft orange light. The glade began to take shape around him, each familiar tree and stone swimming into view. Kurt blinked as he came back to his senses like he'd just woken up from a long dream. Sat in front of him, coming back to her own senses was Nul.

"That place..." Nul whispered as she looked up. As their eyes met, tears began to stream down her face and Kurt could guess as to why. For the first time since they had met she was seeing him for what he really was. He couldn't bear to look at her now she knew the truth but before he could turn away she moved forward and pulled him into a hug, squeezing him so tight that it almost hurt.

"Did you see all of it? All of me?" Kurt asked, pushing her back so he could see her face.

"I saw every moment," Nul replied, raising a hand to touch his face. Kurt found himself reeling back at the sight of her trying to comfort him.

"How can you even look at me?" he asked as tears of his own started to form.

"How could I not?" Nul asked back as she pulled him back into a hug.

"But you saw everything that I did? Everything that I was a part of?" Kurt whispered in her ear. "I don't understand."

"You saw my life and the things I did, what I was still doing right up until I met you?" Nul asked.

"I did." Kurt replied.

"When you opened your eyes, there was no hesitation when you saw me, despite knowing what I've done. The first thing you felt was shame for yourself," Nul said as she pulled away to look Kurt in the eyes. "I saw that place you came from. That whole other world. I don't think I understand even half of what I saw but you know one thing I did understand the moment I saw it?"

"What?" Kurt asked as tears of his own streamed down his face.

"I saw a boy, who grew up in a place where children were starving and people were struggling to survive. You came from a world where you were surrounded by hate and fear for so many years. A world that if you'd made almost any other choice, you'd be dead. And do you know what I saw at the end of it all?" Nul asked but she didn't wait for him to reply. "The moment you truly saw your role in that world, you ran. When I was given a choice, that same choice, I chose to hurt and kill."

"That's not..." Kurt started, but Nul pulled him close to stop him talking.

"You lived in that horrible place for so long that you truly can't see what you really are," she whispered. "Kurt, I just saw your entire life so trust me when I say this." Nul paused for a moment and squeezed Kurt. "You are not the monster you think you are."

"After everything you saw, how can you say that?" asked Kurt, struggling to pull himself free of Nul's grip.

"How?" Nul replied. "Kurt, I couldn't begin to guess how it happened, but somehow you were given a second chance at your life. You could have done anything but what did you choose to do? You chose to fight. You are doing everything you can to make sure what happened in your world doesn't happen here. How could I not love someone who does that?"

"What did you say?" Kurt asked as he managed to push her away enough to look into her eyes. "You love me?"

"Yes, I think I do," Nul replied with a smile.

Kurt was stunned. Thinking back to the Vastupa he'd witnessed before, it dawned on Kurt that he and Nul had just done the same thing. Here was someone who knew the entirety of his life and not only were they not disgusted with him, they'd accepted him. Not just accepted, but loved him. He was at a loss for words, just staring at this impossible woman.

"I love you," Kurt said. He brushed her dark hair out of face and looked into her green eyes for a moment. "And I know you."

"I know you too," Nul whispered. She gave Kurt a kiss on the cheek and once again pulled him close to hold him. For the longest time they sat there enjoying the solitude of the glade, neither of them wanting the moment to end.

# 16

After the most blissful few hours that Kurt could remember, the couple were still knelt down at the glade. When they did finally pulled apart, Nul wiped her face clean with her sleeve and took a deep breath.

"So. Please tell me that all of that was worth it," Nul said as Kurt cleaned his own face.

"Well I think I can talk about the weavers now," he said, shocking himself at how easy it was to say.

"I thought as much," Nul said with a smug smile. "I knew I felt that influence disappear."

"Does this mean that I..." Kurt paused, "...we can go to the surface?"

"I'll need to check in and make sure the Matriarch knows you've had your mind restored, but after that we're free to leave," said Nul with a satisfied smile. "I know you're in a hurry, but do you mind if I go and pack a few things? I get the feeling I won't be coming back down here any time soon."

"Of course," Kurt replied. "I'll head to my room and wait for you there."

Nul gave him one last hug before walking away out of the glade, disappearing amongst the trees. Kurt looked around and smiled. He could feel its power surrounding him, radiating an odd sense of finality, like the glade itself knew he was leaving.

"Goodbye," Kurt said aloud. He felt the power dissipate in response and once it had faded away to nothing, Kurt walked away.

He took his time as he walked back to the gate fort, looking around this underground forest with a newfound appreciation. It had only been his home for a short time, but thanks to Nul's memories, he now felt like he'd been here for years. There was no one around as he entered the fort and walked the stone corridors back to his room. While he was waiting a few orcs passed by him, none of them paying Kurt much attention as they moved crates of supplies further into the fort. Kurt looked up every time he heard footsteps but it was a long while before he was rewarded to the sight of Nul rounding the corner. She had changed into some thick but warm-looking clothes and she was carrying a large stuffed sack slung over her shoulder.

"All set?" Nul asked as she strolled down the corridor.

"I think so. Am I finally free to leave?" asked Kurt, still feeling a sense of disbelief.

"Yes. Yes you are," replied Nul. Kurt let out a breath of relief and he felt like a weight was lifted from him.

"Are you ready to head to the surface?" Kurt asked.

Nul looked back down the corridor towards her home. She stared for a moment and let out a small sigh. She didn't take much time for herself before turning back to Kurt, giving him a resolute nod. They stayed in silence as they walked through the stone corridors that Kurt hadn't been allowed to traverse since he'd been taken captive all those weeks ago. Once they'd left the fort, the carved stone turned back into more natural rocks and stone. Kurt looked back at the large dome one last time, thinking back to when he'd first arrived here and how much had changed for him in such a short time. Not wanting to get distracted the couple quickened their pace as they made their way through the tunnels.

When they reached the threshold that divided the orc's territory from the entrance to the mine, Nul pulled out a small glowstone from her pocket. She grabbed Kurt by the hand and led him into the dark. Their journey up through the mine was soon stopped as they encountered a large wooden door blocking their way. Nul approached and gave two hard knocks in its centre before taking a step back. After a brief pause the whole structure was pulled up, revealing a large orc pulling on a metal chain that was hooked to a mechanism built into the ceiling. Nul and Kurt continued on their way, exchanging a brief nod with the orc guard as they passed.

Once they were through the gate the couple saw many stacked crates, barrels and beds lining every inch of wall as they walked further upward. They passed by a few more orcs resting on the beds who, save for a few passing glances, paid the couple no attention.

The same couldn't be said when they started to see a few humans and dwarves, who upon recognising Kurt, started to whisper amongst themselves. As the beds and supplies ended, the couple came upon various wooden spikes and waist-high walls, slowing their progress upward. Kurt and Nul rounded a corner and discovered that part of the mine had been rebuilt. The tunnel had been expanded to create a large wall made of rocks which was reinforced with heavy wood beams. In its centre there was another wooden gate being constructed by a familiar face.

Cole Berne was hammering a nail into place on the gate, looking up from his work when he spotted Kurt. He dropped his hammer with a loud metallic clang that echoed down the tunnel and stared for a few seconds.

"Kurt?!" Cole blurted out, stunned.

"Cole." Kurt greeted him with a smile. Cole rushed forward and grabbed the younger man by his shoulders.

"Hah! It's good to see you! We all thought you'd be stuck down there with them..."

said Cole, nodding at Nul. "...for a long time. You been treated alright?"

"I'm fine," Kurt replied as Cole stepped back. Kurt looked back at Nul for a moment. "Better than fine actually. They treated me very well. How've things been up here?"

"Not bad. Not great," Cole said with a sigh as he looked past the gate he'd been working on. "Ever since Peyton left you down there, people have been arguing over almost every decision. Things didn't get better when a bunch of orcs started coming up and getting involved either. We've managed to get the town ready despite everything slowing us down but it hasn't been easy. This attack that's coming has people in a panic though."

"That's not good," said Kurt. "This is just the start, we've got hundreds more coming for us."

"Hundreds?!" Cole's eyes widened. "How do you know that? How're we supposed to fight that many?!"

"Well you start by finishing that gate," Kurt replied. "We'll talk about the rest when we've dealt with these scouts."

He and Nul walked past Cole and the sound of hammering started to echo through the stone tunnel again, now sounding a little more frantic.

"You sounded confident back there," Nul praised him as they passed by a few more people building wooden barricades. Nul stopped suddenly when she spotted light coming from further up the tunnel - not light from a torch or a glowstone, but bright sunlight.

"This is the furthest you've travelled from your home," Kurt said, thinking back to her memories.

"It is," she replied. Kurt moved towards her and rested his hand on her shoulder.

"Whenever you're ready," he whispered.

Kurt took a step back and let Nul have a few moments to prepare herself. She took a few deep breaths and began walking forward. Kurt followed close by but let her lead the way at her own pace. Nul walked toward the light, stopping just in front of a sunbeam. She reached out and tentatively let the light touch her palm.

"It's so warm!" she exclaimed with child-like glee. She let the light dance over her fingers for a few seconds and, after bracing herself, stepped into the sunlight.

Kurt watched as she stood still with her eyes closed, bathing in the warm light, enjoying the sensation on her skin. Despite wanting to get going, he didn't interrupt, Kurt looked on and smiled. Nul did, after a few minutes, come back to her senses and turned to face Kurt. Taking the cue, he marched on to step out of the tunnel and back onto the surface.

A wave of cold air rushed into him as he stepped out into the morning sun. Kurt had lost track of time while he'd been living with Nul and the orcs, and finding out what hour of the day it was felt a little strange. His confusion was nothing compared to the pain his eyes felt from the light. It took him a few minutes to even be able to look around without squinting in the daylight. Nul seemed to be having a much harder time, grabbing Kurt by the arm as she struggled to open her eyes at all, but despite being blinded, she still had a huge smile on her face. When Kurt's eyes did adjust enough that he could see a little more, he looked around and saw what had changed in his absence.

The entrance to the mine had changed considerably. There were a dozen spiked barricades forming protective lines all around, some of which were still being hammered into place. After a lungful of the fresh chilly air, Kurt approached the nearest person doing work on the barricades: a young dwarven man he recognised as one of the squad members he'd travelled with before.

"C-Commander?!" The sight of Kurt seemed to put the dwarf on edge.

"Hello there. Could you go and gather the squad leaders and the council? I think we all need to talk," Kurt said. The dwarf didn't say anything but after a panicked nod, he did start running towards the town.

"Is now the best time to call a meeting? Don't we need to be getting ready to fight?" Nul asked, confused.

"We do. But you heard Cole back there, people are disorganised and not working together like they should be. It's something we need to deal with, otherwise this smaller attack will do more damage than we can take right now," Kurt said, thinking back to his first fight with the Dregs.

"Maybe," Nul replied. "What are you going to do about Peyton when you see him again?"

"I'm not sure," Kurt answered. "I guess we'll find out soon."

"Well whatever you need to do, you know that I'm on your side," Nul said, patting his shoulder with her free hand.

"I know," Kurt said with a smile. "Come on, there's someone we need to see before we start all this."

With Nul in tow, he made his way into town. Bismurr, like the mine, had changed quite a bit while he'd been away. Windows had been boarded up, doors had been reinforced or walled off and various crates of supplies were scattered all over the place. While it was disheartening to see the place that had been his home change like this, knowing that people were better prepared for what was coming did put Kurt a little more at ease.

He led Nul through the streets, passing by people who started whispering amongst themselves when they spotted him walking through town. Kurt ignored each voice as he walked past them; he knew rumours were going to spread about his return but there was one person he wanted to tell himself.

He and Nul stopped outside of Cali's bakery and just as he was about to knock, the door flung open to reveal Cali herself. Upon seeing Kurt she dropped the box she was holding, scattering bread rolls all over the ground. With no delay she leapt up and pulled Kurt into a hug, her feet dangling in the air as she clung onto him.

"I'm back," Kurt muttered, gripping her tightly as he lowered her back to the ground.

"You silly boy," Cali said as she stepped back to look him up and down. "Do you have any idea how worried I've been?!"

"I'm sorry," said Nul, drawing Cali's attention and the fiercest scowl that Kurt had ever seen on the woman. "We had to keep Kurt for a time. We'd have released him sooner, but we wanted to make sure he was well again before letting him go."

"And who's this lass?" Cali asked, continuing to look at Nul with scrutiny.

"This is the woman who took care of me down there, Nulkala," said Kurt, beckoning her to come closer.

"Though I prefer to be called Nul," she added.

"Well in that case I suppose I owe you a cup of tea," Cali turned around and gestured for Nul to follow her. "Kurty, clean this all up would you."

While the two ladies walked inside, Kurt gathered the rolls and placed them back into their box. After his time below ground he found it calming to do such a familiar and mundane chore. Once he was done, he went inside, placing the box of ruined rolls by the door on his way in. Cali was already pouring out a third cup which she handed to Kurt when he sat down to join her and Nul.

"I imagine you're not going to stay long?" Cali asked with a serious tone.

"Not just yet," Kurt replied. "But before we jump into dealing with everything, I wanted to come here and see you, let you know that I'm alright."

"That's kind of you, I appreciate that," Cali said before turning her attention back to Nul. "And this young lass is who I have to thank for keeping you fed I take it?"

"No need for that," Nul replied with a smile. "I was happy to help."

"Well even so, thank you," said Cali, gripping her own mug of tea in her small hands as she eyed up the orc in her front room. "I suppose you'd both best be going. I'm sure you've got a lot to do."

"We do," said Kurt. "Once we're done with this problem though, we'd like to come back here? We can catch up properly."

"See that you do," Cali replied with a weak smile. She hopped down from her chair to give Kurt another hug. "Now get going before I don't let you leave at all."

Kurt smiled and put down his tea. As he started to leave, Nul drank her entire brew as though it wasn't still boiling hot and handed the empty cup to Cali. The pair left the bakery and resumed their journey through Bismurr.

"I didn't expect her to be so nice to me," Nul said as they walked. "She seemed kind in your memories, but I thought she'd be a little unhappy about me being there."

"Well she was probably happy to meet the person who's been taking care of me," Kurt replied. "Actually, I wanted to ask you something about her."

"You want to tell her about us," said Nul with no hesitation.

"Yes I do," Kurt said, a little taken aback. "How'd you know that?"

"You're not the only one wishing we didn't need to keep this a secret from everyone," Nul replied with a sad sigh. "I know how much she means to you, so I think once we've dealt with this attack, we should tell her. It'd be nice to have at least one person we don't need to hide this from."

"Thank you," said Kurt. Looking ahead he could see a large crowd gathering outside of the squad leader's tent. Briefly, his new-found confidence wavered but after a deep breath to steady his nerves, he turned to look at Nul. "Are you ready for this?"

Nul nodded and together they approached the crowd. As soon as they drew close, the crowd parted to allow them to walk through. While there was still some whispering, a few people gave Kurt encouraging pats on the back as he passed. The pair arrived at the entrance of the tent, all the squad leaders gathered but only two of the council, Tessa and Melrose. Also standing at the table was Baku, who beamed when he saw Kurt and Nul walk up to the table.

"Welcome back Kurt," said Melrose, smiling at his young friend. "You've been missed."

"Melrose," Kurt greeted. He looked around at each face staring at him. "Is this everyone? Where's the rest of the council?"

"They're occupied at the moment. They did want to welcome you back, but I'm sure you understand that this is a busy time," Melrose replied.

"I do," Kurt said. "Well, let's get to the point of why I called you all here."

"Oh, we have some idea," Soren piped up, shooting Peyton an angry look.

"Peyton," said Kurt, locking eyes with the older man.

"Kurt," Peyton replied. The older man looked to have aged in the short time Kurt had been gone, grey hair now lining his temples. Some of the crowd gathered at the entrance of the tent were already whispering insults under their breath.

"Let's deal with this now." Kurt looked around and glared at anyone still muttering, only turning back when silence had fallen. "What Peyton did, betraying my trust? It was the right thing to do. He had a difficult decision to make and in his place I would have done the same thing."

"Maybe. Doesn't change the fact he made this decision alone, leaving the rest of us in the dark," said Meredith, stepping forward to make sure she had everyone's attention. "Whatever the situation was, you're our leader, we all should've had a say in what to do."

"If there was time to do that I'm sure he'd have brought the decision to you all, but the longer I was left alone, the worse things could have become," Kurt said. "And the fact I was influenced by these 'weavers' proves that he was right, so I think we should move past this. Now."

"It'll be a while before he gets our trust back but if the Commander says we should move on, we should," said Garet, though he still shot Peyton a disapproving look. "I'm sure you've been told, but we managed to set a watch tower further away and they spotted some Dregs heading this way. They'll probably arrive here in the middle of the night."

"Around thirty or so," said Meredith. "No sign of Orlan with them, not yet anyway."

"No, he'll be travelling with his main force," Kurt said, making everyone look at him. "He made a mistake trying to alter my mind; he gave me information we can use. This attack is probably meant to scare us and soften our defences a little."

"His main force?" Lief asked.

"That's right. He's gathered an army of Dregs, five hundred of them," said Kurt, causing a few gasps from the crowd outside. "But that's it. We fight off that force and we're safe for a time."

"But there's so few of us, even with the orcs joining the fight," Melrose said, gesturing around the tent. "Even if we use the mine to slow them down, do you really think we can fight that?"

"I do," Kurt replied, asserting his new-found confidence. "But we'll deal with that later. What's the plan for the Dregs coming tonight?"

"We'll take care of most of them," said Baku as he stepped up to the table. "I'm sure the rest of you can handle any that slip past us."

"Let's not take any chances. Nul, myself and a squad of ours will join you." Kurt said. He looked around and Nul gave him a nod of agreement.

"I'll take my squad then," said Lief. "We'll get some vantage points in the trees and take out any that get by the orc fighters."

"We'll keep your lot safe, I promise," Baku said with a wink. Lief rolled her eyes.

"All the other squads will stand ready in town and we'll all meet up when this is all over," said Kurt, looking around the tent one more time. "Let's get started."

As the crowd dispersed, Peyton started to leave with them but Kurt locked eyes with him and shook his head. Peyton nervously shifted as the last people walked away. Nul gave Kurt a reassuring pat on his shoulder before leaving the tent, leaving the two men alone.

“I'm sorry for what I did to you,” Peyton said, looking down at the ground. Unable to meet Kurt's gaze. “I really thought it was for the best. I thought I was protecting everyone.”

“I meant what I said.” Kurt replied. “I spent a long while thinking about what you did. It was the right thing to do. But making that decision alone has made people feel like you'd betray them at any moment. What do you think we should do about that?”

“I should step down as a squad leader. Let someone else take charge,” Peyton said, he'd clearly been thinking about this since he'd left Kurt behind.

“No,” Kurt said. His firm tone shocked Peyton enough to look up at him. “Do you know why I agreed to be a part of all this? Why I chose to fight and help everyone here fight?”

“Because you were the only one who could help,” Peyton replied.

“I chose to help because I come from a place where people like me did what they were told without question. People did the worst possible things because they blindly followed the orders of people they trusted.” Kurt paused and took a breath. “One of the reasons I agreed to do all of this was because I don't want anyone here to make those same mistakes. I want people to question the choices made by those in charge, including my own.”

“So I'm just supposed to carry on and hope people trust me again?” asked Peyton.

"You'll earn it back. I know you will," Kurt said, placing a hand on Peyton's shoulder. "You already have mine."

Kurt walked out of the tent, leaving Peyton alone at the table. A few eavesdroppers hiding outside scattered as he stepped outside. Kurt didn't mind; the more people knew that he trusted Peyton, the better. Looking ahead at the treeline, he saw Nul leaning against a newly built fence, waiting for him.

"All done?" she asked once he got closer.

"I think so," Kurt replied, yawning as he was overcome with tiredness.

"Well then, we should get ready for tonight," said Nul. "Probably best if we rest up as well."

"Then let's head to my home," Kurt said. He thought for a moment and sighed. "Though it's been empty since I left to go below ground, the place probably isn't in a good state."

"Best to deal with that now then," Nul said with a smile. "You'll feel better knowing the place is already sorted out once tonight is over with."

Kurt knew she was right, but it didn't make the task seem any less exhausting. Nul's good mood was infectious though as he allowed himself to be led through the forest back to his cabin. The chill of winter was much stronger as they made their way further away from the town, enough to have Kurt shivering. When the two of them did reach his cabin they hurried inside to get away from the cold. Even though the sun was still high and bright, Kurt started a small fire to warm the place up.

Looking around, he'd expected the place to be dusty and his food to be spoiled but the whole place seemed to have been taken care of in his absence. As he was checking his cupboards he discovered some of Cali's baked cakes. Knowing that she had been looking after his home brought a smile to his face. He prepared a small meal and while he worked, Nul left her things near the bed and made herself comfortable in his chair by the fire. Kurt handed her a plate and sat down by her feet, resting his head against her knee. He closed his eyes as the heat from the fire washed through him, lulling him to sleep.

"I like your home," Nul whispered.

"Our home," Kurt mumbled as he drifted to sleep with Nul's fingers tousling his hair.

# 17

Kurt woke up some time later when he felt Nul get up and move across the room. Looking up he could see the same log burning away in the fire so he knew he hadn't slept for long. He stood up to stretch and smiled at Nul as he caught her attention.

"I was going to let you sleep a little longer," she said. Nul then gestured towards the fading light at the window. "Sun's still up but I don't think it'll stay around for much longer."

"We'll head out soon," Kurt said. He walked over to the kitchen to join Nul in tidying away the plates, giving her a kiss on the cheek as he passed by.

"Are you worried about tonight?" Nul asked, concern filling her voice.

"A little," replied Kurt. "Everyone seems to be working well together though; I think that'll see us all through. This time at least."

"That's what worries me," Nul said, turning to face Kurt. "After tonight we don't have long to make a plan to face that army. And what happens after that? Will everyone here just expect my people to go back underground again?"

"You know I wouldn't let that happen," Kurt replied, pulling her into a hug and rubbed her back. "And while it's this danger that's brought us all together, I don't think people will want things to go back to the way things used to be."

"You're probably right," Nul said, giving him a tight squeeze before pushing him away. "Come on then, we need to get ready."

The pair set about equipping themselves for the night ahead. Kurt's armour was a little stiff but still fit well and after checking his spike launcher was still in working condition he attached it to his arm. Nul changed into a vest that was slightly padded across her chest and back, with a pair of leather bracers on her bare arms. Once they were both ready, Kurt grabbed his axe and with one final check that everything was in order, they left for the town. The sky was overcast as night was falling, the clouds making the forest much darker than normal.

They walked in silence through the woods, which Kurt was glad for. Despite what he'd said earlier, his worry about the fight to come was making his stomach churn. He did his best to ignore it as they drew closer to the outskirts of town. Waiting for them was a large crowd of orcs, around thirty of them, all of them armed with spears except one: Baku, at the head of the crowd, wielding a huge metal club with a spiked ball at its top. Just as Kurt and Nul reached the group, Lief emerged from the town with her squad of archers close behind her.

"Everyone ready?" Kurt called out.

"All set commander," Lief replied.

"Ready," Baku said, shouldering his heavy weapon. "Lead the way."

"Let's move out!" Kurt shouted, resting his own weapon on his shoulder as he marched towards the forest on the east side of Bismurr.

The large group arrived in good time at the forest's edge and began to spread out as the trees slowed their pace. Everyone stayed quiet while they marched, the only sound was the soft thumping of their feet over the muddy ground. It wasn't long until they reached a large wooden watchtower, its top reaching just above the tree canopy. Lief climbed up the tower, while her squad got themselves situated in the trees nearby. The rest of the group marched on, spreading out more as they moved onwards. Before they covered much ground, a rumbling sound started to emanate from the forest ahead. The group came to a halt and readied themselves as the rumbling came closer, now sounding more like clawed feet pounding against dirt. Kurt looked down the line of orcs, each face staring ahead with determination and not a single sign of fear. Baku moved a few steps ahead of the line and lifted his heavy club, waiting for the enemy to appear. Kurt turned to Nul who gave him a final nod before turning to look out to the shadows. The noise of the approaching Dregs was close now, alongside the sounds of snapping branches and leaves whipping against their bodies. Kurt tightened his grip on his axe and took a deep breath to steady himself.

The Dregs burst forth like a flood, ripping their way through the undergrowth of the forest as they surged forward toward the group waiting for them. The orcs roared at the sight and rushed forward to attack. As the two forces clashed, the first wave of Dregs charged into the spears, killing and maiming themselves as they piled onto the orcs. A second wave burst out of the darkness to move outward and encircle them, but the monsters found Baku blocking their path. The large orc was bringing down Dregs left and right with wide swings of his club.

The battle was spreading further so Nul and Kurt joined the fray. He fired his launcher, obliterating the head of the first monster to approach him. A second Dreg shoved its way past its dead kin and lunged at Kurt. He raised his axe just in time to save himself, but the creature pounced on top of him, sending them both skidding across the ground. The Dreg thrashed around trying to bite Kurt's throat but was blocked by the axe handle. Kurt looked around for something to use as a weapon but found nothing. With every lunge the monster made Kurt lost strength, its fangs getting closer with each bite.

"SOMEBODY!" Kurt cried out. The Dreg got a strong grip on the axe and threw it away. "HELP!"

Appearing from nowhere with blinding speed, Nul sprinted over and landed a hard kick against the Dreg's torso, sending it flying. There was a loud sickening crack as its body almost bent in half around a tree.

"Are you alright?" Nul asked as she helped Kurt back to his feet.

"I'm fine. We need to get moving," Kurt answered through pained breaths. He looked around and saw some of the Dregs were breaking away and getting around the orcs.

Kurt retrieved his axe and hurried to catch up to Nul who was fast approaching the Dregs that had slipped past them. At first he was worried about her, but his concerns were put to rest when he looked ahead. Nul was wrestling a Dreg to the ground and even with the creature's thrashing, she didn't look like she was struggling to hold it down. Kurt ran forward and swung his axe hard into the back of the monster, killing it. Nul kicked it away, its lifeless body skidding into the undergrowth. The sound of arrows flying through the air nearby let them know that their enemies had reached Lief and her squad. As Nul got back to her feet Kurt grabbed her arm, stopping her from running toward the fighting.

"They've got his handled. Let's rest for a minute," Kurt said. At first Nul looked frustrated that he was stopping her, but that expression melted away and was replaced by relief. The pair stood there for a few moments, their hot breath sending out small clouds into the cold night air. The sounds of fighting were dying down, putting Kurt at ease. He looked up and noticed Nul was staring at her own shaking hands.

"Nul," Kurt said. She jumped a little at his voice. "Are you alright?"

"It's just..." She paused for a moment to make sure no one was approaching. "...all this blood and violence. There's something about it all, I can't think straight. I nearly let you get hurt back there!"

"Look at me, I'm fine," said Kurt but before he could say anything else, a group of orcs ran past them, chasing the last of the Dregs into the woods, pushing them towards the distant sounds of arrows.

"We can't stay here any more," said Nul with a sigh.

"No we can't," agreed Kurt. He turned to face Nul and met her gaze. "But I'm with you, alright? You're not alone in this."

Nul clenched her jaw and nodded. Once they caught their breath, the pair rushed towards the sounds of battle to rejoin the fight. As they ran through the forest they saw the bodies of many dead Dregs and many injured orcs starting to gather together. It was hard to tell amongst the chaos but it looked like none of their own forces too hurt, which Kurt was relieved to see. When they reached the watchtower, the battle was drawing to a close. There were at least a dozen Dreg corpses littering the floor, each one filled with arrows. The squad of archers had climbed down from their perches and were walking between each body, checking for any signs of life. Lief herself was standing on the body of a twitching Alpha Dreg. She notched an arrow and aimed downwards, letting loose into the monster's neck, spraying a jet of dark blood up into her face. Upon spotting Kurt and Nul, she jumped down from the corpse and spat out the blood that had splashed into her mouth as she walked over to them.

"I think we're about done here," Lief said, seemingly satisfied with the carnage surrounding her. "How's everyone doing?"

"Not sure just yet," replied Kurt. "Seems like you and your squad had this handled. Looks like you all improved your shooting while I was gone as well."

"Well it's not like we sat around doing nothing while you were stuck down there with those anima-" She stopped herself mid-sentence when she caught sight of Nul. "-with our new friends."

"Can you get your squad building a pyre soon? We need to get rid of these things as soon as possible," Kurt said, trying to move the conversation on as a scowl formed on Nul's face.

"Can do commander," Lief replied before hurrying away. The rest of her squad had been listening in as they all moved in unison to follow her.

"Let's round up everyone else, see how we're all doing," Kurt said, marching towards the gathering orcs with Nul in tow.

As he approached he saw everyone was sporting injuries of different severity, some unable to even stand. Standing in the middle of the group, leaning on his now blood-stained club, was Baku. His clothes were ripped to shreds and he was covered in deep scratches but he was also smiling despite the wounds. A few more orcs appeared from between the trees as Kurt and Nul approached the group.

"Baku. How're you doing? Everyone accounted for?" Kurt asked.

"I'm doing just fine," Baku replied with a chuckle. "I think we're all here, a few of my men are just checking around to make sure none of those things got away."

"Good," said Kurt. "Lief's squad is building a pyre, can you get your people to help burn the bodies? These things have a habit of not staying dead."

"Yeah, we heard about that," said Baku. "We'll get started soon. Could do with someone sorting out our injuries though. You and Nul wanna head back, get someone out here for us? We'll handle everything here if you wanna stay in town too."

"We'll go now," Kurt replied, happy to get away from the carnage. Looking back he could see that Nul shared his relief. Kurt turned to the gathered orcs and raised his voice. "You all did very well tonight. Make sure you all get some rest later, you've earned it."

There were some half-hearted cheers as Kurt and Nul left the orcs and made their way back to town. As they passed by the watchtower, Lief's squad had already laid down several large logs for the foundation of the pyre. Once they had cleared the treeline and were alone, Nul grabbed Kurt's arm to stop him walking further.

"What's wrong?" Kurt asked, resting a hand on her shoulder.

"I think I was wrong to come out with you tonight, you nearly got hurt back there because of me," Nul said, turning to look Kurt in the eyes.

"You also saved me, don't forget that. Whatever happened out there, you still came through for me when it mattered," Kurt said.

"This time. What about next time? What if I'm too slow next time? If I freeze completely?" Nul asked as she paced back and forth.

"You won't," Kurt replied.

"You can't know that," Nul said, shaking her head.

"Of course I can," Kurt said. He dropped his weapon and placed both hands on her face. "I said you weren't alone in this. You and I will face this together, whatever happens. Alright?"

Nul stayed silent, but after a few moments gave an exasperated sigh and nodded. Kurt retrieved his axe and the couple resumed their walk back to town. When they got closer, they saw armed people patrolling the outskirts. As they arrived, someone emerged from the shadow of a tall house and approached them. Once he stepped out of the shadows, the moonlight revealed a tired Peyton, still tightening a strap on his shoulder.

"What's the situation?" he asked.

"Safe for now and everyone up there is getting ready to burn the bodies. We need someone to get back there and see to the injured though," Kurt replied, speaking loud enough so anyone nearby could hear. He knew that news of their victory would be good for the townsfolk.

"I'll get Tessa and head out there myself," Peyton said with a half-hearted smile. He slapped Kurt's arm and hurried back into the shadows.

Kurt and Nul continued walking into the town. Kurt felt like they were being watched and as they passed each building he could see people stepping out of their homes. Soon enough a squad of their fighters were jogging past, telling people the news. Within a few minutes, people were stepping outside with lit candles and steaming mugs. The town was soon flooded with lights and the streets filled with people. Kurt and Nul managed to get away from the crowd without being noticed and made their way to Cali's home. By the time they rounded the corner to her street, there was a light at her window and Cali herself was standing outside holding a large mug of tea. She lit up when she saw Nul and Kurt approaching and ran out to greet them.

"Ah Kurty, you're alright!" Cali jumped up and pulled him downward into a tight hug. "Both of you get inside, I'll get you some tea."

She pushed them both inside before they could say anything, steering the two of them to sit down. Kurt and Nul shed their armour and weapons, leaving them by the door. Cali became a flurry of cups of tea, biscuits and even some blankets as the three of them settled down into the cosy room. They made a little small talk as they shared the events of the evening, the conversation falling into a lull when Cali started a small fire. For a time no one said anything, they just ate and enjoyed each other's company. Once they had all eaten their fill, Kurt looked between the other two and seeing that they both seemed to be in good spirits, decided it was time to share his news.

"Thank you for looking after my home while I was gone Cali. You didn't need to do that," Kurt said.

"Well I didn't know when you'd be coming back and after a while it just felt like the only way I could help," Cali replied with a warm smile.

"Even so, we both appreciate it," Nul chipped in.

"You're planning on staying with Kurt?" Cali asked with a raised eyebrow. "I thought you were just getting ready for the encounter this evening?"

"Yes about that..." Kurt took a breath and looked to Nul, who gave him an encouraging nod. "While I was down there, recovering from what the elves did to me, we became something more than just friends."

"You two are together?" Cali said, seeming only a little surprised.

"We are," said Nul, reaching over to take Kurt's hand into hers.

"It's a bit more than that, we're... married," said Kurt, looking at Nul with a smile as he spoke. "I know it hasn't been that long since we met but there's this ceremony, the Vastupa, it showed us the other's memories."

"What does that mean?" Cali asked, confused.

"It means that we know everything about each other. We've lived through each other's lives," Nul said, turning to look at Cali. "I know how strange it might seem, but you need to know we love each other very much. I know how you feel about Kurt, I've seen it. That's why we wanted to tell you the truth about this."

"I see." Cali became quiet and still for a moment. Kurt was worried for a moment until she looked up with a bright grin. She hopped down from her chair and hurried over to give Nul a hug.

"I guess you approve?" Kurt asked with a laugh.

"Of course I do you silly boy," Cali replied while reaching over to pull him into the hug as well. "I thought there was something going on between you two but I had no idea it was this."

"We still need to keep it a secret from everyone else, at least for now," said Kurt as he pulled himself free of Cali's tight grip. "I know some people in town wouldn't approve and I imagine there's some orcs who wouldn't either."

"Maybe," said Nul, also pulling herself free. "My people certainly won't be happy that I wasn't doing my task correctly."

"You're both probably right about all that," Cali said, as she took the kettle of tea that had been standing near the fire and topped up everyone's mugs. "I'll do my best to keep it a secret but if you insist on living together, people will find out sooner than you think."

"Well I don't think either of us want to keep this hidden forever," said Kurt. He gave Nul's hand a little squeeze and smiled. "However the rest of the town decides to treat us, we'll face them all together."

"Though if they're even half as kind as you Cali, we'll be just fine," Nul said with a smile.

"You're too kind dear," Cali replied. "Now. I need to hear all about this 'Vastupa' and everything else that happened down there."

"We have kept you waiting long enough, haven't we?" Nul said with a small laugh.

Between the two of them talking they spent a good portion of the night telling their story of what happened underground. It took a while with Cali gasping in shock or stopping to dry her tears or even to stop herself from giggling. As they spoke Kurt found himself staring at the two women and enjoyed the sense of love he felt in the room, it reminded him of his own family. By the time they had finished telling their tale, the two of them once again found themselves being pulled into a warm motherly hug from Cali.

“So what's next for the two of you?” Cali said as she sat back down in her own chair. “I imagine you've got a lot to be getting ready for?

“I think I need to prove that I'm to be trusted again,” said Kurt. “People were pretty quick to accept me back, but I think that's because everyone was still upset with Peyton. As things calm down, people will start to think about why I was taken away to begin with.”

“Oh I think you'll be fine there,” Cali replied. “You remember all those books and stuff you pulled out of those ruins? They found some mention of weavers in there, so people definitely think they're real. Not to mention when all those folk came from underground, they started sniffing around to make sure the rest of us were fine.”

“I take it they didn't find anything?” asked Nul.

“Not a thing, which was a relief I can tell you,” Cali said with a little chuckle. “Everyone at least trusts the orcs on that matter, so you shouldn't have to worry about a thing.”

“Good to know,” said Kurt.

“Then I guess the only thing to worry about is the fight to come,” Nul said, her voice trailing off as she started staring at the wall, a look of worry forming across her face. She only came back to her senses when Cali put a hand on her knee.

"Tomorrow's worries are for tomorrow," Cali said, smiling. "I think maybe we should call it a night. I've probably got a lot of hungry mouths to feed first thing in the morning. Though I want you both to come over again for dinner, so we can celebrate properly."

"We should go and get some sleep, since we're going to have to have another council meeting at some point tomorrow," Kurt said, stifling a yawn as he stood up. "We'll be back here tomorrow evening."

"Thank you for tonight though," said Nul, as she too got out of her chair.

After yet another warm hug from Cali, the pair made their way back outside. There was no telling how late it was, but the streets were back to being still and quiet. Seeing that they were alone, Kurt put his arm around Nul, and based on how she gripped his hand back, she was grateful that he did. They were both so full of warm food and drink that they didn't feel the chill night air as they walked back to their home. It wasn't long before they were back inside, starting up a fire to settle in for the night. By the time they had cleaned up and undressed, the couple was too tired to do anything but crawl into bed and hold each other for warmth as they drifted to sleep.

"Kurt?" Nul whispered, turning a little to see if he was still awake.

"Hmm?" Kurt replied but kept his eyes closed and pulled her a little closer.

"I liked spending time with Cali, just us, in the open," she said, kissing his cheek as she nestled between his arms.

He didn't say anything else, tiredness had finally caught up with him and was creeping across his body. With a fire nearby and Nul by his side, he felt like he was sinking into the warmth of it all as he slowly fell asleep. As Kurt sunk deeper into his slumber he felt a familiar chill start to crawl through him. He opened his eyes to find himself standing in the fog yet again.

*The stench of burning flooded around him and his gut was filled with cold dread. He felt a hand touch his shoulder and he already knew what was going to be there if he turned around. Letting out a sigh, he was about to turn when he saw a figure in the fog ahead of him. For a moment he thought he might be Orlan again, but something felt different about it. The figure didn't try to come closer, it just stood in the fog just staring at Kurt. It was then that he realised something. He always turned to face the burned woman. He always let the guilt and the disgust that he felt for himself burrow inside him to do something, anything, to punish himself every time he had this dream. Something about that new figure in the fog made him want to do something different.*

*So this time Kurt walked forward, slipping free from the grasp of the burned woman behind him. Each step he took, the chill melted away and was replaced with a warmth, a kind warmth. Yet no matter how far he walked, Kurt couldn't get closer to the figure ahead of him. He tried to break into a run, but felt like his feet were sluggish as though he was wading through thick mud.*

*Before he could try to do anything else, the fog faded away to blackness and Kurt found himself returning to consciousness.*

# 18

As he opened his eyes, Kurt squinted at the dawning sun's light pouring through the window. Nul was still asleep by his side with one arm over his chest, holding him close for warmth. He watched her for a little while and smiled every time she stirred. Knowing they had to get up, Kurt gave her head a small kiss and shifted out from under her grip. Nul groaned and sat up, her tangled mess of hair completely covering her face.

"Breakfast?" Kurt asked over his shoulder as he walked to the kitchen.

"Toast," Nul muttered before slumping back down onto the bed, dragging the blanket over her head.

Kurt laughed and set about preparing their food. By the time he'd finished cooking, Nul had managed to drag herself out of bed and was poking a small hunk of wood into the fire, all the while still wrapped in a blanket. She looked more awake and energetic once she had finished her meal. Kurt couldn't help himself from staring as she walked across the room, the sunlight glinting over her soft-looking grey skin and Nul smiled at him when she noticed him looking.

"So what are we doing first today?" she said, stretching her arms with a yawn.

"First? Head into town and talk with the council," Kurt replied as he tidied away the crumb-covered plates. "I think we need to see how everyone is doing. The townsfolk and your people seem to have been working together well enough, but I know there's a lot of bad blood there. Things might not be as calm as they seem."

"Maybe. That woman, Lief, did almost call me an animal last night," Nul said as she cracked her knuckles.

"I hated that," said Kurt, glaring at the window. "I'm going to talk to her about that."

"It's alright. People aren't going to change their opinion of us overnight," Nul said, a hint of sadness in her voice. She walked over to Kurt and hugged him from behind. "But it's nice that you want to do something about it."

"Though before we go and do anything, we need to talk about last night," said Kurt. He turned around and gently took Nul's hands into his own. "Is that alright?"

"I suppose we have to eventually," Nul said with a resigned sigh.

"Look, when we talk with the council later, we need to be making plans for the future of the town," Kurt explained. "Whatever choices or plans we make, everyone needs to be certain about what they are doing as we go forward and that includes us."

"What are you trying to say?" Nul asked, sounding a little defensive.

"I'm saying that if you don't want to fight, you don't have to," Kurt replied.

"You don't want me with you?" Nul asked as tears began to well up in her eyes.

"Of course I want you with me," he replied, squeezing her hands in what he hoped was a comforting way. "If you asked me a month ago, I'd have said there was nothing more important than defending this place. But now? The most important thing to me is you. If you want to fight, I'll stand at your side. If you want to run, I'll leave everything and we'll run together. If you want to hide then I'll keep you hidden. I am with you but we need to make ourselves ready now, while we still have time."

"You really mean that don't you?" Nul smiled, drying her eyes with Kurt's sleeve. "You'd really leave all this behind?"

"If that's what you wanted, yes," Kurt replied. "I've spent too long holding on to guilt, refusing to move forward. I'm not doing that any more. Whatever happens next, we're going forward together, no matter what that means for this place."

"That's good," Nul said as she looked down, her brow furrowed in thought.

"So, what are you thinking?" asked Kurt, lifting Nul's head to look up at his face.

"I'm going to fight with you," Nul said, filled with a sense of resolve. "We're going to stay here and fight off Orlan and his army. Even if Bismurr gets destroyed, we'll find a way to win."

"I..." Kurt was about to speak but after hearing Nul's words, an idea started to form in his mind. "Wait, what did you say?"

"Even if Bismurr gets destroyed?" Nul asked, confused.

"That's it!" Kurt declared.

"What's it?" Nul asked, smiling now as she got caught up in Kurt's excitement.

"We destroy the town!" Kurt revealed, staring at Nul as though she should be excited with him. Instead, she stared back at him with even more confusion.

"You've lost me on that one," Nul said, looking concerned at how frantic Kurt was becoming.

"It might sound like I've gone mad but just listen," he said. "We get everyone into the mines except for a small force of fighters."

"How's a small force supposed to destroy the town? Also won't destroying the place with them in it be dangerous?" Nul asked.

"They won't be there for long," Kurt explained further. "They're only there to lure as many Dregs as they can. When there's too many for them to deal with, they'll retreat to the mine as well. Once they're safe? We blow up the town and take as many Dregs out as possible. Then we send out everyone who can fight to finish off whatever is left."

"That...." Nul thought for a moment. "...might be a good idea. How exactly do you plan on doing this?"

"With sparking powder," Kurt said. "We line each street and fill every building with the stuff. If we do it right, we can make their numbers mean absolutely nothing."

"It's a good plan," Nul replied, more than a little surprised. "Might be a bit difficult convincing people to destroy their homes though."

"Shouldn't be too difficult, what with the alternative being to face an entire army of those things. Not to mention Orlan himself," said Kurt.

"Good point," Nul replied. "Do you think he'll be amongst the Dregs? If we could catch him in town with this, it'd end the whole thing quickly."

"I don't think we'll be that lucky," Kurt said, thinking back on his previous encounters with Orlan. "He'll want to enjoy the victory without having worked for it, so he'll probably hide and wait until the fighting is over. Though if we manage this, he's likely to come out and fight since he doesn't think he can lose."

"Well whenever he does show up, you don't face him alone," Nul said, gripping his hand. "Doesn't matter who you're with, you just don't go alone."

"Oh I won't," Kurt replied. "I've seen his powers first-hand - it'd be stupid to fight him alone. But the moment he does show himself, he needs to be the priority."

"Agreed," Nul said.
"Good," said Kurt. He let out a long sigh of relief; he felt lighter and more ready to start the day after everything that had been said.

"We should get going soon," Nul said, walking across the room to get dressed.

Kurt joined her without speaking and within a few minutes they were both ready to leave. As the couple were leaving, they took the time for one last kiss, knowing that they might not have another opportunity for the rest of the day. The couple were in such a good mood that they were almost running through the forest as they made their way towards Bismurr. When they reached the outskirts they saw the town was bustling with people: orcs, humans and dwarves alike. Everyone seemed busy either reinforcing the town's defences or moving supplies around and the town appeared to be in good spirits. Kurt and Nul even had a few people say thank you for the night before as they walked past them. They arrived at the squad tent without much delay and discovered Garet and Meredith having a conversation. They both jumped a little as Kurt and Nul came into the tent.

"Commander," Garet said, standing up straight but sounding a little nervous.

"Garet. Meredith," said Kurt, greeting them both with a small nod.

"Good morning commander," said Meredith with a pleasant tone. She then turned to look at Garet and smirked. "Relax a little, Garet. It's not like he came back from the dead or something."

"Sorry. It's just-- you've changed. You don't seem much like the same man who left us, at least to me," said Garet, calming down a little after he spoke.

"Changed?" Kurt asked.

"You're a little more self-assured is all," said Meredith with a small smile. "Anyway, what can we do for you? I imagine you need to talk about last night?"

"As long as people are alright and those Dreg bodies have been burned?" Kurt replied.

"Everyone is fine I think. The Dregs were dealt with, a few of those orcs stayed overnight to make sure," said Garet, still a little nervous when he was speaking to Kurt.

"Not just the orcs," said a voice from outside the tent. Everyone turned around to see Peyton arriving. "Morning everyone."

"Lief was asking for you," said Peyton, looking at Kurt.

"Is she alright?" Kurt asked. He then looked around the table. "In fact, where is everyone else?"

"I know Soren and Yvette took their squads out to make sure the woods surrounding the town were clear, they'll probably be gone for most of the day," said Meredith, looking around to the others, also curious to see what they knew.

"Sig was up at the mine when I last saw her. Checking to make sure the new gates were strong enough," Garet said.

"And Lief is at the Jumping Canary, waiting for you," Peyton said, yawning.

"Me and Nul will go there next then," Kurt said. He was curious why Lief wanted to speak to him, but he was glad she was somewhere private since he wanted to have words with her. "Peyton make sure you get some sleep. We'll be calling another meeting later, so I want all of you ready."

He looked between the three squad leaders and after each one acknowledged his orders, Kurt left the tent with Nul in tow, to make their way across town. Things seemed much quieter as they got closer to the town centre, but there were still a fair few people making their own way back and forth through the streets. The couple arrived at the tavern and could see that Lief was waiting outside its front door, looking around nervously at each person that passed by. Upon spotting Kurt and Nul arriving, she let out a long sigh of relief, though she continued to look uncomfortable every time someone walked close to her.

"Good morning Lief," Nul said when they arrived at the entrance to the tavern.

"Nul. Kurt," Lief said, nodding at them both.

"You seem a little nervous. Everything alright?" Kurt asked.

"I think it's best if we talk inside," Lief replied. She didn't wait for a response as she turned around and walked inside.

Kurt and Nul looked at each other, confused, but they followed the dwarf inside regardless. The tavern was empty and once the pair had walked in Lief shut the door and set about drawing all the curtains closed. Once the room was dark with only slivers of light making their way inside, she walked to the middle of the room and gestured for the two of them to sit down. Kurt and Nul made themselves comfortable while Lief paced back and forth in front of them.

"What's the matter?" Nul asked, breaking the silence.

“Okay,” Lief stopped pacing and took a deep breath to steady herself. “This is gonna sound weird, but you remember the creature from last night, the alpha that I killed?”

“Yes?” Kurt replied, looking over to Nul who was also still looking confused.

“Well when I fired that last arrow into it, some of its blood splashed into my mouth,” Lief explained.

“I remember. You spat most of it out, you're not feeling sick are you?” Kurt asked, leaning forward.

“No, I'm not sick. That would be something normal,” she replied, shaking her head before resuming her nervous pacing.

“Lief, please. What's going on?” Kurt asked, getting a little frustrated.

“It'll be easier if I just show you,” Lief replied, stopping in place.

She reached into her pocket and pulled out a small stone, placing it onto her palm. Lief closed her eyes and for a moment or two nothing happened. Just as Kurt was about to say something to interrupt, the stone began floating above Lief's hand. Nul gasped while Kurt was wide-eyed with surprise.

“That's magic. You can do magic! How can she be doing magic?” Nul asked with frantic excitement.

“I don't know!” Lief replied in a panic. “I felt strange as soon as I got home. Then I just found that I could make this happen.”

“Have you told anyone else?” Kurt asked.

“No, I wasn't sure what to do. Since you're the only one I know who's had the elves do something to you, I thought I'd ask you first," Lief replied. Her eyes welled up as she spoke. "What am I going to do?"

"Well first, stay calm," Kurt said, standing up to place a hand on her shoulder. "Second, other than this power, how do you feel?"

"I'm not sure. I think I want to throw up?" Lief took a moment to think, breathing slowly to try to calm down. "I think I feel fine, just this power."

"What's it like?" asked Nul, walking around Lief, inspecting the small dwarf.

"It's like I can feel where rocks are in my head. Below us, in the walls, scattered outside, they're everywhere," Lief replied, her eyes darting all over the room.

"Nothing else, just rocks?" Nul asked, sniffing the air around Lief.

"I haven't tried much else to be honest," said Lief. After a few more deep breaths she seemed to be calming down.

"It might be best for you to get yourself over to Jessie and Tessa, have them take a look at you," Kurt said. "Don't tell them the truth, just say you feel a little sick or something."

"Do you think this is permanent?" Lief asked, grabbing the stone out of the air.

"There's no way to know," Nul replied as she sat back down. "Even with some of things we have underground, this is something I've never heard of before."

"Regardless of what it means, the first thing to do is make sure that you're alright. We can worry about what happens next later," Kurt said, patting her shoulder.

"Sure thing," Lief replied, pocketing the stone. "Can I come back later to talk about this?"

"Of course. Nul and me will be around if you need us," Kurt replied. "Just try your best to keep this a secret for now, at least until we learn what it means."

Lief nodded and hurried out of the tavern, leaving Kurt and Nul alone in the darkened room. As the door closed, Nul let out a long sigh.

"So that was unexpected," she said while staring at the closed door.

"I swear every time we think we understand our enemy, something new comes up," Kurt said. "Did you sense anything we should be worried about, weaver influence or anything?"

"That was the strange thing. Lief seemed perfectly normal to me, even when she was using that power," Nul turned to face Kurt. "I don't think those healers are going to find anything either."

"Better to be absolutely sure," said Kurt. "Do you think it might be permanent?"

"No way to tell," Nul said as she stared at the ceiling. "I'm actually more curious how strong she might be now. That power could be useful in the battle ahead, especially with a whole mountain of rock right here. What do you think?"

"I'm not thinking about that at all. You saw how scared she was, she's in no state to try anything like that just yet," Kurt said, but as he spoke he did start considering the possibilities. "It does raise some questions though. Most important one being, did the Dreg blood do this?"

"It's the only thing that makes sense at the moment, but it'd be something to worry about if it did," Nul replied, scratching her head in thought. "No use worrying about this until she's done with the healers though."

"Right," Kurt agreed. "Come on, we should get the council gathered."

The pair left the tavern, squinting as they emerged back into the morning sun. They stood in the light for a few moments, unsure where they should go first to begin rounding up the council. Kurt made his decision and with Nul at his side, began to walk down the street, together making their way to talk with Cole at the smithy. Now that the entire town had woken up, the streets were much busier, making their walk a little more difficult. Not that the couple minded, since they were still receiving praise from most people who passed them by. Kurt was glad for the distraction though, since he didn't want to dwell on Lief's predicament right away.

As they were walking, Kurt noticed something about the people that passed them by. While it was subtle, the orcs and the people of Bismurr stayed apart from one another in the streets. His frustration grew as he looked on, realising that both sides were avoiding each other. Nul soon noticed that he was staring around at everyone that passed them by and followed his gaze.

"We need to deal with this," Kurt muttered.

"One problem at a time," Nul said, placing a hand on his back. Her touch calmed him a little, but he still felt a small simmer of anger as they continued walking.

The rest of their journey was uneventful and as the people in the streets began to thin out, Kurt even managed to calm down a little more. When they arrived at the smithy, everyone was too busy with their work to notice as the pair entered the building.

"Kurt! Good morning!" Cole called out, stepping from the shadows. "Good work last night. From what I've been hearing our side only received light injuries - that bodes well, eh?"

"I think we can thank our new allies for the win," Kurt replied, looking at Nul with a smile. "How're things? The defences around the town look like they're coming along great."

"They are indeed!" Cole exclaimed. "We're nearly done reinforcing the entrance to the mine as well. There might even be time to start trying to make ourselves a bit more comfortable down there."

"That's a good idea," said Nul. "Kurt's come up with an idea that might mean the mine will need to be a much better place to live, and soon."

"Oh?" Cole turned to Kurt.

"Maybe," Kurt replied. "Whatever we decide to do, we need to call a council meeting before we make a decision. We've got a lot to talk about if we want to be ready for Orlan's arrival, among some other things."

"Other things?" Cole asked, a little confused.

"I've noticed some things about how people are treating the orcs around town," said Kurt, trying to keep himself calm while he spoke. "We need to do something to bring everyone together. What's the point of fighting to get the town free if we're still treating each other the way the elves want us to?"

"I haven't noticed much of anything myself. Maybe a small amount of tension, but I'd assumed that was going to be inevitable," replied Cole, scratching his scruffy hair in thought. "But we can bring it up with the council if you feel we need to. I'll head off soon and get the others to the tavern for the meeting. I'll keep it quiet though, best not to have a crowd for this one."

"Thank you. We'll head over and wait for everyone," said Kurt. "Look around town when you get the chance. Really try and see how people are acting around one another."

Cole gave Kurt a nod as he walked past to a back room. Seeing that they were now alone in the workshop, the couple wandered back out onto the sunny streets. A chilly wind was starting to blow through the town, bringing dark grey clouds over their heads. The couple huddled closer together as they retraced their steps back to the Jumping Canary. As they were walking it started to rain, clearing the streets and forcing the couple to hurry back to the tavern as fast as they could. The tavern itself was still empty when they arrived, so Kurt set about dragging some chairs out to form a large circle. Nul went to the fireplace and started a small fire, spreading a warming orange glow across the dark room. Once they'd finished their work, the pair stood close to the fire, allowing themselves to dry off as they stared into the flames. Kurt and Nul enjoyed the quiet for a time, the sound of wood crackling away was soothing to both of them.

"Do you think your council is ready to deal with what's coming?" Nul asked, not looking up from the fire.

"We've all come a long way in a short amount of time," Kurt replied. "Even as we keep learning new things about our enemy, everyone here keeps proving themselves to be better everyday. If I thought we couldn't face down Orlan's army, I'd come up with another plan."

"Like what?" asked Nul, turning just a little to look at him.

"Before I might have suggested going up the mountain, covering our tracks with snow or something. Now? I think I'd plead with the Matriarch to let us move the town underground and blow up the entrance to the mine behind us,"said Kurt.

"I'd like to have seen you ask for that the first time you came to see us," Nul said with a laugh.

"Well I never said it was a smart idea," Kurt replied with a small laugh of his own. He placed his arm around Nul's waist and pulled her close to him.

"The council might arrive at any time," she warned, but didn't move away.

"I've been thinking," Kurt said, turning to face Nul. "I know we're both worried about what might happen, but how would you feel if we were discovered?"

"Honestly? I think a part of me wants to be found out," Nul replied. "But we need to think of what's best for the town, at least for the time being. We don't want to be the cause of people getting distracted, do we?"

"I suppose you're right," Kurt said with a disappointed sigh.

"When am I not?" Nul said with a smug grin. She gave Kurt a quick kiss before pulling away.

Kurt walked across the room feeling a little warmer - and not because Nul was adding more logs to the fire. He moved to the window and pulled the curtain back a little. The rain was coming down heavy and thick now, almost emptying the streets, but a short way down the road he could see hooded figures making their way towards the tavern. While Nul was still stoking the fire, he went to the door and waited for the other council members to get closer. After a few moments he heard some hurried damp footfalls from the other side. Kurt had time to open the door as the rain-sodden group pushed their way inside. One by one the council members took off their cloaks to hang them by the door and moved over to the fire to warm themselves. When they'd each decided they were warm enough, they all took a seat in the circle and after some brief muttering, everyone soon fell silent, waiting for someone to start the meeting. A small nervous knot was twisting in Kurt's stomach now, but he still rose to his feet, letting all eyes fall on him before he began.

"Thank you all for coming today. I did want to do this as soon as I came back, but obviously with the situation yesterday, we all had other priorities," Kurt said, keeping his voice a little quiet in case someone was braving the rain to eavesdrop.

"We're all quite happy with your return, young man," Ollie said, drawing everyone's attention. "While there was some suspicion about what was happening to you, the history we found in the southern ruins helped us trust in the orc judgement a little more. Seeing you here now though? I see you've been treated very well indeed."

"Well I have Nulkala here to thank for that," Kurt replied, gesturing to Nul who was leaning on the bar. She waved as everyone looked over at her.

"As lovely as this all is, let's get to the point of why we're here," Pete spoke up. He looked a lot better than the last time Kurt had seen him, his wounds had healed well, leaving only some faint scars across his face. "You said there were hundreds of those things coming for us. If that's true then we need a better plan than hiding in a hole and hoping they run out of bodies before we do."

"Don't be so dramatic," said Keiran, causing Pete to lean back on his chair to sulk. "But Pete does have a point. Even if our new allies took up the front line, we still need to survive a much larger force than we're prepared for."

"I have an idea about that," Kurt replied, his frustration resurfaced at Keiran's words. "But before we get to that, we need to deal with how people are treating the orcs."

"How we've been treating them?" said Melrose, with confusion in his voice. "We let them keep you, we allowed them to come through town and even let them fight with us. There has been years of fighting and distrust between us and them, we can't just expect that to disappear overnight."

"Maybe not, but don't act like you can't see what's happening around town," Kurt replied, struggling to keep his calm. "Out there on the streets people avoid them like they're something to be afraid of, where do you think that will lead?"

"Where will it lead? You don't think the orcs are going to stay if we manage to win this battle do you?" said Keiran, his question filled with venom.

"Wait, were we not going to let them come and go as they please?" Mary asked, looking around the room concerned. "I thought when this was over they'd be free from the mine if they wanted to be."

"You can't seriously think we'd allow those animals to come and go as they please?!" Keiran spat.

"Watch your mouth," Ollie warned, glancing over to Nul.

"My apologies Ollie, but I thought we were all clear on their role here?" Keiran replied, looking around the circle.

"Obviously not," Mary replied as she looked at the older man with disgust.

"ENOUGH!" Kurt shouted as he stood up. He waited until all eyes were on him before continuing. "The elves spent years doing what they could to divide everyone here, above and below the surface. If you continue to spread the same hate they had for us all, then what's the point in fighting to be free? The orcs are people, the same as you or me and they should be treated the same as everyone else in town. They shouldn't be made to fight instead of us, they need to be fighting with us," Kurt sighed and felt a little calmer as he spoke. "I came from a place where people who were no different from me were driven from their homes and treated worse than animals. It was disgusting, I was disgusting for even being a part of it. Seeing even the smallest chance of history repeating itself makes me doubt what we're doing here. So I need to know, what is the council's plan if we win the coming battle? I can't speak for everyone in Bismurr, but I don't want to be part of a place that refuses to treat people the way they deserve."

A stunned silence fell over everyone in the room as Kurt sat back down. Looking at each member of the council, most of them were looking down, deep in thought.

Keiran simply sneered as Kurt's eyes landed on him. Kurt turned his gaze to Nul instead, who was beaming at him. Kurt gave her a small smile in response before looking back at the council.

"I think it's time this council made a decision for our people," said Melrose, breaking the silence as he stood up. "Since there are differing opinions on this matter, I suggest we vote on this."

"Pointless," Keiran muttered, earning a few more scowls from others in the room.

"All those who want to allow the orcs to come and go as they please, raise your hand. All those who'd rather they be sent back below ground when this crisis is resolved, keep your hand down," Melrose said as he sat back down.

Kurt was the first to raise his hand but there was an odd pause in the room as everyone else spent a few moments thinking about their own decision. Soon enough though, Melrose and Mary raised their arms. Ollie was quick to follow along with Pete, Jessie, Cole and Tessa. Keiran folded his arms and glared around the room. Rick, the last council member yet to vote, leant forward in his chair.

"I'm undecided but I can see the council has made a decision," he said before leaning back again. Kurt couldn't tell if Rick was happy with the decision but he at least seemed willing to accept it.

"Well this is a waste of time!" spat Keiran as he stood up. "If this council is going make stupid decisions, I want no part in it."

Before anyone could respond, he strode across the room and walked back out into the rain, slamming the door behind him as he left. Despite Keiran's outburst, Kurt felt relieved that the rest of the council seemed to embrace the changes in Bismurr.

"It would appear there is now a free seat on the council," Ollie said with a disappointed shake of his head. "Nulkala, would you please take his seat?"

"Me?" Nul asked, a little taken aback.

"Indeed. We'll need one of your kind on the council if we're making decisions that affect us all," Ollie replied with a smile. "You'll need to talk with your people and see if there is someone who'd be better suited to join us, but for now it would probably be best to save time."

"Thank you," Nul said with an awkward bow. She hurried across the room and took Keiran's seat for herself. She looked uncomfortable with the sudden attention, but relaxed after a few encouraging nods from people around the room.

"Now, back to the matter in hand," said Melrose. The entire room felt like it was less tense, as though a weight had been lifted off the entire building. "Kurt, please continue."

"Firstly, thank you, all of you. I wasn't expecting so many of you to agree, I appreciate that. Secondly, we need to look over everything we're doing to prepare the town and make sure we are including orcs in all things," Kurt said, earning murmurs of agreement from everyone. "As for my plan to deal with such a large number of Dregs? I want to use the town itself as a trap."

"What do you mean?" asked Pete.

"I want to place sparking powder all over town, lure as many Dregs as possible and then blow them all to pieces," Kurt said. There was another stunned silence but he continued talking through it. "We'll need to time it carefully if we're going to use our forces to do this, but if it works? Orlan won't see it coming, and every able fighter can come out of the mine to finish off whatever is left standing."

"That's... quite the plan," said Melrose, still shocked, but considering the idea.

"You really think destroying our home is the best option?" asked Tessa, sadness filling her voice. "Even under the elves. control, this is all we've known. It's our home."

"That may be true, but what other options are there?" Cole asked, looking around the room. "I've been thinking of ways to combat such a large force and can't come up with anything that doesn't end in bloodshed. This plan? Might not just be our only option, it may be the very thing that keeps most of us alive."

"Sparking powder won't be enough," said Rick, his brow furrowed in thought. "But I think we can come up with some ways to increase the damage."

"We're really set on this then?" Tessa asked.

"I think we are," Ollie said. "As painful as it may seem to destroy our homes, protecting the people is the most important thing."

"I'm not sure it's the best idea either, Tessa, but we don't have time to argue," said Jessie, though she sounded reluctant, her voice was still warm and sympathetic. "Though I think convincing the rest of the town might be a problem."

"They'll listen," Melrose said, his stern expression implying an order rather than an assumption.

"We'll need to come up with a more detailed plan, but we can do that later," Cole said, scratching his tired eyes. "I think we should end this here for now and meet again in a few days."

"Agreed," replied Ollie, standing up. "Nulkala, will you talk to your people and find someone to sit on our council?"

"I will," Nul replied with a smile.

"Good. Kurt, I trust you'll take charge of making sure the orcs get mixed in with our own fighters?" Ollie asked.

"Of course," Kurt said.

"Then we're done," said Ollie. He let out a sigh and the old man seemed to shrink a little. "Keiran is probably going to try and gather some people who think like he does. Hopefully there won't be many but if everyone could do their best to convince people he's wrong, we could keep this under control."

"I'll speak to the hunters. They'll listen to me," said Pete. "What are we going to do if he keeps pushing against this?"

"Let's worry about that later, see what he does first," said Melrose, worry filling his voice.

The council was quiet as they donned their wet clothes and started to leave the tavern. Kurt held the door open as one by one they left, back out into the rain. They all gave him smiles and nods as they walked outside, except for Melrose who gave Kurt a couple of pats on the back before walking out as well. By the time he closed the door and turned around, Nul was already clearing the chairs away.

"That went better than I expected," Kurt sighing with relief. "I honestly thought more of them would have reacted much worse. Maybe not as bad as Keiran, but still."

"I really didn't like him," said Nul as she dragged the last chair away. "He just seemed so filled with hate for my kind, you know?"

"You know I do," Kurt replied, placing a hand on her shoulder. "There were plenty of men like him where I come from. I don't know him well enough to know if he can change though."

“You think someone like him can change?” Nul sneered.

“I hope so, otherwise what does that say about me?” Kurt said, feeling a little hurt at her words.

“Oh, please,” Nul said, rolling her eyes. “Don't start moping again. You're a good man, whether you think so or not.”

“Understood,” Kurt replied. He smiled to himself, even though he didn't agree with her, it was still nice to hear.

“I guess we're waiting for Lief to show up again?” Nul asked, moving closer to the fire.

“No sense going into the rain for nothing. I'm sure she'll hurry back as soon as she can though,” said Kurt. Nul nodded as she picked up a small log, pushing it deep into the flames with the poker.

Kurt moved over to the window and stared out into the rain and while a few people were walking through the streets, Lief was not among them. The pair stood in silence for a time, waiting whilst both deep in thought. As Kurt's thoughts wandered he found himself coming back to the problem of how to lure as many Dregs into the town as he could. A slight chill started to wash over him as he realised what they might need to do. He looked across the room at Nul, she had a content smile on her face whilst staring into the flames. Kurt decided against telling her what he was thinking, at least not right now. She seemed so happy in this moment that spoiling it just felt cruel.

He pushed the thoughts away for the time being and resumed looking out of the window. The raindrops were hypnotic, distracting enough that Kurt closed his eyes and listened to the water tapping against the glass. He only came back to senses when a figure came up to the door and started knocking frantically. Kurt rushed over and opened the way for a drenched Lief to barge her way inside. She seemed to be in better spirits as she hung her cloak up and hurried over to warm herself by the fire.

"H-how'd the council meeting go?" she asked, shivering a little as she spoke.

"Better than I thought," Kurt replied. He glanced at Nul before continuing. "Most of them agreed we need to treat our orc allies better and decided that once we make it through this coming battle, they'll be allowed to come and go as they please."

"Oh," Lief seemed confused for a moment and then became wide-eyed before turning to face Nul. "Is this about what I said before?"

"Words can only hurt if people mean them," Nul said. "Did you mean what you said? Truly?"

"I may have done a while back, but now? Not at all," Lief replied, looking downwards in shame.

"Then we're fine. All forgiven," Nul said with a smile. Lief looked up, dumbfounded.

"Just like that?" the dwarf asked in disbelief.

"I think we've all had to question everything we thought we knew about each other. Seems only fair to give someone at least one more chance, don't you think?" replied Nul.

"That's more than fair. Thank you, Nul," Lief took a breath and let out a sigh of relief.

"I take it you managed to get yourself looked over?" Kurt asked, distracting the ladies from their much-needed reconciliation.

"Yes I did." Lief replied. "I'm as healthy as I can be. Though I didn't tell her about the, I guess we can call it a gift?"

"Can you still use it?" Nul asked, once again walking around Lief like she was studying her.

"Seems so," replied Lief, and proved the fact by making a rock float from her pocket and hover in the air for a moment before Nul grabbed it.

"You seem less nervous about it now," Kurt said, scratching his chin in thought.

"It was terrifying at first, but once I was told I wasn't sick, I calmed down a lot," Lief replied. She managed a small smile. "I think I'm alright with it, happy even. Especially if I can maybe use this to help protect the town."

"About that, we're going to blow the town up," Nul said, smirking.

"What?!" Lief said, confused.

"It's a bit more complicated than that," Kurt explained. "We're going to lure as much of Orlan's Dreg army as possible into a trap. The details will need to be sorted, but everyone will be safe in the mine when we go through with it all."

"Seems a little extreme but I suppose it's only buildings, we can rebuild those," said Lief, scratching her head in thought.

"You don't need to worry about that for now though," Kurt said. "For now just focus on seeing what you could do with this new power. Secretly."

"Do I have to keep this a secret? I think people might be happy that we have another weapon to use," Lief replied.

"We don't know enough about any of this," said Kurt. "For all we know other people will try to repeat this and start trying to drink any Dreg blood they can find, which probably won't go well. Until we learn more, I really think we should keep this to ourselves."

"Speaking of learning more. Lief, do you know who's going through what you found in those ruins?" Nul asked.

"I think Ollie and a few others have them at the moment. Do you think they might mention something about all this?" Lief asked in reply.

"I'm not sure, but apparently they did mention the weavers so I'm wondering what else your people may have learned," Nul said, staring into the fire.

"We found those books and notes among ruins, so I doubt whatever they learned did them any good," said Lief, a hint of bitterness in her words.

"That doesn't mean we can't learn from them," Nul countered. "It might not be much but anything we could learn about the elves is worth knowing. Wouldn't you agree, Kurt?"

"You're right," Kurt replied. "We'll go and see what else they might have learned. Lief, can you please keep this a secret, at least for now?"

"Fine, fine," Lief agreed. "But if you find out anything that might be related to all this, you tell me straight away - whether it's good or bad."

"We will," Nul said with a smile, trying to lighten the mood. She looked to the window and her smile dropped a little when she saw the rain was still coming down strong. "Shall we leave now?"

"Might as well," Kurt replied with a sigh, also not eager to go back out into the cold rain. "Will you be alright Lief?"

"I'm a big girl, I think I'll be fine," she replied with a chuckle.

"Alright then. We'll see you soon," Kurt said, turning to leave.

He walked to the door and waited for Nul to join him before opening it up to the pouring rain that awaited them. Once again the couple huddled close together as they walked across the town to Ollie's home. Kurt hadn't been there in person but while he was training the recruits he'd heard about where all the council members lived. He suspected Ollie would be home, if the old man was in any way curious about looking over a lost trove of unknown history.

As the pair walked on, they both started to shiver, the freezing wind that battered against their waterlogged clothes was showing them no mercy. On the way through town Kurt noticed a group of orcs struggling against the weather to carry some large crates towards the mine, but they seemed to be in high spirits regardless. Their energy was infectious as Kurt started to smile as they passed by. It wasn't long before the pair reached the threshold of a small house at the eastern edge of Bismurr. Despite the fact the couple were wet and freezing, Kurt knocked and waited for someone to answer. After what felt like the longest few moments of his life, the door opened just a little to reveal Ollie looking more than a little confused. He stared at the couple on his doorstep before swinging the door open and gestured for them to come inside.

"Thank you!" Nul and Kurt said at the same time as they hurried inside the candle lit hallway.

"Wait here," Ollie said, closing the door before marching past them. "Let me grab you something to dry off with, I'll not have you dripping all over my house, and take off your damn muddy boots."

As the old dwarf disappeared around a corner, Kurt realised they had already tracked a lot of mud all over the hall. The pair removed their shoes and were only waiting for a moment before the old man returned holding two large blankets, and waved the couple to follow him through to the next room. After wrapping themselves in the warm fabric, taking care not to drip any more water on the floor, the pair walked into the cosy sitting room. Ollie took his place in a large armchair and pointed to two smaller wooden chairs for the other two to use. As they were about to sit down, Kurt noticed a table that was covered in some of the tattered pages that he'd seen back in the ruins.

"I wasn't expecting to see you both so soon after our meeting. What can I help you two with?" Ollie asked, frustrated that he was being disturbed.

"We were curious about what you've learned from those things found in the southern ruins?" Nul said. "We've heard they already mentioned some things that this town wasn't aware of before, so we're just wondering what else might be hidden in those pages."

"Oh I see!" Ollie lit up at Nul's enthusiasm. "We've found out a great deal of things - not all of it useful to our resistance efforts, but fascinating nonetheless. For instance, those ruins used to be a trading post for people passing through the region. It used to be a part of Bismurr! Most of the buildings there were made by stone harvested from our very own mountain. They even start to explain why our town is mostly built with--"

"Was there anything more about the elves? I'd heard the weavers were mentioned somewhere," Kurt interrupted, worried that the old man was going off-topic.

"There's many mentions of elves in the newest of the pages," Ollie replied, sighing with disappointment as he seemed to want to talk more about the buildings. "They only learned of the weavers when they saw people starting to turn against each other. Distrust, refusing to help one another, hoarding food, it all became rampant towards the end. They did manage to learn that those soldiers they turn into Dregs seem to be some sort of lower caste with lesser powers. Only when they were turned into monsters did they become a real threat, especially when they kept increasing in number. The ones like Orlan? They seem to be some sort of nobility, but still quite low within the elven society. It seems like the ones who have to go out into the world and perform tasks are some sort of lower class."

"So despite what Orlan says, he's actually not very important," Kurt said as he relaxed in his chair. To hear that his enemy wasn't as powerful as he made himself out to be, gave Kurt some relief. "Though if he manages to deal with us, it might improve his standing with the people he answers to."

"That's not likely to happen with the elves," Ollie explained. "You see, the people who lived here before did manage to learn more. It seems as though the more powerful an elf's magic, the higher value they hold in their society. It does seem like certain families always produce strong wielders of that power, but those families are very few in number - not sure how few exactly though. Those rankings don't seem to change often, whatever talent an elf is born with seems to be what they have for the rest of their life."

"How did these people find all of this out?" Nul asked.

"Ah now that is another interesting thing," Ollie said with a smile. "Some of what we found mentions when the elves first came to this region. They seemed to come in small numbers at first, simply as travellers, but once they understood the lay of the land, they changed their tune. Attacks from creatures, most likely Dregs, started to occur on the roads near town. So Bismurr decided to send a group to the east to investigate the elves - and when they eventually returned? They had learned more of these strange visitors and their true intentions. Of course by then it was far too late to do anything."

"It's a bit strange how they seem to come to town in smaller numbers as the years passed," Nul said, tilting her head in confusion.

"No need for more of their people I suppose, as long as someone comes along once in a while to keep us in our place," replied Ollie, scratching his chin in thought for a few moments before continuing. "What I find most interesting is that I find no reference to any kind of weapons that our people would have used, and I find it hard to believe the group that went to see what our enemies were doing were unarmed. Doesn't that seem strange to you?"

"Maybe they had some other means to defend themselves?" Nul said, shooting Kurt a knowing look.

"I guess we'll never know," Kurt muttered while shaking his head, hoping Nul would get the hint. "Was there anything else? Anything more about the elves?"

"Nothing that we don't already know, but we've so many more pages to go over so there's no telling what else we might find," Ollie said, stifling a yawn. "I'd rather like to return to my nap unless there's something else?"

"No, I think that'll be all," Kurt replied. "Thank you for seeing us we appreciate it."

"You're welcome," Ollie said with a small nod. "Now please leave an old man to get his rest."

The dwarf didn't get up to see his guests out, but Kurt and Nul obliged his request and left the room to don their mud-caked shoes. The couple were both thankful the rain had stopped as they walked back out onto the damp street. While the light was starting to dim, there was still a long while before the evening so Kurt and Nul started the journey back to their home. They walked in silence through the town, each of them thinking about what they had learned. Once they had reached the forest, Kurt remembered something he was curious about.

"Nul," said Kurt, breaking the silence. "Can I ask you something about your people?"

"Of course," Nul replied, turning to look at him.

"I've noticed you're much stronger than the others. I know that the female orcs are strong, but you seem to have so much more strength than any of the others. I was thinking over the memories we shared but I still don't understand," said Kurt.

"Ah, that." Nul's expression looked pained for a second, but she took a moment and let out a long breath before talking. "When your kind or my kind train, we become faster and stronger - but with one small difference. My kind has much higher limits than yours."

"Alright, but why are you so much stronger than the others I've seen?" Kurt asked.

"Because of my father," Nul replied, stopping in her tracks.

"That monster?" Kurt stopped also and turned to face Nul. "From what I saw all he did was abuse and hurt you."

"True," said Nul, her eyes welling up as she remembered her past. "But there was a point to all his anger. He wanted me to be strong. Stronger than anyone else. So he pushed harder and harder, breaking me down over and over again, right up until the day he died. And do you know what the ironic thing is about all that pain? It didn't even make me the strongest of my people. The Matriarch and a few others can make that claim, but not me."

"Getting strength that way was wrong," Kurt said through gritted teeth. He didn't know where to direct his anger, but did his best to let it go as he pulled Nul into a tight hug.

"I know," Nul whispered in his ear. She gave him a small squeeze before breaking away, a warm smile on her face. "But as far as I'm concerned if I can at least help the two of us and this town then all that pain was worth it."

Kurt had no response as she resumed walking through the forest. He stood frozen in place for a few moments, stunned and amazed at her attitude. Having experienced her memories, he had no idea how she could keep bouncing back with joy but was glad when she did; it made him happy to see her smile. Kurt had fallen quite far behind while he'd been staring so he ran to catch up with her. Nul laughed as he caught up and pulled him close to walk arm in arm for the rest of the way.

When they got back inside, Kurt started a fire while Nul stepped into the kitchen. By the time he was done, she presented him with some hot tea he'd forgotten was there. The pair changed into dry clothes and spent a long while in thought, warming themselves by the fire. It wasn't until Nul's stomach broke the silence with a huge gurgling noise that they realised how much time had passed. Kurt looked to the kitchen but thought better of spoiling their appetite before heading to Cali's for dinner. The light from the window was already beginning to fade to a soft orange glow as they quickly grabbed their thick jackets and left their home once again to head back into town.

Despite the now-biting cold of the evening air, they rushed through the forest as the thought of the meal Cali was preparing made their growing hunger almost painful. Their brief journey was nothing more than a blur as they came up to the door of the bakery. It swung open just as they were about to knock and a wave of delicious smells engulfed them, leaving them both trying not to drool on Cali's head as she greeted them with a warm hug each. She then pulled them inside and within a few minutes the three of them were talking and laughing over the huge spread that Cali had prepared.

She'd laid out such a huge array of pies, sweet pastries, fruits and cheeses, that the two tables that held everything looked like they were going to collapse at any moment. There were even a few bottles of spiced wines to choose from, which after a few sips left everyone very red in the face. As the evening gave way to night, they ate their fill of food, drank their way through cup after cup wine and even started to sing, leaving them all giggling at the slightest slurred word or hiccup. Their merriment continued well into the night, only coming to a close when Cali fell asleep with a bottle in hand, snoring so loud it was a mystery how she didn't wake herself. Being careful not to wake her, Kurt and Nul stumbled their way out of Cali's house.

Their journey back was something of a haze but the couple were soon tumbling through the front door of their home, giggling all the while. It wasn't long before they gathered some blankets and cuddled together in front of the last embers of the dying fire. Too tired and full of food, Kurt and Nul drifted into a drunken slumber. While they slept, the cold wind outside brought a frost across the forest outside. Little by little a soft white topping of snow began to spread across the treetops. As the white coat grew it began reflecting the bright moonlight, illuminating the entire valley and its surrounding forest. Winter had come to Bismurr, and the townsfolk shivered in their sleep.

# 19

Over the next couple of weeks the town changed to match the season. People began wearing heavier clothes, making the work slower but with certain people passing out warm drinks, they remained in good spirits. Most of the town's food had been moved to the mine along with the remaining livestock, leaving the farms surrounding Bismurr eerily empty. With the orcs' help the entrance to the mine was reinforced with enough metal, wood and stone to seal it off forever if the town wanted. Each of the squads that Kurt had helped form had doubled in size with a mix of orc, dwarf and human fighters. A new tavern had also been built in the mine, taking all its supplies from the Jumping Canary, leaving the building empty save for the occasional council meeting. Despite all their necessities having been moved into the mine, the streets of Bismurr were still busy with people preparing for the battle to come.

"You know another thing I hate about snow?" Nul asked Kurt as they were trudging their way into town.

"I know I should start making a list," he muttered to himself.

"It makes everything that touches it just so damp," Nul said, ignoring Kurt as he sighed with annoyance.

"Can we please focus?" Kurt asked. He'd grown tired of hearing that same question every day since the snow had first appeared.

"Fine, but I still don't appreciate having to walk through this cold slush every day,"

Nul replied, folding in her arms with a dissatisfied grunt.

"I know you don't, but after today we should be able to take a break for a few days," Kurt said, patting her on the shoulder.

"We'd better," she mumbled, shrugging away his hand.

Kurt knew she was still sulking but knew better than to press further; better to focus on the meeting that was waiting for them in town. The council had been arguing back and forth on the best way to execute his plan for almost a week now and in that time they'd made no progress at all. Kurt could understand Nul's frustrations as they were something he shared over recent days. He pushed those feelings down when they entered the town, making sure to exchange smiles and polite nods to anyone they happened to pass by in the streets. Kurt didn't want the people in town to think that he and the council didn't have everything in hand. The couple entered the tavern and were greeted to the familiar sound of raised voices bickering amongst each other.

"--and I'm telling you that there isn't enough powder to waste on experimenting with your foolish idea!" yelled Cole, who upon seeing Kurt and Nul arrive to take their seats, took a breath and waited for them to get situated.

"It's not foolish. We need to make sure anything we build is going to work, so of course we need to test it first otherwise everything could fall apart when the Dregs start running rampant," Rick countered. He didn't acknowledge the new arrivals as he continued arguing with his brother.

"Enough for now," Ollie said, rubbing his brow to nurse his growing headache. "Baku, any reports from the scouts?"

"Nothing yet. Wherever that elf is coming from, we've still got plenty of time," the large orc replied. He looked over to Kurt and Nul and nodded in greeting. Baku had joined the council at the Matriarch's order and while he seemed bored most of the time, he was doing a good job making sure the orc's voices were being heard.

"On a lighter note, we're completely finished moving everything into the mine," said Jessie, leaning back in her chair as though she had only just finished the task. "A few people don't want to leave their homes until it's necessary but when the time comes, they'll head underground with no complaints."

"We should stop calling it that. It's clearly a shelter now and I'm sure no one has any plans to start using it as a mine again," said Pete, earning some murmuring agreement from the room.

"Well people aren't making any plans at all," Mary muttered to herself.

"What was that?" Ollie asked, drawing the attention of the entire room onto Mary.

"I said people aren't making any plans," Mary repeated with a raised voice, taking the time to look around at the other council members. "Everyone is hoping to make it through this coming fight but no one is thinking about their future beyond that. People are being made to uproot their lives and be shepherded around like farm animals. If this keeps up, I dread to think how they'll be after being made to live in tunnels and caves for goodness knows how long."

"Hmm. That won't do, not at all," Ollie said whilst stroking the scruffy grey hairs on his chin.

"That's an easy thing to solve," said Nul, looking around the room with a confused expression. "People need a distraction. Something where they can just enjoy themselves without needing to think about what's coming."

"Not a bad idea," said Mary. "Doesn't have to be very impressive I suppose, just a lot of food and drink will probably do the job. I'm sure once the drink starts flowing people will get into the spirit of things."

"They'll need more than that," Kurt said. An idea then dawned on him. "We should get people to start thinking of a new town to build. No matter how the coming battle goes, the town as it is now won't be here when we're done. I think if people feel like they can rebuild Bismurr into something new then maybe they'll start to look forward to the future again."

"You think that'll be enough?" Ollie asked.

"It's a start at least," Cole answered. "Now for any of this to actually mean anything, we need to agree on the final plan for the town."

"We've argued back and forth on this for far too long, so let's just put it to a vote and we can be done with this," said Rick, the tired bags under his eyes almost growing larger as he looked around the room.

"Fine," Cole replied. "We've got mostly everything planned except for how we're going to place the last of the sparking powder. I suggest we simply place barrels all over town and lay out enough dry firewood to make sure there's fires burning when the first blast is done."

"And I want to build a few special barrels that burn hotter and spread fire without the need to waste wood we could use elsewhere," said Rick. "I just need to get the formula balanced first."

There were a few moments of silence as each council member thought to themselves but soon enough everyone was looking at Cole and murmuring their agreement.

"It's decided then," said Ollie as he shot Rick a stern look, who simply sighed but nodded his agreement to the plan.

"So how long do you think it'll take to plan this feast?" Mary asked, now smiling with excitement as she changed the subject to something she had more control over.

"Well in the interest of building something new, we can provide some of the food and maybe some music," Baku spoke up, everyone in the room murmured with approval.

"I think we'll end this here then," Ollie said, standing up. "I don't think we'll need to call any more of these meetings until after we deal with the coming attack, so I just want to thank you all. No matter what happens, I'm proud of what we tried to do here."

There was a brief moment of silence before people in the room started clapping with smiles on their faces. Kurt felt a little lighter as well, knowing that they were done planning the town's defence put his mind more at ease. The council began to leave the tavern one by one, a few of them already discussing what food they wanted to see at the feast, Cole and Rick on the other hand were already arguing about the best places to stash barrels across the town. Kurt and Nul were the last to leave, wrapping their coats tightly over themselves to brace against the cold. Even though the sun was still shining through the small gaps between the clouds, it had started to snow again. Nul grunted her disapproval as they walked, but otherwise she kept quiet as they made their way through town.

The pair tried to stop by Cali's bakery for some warm food but had second thoughts when they saw the large crowd of people waiting outside. Judging by the pile of weapons propped up by the front door, some of the squads had the same idea and were taking a break from training to warm themselves up. Coming in and out of the building was Cali, looking pleased to see such a large crowd as she walked between people, handing out small pies to everyone. Kurt heard his stomach growl as he watched a few people eat. Nul was having the same issue as she grabbed Kurt by the arm and marched through the crowd until they reached the open door to the bakery. As they entered, Cali was already placing another tray of baked pies onto a table to cool. Although she was already smiling, she lit up even more when she saw Nul and Kurt.

“Ah! I wasn't expecting you two today!” Cali exclaimed as she rushed forward to hug the couple.

“Well since this one decided to drag me out into the snow again, where else are we going to go?” Nul asked with a smile.

“Oh shush,” Cali said as she squeezed Nul with a tight hug. She pulled away and from nowhere revealed two pies which she handed over to the eager couple. They didn't hesitate and started devouring the hot pastries, almost drooling on the floor while they ate. Cali disappeared for a brief moment only to return with yet another tray of pies.

“Why so much food?” Kurt asked once he finished the last bite of his own pie.

“Well since you lot decided we need to move into the mine I figured I would bake the last of my stock before finishing up,” Cali replied. She looked around the room and a brief flicker of sadness lessened her warm smile but only for a moment. “I've got one more batch cooking and then I'm done.”

“I hope they've got something prepared for you in the shelter, people are going to need some good food soon,” said Nul.

“Oh? You know something I don't?” Cali said with a raised eyebrow.

“The council decided that since we have some time, we're going to have a little party. Have people think about what they want the town to be like when this is all over,” Kurt explained. “And of course if we're having a party we'll need the best cook in town to help out.”

“Well if I found I wasn't making the food for such an event, I think I'd be pretty mad,” Cali laughed.

“Not to mention you can think about rebuilding all this into something new when you come back here,” Nul said as she pocketed another pie from the table.

“I don't even want to think about that just yet,” Cali said, again looking around the room with a mix of emotions on her face. “My husband and I built this place. Even if the elves were making sure we cooked enough food to supply the town, it was still our place, you know?”

“Whatever you want to do, we'll be here for you,” Kurt said with a smile. Cali winding him as she moved forward and pulled him down for yet another hug.

“You'd better be,” she muttered as she pulled away to head back into the kitchen.

“What's next for us today?” Nul asked, looking over at the door to the outside with a slight frown.

“I have to check in with the squad leaders, make sure everyone is ready to get the town evacuated when the time comes, but nothing after that,” Kurt said, helping himself to another pie.

“In that case, do you mind if I head through the shelter and talk with some of my people?” Nul asked. “I think they'd like to be involved with this party, it'll definitely be good to get more of us up here when fighting isn't the only thing going on.”

“That's a good idea,” Kurt responded. “I should really get going, see you at home later?”

“I'm not meeting you or anyone else in this horrible weather,” Nul said with a grimace. She then looked to the door and once she was sure no one was going to come inside, she gave Kurt a quick kiss on the cheek.

He was smiling as he walked back outside, ignoring the chilly wind that had started blowing through the town. Kurt followed some of the squad members, who had finished their own food and were making their way back to the defence encampment that had been formed over the past weeks. Thanks to the orcs who had joined, they'd managed to flesh out their training area with wooden mannequins, new weapons and several more supply tents to keep all the fighters equipped and ready. Kurt separated from the group and headed towards the command tent, which had now become much larger with tall wooden posts holding up each corner. As he approached, Kurt could hear muffled voices from inside. Pulling back the thick fabric door, he stepped into the dark tent. Once the fabric fell down behind him, it took a moment for his eyes to adjust to the dim light. The inside of the tent hadn't changed too much, but they had added various rugs and candles to make it warmer. As Kurt took off his coat he saw that Lief and Peyton were the only two people inside, they had gone quiet when he entered but went back to their discussion while he was still brushing the snow off of himself.

“And you're sure there's nothing coming from any other direction?” Peyton asked.

“I've had a few people head south past the ruins and they've found nothing. The mountain is too dangerous to climb now that winter is here, people would lose their way too easily. A few scouts did manage to climb up some of the way though, they didn't see a thing,” Lief replied, whilst marking the map in front of them. “We even had a few people head west, all they found was animal tracks.”

“Good, good,” muttered Peyton, scratching his head in thought.

“Nice to have another piece of good news,” Kurt said as he sat down.

“Council meeting went well, I take it?” asked Lief as she finished scrawling some notes on the map.

"Very well," said Kurt. "We decided on a couple of things, but the important one is that we finally agreed on how we're going to set the sparking powder all through the town."

"We were just talking about that," said Lief, looking over to Peyton.

"Yes. We've been thinking about how best to lure the most amount of Dregs into the town and we realised something," said Peyton. Kurt already knew what he was going to say next. "We're going to need bait."

"I've been thinking the same thing," Kurt said with a sigh. "I'm the one that started this, so I'm going to be the one staying behind to make sure it ends."

"Not alone you're not," said Peyton, leaning forward to meet Kurt's gaze. "Besides, we came up with an idea that would be a little better than leaving someone to die."

"What?" asked Kurt, confused.

"We'll need to talk to Cole about making the parts we need, but we think we can build a sort of underground chamber out of some Valentail-treated metal," Peyton explained. "It wouldn't have much room, but it should protect anyone, assuming they can get inside in time."

"It'll still be dangerous," said Kurt, but as he thought about it, the more the idea started to seem workable.

"Timing would be the most important thing," Lief said, a smile forming on her face. "But if we do this right, we can really take Orlan by surprise and end the bastard."

"What do you think?" Peyton asked, looking apprehensive.

"I think I might need to stand down and let you two take charge from now on,"

Kurt replied with a small laugh. "Talk to Cole as soon as you can and get this thing built."

"I'll get on that now, I need to check in with the other squad leaders anyway," said Peyton, standing up.

"One more thing before you leave," Kurt said. "The council also decided that while we have time, we're going to have a feast, a celebration of sorts. People need to have some fun, so spread the word."

"A party?" Lief asked, as Peyton left them and walked out into the snow. "Not a bad idea. I might even have a few tricks to keep the kids entertained."

"Speaking of your tricks," Kurt fell silent for a moment, listening to make sure no one else was coming into the tent. "How is your other training coming along?"

"I'm getting stronger every day," Lief said, pointing at a stone on the table. The stone then began to float and spin in the air as she twirled her finger back and forth. After a few moments of making it dance across the table, she clenched her hand into her fist and the stone broke apart as though it had been smashed by a hammer.

"Do you think you could use it in a fight?" Kurt asked, impressed at the display.

"Oh definitely," Lief said with a smile. "Though I wish I could share this with a few more people. Keeping this a secret has been annoying to say the least."

"Well once this fight is over, everyone is going to know," Kurt said, patting her on the shoulder. He looked over the map, taking note of all the changes since he'd seen it last. "These eastern towers are further out than I thought. How recent can a report from them be?"

"They have a signal fire ready to go if they see Orlan's forces, so we'd see that straight away if it gets lit. As for anything else, we have people going back and forth at least once a week to change shifts," replied Lief, tracing the route on the map with her finger. "Of course if they end up lighting the fire, I imagine we'll see them a lot sooner."

"We should make sure whoever goes out there next gets something of a reward for missing the party," said Kurt.

"Good idea," Lief agreed."I'll handle that, might even go myself."

"Fair enough," Kurt replied. "I'm going to take a walk, unless there's anything else?"

"Nothing that I can't handle by myself," said Lief.

Kurt nodded and got up to grab his coat. He looked back one last time to see Lief staring at the map, muttering under her breath. Kurt didn't disturb her as he stepped back out into the cold. Knowing that Nul wasn't going to come home any time soon, he didn't feel a need to return there himself just yet. He soon found himself wandering around the outskirts of Bismurr.

When Kurt had first arrived here the snow had melted but seeing the white-coated landscape felt familiar to him. He couldn't figure out why for a short while but then he remembered. It looked like his old home. He couldn't believe he had almost forgotten what his home used to look like but as he stared out over the snow-covered fields, those memories began to flood back into his mind. Playing as a child, snowball fights, gathering around a fire that was far too small to warm his family and huddling together for warmth during the colder nights of winter as their meagre meals were never quite enough to fill their bellies. Even though life back then was hard, Kurt couldn't help himself from reminiscing about some of the more happy times, or at least the times before he learnt about anything else happening in the world.

As he continued his walk around the town he spotted a few children play-fighting near what looked like a collapsed attempt at a snowman. The children stopped what they were doing when they noticed Kurt was watching them. He smirked as he walked on by, happy to see children just acting like children for a change. The sounds of their playing resumed as he got further away, fading into the noise of people moving around Bismurr. Not wanting to be pulled back to his worries just yet, Kurt made sure to keep on the outer streets of the town. It had been a while since he'd been alone with his thoughts. Not that he was unhappy about having people in his life care about him, but some time to clear his head without being distracted was nice. Kurt stopped thinking about anything in particular and just let himself enjoy the fresh air as each chilled breath he took refreshed him.

It wasn't until the sun began to set that Kurt came back to his senses and realised how much time he'd spent wandering. As the townsfolk nearby began getting back inside their homes to settle in for the night, he decided to do the same. Walking through the forest back to his cabin was slow going, as his lack of attention through the day had made his feet start to go numb. Kurt didn't mind though, he was in too good of a mood to let a bit of cold bother him, though in the time it took him to hobble his way home, the sun had sunk away behind the trees, taking the last of the day's warmth with it. When a shivering Kurt reached the end of the forest path, he saw Nul waiting outside the house cradling a hot drink, the steam from it spreading out like a small fog.

"You're late back," she said, taking a sip from her cup.

"I lost track of time," Kurt said. Despite how cold he was now, he didn't rush to get past Nul. He eyed her hot drink and all he wanted was one of his own. "Can we get inside? I'm freezing."

"We can, in a second," Nul said with a smile. "I have a surprise for you."

"Oh?" Kurt said, shivering. "Can I be surprised in the warm?"

“Come here,” said Nul, holding out a hand for him to take. “Close your eyes.”

Kurt did as she asked and felt himself being led inside. He almost melted when he crossed the threshold as the heat from the fire inside had been burning for a long while, filling the home with a much-needed warmth. Nul let go of his hand to close the door behind him and then guided him forward a few more steps before stopping him.

“Now open them,” she whispered.

Kurt opened his eyes, squinting for a moment as his eyes adjusted to the brighter light. His jaw dropped as he looked around his now-unrecognisable home.

Hanging from the ceiling were dozens of coloured streamers made of paper and fabrics. There were several new thick blankets laid over the chilly wooden floorboards, making the room look much more cosy and inviting. From the kitchen he could smell something he'd not smelled in over a decade, the smell of a beef and carrot stew like his mother used to make every winter. But standing in the corner of the room was the thing that shocked Kurt the most. A large tree, almost completely wrapped in green and red fabric strips, with a variety of carved wooden animals hanging from its branches, along with some small glowstones that glimmered in the firelight. Kurt was stunned at the sight of it all, but when he did manage to turn around to look at Nul, she was wearing the biggest grin he'd ever seen on her.

“You did all of this?” Kurt asked, not knowing what else to say.

“I did,” Nul replied, beaming at her work with pride. “You like it?”

“This is amazing,” Kurt replied, looking around the room, still trying to take it all in. “How? Why did you do all of this?”

“It's something that I've been thinking about since the Vastupa,” Nul explained as she moved to the kitchen to pour out some drinks for the two of them. "In your memories, I saw that you hadn't done this for years, even before you arrived in Bismurr. I just felt like it was something you missed doing, so I wanted to take something good from your old home and bring it here."

"And my mother's stew?" Kurt asked, stumbling forward to sit down whilst discarding his coat and boots on the floor.

"Oh, I just thought that looked delicious so I wanted to try some," Nul said with a smile.

"This is..." Kurt felt himself starting to well up with tears and couldn't think of anything to say. The feeling of love that Nul had filled the room with was a struggle for him to accept.

"Why don't we sit down, eat a meal and sit by the fire?" Nul asked, pushing Kurt down into a chair before moving to the kitchen to pour the stew into two bowls.

After a short while, Kurt regained his composure and began to enjoy himself. Nul had poured him a cup of Berry-Finka she'd managed to hide away until now, the warm taste relaxing him and helping him sink further into his warm chair. When he took his first bite of the stew, he almost lost himself again at the taste as memories of many winters from his childhood filled him. While they ate, the couple also managed to go through the entire bottle of Finka and as Kurt was settling by the fire, ready to fall asleep on the spot, Nul pulled a second bottle out of nowhere. They only managed to share half a glass each before they were moving across the room, hurrying to get to the bed while peeling their clothes off. As they clung to each other, the fire struggling to stay alight, the cold winter air forced them to hide away under the blankets. The night grew colder once the fire collapsed into embers, but Kurt and Nul didn't notice a thing, wrapped tightly in each other's warm embrace.

# 20

It didn't take the town long to prepare for a celebration. Within two days the people of Bismurr had already built a large tent in a now-unused field. When the day of the party arrived, the whole town erupted in delicious smells as everyone decided to cook something to bring with them. The entrance to the mine was bustling with orcs coming out, all of them carrying some sort of food, drink or musical instrument to share in the festivities.

By the time Kurt and Nul were arriving into town, the excitement in the air was palpable. As the couple passed through the streets filled with happy-looking people, Kurt could see how even trying to throw a party was affecting everyone for the better. Even Nul had nothing to say about walking through the snow as they arrived at the main tent.

"Kurt! Nul!" A voice called out, followed by the sounds of several complaints as a large figure pushed their way through the crowd.

"Baku!" Nul exclaimed, rushing forward to greet him. "How's everything going? No problems setting up?"

"Not one," replied Baku, ignoring the angry voices behind him.

"I'm surprised to see so many of us above-ground." Nul said. "I know a few more of us have been curious about coming up here, but I didn't think it would be so many."

"Things have been changing in our home, Nul," said Baku, glancing toward the entrance of the mine-turned-shelter. "Ever since we started coming up and helping

to defend this town, our people have started asking questions whenever someone returns. Even the Matriarch has been getting curious."
"Any issues with the townsfolk and your people?" Kurt asked.

"Not really. A few disagreements over pathetic things, but nothing so bad that anyone felt a need to step in and deal with it," Baku replied. The large orc then smiled and placed a hand on Kurt's shoulder. "I've been keeping an eye on anyone stepping over the line, so don't worry yourself, we've got it handled."

"Thank you," said Kurt.

"Not a problem," Baku said, stepping back. He looked into the crowd and rolled his eyes when someone dropped a large crate onto the floor, spilling its contents of fruits and nuts under the feet of other people trying to unpack their own additions to the feast. "I need to deal with that. Have fun you two, hopefully I'll see you later."

Baku dashed off, ordering people to move back or to stop what they were doing to help clean up the mess. Both Kurt and Nul smirked at the sight of him acting like a parent to a group of adults. The chaos was dealt with and the crowd resumed setting up various tables and seats along with a large wooden stage that took up the entire back portion of the tent. A few orcs had begun setting up a large variety of instruments on one side of the stage, and Mary stood on the other side, looking over everything in sight and marking things off on several sheets of paper.

A familiar smell filled Kurt's nostrils and his stomach growled in response. Looking at the entrance he spotted Cali pushing a large cart packed with several crates – all of which were almost overflowing with cakes, pies, rolls and a few other delicious-looking things that Kurt hadn't seen before. Seeing her struggle to move the cart into the tent, Kurt hurried over to help.

"I don't think anyone expected you to feed the entire town," he said with a laugh as he moved alongside her to push the cart.

"What did you expect I was gonna do?" Cali replied between panting breaths. Together they pushed the cart to a free space that Nul had managed to clear.

"Are you sure you made enough stuff?" Nul asked, as she leaned forward to look at the mountain of food.

"I could take all this back you know," said Cali, slapping Nul's hand to make her drop the pie she was attempting to take. "Now both of you help me get all this ready."

The three of them proceeded to transform the cart into something almost resembling a stall. By the end of it all Cali was red in the face, sitting on an upturned barrel. Even Kurt was a little short of breath when he placed the last crate down, so he could only guess how Cali had managed to get all of the food out of the shelter by herself. Nul was eating a pie from the top of the display she'd constructed out of a variety of other baked goods when someone called her name from across the tent. Kurt didn't see who called, but Nul did as she shrugged at him while mumbling something unintelligible. She disappeared into the crowd, leaving Kurt and Cali to rest. Everyone else in the tent had also finished setting up, there was even a band on the stage starting to tune their instruments.

"It was good of you to help sort all this," Cali said, having caught her breath. "I think it's just what people needed."

"I hope so," Kurt muttered.

"You alright Kurty?" Cali asked, concern in her voice.

"I'm fine, just a little distracted is all," Kurt said, shaking his head a little as though he could push his worries out of his mind.

"Well try and enjoy yourself, you deserve to have a little bit of peace before you go off to fight again," said Cali as she gave his hand a comforting squeeze.

"You take some time for yourself as well," Kurt replied with a smile. "If I find out you spent the entire evening here just giving people your delicious food, I'll be having words with you."

Cali laughed and gave him a small thump on the shoulder. Soon enough the band started to play, causing the tent to erupt in cheers. The music was slow at first but the tunes were all happy-sounding ones, which coupled with slowly spreading drinks, put anyone coming and going from the tent into high spirits. Even Kurt got into the spirit of things, enjoying a cup of wine whilst tapping his foot along with the songs being played. He'd found a quiet spot near the entrance to the tent, watching people arrive, raising his mug in greeting whenever someone noticed him. No one paid him much mind as the sounds of music and smells of food were too enticing to ignore. Kurt didn't mind though, he was content to watch people enjoy themselves. He was pleased to see the orcs and the townsfolk getting along as though they'd been friends for years. Night fell as the party started to get into full swing, with people starting to laugh and dance all around. Kurt smiled as he drained the last of his cup, letting the warmth of the drink stave off the cold night air.

"Want another?" said a voice from behind him. His smile grew larger when he turned to see Nul with her own mug in one hand and a new bottle of wine in the other.

"Of course," Kurt replied, letting her refill his cup. "Enjoying yourself?"

"I am. I just missed you is all," Nul muttered. "This is nice, seeing my people up here, like this is how we've always lived our lives."

"Agreed," said Kurt with a smile. "I'm glad we made this happen. It's nice to do something normal and fun for a change."

"Well I think you and I have been having plenty of fun regardless," Nul said with a raised eyebrow.

"That's true," Kurt replied with a small laugh. "But you know what I mean."

As the couple were about to walk away from the party, the music inside the tent abruptly stopped and raised voices began to echo out into the night. For a moment Kurt and Nul considered walking away but as the voices grew in volume along with the sound of smashing glass, they sighed with resignation. They walked back inside to discover a crowd of people had formed in the middle of the tent, surrounding someone who was arguing with anyone who strayed too close. As the couple approached, a few people from the back of the crowd moved away to let them through. Stood in the centre, swinging a half-drunk bottle of some clear spirit was Keiran Stone, hurling insults at people he recognised. Kurt sighed again and stepped forward drawing Keiran's attention.

"Oh and here he is, our precious hero!" Keiran spat, swaying as he walked forward.

"I think you've had enough. Time for you to head home," said Kurt.

"You don't get to tell me what to do!" Keiran replied, jabbing Kurt in the chest with the bottle. "If everyone here knew what you really are, do you think they'd still fall in line to do whatever you say?!"

"Everyone here asked me to help and I did," said Kurt. "Despite that, I'm not going to pretend that people didn't get hurt because of me before I came here."

"I'm not talking about that!" Keiran said through gritted teeth. He then shot a glare over Kurt's shoulder before leaning close so only the two of them could hear him.

"What?" Kurt asked, confused. He looked over his shoulder to see Nul staring, her fists clenched as she waited to see what was going to happen. He turned back to see a twisted grin spread across Keiran's face.

“Do you want to tell everyone here about what you've really been doing? Or do you want me to?” he hissed into Kurt's ear.

“Don't do this,” Kurt muttered as a cold sobering sensation washed over him.
“Don't do what?” Keiran stepped back to look around at the crowd. “Don't tell everyone here the truth about you and this orc whore?!”

There was a few gasps from the crowd followed by hushed muttering. Kurt turned to see Nul with a look of shock and anger on her face. A part of him wanted to take her away and leave the tent, but Keiran's words pushed Kurt.

“Fine. You want the truth?” Kurt took a step forward and turned slowly to speak to the crowd. “Me and Nul are together. We have been since before I returned to the surface.”

“So you admit that you and this whore have been treating this town like fools?!” said Keiran, a smug grin now plastered to his face.

“No,” Nul said, stepping forward to stand alongside Kurt. “We didn't know how the town would react and we didn't want to add another problem for these people to deal with.”

There was more muttering from the crowd and Kurt couldn't see anyone looking angry or disgusted. In fact, judging by the faces of the closest people, everyone was just staring at the situation unfolding in front of them, unsure how to respond.

“We never intended to lie to any of you. Once Orlan and his army were dealt with, we planned on telling the truth about this,” Kurt said to the crowd before turning to look at Nul. “But when you're in love, you don't always make the smartest choices.”

"Love?! With this orc whore? Don't make me laugh," Keiran spat.

"I think we've heard just about enough from you," said Cali from the back of the tent. Her voice, though muffled, still had the crowd murmuring in agreement.

"You're all fine with this?!" Keiran asked the crowd angrily. "This is disgusting! Unnatural! How could any of you be fine with this?!"

"That's enough," said Kurt, stepping up to the taller man. "You might be drunk, but if you don't finish talking right now, then you're going to have trouble."

"What did you say to me?!" Keiran hissed, dropping his bottle and walking forward to square up to Kurt. "You think you're a big man?! Think you're gonna prove to all these people that you're somehow right just because you win a fight?"

"I don't really care about any of that at this point," Kurt said, his own anger fighting to take control. "But I was raised with some manners so I'm just giving you one last chance to walk out of here, which is far more than you deserve right now."

"One last chance?! You're pathetic. Why don't you do this town a favour and take your filthy orc whore back under the dirt where you both belong!" Keiran said, his voice filled with anger and venom.

"Kurt," Nul placed her hand on his shoulder with a tight grip, stopping him from moving forward. "As much as we both want to. We shouldn't do this."

"Stay out of this!" Keiran said. He then turned to the crowd. "All of you stay out of this! If none of you have the guts to admit how wrong this is, then I'll do it myself!"

The drunk Keiran then swung a fist towards Nul. Even though she leaned back to dodge the blow, it wasn't anywhere close to touching her - Kurt had broken free of her grasp and lunged forward with enough force to floor the taller man. The two men scrambled in the dirt for a few moments, the crowd started shifting back to give them space. Keiran ended up on top and landed a few punches before Kurt managed to kick him off. Nul ran forward and pulled Kurt back up to his feet. She grabbed Keiran by the leg and dragged him out of the tent, with the crowd and Kurt following behind. The drunken man started shouting whilst flailing to free himself, only stopping when Nul let his leg go. As he tried to scramble back to his feet, Nul landed a kick straight to his chest, sending him sprawling into the snow. She then marched back to Kurt, completely ignoring the stares of the crowd.

"I'm beginning to think this might be a good idea after all," Nul muttered.

"He's getting back up." Kurt replied, looking over Nul's shoulder to see Keiran getting back to his feet. "Do you want another go, or would you mind if I jump in?"

"Only if you make him regret everything he said in there," Nul said, as she walked past Kurt to join the crowd surrounding them.

"Will do," said Kurt. He turned back to see just in time Keiran running towards them.

There were a few cheers from the crowd as Kurt rushed forward and landed a punch to Keiran's gut. Before the taller man could react Kurt threw another punch that landed under his jaw, flipping him upside down before he smashed back onto the ground. Kurt didn't wait for him to get up again, he threw out a few kicks until Keiran managed to roll away. The two men exchanged blows, each of them refusing to back down. The crowd had turned almost primal at this point, cheering with every blow and gasping whenever someone got hit. As both men grew tired, Kurt managed to land a solid hit to the side of Keiran's head, stunning him. Seeing his advantage, Kurt stepped close to the older man and after three more punches, sent Keiran down to the ground for the final time. Everyone fell silent as all eyes were fixated on the two men. After a few moments of bated breath, Keiran groaned and the crowd erupted with cheers. Kurt limped back over to Nul who was waiting with a smile on her face.

"How'd I do?" he asked, wiping away some blood from his throbbing lip.

"Well, he's still breathing and you're still standing so I think we'll call it a win," she replied.

The music picked up again and a few dwarves moved in to take Keiran to the shelter. The rest of the crowd went back in the tent, giving Nul and Kurt smiles and pats on the back as they passed. Within a few moments, Kurt and Nul were left alone and there was no sign there'd been a fight at all.

"This town keeps surprising me," said Kurt with a pained smile. "Every time I think I'm going to be judged harshly for something, they just accept me. They're all just too kind."

"I don't think it's the town," Nul replied, stepping forward to take his hand into her own.

"Oh?" Kurt said as he took her hand. Despite the reason why, knowing that he could now show even this small amount of affection in front of the few stragglers still outside the tent, filled him with enough warmth that he barely noticed the cold winter night around them.

"If you can't figure it out, then you're not nearly as smart as I thought," Nul said with a small laugh. She then started to steer him back inside. "Come on, I want another drink."

As they walked arm in arm heading toward the entrance of the tent, a hooded figure stepped outside and stopped in their path.

"Can we help you?" Nul asked. She took a step forward to shield Kurt from the stranger.

“Yes. Yes you can,” replied a familiar voice. The figure lowered her hood and Nul gasped. Even Kurt was shocked to see the Matriarch.

“I-I'm sorry,” Nul said, lowering her head. “I had no idea you were going to come tonight. If I'd known I would have made some changes around here.”

“There's no need to be so formal my dear. I came here in secret for a reason,” said the Matriarch. “My intention was to stay hidden and enjoy the festivities but after what I just heard, I decided that we should have a little talk.”

“Should I go?” Kurt asked, letting go of Nul's hand.

“I think not,” said the Matriarch. “If what was said earlier is true, then I would definitely want to have words with you as well.”

The Matriarch walked away from the entrance and gestured for the couple to follow her. Nul shot Kurt a worried expression as they began to move away from the warm inviting entrance and followed the Matriarch to a shadowy spot at the side of the tent. After they were satisfied that no one else was nearby, Nul and Kurt stood close together to brace against the chill wind, while the Matriarch seemed completely unbothered by the cold.

“So I presume you two have something of a clue why I want to talk to you both?” the Matriarch asked in a hushed tone.

“We do,” replied Nul, staring at her feet.

“Anything either of you would like to say first?” the Matriarch asked, her expression and tone both neutral. Kurt and Nul looked at each other and without saying anything, both knew what their decision was.

"No," said Nul, tightening her grip on Kurt's hand.

"Well then let's begin," the Matriarch looked upon the couple for a few moments before continuing, almost as if she was trying to read their thoughts. "Nul, did you and Kurt start your relationship while he was under your care? Did you neglect your duties to us?"

"I didn't neglect anything," Nul sighed. "But yes, we started to have feelings for each other while he was under my care and even though that might have been wrong, I do not regret what we started."

"Very well," replied the Matriarch, not giving away any hint of how she felt about Nul's answer. "Kurt, did you pursue Nul to try to manipulate her? What was your motive for starting all this?"

"I didn't have a motive," Kurt answered, not trying to disguise the anger he felt at hearing that accusation. "She was kind to me, showed me affection and accepted my own affection back. That's all there is to it."

"I see," said the Matriarch. She tilted her head for a moment, considering the couple's answers. "Do you both understand what your actions mean for the people above and our people below?"

"I think so," Nul replied, looking at Kurt. "Yes, I do."

"And you?" asked the Matriarch, staring at Kurt.

"I'm not going to pretend to understand the full weight of it, but I know it's something I don't plan on ending," Kurt replied.

"I see," the Matriarch repeated. Again she spent a moment considering their answers before looking up at them. She had a small smile on her face. "In that case, I happily support you both and I'll see to it that the rest of our people do the same."

“Really?” Nul asked, her eyes welling up with happy tears.

“Of course,” replied the Matriarch, giving Nul a comforting pat on the shoulder. “Though I'd ask you to have some better sense going forward. This kind of thing tends to make others look upon you rather harshly.”

“Yes! Yes I promise,” Nul said.

“Excellent. Now that's settled, I'd very much like to return home,” said the Matriarch. She then walked past the couple and headed towards the entrance to the shelter, disappearing into the shadows.

Nul grabbed Kurt by the hand and started pulling him out of the cold and towards the entrance of the tent. The music, the warmth and the smell of food were all still going strong even as the night was growing late. The couple felt refreshed as they walked back into the festivities, even as Kurt was nursing various aches and newly formed bruises. There were even some cheers from the townsfolk when the couple came back inside to enjoy the rest of their night. The merriment would have continued until dawn, but a young man came running out of the dark night, with steam rising off his skin. He took a moment to catch his breath before speaking out to the crowd.

“We've spotted things moving close to the eastern tower!” he yelled, still trying to catch his breath. The crowd fell silent. “They'll be here in two days!”

# 21

News of their enemies arriving had sobered the town in a matter of hours. The following day there was no complaining about hangovers or lack of sleep while everyone worked. If anything the people of Bismurr were filled with a strange zeal while they set about making the final touches to everything they had built over the past few months. People finished the last of the defences while it was still morning and all the townsfolk moved into the shelter, leaving the town empty and eerily quiet.

Despite everything, Kurt felt satisfied as he marched through the empty streets, the crunch of the snow echoing with each step. After the night before, he felt more acceptance in Bismurr now than he'd ever had in the year he'd spent living here. Even with his mood and the tension he saw in some of the recruits' faces as they patrolled the streets, Kurt didn't let himself get distracted while he checked on the town's defences. Each barricade looked sturdy and all the traps the recruits had built were well-hidden, bolstering his confidence in his plan. Once he was satisfied that nothing was out of place, Kurt went to the centre of town where a large gathering was taking place. Nul, Lief, Baku, Peyton and a mix of human, dwarf and orc fighters were talking amongst themselves waiting for him to arrive.

"Commander," Peyton said, causing a silence to fall over everyone who had gathered.

"Morning everyone. The town is looking ready for a fight, how're things here?" Kurt asked the group.

"Better than we expected," said Lief. "The people we placed on the watchtowers are making their way back and we should see them all by nightfall. Everything we've built around town is holding steady, even with the cold. I think we're all set."

"All your recruits and our fighters are ready as well," said Baku, gesturing at the crowd. "I think the only thing left to do is sharpen our weapons and get a good night of sleep."

"So this is it then. All that's left is to wait," Kurt said to himself. Not knowing what else to say, he looked around at the men and women surrounding him as a sombre silence fell over the group.

"Would anyone mind if I say a few words?" Peyton asked, breaking everyone free from their worried thoughts.

"I think we could all do with something else to think about." Nul replied, with a small smile.

"Alright then," Peyton said, taking a moment to clear his throat with a cough. "I just wanted to say; no matter what happens tomorrow, no matter who is left standing and no matter where we go from here, I've never been happier or prouder of what we've done here. I'm so grateful to have met each and every one of you. I can't speak for every person here, but I'm almost certain the rest of the town feels the same."

"Well said," Lief muttered, wiping her eyes on her sleeve.

"So what's the plan for the rest of today?" asked Baku.

"I think it'd be best if we spend our time resting," Kurt replied. He locked eyes with Nul before continuing. "Spend some time with your loved ones. Hopefully we'll have one more day, but we need to stay ready just in case."

"Right," Lief agreed.

"So if that's everything, I'd very much like Nul to join me and we'll see you all tomorrow," said Kurt, holding out a hand which Nul took.

The couple walked away, leaving the group to say their own goodbyes to one another. Neither Kurt nor Nul said anything as they walked out of the town and back onto the snow-covered fields leading back to their home. It wasn't until they were approaching the edge of the forest before either of them spoke.

"How do you think tomorrow is going to go?" Nul asked, her grip on his hand tightening.

"Honestly?" Kurt asked back, keeping his gaze facing forward.

"Always," replied Nul.

"I think we'll win," said Kurt. He then let out a long sigh before sharing his thoughts. "But I think a lot of us are going to get hurt, we're going to lose people. I'm sure everything we've prepared will work but I know Orlan will have something up his sleeve we're not ready for."

"We all know there will be some losses, but you're thinking about something else. So what's bothering you?" Nul asked.

"It's just..." Kurt hesitated and took a deep breath. "It's just that I'm the one that has to give the orders that allow all of this to happen. Win or lose people are going to get hurt and die because of decisions I make, again."

"Wait," Nul stopped them both from walking and grabbed his other hand. They stared at each other for a few moments in silence before she continued. "You and I both know what you were a part of. This is not the same thing. No one here is being forced to do anything they don't want to."

“I know that,” Kurt said. He tried to pull away, but Nul wouldn't let him go. “It's difficult not to see the same thing repeating itself. I just hope that when this is all over enough good people are left standing to rebuild this place.”

“You've changed,” Nul said with a smile, before pulling Kurt into a hug.

“Oh?” Kurt asked.

“You're not letting all of this drag you down any more. You're looking forward and keeping focused on what you need to.” Nul replied, squeezing his midriff tightly as she held him. “It's good.”

“I hope you're right,” Kurt whispered.

The couple stood there for a time, only breaking apart when they noticed more snow starting to fall around them. The chilly air chased them all the way through the forest back to their home. They hurried inside, removed their winter clothes and while Nul got the fire started to warm the place up, Kurt went to the kitchen and started to prepare some food. The couple were soon sitting next to each other by the fire, both of them too distracted to eat anything. As they sat, Nul rested her head on Kurt's shoulder and he felt her start to fall asleep at his side. He smiled as he pulled a blanket from nearby to cover the two of them, being careful not to wake Nul. Looking out the window, he saw that the sun was already setting and his smile faded. The day was coming to an end. He didn't dwell on it, choosing to place his arm around Nul and hold her close. Kurt didn't know what was waiting for them tomorrow, but he did know that right now, in this moment, he'd rather keep his attention on the woman he loved and nothing else. He drifted into his own slumber.

* * *

The next morning started like any other. Nul prepared a small breakfast for the two of them which they ate, both trying to spend their time avoiding what they needed to do. Soon, the time came for them to leave for Bismurr. After grabbing their weapons and armour the couple stepped outside, ready to face the day ahead. The snow in the forest surrounding their home had grown heavier overnight, as though it was trying to stop them from reaching the town. Hand in hand the couple pushed forward, each cold-soaked step harder than the last but they managed to reach the edge of the town.

The mood in Bismurr was a sombre one as they walked past the warriors waiting in the streets. It was odd to walk through the town and not see the familiar faces performing their daily routines. Kurt took in all the changes they'd made to the place he'd called home. It was saddening that it had become such a harsh shadow of its former self but he knew it was going to be worth it, if they could make it through the night.

"Commander. Nul," greeted Lief as she emerged from an alleyway to walk alongside the couple.

"Morning," replied Nul. "What's the word on Orlan and the army?"

"Last of the people we had on watchtowers came back in the night. If they keep up their pace, it looks like they'll get here just after the sun sets," said Lief. "We've got a few traps set up that should give us warning when they get close though."

"How's everyone doing? Ready and rested?" Kurt asked.

"Ready as we can be," Lief replied with a shrug. "We could probably do with more time, but I'm sure I'd be saying that no matter how long we had left."

"What about you? You think your powers will be helpful?" Nul asked, with a look of concern.

"I think so," Lief said, looking around to make sure no one nearby could hear them. "I'll probably stick to using my bow as much as I can but when the time comes, I'll use everything I have on those monsters."

"Good," said Nul, patting Lief on the back while they walked.

"Are the squad leaders waiting for us?" asked Kurt.

"Gathered them myself. Even managed to grab Baku and a few of his more capable fighters," replied Lief with a smug smile.

"Well done," said Kurt. He started to walk quicker, eager to meet the others.

The three of them arrived at the centre of town where the remaining squad leaders were waiting, along with Baku and two orc women that Kurt didn't recognise. Lief walked around the group and took a place between Yvette and Garet. Nul left Kurt's side and greeted Baku with a hug before taking her own place in the circle. Once they had all settled, each of them looked to Kurt and waited for him to speak.

"We all know what's coming for us tonight. I know we are ready but if any of you want to be with your loved ones, now would be the time to go down into the shelter. No judgement. I don't want anyone here who doesn't want to be," Kurt said, taking the time to look at as many faces as possible. No one moved from the circle. They had all come so far in such a short time and Kurt was proud of all of them. When his gaze landed on Nul, she gave him an encouraging nod which gave him a sense of calm he needed. "Not all of us are going to be walking away from this. That being said, I promise when the dust is settled, the only people who'll be left standing will be us."

"Damn right we'll be the ones left standing!" said Baku. Everyone started to laugh as the mood lightened and even Kurt couldn't help but smile along with them.

"Alright then. You all know where you need to be. Go, and be ready." Kurt ordered. The group dispersed, spreading out through the town to meet with their own squads.

Soon Kurt and Nul were standing alone with a few orc fighters walking nearby, patrolling the town. Not wanting to sit around in the cold, the couple made their way through the town until they arrived between the last two buildings before the road to the shelter. The buildings themselves used to be warehouses for food but now they were full of barrels packed to brim with sparking powder. Kurt wasn't interested in the warehouses, he'd checked on them enough over the past few days – his interest was waiting in the middle of the path between them. The couple walked forward and stopped when the sound of their footsteps stopped crunching with the snow and started creating metallic clangs. Kurt leaned down and brushed away the snow that had gathered to find the handle to the bunker hidden in the ground. As he pulled open the hatch, the hinges creaked slightly and snow started to pour into the small dark room below.

"How's it looking in there?" Nul asked, leaning over his shoulder.

"Looks like it'll be a tight fit and looks a little damp down there, but it should do the job. Cole did some good work," said Kurt as he lowered the entry hatch back into place.

"When has he not?" Nul asked with a chuckle.

"Good point," Kurt replied with a smile.

"So what now?" asked Nul.

"It'll be a few hours before the sun sets, I guess we find a warm place to wait," Kurt replied. He walked back into town with Nul at his side. Kurt took a deep breath of cold air before asking a question that had been on his mind for a few days. "How're you doing? You feel up to this?"

"Of course," Nul replied. "After everything we've been through and everything we've planned. I am not leaving your side until this over."

"Thank you," said Kurt, taking her hand into his and squeezing it while they walked.

The couple wandered for a while before they found themselves outside the Jumping Canary. The doors were left ajar, so Kurt and Nul stepped inside. The place had been torn apart, all that was left were a few chairs and some empty crates tossed into a corner. After laying their weapons by the door, Kurt and Nul both took a chair and sat down near the door. There was quiet for a time, as they both lost themselves in their thoughts.

"What do you want to do tomorrow?" Nul asked.

"What?" Kurt replied, confused.

"Tomorrow. What do you want to do?" she asked again.

"I'm not sure," Kurt said. "Do you have anything in mind?"

"Well, assuming we don't die horribly. I'm thinking we have a big breakfast and stay inside all day," replied Nul so matter-of-factly, that for a moment Kurt forgot why they were there in the first place.

"That sounds like a perfect plan," he said, before his smile faded.

For a long while the couple sat there in silence, until Nul dragged her chair next to Kurt and sat at his side. She rested her head on his shoulder and grabbed his hand. They were both grateful for the warmth and would have been content to stay holding each other for the rest of the day. Time caught up with them and the pale light outside began to drift away. Almost on cue with the setting sun, the sounds of people rushing around and shouting began to break out all over Bismurr. The couple hugged, retrieved their weapons and just before they reached the door, Kurt turned around to face Nul. They shared one last kiss before heading out, ready to fight.

# 22

Kurt and Nul didn't feel the cold as they joined everyone else running towards the edge of town. Once they reached the line of people, each one of them eager and ready. Archers were on the rooftops, readying their first arrows. The orc, human and dwarven fighters all formed lines that stretched from the town, all the way up to the shelter entrance. Kurt didn't spot any of the squad leaders, but he knew they'd be standing ready. Nearby, two people rolled a large cannon to the front of the line, while a few others were dragging a large crate filled with cannonballs ready to load into it. Looking down the line, Kurt saw a few more cannons being pulled into place further up the lined up fighters. Just as the last of the fighters got back into place, a low rumble echoed from across the field in front of them.

Everyone tightened their grips on their weapons as the first Dregs emerged from the trees ahead. At first there were only a few, then a dozen and before long they were pouring out of the woods without an end in sight. Kurt took a moment to load his spike launcher and then grabbed his axe with both hands.

"FIRE!" Kurt shouted.

The fighters passed word down the line and people began to load the weapons with sparking powder. After a few seconds the deafening sound of cannons firing filled the entire valley. A few Dregs were ripped apart, spreading a dark red mist as the first volley made contact. More monsters charged forward, trying to get across the field quicker now that their prey was in sight. As some of the Dregs managed to get closer, the archers on the rooftops let loose their arrows. Between the cannon blasts and the raining arrows, the line of fighters at the front needed only single blows to finish off the few monsters that managed to get close.

Kurt kept his eyes on the treeline, scouring the shadows for any sign of Orlan. Instead all he saw was more and more Dregs pouring from the forest. The cannons were still firing, but each blast was less effective as more of the monsters charged toward the line of warriors. Even the archers were starting to have trouble picking off their enemies as the Dregs pushed through their fallen to reach the town. The first row of axe-wielding fighters surged forward to fight the monsters. Most of the front row were orcs so they made quick work of the injured monsters but as more of them began to push in, the fighters began to have trouble holding the Dregs back. As Kurt tried to keep an eye out for Orlan, he almost didn't see a Dreg pushing its way forward to leap over the dead and lunge towards him. Nul was quicker than the monster and with a single swing of her axe chopped its head off, letting the body slide into the snow away from them. Kurt nodded his thanks and together they rushed forward to join the fray. The line of warriors held strong against the ever-increasing tide of monsters, but had to start retreating as the bodies of the fallen Dregs began to block the cannons from firing. As the battle raged around him, Kurt felt a chill creep over him and something in the back of his mind compelled him to look towards the forest.

Slowly approaching, amidst the Dregs still swarming forward from the darkness, was a cloaked figure. It was shorter than the monsters and its face was obscured but Kurt knew exactly who it was. He could feel it in his gut.

"HE'S HERE!" Kurt called out to Nul. With a hefty swing of her weapon she dispatched the Dreg which was trying to crawl past her and she ran to Kurt's side. "EVERYONE PULL BACK! GET TO THE SHELTER!"

Despite the noise of battle, enough fighters heard the order and began to retreat, shouting for others to follow them. Kurt and Nul took off in the opposite direction, heading into the streets of Bismurr, rushing to get to the bunker. As they ran through the town, the sounds of fighting surrounded them. When they rounded a corner the couple came face to face with a Dreg, fresh blood dripping from its mouth as it tossed its human victim down into the red-stained snow. Before it had time to react Kurt lunged forward and swung his axe straight into the head of the monster, sending its lifeless body sprawling alongside its recent prey. Kurt started to move on but realised he was running alone. He turned back to see Nul facing two more Dregs that were charging towards them. Kurt skidded to a halt and ran to join her.

But before he could reach her, Kurt spotted a third Dreg climbing over a rooftop just above Nul. The two monsters rushed forward with their fangs bared, ready to rip their prey apart. Kurt shoved Nul to one side as he rushed forward to fight. He swung his axe upward with all his might, just in time to bifurcate the skull of the Dreg jumping down from the roof. Nul recovered as the remaining two monsters reached her. She swung her own axe in wide arcs, keeping them at bay as Kurt struggled to remove his weapon from his slain foe. One of the Dregs became enraged enough to lunge forward, using its fangs to bite down on Nul's axe mid-swing. It tried to rip the axe free but found the orc's grip to be too strong. The monster leapt forward, flailing as it and Nul tumbled back.

The other Dreg dashed forward and slammed into Kurt, sending him colliding into a wall. His armour took the brunt of the blow, but he still felt winded as he collapsed to the ground. Kurt looked up to see Nul struggling to get a grip on her opponent as they wrestled across the blood and snow. As he was about to get up, a large foot pinned him to the ground. Kurt tried to raise his spike launcher but the monster grabbed his arm and pushed it down. Kurt struggled under the Dreg's immense strength and found himself completely at its mercy. The monster lunged down to rip out his throat and having no other options, Kurt shoved his free arm in the way to protect himself. His armour once again protected him a little, but he still felt sharp pain across his arm as the Dreg's fangs managed to find flesh.

Kurt screamed in frustration, not because of the pain, or the danger he was in, but because Nul needed him and he was powerless to help her. Frustration shifted to despair when he heard the sound of the monster with Nul howling into the night. He couldn't even look over to them now that the Dreg above him was gnawing at his arm, trying to tear its way through the leather and metal to taste more of the blood that was now dripping from its mouth. When the howling stopped, Kurt felt his gut turn to ice.

Steeling himself against the pain, Kurt shoved his arm deeper in the Dreg's mouth, ripping more metal, leather and flesh off his forearm. Kurt found what he was looking for as his hand brushed against the monster's hot and wet tongue. He grabbed it and wrenched his hand back with all the strength he could muster. As his arm moved back through the Dreg's sharp fangs, his armour ripped completely apart, but the pain was worth it as Kurt kept his grip on the twitching flesh in his hand. The Dreg reeled its head back in pain as dark blood began spurting from its mouth. Kurt tossed the fleshy lump that used to be a tongue away but the monster still had him pinned. He looked over and saw there was no sign of the other Dreg or Nul. When he looked back at his own enemy he felt his heart almost stop in his chest.

Standing behind the monster, drenched in blood and viscera stood Nul, her expression of rage obvious even under the gore. She grabbed the upper jaw of the raging Dreg with one hand and its bottom jaw with the other. With what looked like no effort at all, Nul flung her hands in two separate directions and the monster's head ripped apart like it had been made of paper, spraying dark blood upward in a red geyser. Nul kicked its lifeless heavy body to one side and knelt down so she was face to face with Kurt.

"I'm so sorry," she whispered, grabbing him into a hug so tight that Kurt almost wished he was pinned under the monster again.

"Are you alright?" Kurt asked, pulling himself off the blood-soaked ground and picking Nul up onto her feet as well.

"I'm sorry," Nul repeated, not meeting his gaze.

"Nul, look at me." He pushed her chin up to look him in the eye. "We're fine as long as we're together right?"

Nul looked at Kurt's injured arm like she was going to disagree but seemed to think better of it.

"Right," she replied, her expression changing to resolve.

Kurt nodded and the couple started running down the street again. As they approached a corner leading to an open space in the town, they stopped to look around whilst trying to stay hidden. The street was filled with dozens of dead Dregs with several human and orc corpses as well. Ignoring the carnage, Kurt and Nul dashed from their hiding spot to another alley on the opposite side of the street. While they kept out of sight as they hurried across town, the couple heard fighting all over the place. It wasn't clear through the chaotic noise which side was winning, but the fallen bodies from both sides were everywhere as the couple made their way to the bunker.

"How long do we have?" Nul asked in a hushed tone.

"They'll set off the sparking powder around the shelter entrance as soon as they can't see anyone else trying to retreat," Kurt replied between heavy, pained breaths. "We haven't heard anything yet, so they must still be getting people inside. Once we reach the bunker we need to get as much attention on us as possible before we set off our own trap."

"Hopefully the Dregs aren't giving them too much trouble," Nul said as she peeked around a corner.

"They're fine. If things go too far, they'll blow up the entrance and seal themselves in. Your home and the townsfolk have to take priority over our fighters," Kurt replied as he kept looking around for any movement nearby. Noticing that his arm was still bleeding, he took the time to rip off the remains of his tattered sleeve and wrap it around the wound. It stung as he pulled it tight but he ignored the pain and got back his feet just as Nul was done looking ahead.

"Ready to move?" she asked, eyeing his arm.

"I think so," Kurt replied, stretching to make sure his makeshift bandage didn't slip. Satisfied that it wasn't moving any time soon, he grabbed his axe. "Let's go."

The couple carried on moving through the town as silently as possible, keeping their eyes and ears peeled for any danger all the while. Kurt caught sight of a few Dregs smashing their way into the buildings and roaring with rage when they found nothing inside. He saw more bodies of orcs, humans and dwarves he recognised but no one he knew by name. Even though seeing his fallen comrades made him angry, Kurt was still a little glad that there weren't as many losses as he worried there would be. All the preparations and training for this fight had paid off.

Kurt and Nul managed to get to the bunker without any more trouble and after checking the entrance was still secure, they got inside the building nearby and shut the door behind them. Inside were dozens of barrels filled with sparking powder. Hung by the door was a small lantern made mostly from glass, blackened with soot so that its light would be dim, and filled with oil so when smashed, it should spread a fire quickly. Kurt grabbed the lantern and hooked it onto his belt, then shoved a barrel over to spread sparking powder all over the floor. Nul left the door open just a crack so she could keep her eyes on the bunker, and once Kurt was done preparing the room he joined her.

Together they waited and listened. The sounds of fighting had died down and all they heard now was the sounds of Dregs running and smashing their way through Bismurr. They stayed hidden, relieved to have a few moments of rest. After a short while, quiet fell over the town and for a brief moment it sounded like the fighting was over. Then the distant sound of an explosion ripped through town, followed by a small rumble. Nul and Kurt exchanged a nod and steeled themselves before pushing the door open to step back outside. Even though it was dark, a huge cloud of smoke coming from north of the town could be seen snaking its way into the night sky.

“Are you ready for this?” Kurt asked, keeping his voice quiet.

“I am,” Nul replied. “Let's end this.”

In unison the couple screamed out into the night. Several Dregs appeared on rooftops nearby. As one of the monsters jumped down, Nul swung her axe and decapitated it with ease. She had no time to rest however as two more Dregs jumped down to surround her. Kurt lunged forward and smashed his own axe into the skull of one while Nul kicked the other with enough force to smash the monster through a wooden wall nearby. More Dregs appeared from the shadows and within a few seconds, the couple were surrounded by more than a dozen of the monsters. Nul was a blur as she dashed back to open the bunker hatch. As the monsters started to move in to overwhelm their prey, Kurt grabbed the lantern from his belt and tossed it through the door towards the open barrels. He then jumped into the bunker, almost tackling Nul inside as well. She managed to grab the handle and slam the hatch shut behind them, shrouding them in complete darkness. The noise of scratching and pounding on the metal hatch from inside the chamber was overwhelming.

After only a few seconds the sounds were swallowed up by an earth-shattering explosive blast, so violent it shook the walls and floor of the small chamber. Both Kurt and Nul gripped their heads in pain as the noise deafened them but before they could relax another explosion rocked the bunker. Then another and another as each home stuffed with sparking powder ignited and the town of Bismurr erupted into fire.

Just as quick as the explosions started, they ended. Even though silence had descended on them, Kurt and Nul were still deafened, holding each other in the dark. After a few minutes, the ringing in their ears faded, and the couple realised that all they could hear was silence. Kurt approached the door and started to push it open. The metal was hot to the touch and something heavy had landed on top of it but after a brief struggle he managed to throw it open.

Although it was still night, everything nearby was lit up with a bright orange glow. The town itself was unrecognisable as all the buildings had been blown apart, leaving only the odd barely-standing wall and scattered debris. Fires were burning all over the place, illuminating the countless Dreg corpses scattered amongst the burning rubble and scorched wood. As Kurt and Nul began to walk through the town, it was soon clear that there were in fact hundreds of dead monsters. The plan had worked. Kurt let out a small sigh of relief, careful not to breathe too from the thin layer of smoke that was hanging in the air. He then felt Nul rest a hand on his shoulder.

"Do you think it's over?" she asked.

"I'm not sure," Kurt answered.

He turned to look at Nul and wiped away a little blood that had sprayed onto her cheek during the fight. Kurt took her by the hand and together they headed towards the shelter. Just as they left the edge of town, passing by the burning debris that had been flung into the fields nearby, Nul stopped in her tracks. Kurt turned and saw that the air around her began to ripple and warp. She was then pulled away, tearing free from his grip as an invisible force flung her back towards the ruined still-burning buildings. Before Kurt could react, a cold gripped him when he saw the cloaked figure hobbling out of the smoke nearby, his cloak still smouldering in places as though it had been aflame.

"I really have to give you and your filth kind some credit," said the hoarse yet familiar voice of Orlan. Each word he spoke was seething with rage as he struggled to speak through pained breaths. "I never expected you'd have much of a fight in you, let alone the sheer idiocy to destroy this place."

Kurt didn't respond. He tightened his grip on the axe in hands and started running forwards. He didn't get far as Orlan raised a hand and that same invisible force pushed Kurt onto the ground. The elf doubled over as a small coughing fit racked through him.

"It took a lot out of me to protect myself from your little trap here, but I think I still have enough left in me to deal with you," Orlan said once his voice returned to him. He gestured upward and Kurt found himself flung up into a standing position.

The elf approached, limping while keeping his arm raised to hold Kurt in place. He'd only taken a few steps before an axe flew out of the surrounding smoke, aimed straight at Orlan's body. With inhuman speed he raised his other hand and the axe froze in place in the air before dropping to the ground. A grey blur dashed past Kurt trying to reach the elf, but with another flick of his wrist Orlan stopped his new attacker. Nul was now frozen in place as well, one fist still raised ready to strike.
"Be patient cave-dweller. I'll get to you when I'm done with him," Orlan spat. Now holding two people in place, the elf's hands began to tremble from the effort of restraining them. As Orlan again tried to walk forwards, Kurt spotted two figures emerging from the smoke behind the elf.

"LET THEM GO, MAGIC MAN!" shouted Baku as he ran into the firelight. He was covered in scratches and cuts with one arm dangling useless at his side but the large orc gave no hint that he was in pain, as his face held only anger.

"More of you?!" Orlan hissed through gritted teeth. He turned to face the newcomers. "What other creatures are going to crawl out of the dirt to delay me?! Are the worms going to rise up next?!"

"The worms don't want to waste their time with scum like you," said Lief as she stepped into the light alongside Baku. Her clothes looked torn, but unlike her orc companion she appeared to be uninjured. "Now like the big man said. Let our friends go."

"And what if I don't?" Orlan asked with a smirk.

Baku dashed forward, throwing a rock he'd kept hidden in his injured hand, though the orc winced with pain at the effort. The rock struck Orlan in the head, sending the elf stumbling backwards. Kurt fell to the ground, free from the invisible force gripping him and looking up, he saw that Nul had also been released. In unison they all sprinted towards the distracted Orlan, still clutching his head in pain. Just as they got close enough to hit him however, Orlan flung his arms wide and everyone froze in place. The force he expelled knocked his hood back, revealing his face. Orlan still looked as pristine as ever, save for his right cheek which was a melted mess of burned flesh. The burns stretched down his neck until they met his shirt, where the silken material had fused painfully to his skin.

"I hope that stings you son of a bitch," muttered Lief as she struggled to move.

"All this?" Orlan asked, looking down at his burns. "This is nothing. Do you know how my kind treated me when I returned from here last? Do you know what happened to me when this pathetic creature found a way to resist our weavers? You honestly think this paltry amount of physical pain even compares to what I've been through? DO YOU?!"

Orlan jerked his wrist and the invisible force holding Lief in place flung her back, dragging her through the ash and snow until she disappeared into the smoke. Baku grunted in frustration, trying to break free, but all he managed to do was draw the elf's attention. With another flick of his wrist, Orlan lowered Baku down until he was on his knees.

"I think maybe we should bring this to an end," Orlan said, a twisted grin spreading across his face. The elf made a fist and as he did, Baku growled in pain. Orlan then tightened his grip until Baku was roaring in agony.

"ENOUGH!" shouted Kurt. Orlan released his grip and Baku's large frame collapsed onto the ash-covered ground, unconscious.

"Enough? After all you've done, you dare to tell me when it's enough?" Orlan asked, his twisted grin fading as anger filled his face. "Tell me Kurt, how many lives have you ruined since you came here? No, better yet, tell me how many bodies need to lie at your feet before you become a fair judge of what's enough?!"

"SHUT UP!" screamed Nul. Using all her strength to struggle against the invisible force was making the air around warp as though it was hardening into something solid.

"Oh, did you think this pathetic human was innocent?" Orlan asked, turning his attention away from Kurt. "How much do you know of his past? Did you know that simply by existing, people suffer and die all around him. Just look around you. Look at all this destruction and death. Everything that's happened here is because of him."

"That's not true!" Nul yelled through gritted teeth as she still struggled to break free. "I've seen his life. If he fought before then he would just have been another body on the pile. Everything that's happening now, isn't his fault!"

"Is that so?" Orlan said before laughing, his voice breaking a little. He turned back to Kurt. "I don't know or care how she saw into your mind, but are you so deluded as to what you are that you'd drag these other ignorant creatures down with you?!"

"I know what I am," Kurt muttered through gritted teeth. He met Orlan's gaze with a scowl of his own. "I was and am a monster. People have suffered and died because of me and there will never be justice for any of them. But don't pretend for a second that any of that has anything to do with what you're doing here!"

"And again you try to hold me to the same standards as your pathetic, mortal lives," Orlan spat back. "Why can't you just learn your place?! Why do you keep fighting against your betters?!"

"I keep fighting because you and I? We're the same kind of monster," Kurt replied. He looked to Nul, who was still struggling to break free, but as their eyes met, she knew Kurt believed his own words. Even as tears started to fall down her face, she didn't stop trying to escape from the elf's magical grasp.

"The same? THE SAME?" Orlan screamed in rage. He then flung his arms down and the force gripping Kurt and Nul dragged them both down to the knees. "YOU THINK YOU'RE AN EQUAL TO ME? ME?"

Kurt tried to speak, but the force surrounding him gripped tighter until it was strong enough to stop him from breathing.

"LET ME SHOW YOU EXACTLY HOW INFERIOR YOU ARE!" Orlan shouted. With another flick of his wrists, Kurt and Nul were thrown back. They both recovered but stopped before rushing in to attack.

Orlan's body was twisting and convulsing, his bones cracking with each jerk of movement. His arms and legs began to stretch and grow, tearing his clothes apart like they were made of paper. As his torso grew to match the new size of his limbs, thin pieces of bone ripped through the skin on his shoulders and arms, each grey shard dripping with dark blood. The elf's hair lengthened down the length of his spine, shifting in colour from blonde to silver. When the transformation reached his face, his teeth grew longer and sharper as his flesh darkened to a blood red. His cheeks ripped away and shifted into something resembling insect-like mandibles that covered his long fangs. Orlan's change finished, leaving his new Dreg-like body standing almost twice as tall as he was before. The creature then roared, an inhuman noise so loud it felt like it was scratching the back of Kurt's mind. Whatever this monstrosity was, one thing was clear, Orlan was gone.

Nul was the first to rush in, leaping through the air at blinding speed to strike the monster. Orlan's new form was too quick however, grabbing Nul's fist with ease. Kurt had managed to grab his axe and move in as well, just in time to see Nul get tossed aside. He swung his axe with all the force he could muster but the monster grabbed the weapon and wrenched it free from Kurt's grasp.

With his new monstrous strength, Orlan shattered the head of the axe by squeezing it, his own blood dripping down as he tossed the metal shards aside. He punched Kurt in the gut, sending him flying over the ash-covered ground. As Kurt skidded to a stop, he struggled to breathe in the cloud of ash around him but he managed to get back to his feet just in time to see the monster start to walk towards him. Orlan stopped and snarled at something behind Kurt. He soon heard several footsteps crunching in the ashen snow behind him. Baku and Nul joined Kurt, and the three of them stared down the monster. Orlan roared at them, the sound was loud enough that the smoke that had been drifting around them cleared away. Before the monster could move, a large rock collided into his chest and sent him smashing into the ground. Lief then appeared, wincing with each step as she limped forward. She hobbled over to join the others, keeping her eyes on the enraged Orlan as he thrashed around in pain.

"I take it that thing is our elf friend?" Lief asked, spitting on the floor as she caught her breath.

"He looks better this way. Don't you think?" Baku said with a laugh.
"More like a monster anyway," Nul muttered, looking at Kurt.

"How'd you manage that rock thing?" asked Baku, eyeing Lief up and down. "Looked a little like magic to me."

"Just something I picked up while fighting these things," Lief replied with a smile. Baku laughed.

Orlan managed to get back up onto his clawed feet and turned to face the four smaller creatures staring at him. He growled as he walked towards them with menace in his dark eyes. Kurt stepped forward and rested a hand on Nul's shoulder.

"Do you really still think so little of yourself? That you're a monster like him?" she asked in a whisper.

"I did," Kurt whispered back, "but I think seeing Orlan again, especially like this, was exactly what I needed to see."

"What? Why?" Nul asked, confused.

"As he was ranting he made me realise something," Kurt said, turning to look at Nul with a smile. "I can't change the past, no matter how much I want to. What I can do is try and be better. Be on the side of right."

"It'd be nice if the person you loved could have convinced you of that instead of that piece of filth," Nul replied.

"Are you two done?" Baku asked, stepping in front of the others. "I don't think this beast is gonna wait for you much longer."

While they were talking, Orlan had approached. He snarled at the four, his mandibles quivering slightly as he bared his sharp fangs. In response, Lief made two fist-sized rocks float up to her hands while Baku beat his chest with his one good arm. Nul and Kurt both rushed forwards past their friends, roaring at the monster as they started the fight.

Kurt moved in close, ducking under a swipe from Orlan's clawed hand. He aimed his spike launcher at the monster's arm and pulled the trigger, separating the long limb from its owner with an explosive crack. While Orlan howled in pain, two rocks struck him hard in the gut. Before he could recover, Nul leapt up and punched with all her strength, flooring the monster so hard that ash scattered all around the fight. Baku then joined the fray, leaping high in the air only to crush Orlan's head, their combined weight crushing one of the monster's mandibles with a wet crunch.

The monster flailed in the chaos and his remaining arm collided with Lief, knocking her away. Baku screamed in pain as Orlan lunged forward and sunk his fangs into the orc's shoulder. He soon released his bite as Kurt leapt up onto his back and pulled back his other mandible, trying to rip it off. Nul helped by tackling the monster off Baku. The three of them tumbled down into the ash, scattering a grey cloud into the air around them. Kurt was thrown off the back of the monster, but Nul kept her grip and did her best to keep Orlan off his feet. The monster managed to grab her hair and rip her away from him, tossing her aside as he scrambled back to his feet. Kurt picked himself up and as he was getting up, his hand brushed against the wooden handle of his axe.

He grabbed it just in time as Orlan was already rushing towards him. Kurt used the axe to block the first strike but wasn't quick enough to stop the second swipe that slashed across his chest, tearing several large holes into his armour. Orlan roared in frustration at the lack of blood and as he raised his clawed hand to strike again, dozens of rocks and stones pelted into his head, forcing him to try to shield himself. Seeing an opportunity, Kurt rushed forward and swung his axe into the Orlan's leg. He tore the weapon free, taking a chunk of flesh away as more rocks under Lief's control continued to push Orlan back. Nul returned, leaving a trail of ash in the air as she leapt upward. She grabbed the back of the monster's head and shoved it face down into the ground. Kurt didn't hesitate, moving in he brought his axe down into the monster's spine. Orlan howled in pain as he thrashed around, catching Kurt with a kick to the stomach which sent him flying back to collide with Baku, who'd only just managed to get back up before the two of them crashed back onto the ground. Nul grabbed Orlan by the leg and with a grunt of effort swung him around, launching his large body upwards. While he was in the air, Lief gathered dozens of rocks above the monster and used all of them to smash into Orlan, bringing him back down with a sickening crack of bone when he collided with the floor.

Orlan's monstrous form was still as the four approached him, each of them battered and out of breath. The monster's body twitched as though it was going to start changing again. His flesh hardened and turned to a stony grey. Cracks appeared all over him and as bits of the stone fell away, Orlan's pale skin came into view like he was emerging from a cocoon. The cracks spread and the frail, naked elf rolled onto the blood-caked ground. Orlan's body was whole again except he now looked drained as though he'd been starved of food for some time. As he came to, seeing the four people glaring down at him, Orlan tried to raise an arm to defend himself but found himself too weak to move it more than a few inches off the ground. Kurt leaned down and picked up his axe.

"You're done," Kurt said, using the blade of the axe to lift Orlan's head to face him.

"Done?" Orlan said, spitting on the ground. "This isn't over with me you ignorant filth! You think any of this means anything?! All you've done here is prove that this entire disgusting town needs to be wiped clean from this land! More of mine will come for you all and when they do, no amount of begging will spare any of you from death!"

"You have a point," Kurt replied, pulling his axe away. "I don't know what the future holds for us or how long we'll need to fight for, but right now? In this moment, I do know one thing."

"What?" Orlan spat.

"There's no more monsters in this town," He raised his weapon and as Orlan screamed with a helpless fury, Kurt slammed the axe down.

# 23

The days that followed were spent clearing the entrance to the shelter, with people from the inside struggling their way out while the four outside tried to get in. It seemed blocking the entrance had proven to be a little too successful, but once the tunnel was open again, the four survivors were treated to a heroes' welcome. The townsfolk carried them into the tunnels and sat the four down in the makeshift tavern, handing an overflowing cup of mead to each of them. As they shared drinks with the townsfolk, many of the fighters emerged to join the celebrations, each one sporting injuries but happy to be alive nonetheless.

It wasn't long before the congratulations ended and was replaced with a sombre mood as people began to venture outside to deal with the aftermath of the battle. Kurt and Nul were grateful to be spared from this task and found themselves holed up in a room near Cali's. The older woman burst into tears when she was reunited with the couple, squeezing them both into a hug so tight it threatened to be the very thing that finally ended them both. She helped to tend to their wounds, possibly going a bit too far with the bandages and constant cups of tea, but Nul and Kurt were far too tired to argue. They were just happy to take the time to rest.

The days underground came to an end as more and more people returned to the surface to start rebuilding. Bismurr was still a complete mess, but the bodies of the fallen were buried and any Dreg remains that weren't reduced to cinders were found and burned, adding more ashes to the large piles all over the ruined town. After they'd rested for a few days under Cali's care, Kurt and Nul returned to their home. The Dreg army had destroyed everything in the glade and though the walls of the cabin were still standing, the place was a ruin. It took a few days to make the structure serviceable again, and while it was smaller than what it used to be, Nul and

Kurt were happy to have a place to rest.

A new sense of normality began to take shape in Bismurr. More orcs had come to the surface to help start building new homes, while the townsfolk were invited further into the tunnels to see how their underground neighbours had been living beneath the surface. There were even enough people to begin work on tall wooden walls that would circle the entire town.

Days turned into weeks as wounds were healed and people took the time to mourn those who fell in the battle. Even as the town grieved for the losses however, their spirits were lifted as they all joined together to forge Bismurr into something new. Despite the hope that was spreading throughout all the people of this different yet stronger town, Kurt found himself feeling a growing apprehension with each passing day.

At first he'd been content to rest and heal but once he'd recovered he found himself dwelling on Orlan's final words. Even though he believed the elf had been insane with rage at the end, there had been a truth in his words that had sunk deep into Kurt's thoughts, pestering him whenever he tried to relax. On one particular afternoon, Kurt was standing in the doorway of his home, looking at the setting sun through the trees, the mug of tea he was holding having long since grown cold in the winter air.

"Food's ready, come inside," Nul called out from inside the house.

Kurt did as he was told, closing the door behind him. The heat from the fire had filled the small cabin, but like the cold outside, he didn't feel much of it. Nul had sat down with two steaming hot bowls of stew next to her and as Kurt approached to sit beside her, she threw a blanket at him.

"You just get that," she said with a playful smile. "I'm warm and want to stay that way."

“Fair enough,” Kurt said with a small laugh. He wrapped the blanket around himself and took his place next to her, falling silent as he started to stir his stew as his thoughts continued to drift.

“You've been quiet lately,” Nul said after a while, pulling Kurt's attention to her. “What's on your mind?”

“It's what Orlan said before he died,” Kurt said, putting his bowl down as his appetite faded.

“You don't think he was just spouting lies to scare us?” asked Nul.

“I doubt it. Whatever kind of monster he was, he wasn't really much of a liar,” Kurt replied, sighing with frustration.

“The town's already building walls and every day more of my people have started trying to make a home on the surface as well. I think Bismurr will be able to protect itself even better as time goes on,” Nul said, pushing her own bowl of food to one side so she could take Kurt's hands into her own. “We won, Kurt. You brought all these people together and helped them learn to fight for themselves. You even shared ideas from your own world that I still can't make any sense of, but all of it has made this place better. What more could you possibly do?”

“That's the point,” Kurt replied, holding Nul's hands tighter as he was worried his next words might make her upset. “There's nothing more I can do here.”

“You want to leave the town?” Nul asked, realising what he meant.

“We still know so little about the elves,” explained Kurt. “I think the longer we spend in the dark, the more danger the town will be in as time goes on. I think I should leave as soon as possible.”

“And you think it needs to be you who leaves?” asked Nul, her grip on his hands tightening.

“I do,” Kurt replied. “No matter how much of a home this place has been for me, I've been here the shortest time. I can't make someone else go.”
“And I was just starting to get used to the place as well...” Nul said, pulling her hands free to resume eating her stew. “We'll have to get a lot of supplies for the journey. There's no telling how long we might be gone for.”

“What? No, I can't ask you to-” Kurt started, but was interrupted by a raised finger from Nul.

“No, you can't ask because you don't get to. There isn't any chance of you going alone so don't even think about it,” said Nul, looking at Kurt with a warm smile. “We're in this together, remember?”

“I-” Kurt was speechless for a moment before smiling back. “I love you.”

“I know. I'm pretty great,” Nul said, her smile growing wider. “Now eat your food, seems like we have a big day tomorrow.”

Kurt did as he was told. Once the couple had finished their meal they spent the rest of the evening starting to pack up things they might need for a long journey. By the time they were tired enough for sleep, there were two large packs waiting at the door, both stuffed to bursting with food and clothes. As they were finishing up with the necessities, Kurt looked over his collection of weapons. As the town had started to recover he'd acquired a new axe and a smaller version of the spike launcher, as well as several daggers. He was planning to take the entire arsenal with him, but something in the back of his mind made him hesitate for a moment. Opting to leave the axe behind, he stashed the daggers and spike launcher into his bag. Kurt had no intention of getting into a fight but he knew better than to leave without any weapons. When the couple were finished, they crawled into bed and despite both their minds thinking about the next day, sleep found its way to them.

The next day the couple trudged their way through the snow and made their way into town. Bismurr had started to resemble a shadow of its former self, but where the buildings used to be were hundreds of large tents replacing the homes that still needed to be rebuilt. It was a temporary measure but with everyone chipping in, the place was starting to feel like a home again. Nul and Kurt walked past people busy with their morning routines, until a wave of familiar smells washed over them. They quickened their pace and soon found themselves standing outside the only tent that had an oven sat outside its entrance, its large chimney leaving a cloud of smoke above their heads.

"Good morning Cali," Kurt called out. Looking inside, all he could see was the top of head bobbing around between large sacks and wooden crates.

"Ah. Morning Kurty!" an excited voice called back. Cali emerged from behind her towers of baking supplies, wiping her hands clean of flour and scraps of dough. She pulled Kurt into a hug before noticing Nul and the two packs the couple had brought with them. "What's all this? Are you heading underground for a bit?"

"Not exactly," Nul replied. She turned away and moved over to a tray of freshly baked pies Cali had left out to cool, casting hungry eyes over all of them.

"You'd better sit down," said Kurt, taking a seat on top of a barrel.

After Cali took a seat of her own, he explained his plan to leave. She sat and listened but as Kurt spoke he noticed tears beginning to fall down her face. Even though it pained him to do so, he continued talking until he had finished sharing everything he planned to do. Once he was finished, Cali got off her seat and pulled him up to his feet so she could hug him. She sobbed for a few moments before gesturing at Nul to come over to them, pulling her into the hug once she came close. The three stayed there for a short while, only breaking apart when the slight smell of burning filled the tent. Cali dried her eyes on her apron and rushed over to take out the tray of too-dark bread rolls. She collected herself before joining the couple once more.

"So you'll both be leaving today? So soon?" Cali asked.

"It's for the best. The town is doing so well now, I-" Kurt looked at Nul, her mouth still full of food, causing him to stifle a laugh, "-we want that to last."
"I suppose I understand," Cali said with a sigh. "I'm not happy about it, but as long as you two stick together then I'll make my peace with it."

"He'd have to do something drastic to get rid of me," said Nul, after swallowing the final bite of her stolen food.

"I take it you're both off to tell the council next?" asked Cali, still with a look of sadness but she managed to force a weak smile onto her face. "Come see me after, I'll pack you up some extra food for the trip."

"Of course," Kurt said, pulling her into another hug.

Sooner than he would have liked, Kurt and Nul found themselves walking away from the bakery. They had left their packs with Cali so she could stuff them with more food. Being lighter made their walk much quicker, arriving at the council tent in the centre of town in good time. As they approached, the sounds of voices became louder and when Kurt pulled the entrance open to step inside, a silence fell over the tent. Jessie and Cole stood over a redrawn map of the town, they shared a frustrated expression as they stared down at the mess of papers and building plans scattered across the table. Their mood brightened briefly as Kurt and Nul entered the tent but darkened again as the couple explained their plan. There were a few moments of quiet as the two council members thought on everything they'd been told.

"And you both plan on leaving today? In the middle of winter?" Jessie asked, concerned.

“It'll be a hard journey but their tracks will be covered. Not to mention, it would probably make it easier to sneak around when they find whatever it is they're looking for,” Cole replied while scratching his chin.

“That's the idea,” Kurt said. “We're not looking to draw any attention. We just want to learn what we can and get back here, hopefully without a fight.”

“Are you sure it should just be the two of you?” Cole asked. “Surely taking a small force with you would make your task easier? Not to mention if things go wrong, you'd be better able to defend yourselves.”

“I think if we get caught with a small army, our intentions won't exactly look peaceful,” Kurt replied. “I think if it's just the two of us, things will be easier. And if things do go wrong, better that the town doesn't lose too many people.”

“Don't undermine your value here - but I see your point,” said Jessie. “I suppose your plan was to leave without much of a fuss?”

“You know what he's like,” Nul said, patting Kurt on the back.

“Then on behalf of the town. Thank you, both of you,” said Cole with a smile. “We'll speak to the rest of the council and we will all eagerly wait for your return.”

The couple went back outside and despite the cold, took their time walking back to Cali. Kurt looked at all the people they passed, going about their lives as though everything was normal. He hadn't paid much attention to goings-on of the townsfolk while he'd been recovering from the battle. Now that he could see how much things had changed since he'd first arrived here, he could feel what he'd been a part of by helping the town fight. The pride he felt in what this town was becoming filled him, giving him confidence that he and Nul were doing the right thing.

They arrived back at the bakery to collect their packs, now almost twice the size as they were before, stuffed to breaking point with enough food to feed the couple for weeks. Cali herself emerged with a fresh coating of flour and dough. She said nothing as she rushed over and pulled the couple into an awkward three-person hug.

"Don't take too long, you hear?" Cali said between sobs.

"We'll hurry home as soon as we're done," Nul whispered, stifling some tears of her own.
"I'll miss you," Kurt said, trying and failing to keep his composure. Seeing Cali like this was almost enough to make him change his mind about leaving.

After a shorter time than any of them would have liked, the couple broke free from Cali's embrace. Kurt and Nul wandered away to begin their journey, leaving Cali to wave at them until they walked out of her sight. Taking care not to draw attention from any of the townsfolk as they moved through the tents. They walked through the snow until they reached the eastern edge of the town and saw three figures waiting in the field nearby, blocking their path. When the couple drew closer, their footsteps crunching in the snow, they recognised the figures waiting for them. Lief, Baku and Ollie, each of them wearing thick travelling clothes and carrying a large pack of their own.

"What's going on?" Kurt asked.

"Did you two really intend on leaving town on your own?" Lief asked.

"I think they did," Baku answered before the couple could respond. "I'm a little hurt that they didn't even try to ask for help."

"Well you're all young. You lot tend not to think things through nearly enough," Ollie said with a chuckle.

"You all know that we're going to be gone for months, if we even come back at all?" Nul asked, brightened to see them all.

"Possibly. But think of all we could learn," Ollie replied looking up at the couple. The excitement on his face seemed to shake off his years, even his hair seemed less grey. "We know almost nothing about the world outside of our tiny town. I'm old enough to have learnt everything our home has to offer, so when a chance to see more of our world crops up, of course I'm going to be first in line to see what's out there - and I dare you to try and stop me joining you."

"I would never," Nul said happily, looking at Kurt.

"Are you all sure this is what you want to do?" Kurt asked. He wanted to give them an opportunity to change their minds, but a part of him was just filled with more pride in these friends he was more than happy to welcome along for the journey.

No one said a word, the three adjusted their packs and walked away across the snow-covered field, leaving the couple behind. Nul grabbed Kurt by the hand and together they followed their friends. The group walked across the fields, approaching the treeline that acted as a boundary for the town. Kurt stopped and turned back to look at Bismurr one last time.

Though he didn't know how long it would be before he would return and he had no idea what dangers they would face on the journey, Kurt did know one thing. He was reminded of it as he felt a slight tug on his hand. Whether he was in Bismurr, or underground, or travelling to unknown lands.

Kurt gripped Nul's hand tighter as he walked into the forest. He was exactly where he was meant to be.

Printed in Great Britain
by Amazon

82416978R00185